I0673916

This is a work of fiction and any resemblance to any person, living or dead, any place, events or occurrences, is purely coincidental. The characters and story lines are created from the author's imagination or are used fictitiously.

Wishing Well: Copyright © 2018 by Lily White

lily@lilywhitebooks.com
http://www.facebook.com/authorlilywhite
www.lilywhitebooks.com

A Romantic Suspense by Lily White

LILY WHITE
BESTSELLING AUTHOR

If you are interested in reading additional books by Lily White or would like to know when new books are being released, Lily White can be found on:
Facebook, Instagram and
Twitter

Join the Mailing List!
If you are interested in receiving email updates regarding additional books by Lily White or would like to know when new books are announced or being released, join the mailing list via this link.
http://eepurl.com/Onoeb

Join the Facebook Fan Group!
If you are interested in receiving exclusive previews for upcoming novels, or to participate in giveaways, join the fan group for Lily White Books.
FAN GROUP LINK

Follow Lily on BookBub!
https://www.bookbub.com/profile/lily-white

OTHER BOOKS BY LILY WHITE

<u>MASTERS SERIES:</u>

Her Master's Courtesan
(Book 1 of the Masters Series)
(Available on Smashwords and lilywhitebooks.com)

Her Master's Teacher
(Book 2 of the Masters Series)

Her Master's Christmas
(Novella in the Masters Series)

Her Master's Redemption
(Book 3 of the Masters Series)

Her Master's Reckoning
(Book 4 of the Masters Series)

<u>STANDALONE NOVELS:</u>

Target This

Hard Roads

Asylum

Wake to Dream

Four Crows

Crazy Madly Deeply

Rules of Engagement

Wishing Well

The Five

ILLUSIONS DUET

Illusions of Evil
(Book 1 of the Illusions Duet)

Fear the Wicked
(Book 2 of the Illusions Duet)

**DARK EXCLUSIVE - Available only on
LilyWhiteBooks.com:**

The Director

Table of Contents

CHAPTER ONE

They are far too bleak, these places with their metal bars and razor wire, these holes where doomed men are tossed, awaiting the day when their numbers would be pulled and they would be walked down long halls to a room that would forever remember their last breath.

Even the sun couldn't penetrate the low hanging dark clouds, the sky a grey haze welcoming Meadow Graham to Faiville Prison, the hole that held a criminal who had taken everything she had left.

Seeing him would shred what remained of her barely beating heart, but she made her way up the long winding sidewalk regardless. In the distance she could hear the muted shouts of men, both criminal and security. She could see the rigid, cement buildings, could smell the taint of violence and fear that doused the grounds in misery.

How long had this man - this monster - been chained? Three days remained for him, seventy-two hours that he'd set aside for one interview, one meeting where he would explain the reasons for his crimes. Approaching the outermost gates of the high security institution, Meadow was unsure why Vincent Mercier had allowed this last conversation, why he'd chosen her out of numerous investigators, journalists and rabid fans, to hear his tale of a life lived in luxury, elegance and decay. If anybody would hate him most, it would be her, yet one month prior, she'd received a note inviting her to the prison to record his last confession.

1

Smiling at the guard, she withdrew her identification and journalist credentials, allowing him to inspect the materials she'd brought to record the interview that many had requested but been denied.

Apologetically, the guard explained, "Given Vincent's antics while in the facility, we can't allow you to take much inside the interview room. Only a tape recorder, your tapes, and that's it. Even these pens can be used as weapons. You'll have to leave them with me until the day's end."

She wasn't surprised. From what she knew of Vincent, he could create havoc in any place he roamed. "I understand," she answered, forcing another smile, even though she felt like screaming. A month hadn't been enough time for her to prepare her heart for this meeting, had been too little time for her to adequately steel her spine.

After flitting his fingers over an electronic keypad, the guard used a physical key to unlock the large, iron gate, the pneumonic hiss that of a serpent welcoming Meadow to Hell. Ignoring the chill that coursed down her spine, she brushed her long, brown hair away from her face, wondering why she'd chosen to wear it down rather than up and out of the way. It wasn't that she wanted to impress Vincent with her appearance, it was that she wanted him to remember her face - to remember the face of his last victim before his incarceration.

The guard led her down a maze of halls, his steps regular, yet lethargic, his shoulders squared and his head balding at the top. Meadow would have aged him at least in his late forties, but she surmised he could be younger and that a life around violent men had stolen his youthful appearance, replacing it with a menacing resolve.

Approaching another set of ominous gates, two guards stood at the ready, their expressions hardened, their hair clipped close to their heads. They wore the standard slate grey uniform, their belts heavy with the tools of their dreary trade.

Snatching a set of keys from his belt, the older guard unlocked the gate, the younger entering a small booth to tap in the electric key, the gate opening with the same hiss as the first.

Meadow's escort approached the men. "Ms. Graham is here for her interview with Vincent Mercier. Is he secured already?"

"Interview room three," the older guard answered, confusion riding his tone. His eyes lifted to hers. "Although I have no idea what you would want with him. He's worthless. A no good sadist that deserves the needle. Why give him the time to brag?"

Understanding filtered through Meadow's bones. It was true that a man like Vincent would enjoy the theatrics of such an interview. His crimes weren't solely physical, his cruelty wasn't restrained to death of the body alone. He enjoyed imparting his control over the psyche of those around him. Knowing this, Meadow had attempted to prepare, but how does one ready themself for a man as refined in his games as Vincent? However, knowing he would enjoy this time wasn't enough to deter her. She wanted answers, and she was willing to play whatever games Vincent demanded to get them.

"Perhaps the information I obtain in the next three days will give solace to his victims' families," Meadow mused aloud.

The guard huffed while stepping aside to let Meadow and her escort through. "The only solace those families will have is watching him die. He's drawn a full crowd. There won't be one empty seat in the viewing room."

Meadow's heart lurched, her mind warring with her soul. It wasn't that Vincent didn't deserve to die for his crimes. It wasn't that she didn't hate him for killing her sister. But there was more to him that she knew, secrets that had been revealed to her by a gift she'd received following her sister's death. There was more to this monster than most understood, and for that small part of him, she mourned.

"Thank you for letting us through," she responded in order to appear polite. The guard's disgust was not without merit, not after what Vincent had so callously done in his life, but to celebrate his death was almost as bad. Refusing to meet the older guard's eyes as they passed, she was thankful to turn a corner into a long hall marked by equally spaced steel doors.

Small numbers were indicated above the door, Meadow's steps coming to a stop outside room three.

"Here we are. Are you sure you want to talk to him?" Her escort attempted to smile, but the expression was lost within the concern written over his face. "He's not the nicest of people."

Unable to stop the burst of laughter, Meadow tucked her tape recorder beneath her arm. "I assume none of the men currently on death row are."

Nodding, the guard rubbed at the back of his neck. "Yeah, but some are worse than others."

Meadow inclined her head, sucking in a steadying breath as the guard opened the door and led her into the room. The moment her eyes met Vincent's her heart

4

screeched to a stop, one heavy beat bringing it back to life as the room spun around her.

"Good luck," the guard whispered on his way out. Casting a glare in Vincent's direction, he warned, "Best behavior, Mercier. We're watching."

With a smile that could only be accomplished by the most devious of lovers, Vincent responded, *"Bien sûr."*

The guard hadn't closed the door before warning Meadow, "He tends to mix his native language with English. I hope you understand French."

With that, the door slammed closed and Meadow was left to stare at a devil with the face of an avenging angel. Prison had done nothing to strip him of his masculine, feral beauty.

With dark brown hair swept back and dusting his collar, Vincent leaned back in his chair, his shackles jangling against the table. Green eyes studied her, the emerald color glimmering beneath the lights above their heads. His cheekbones were aristocratic, his jaw square and dusted with stubble, and his lips as sultry as she remembered them.

"Meadow Graham, how lovely of you to accept my invitation. I'll enjoy my last days of life with a woman as beautiful as you to gaze upon."

"Cut the shit, Vincent. I'm not here for your benefit."

He laughed. The deep, smooth sound tugging at Meadow's resolve. "And here I thought you'd be more elegant than your sister, especially with the benefit of your European education."

Meadow didn't have to look beneath the table to know his long legs were stretched straight, a lazy pose that masked the predator staring her down. "We were identical twins, our personalities as alike as our appearance. And you're not exactly the type of person I would consider worthy of my most polished of behaviors."

Vincent's eyes locked on her, but Meadow couldn't shake the feeling he was looking straight through her. "I have no doubt you're as delicate as Penelope, despite your lack of *savoir-faire*." His deep voice held a hint of his French accent, still a rolling lilt despite the brusque tone of his American English.

"Penny," Meadow said, stressing the name her sister preferred, "was anything but delicate."

He grinned, the cruelty of the expression bleeding into the room. "Inside, she was as delicate as a flower. Even if she attempted to disguise it with her rebellion." Regarding his fingernails, the superficial gesture at odds with the shackles cuffing his wrists, he murmured, "A rebellion that didn't last long."

Meadow's blood boiled. Vincent glanced up and grinned. "You should sit so we can begin. Only seventy-two hours remain of my life, and this story is quite long. Why come if you only intend to glare at me like a cat with her fur stroked the wrong way?"

Ignoring his attempt to manipulate her emotions, Meadow slowly prepared her recorder, setting the tape and closing the lid before hitting record. Turning, she eyed the beautiful man chained to a table, fought against the pull she had towards him. "I'd like to discuss what I already know about you first. Although I didn't bring it today, I want to begin this interview with a question. Specifically, why did you feel the need to have someone deliver to me my sister's diary?"

He didn't need to answer for Meadow to know exactly why Vincent had the gift delivered shortly after his arrest, but she wanted the confession on tape, wanted to ensure she did, in fact, know him as well as she believed. As far as Vincent knew, her only knowledge of him came from that journal, but there were other communications, other means for her to understand the nature of the man staring back at her. Vincent Mercier held his secrets close to his chest, but in that, so did Meadow. The next three days would be a game on both their ends.

His responsive grin confirmed her beliefs before his words broke the stiff silence in the room. "Ah, *ma chèrie*, but I think you already know the answer."

Leaning against the table at her back, Meadow's palms were planted against its surface. "You can stop there with the pet names. Thanks to my *European education* as you so deemed it, I understand enough to know what you're saying to me. And I'm not your anything."

"*Pas vrai*, you are my interrogator, are you not? By standing where you are, you have a relationship with me already. Not only that, but you are my last victim, the woman who will forever mourn the last life I took. I will die in three days, but you will live on in your grief...and your hatred. And for that, I will also live on, until the day you take your final breath. It's poetic, is it not?"

"It's too bad I never liked poetry." Meadow said in bitter retort. "Let's just get this started and stop playing around. The seventy two hours you have left are winding down." She grinned. "Tick tock."

Returning her caustic smile with a look that you would expect a lover to give in bed, Vincent relaxed his shoulders, unaffected by her anger. "Will you be there when I take my last breath? Will you escort me into the

7

afterlife? I would love to look at you through the viewing glass."

Refusing to answer, Meadow dropped the subject of her sister's diary, choosing instead to begin his story at the beginning. "Let's go back to the night you met Penny. Why did you approach her on the street? What value did she have to a man like you?"

Seconds passed before, "If you will take a seat, I'll talk. A conversation should be had between people at equal comfort. And you, at the moment, appear to ready to take off."

Knowing he wouldn't begin until she sat, Meadow grudgingly took her seat.

"Thank you," Vincent said, his fingers braiding together over the surface of the table. "If we are to begin on the night I met your sister, then I can tell you that you won't be pleased with why I decided to take her under my wing. Romance is lost in those details."

Staring, Meadow crossed her arms over her chest, knowing fully that the body language wouldn't be lost on Vincent. His eyes darted to her arms and back to her face, a small smile stretching his lips. Ignoring her behavior, he fanned his fingers out to the sides. "As is true with many stories, mine starts with a conversation with a friend, and I must confess that the only interest I had in Penny, the only reason I approached her on that lonely, rain drenched street, was because of a bet."

Eyes widening, fury coursed through Meadow's veins. "A bet! My sister is dead because of a bet?"

Puckering his lips, Vincent tsked. "Perhaps this interview should end. You seem to have a problem already."

"No," she answered quickly. "I want to know."

8

His lips stretched wide. "Then I'll begin as any good story should begin."

Vincent settled into his seat, his shackles rattling.

"Once upon a time, there was a dirty girl on the streets and the man who would make her his..."

CHAPTER TWO

Vincent

I've never loved America. The country was missing something, a certain *joie de vivre* was absent, the history lacking, the soul having been torn from a body of people who rushed about from place to place, never stopping to experience the moments of their day. On every sidewalk I watched them bustle, refusing to slow down, not even to eat. With bagel in hand, or some other portable lunch that tasted like cardboard or week old starch, they hurried. Occasionally I'd call out *Bonne Appétit*, a Frenchman's pointed admonishment of those who couldn't even slow down long enough to take pleasure from food.

It was never like this in Paris, and often I found myself staring out cafe windows longing for the city where I was raised, hating my father for dragging me to a country of cement and steel, of dying and leaving me tethered to the business he'd created in a foreign state.

Yet, here I was, staring out another random window, reclining in my seat as my friend and business acquaintance rattled on about some deal he'd made that afternoon. The sun had long ago set, the sky lit not by stars but by glittering lights dotting the tall buildings of the city skyline. Inside, the cafe smelled of coffee and baked goods, and outside I knew the stench of dank alleys and smog awaited me, its path winding between cars and sweaty bodies. There was nothing of interest here, not on this street, not outside the walls of

The Wishing Well, the only hotel I owned that I had designed to remind me of home.

"Are you listening to me, Vincent? I've finished with my story and have been reciting nonsense for the last five minutes. Yet, you've said nothing."

Barron laughed, his blond hair swept back and styled professionally, his grey eyes sharp despite the humor behind them. Even while relaxed, the man was a shark any intelligent person would fear. "What's on your mind?" he asked, his hands folded around his ceramic mug. "Has something happened I should know and use against you later?"

The corners of my lips curled. "I'm bored of this city. Bored of these hotels and of these people."

Suspicion arched his brow. "Even all the women you enjoy. You can't be bored of them."

A sigh rolled over my lips. "Even them. They're all the same. Their personalities leave much to be desired, their bodies plastic and far too perfect. Not one of them holds my interest for long, and once I walk away, they screech and cry, begging me to give it another chance only so that they can cry even more when I introduce my desires into the mix." Throwing out my hand, I brushed my frustration aside. "I haven't found a woman yet that can endure me."

Flippantly, Barron suggested, "Then make one."

My brow crooked. "Should I fashion her from clay? A golem I'll bring to life through some extraordinary power? You're insane."

"And you give up too easily."

Setting aside his words to consider later, I watched a woman walk down the sidewalk, her hands tucked into the pockets of a tattered hoodie, her head ducked down, her shoulders rolled forward. Even in the cold,

11

she wore jeans with holes in the knees, rain coming down harder as the minutes passed. Rather than moving inside like the rest of the crowd, she continued on, her face peering up so I could see the dirt that smudged her cheek. She'd be pretty if not so filthy, her youth shining through the grime.

"I mean it, Vincent. Perhaps I can make my suggestion more palatable for a man like you. A wager?"

I stripped my eyes from the dirty girl to meet his gaze. "And what is it you'd like to wager?"

Craning his neck from side to side, the muscles stretching as he tipped his gaze up in thought, he answered, "The Castle versus the Wishing Well. I would love to get my hands on your home."

A bark of laughter burst from my lips. "You're offering your club? How is that supposed to interest me when I'm not in the business of managing those types of establishments? It would only be more work on my part."

"Fine," he grinned, "the profits from each for a full year. We keep ownership. We do the work, but whoever wins the bet keeps the money the businesses make for a year following the end of the agreed upon time period for you to complete your mission."

Eyes drifting back outside, I saw the rain now pouring in sheets, Dirty Girl turning a corner into an alleyway with a small overhang for cover. Crouching down, she wrapped her arms over her shins and laid her head atop her knees. Her soaked hoodie concealed her face. "And what is my mission?" I asked.

"To create the perfect woman, tailored precisely to your specific tastes."

12

Dirty Girl huddled closer to herself, the winds sending the rain sideways. "Not many women are willing to be a slave, Barron. Not for a man like me. My tastes are cruel."

His laughter flowed across the table. "I never said it would be easy. Especially with the pampered women you date."

My perception shifted, the reflection of my face in the glass superimposed over the young girl crouched and huddled. Her fear, her obvious lack of class, her narrowed stare on the businessman that whipped past her with their briefcases held over their heads to block the rain, the allure of her *je ne sais quoi* calling to me. Always up for a challenge, my lips twitched, the muscles in my body tightening as I considered Barron's bet. "Do I choose the woman?"

"Of course, but I have to meet her before and after to ensure you've adequately changed her."

"Meet her how?"

"An introduction at first, a taste in the end." He paused. "How else will I know if she's as well behaved as I'm sure you'll claim she is?"

When my eyes shot to him, he shrugged. "We're talking millions here, Vincent. I won't simply take your word for it."

"Any adequate businessman wouldn't, or else I'd tell you now that I've completed the task and steal the money from your pocket." Eyes darting to Dirty Girl, I asked, "What's my time limit?"

"Three months. By the end, she will crawl if you tell her to. She'll eat dirt if you demand it. She'll thank you for letting me taste while you watch. Regardless of how I use her. Those are the terms."

"Done," I agreed, tossing the napkin from my lap to the table. I didn't bother finishing my coffee before standing from my seat. Barron's eyebrows shot up.

"Where are you going? It's pouring outside."

"To begin. I only have three months, might as well make the most of it." *Might as well steal a girl from the streets before she's out of sight.*

"You'll get soaked," he argued.

A smile curved my mouth. "That's precisely the point." Without bothering to button my jacket, I tossed cash on the table and bolted for the door, but stopped to turn to Barron at the table. "Come by the hotel tomorrow. I'll let you meet her so you can gauge her behavior prior to my training."

His expression was one of bemused confusion. "Have fun in the shower, my friend."

With laughter on my voice, I called, "*Au revoir,*" before stepping out into the storm, my steps hurried regardless of the fact I wouldn't be seeking shelter until I'd secured my catch. I hated to admit that Barron's wager added a spring to my step, a lightness about my shoulders I hadn't felt in a long time.

Crossing the street, I winced in response to the dampness of my shoes, my suit sticking to my skin, the fabric drenched and possibly destroyed. However, the suit was a small sacrifice to this mission, a non-issue in contrast to the girl I approached on hurried steps. She flicked a glance at me as I slowed to a walk, my heels barely audible against the concrete beneath the drumbeat of rain.

Reaching her, I glanced down, my expression amused as she peered up at me from beneath her waterlogged hoodie. "Can I help you?" she practically grunted. Perhaps she would be too much of a challenge, her demeanor was sorely lacking.

Stepping beneath the overhang, I rolled my eyes at the sideways rain from which the small top did little to shelter us. "I was wondering if you enjoy sleeping on the streets."

"Fuck off, old man. I'm not a hooker. Go get your thrills elsewhere."

Taken aback by the comment, I focused on the one word that struck deep. "I'm not old."

"The grey hairs say differently," she retorted, satisfaction gleaming in her glare.

"*Mademoiselle*, perhaps you-"

Her head tilted up, brown eyes pinning mine. "What did you just call me?"

Stinging rain assaulted my skin, the fierce wind like ice. "I apologize, my native language tends to bleed out when I'm in shock. But, back to what you said to me, I'm not old, Dirty Girl, I'm only-"

"Dirty Girl? Are you serious right now?" Ire coated her voice, her eyes narrowing into slits as her mouth pulled into a line to match her fury. "Take off, jerk. I'm not into whatever it is you're offering."

Grinning despite her growing rage, I crouched in front of her, bringing my eyes level to her twisted expression. "How about a warm, dry place to sleep -"

"In your bed, I'm assuming. No thanks," she interrupted, kicking her foot out as if to knock me over. I caught her ankle easily, giving it a firm squeeze with my fingers until she yelped and pulled away. I regretted having to cause pain, but a man like me would only tolerate so much before losing his patience.

Fear widened her eyes. "You hurt me!"

"I did," I responded, my amusement fading as frustration took hold. "Only because you so rudely interrupted. Had you not accused me of taking you home to fuck you, I could have finished my sentence. I'm offering you room and board, as well as a job." Reaching out, I traced my finger along the smudge of dirt on her cheek. "When's the last time you've met a shower?"

Flinching in response to the curt tone of my voice, Dirty Girl glared again, her fear lost to the rain that slashed against us. "When's the last time you met a person who gave a damn about your opinion or anything you have to offer?"

"Just this morning, actually." A quick grin and I raised my voice to be heard over the pounding rain. "You can take my offer or leave it. But I'm not waiting out in this storm for you to answer. If you want a decent job, and to get out of this alley, you can follow me. Otherwise, *Bonne soirée*. Perhaps the rain can clean the filth from your body."

Standing, I refused to look back at the uncouth girl huddled over herself in a pathetic effort to keep dry. She'd accept the offer. She had no reason not to, she just needed to convince herself that she was tougher than she appeared. I'd made it a block without glancing back, was about to turn a corner when a small voice called out to me from behind. The wind almost snatched the sound away from me, but I'd caught enough to peek at her from over my shoulder, to stand tall in a downpour that had chased the residents of the city from the streets.

Holding my hand to my ear, I yelled back. "What was that? You'll need to come closer so I can hear you. We're in the middle of a storm if you haven't noticed."

The corner of my mouth quirked. Thunder rolled overhead that threatened to shake the buildings from their foundations. She shuffled her feet, unsure whether to approach.

Smart girl. If I were her, I'd turn and run from a man like me. But money is always the ultimate lure.

Finally taking measured steps forward, she tilted her chin, crossing her arms over her soaked chest. "What's the catch?" she yelled over the pouring rain.

You are, ma trésor...

"I'm not sure what you mean," I answered, stepping toward her, heel to toe, so slowly as if she would fly off should I move too quickly. "My offer is as I said. A job and a warm place to sleep."

Consternation wrinkled her brow, drops of rain dripping from her eyelashes. "Why would you approach a stranger and offer her something like that? There has to be some reason. Men don't just approach homeless women and give them jobs. It doesn't work like that."

Her voice barely audible over the violent storm, she jumped when lightning cracked across the sky. Carefully, she stepped away from me, her muscles tense as if she remained primed to run.

Smiling despite the water stinging my skin, I shoved my hands into my pockets. The sodden material struggling to remain plastered to my legs. "There's no catch. Not yet anyway. But isn't this a conversation we can have inside and out of the rain? I really must get back."

Lacking trust in my honesty, she began to turn, but I moved quickly to grab her shoulder and hold her in place. Jerking away, she narrowed her eyes on me, her chin tilting higher. I was a good six inches taller, which didn't make her short, not when compared to most women. Standing at six foot five, most people were shorter than me. "There is no catch to which you won't agree," I explained hastily. "At any point, if you decide to leave, the door is open for you to go. My hotel is a public place. It would be impossible to trap you, if that's your concern."

"Hotel?"

My lips tugged wider, my eyes scanning her face, finding that the blistering cold wind had deepened the color of her lips, the pink becoming purple, threatening to turn blue. "Yes, I own several. But I'd planned to take you to Wishing Well, my favorite. It's just around the block. I promise you it's safe."

Laughing, she said, "Yeah, I'm sure that's what H. H. Holmes said to his victims as well."

Genuinely confused, I arched a brow. "Who?"

Dirty Girl shook her head, water droplets flying from the ends of her hair. "Nothing, Just...never mind."

I wasn't the type to beg. "Have a good night then. I hope the rain suits you."

I hadn't finished my turn before she yelled, "Wait!" Pausing, I watched her run in my direction. "Is food included in this deal? I'm starving."

And there it was, the moment I knew she was mine for the taking. The moment her cloak of rebellion faltered just enough for me to reach inside and take hold of the desperation within.

"I can arrange it. But only if we hurry." Lightning cracked the sky, the timing almost too perfect.

Reluctantly, she nodded. "Yeah, let's go."

It wasn't the level of enthusiasm I'd hoped for, but it would do. It appeared Dirty Girl had accepted the challenge of trusting me, while I had accepted the challenge of transforming and owning her.

CHAPTER THREE

"I don't even know your name."

It was the first time she'd spoken since accepting my offer, her voice weak and unsure. With my hand locked over the handle of the gate leading into the private entrance wall of Wishing Well, I turned and peeked at a face that was tinged pink with embarrassment...or something else.

The rain continued to beat down on our heads, the winds ripping past to dot our skin with icy needles. Releasing the handle, I turned fully to gaze upon her, tucked my arm beneath my ribs and bowed shallowly before reaching for her hand to place a kiss on her knuckles. She snatched it away before my lips could touch her skin.

Grinning at her continued rebellion, I answered, "My name is Vincent Mercier. And yours?"

"Penny," she answered, not offering me a last name to go with the first. As I straightened my posture, she wrapped her arms around her abdomen, her shoulders shaking in response to the wind that snatched at our hair. I could only see the long ends that hung out from the opening of her hoodie, my eyes tracing the deep mahogany color.

"It's lovely to meet you, Penny. Shall we go inside?"

Lifting her gaze, she stared at the top of the six story hotel. All that stared back were windows. I'd made sure that the discreet gardens and small private niches were out of plain sight in the design. "I'm not dressed for a place like this," she admitted.

"I agree, which is why we're entering through a private entrance, one used by the staff and myself. I can give you the grand tour once you're...respectable."

Her eyes locked on mine. "These are the only clothes I have. I'm not sure how I can be respectable."

Nodding, I responded, "We have some small boutiques in the lobby. I can buy you some clothes."

Opening her mouth to argue, I raised my hand to silence her. When whatever words she'd wanted to say became trapped in her throat, I spoke as softly as possible, yet loud enough to be heard over the rain. "You can repay me from your first several checks. That is, if you accept the job I'm offering."

"What kind of job is it?"

Laughter shook my chest. "Can we talk inside? Any more time out in these conditions and we'll both be sick by tomorrow."

Begrudgingly, she nodded, following me inside once I'd unlocked and opened the gate. It took all my will power not to glance back and gauge her reaction to the interior gardens, not to stare at the reflection of twinkling lights in her eyes. During the tour I planned to give her once the weather improved, I would memorize each reaction, every subtle change in her expression as she discovered the wonderland I'd created in memory of my first home.

For now, I would get her inside, I would assign her a room and I would enjoy dressing her for dinner. "This way," I directed, opening a side entrance door and running into Émilie as she rounded a corner into the hall.

"Monsieur Mercier!" Running toward me in the black and white maid uniform that was popular in the kitsch lounge on the first floor, Émilie ran her hands

21

over the lapel of my sodden suit. "You're soaked," she complained, her accent thick because she hadn't been in the States for longer than a year. I'd hired her directly, *imported* her as I liked to think, only because the businessman enjoyed listening to her voice and looking at all her assets while winding down for the night.

Gently pushing her away with my hands on her shoulders, I smiled. "It's fine, Émilie. I have dry clothes upstairs. You should hurry back to the lounge. Theresa will be furious with you if you're late again."

She stepped toward me, her ruby glossed lip caught between her teeth. Unsure what to do, she flicked a glance behind me to see Penny standing silently. Disgust wrinkled Émilie's brow. Jealousy colored her cheeks. I knew better than to sleep with my employees, but sometimes a man enjoys a taste of home.

"I should go," she finally agreed, her words clipped and hasty. I waited until she was out of sight before turning to Penny.

"There are rooms available on the fifth floor. I'll grab a key from the lobby and escort you up."

Penny didn't answer immediately, instead choosing to shrug, the mannerism ineloquent. "Should I just stay here or whatever?"

Arching a brow, I answered, "Whatever works. Just stand there and ... drip ... or whatever."

She glared at me, obviously not pleased with my mocking tone. Molding her would be an amusing task, although I wanted to kick myself for choosing a gem not yet hewn. Someone like Émilie would have been far more simple a project, but simplicity is never as much fun. Making quick work of the halls, I approached the lobby desk and drew the same reaction from the staff as

I had from Émilie. Waving it off, I explained, "It seems I forgot an umbrella."

John, the hotel's manager approached the counter. "What can I do for you Mr. Mercier?"

"I need a key for one of the rooms on the fifth floor. I've brought in a new employee."

His gaze flicked past my shoulder, and finding nobody standing close by, he returned his confused stare to me. Shaking my head, I explained, "She was caught in the rain as well. I left her in the employee hall since it didn't seem safe to have both of us dripping through the lobby."

John's face was carved from stone. Rarely did he smile, his professionalism a constant mask. "Yes, I've already called housekeeping to clean up your trail. We wouldn't want our guests slipping and injuring themselves."

Inclining my head in agreement, I drummed my fingers on the counter as he keyed in a code to select a room for Penny. Glancing at me, he asked, "What is the new employee's name? I'll assign her a room now."

"Ah, well, I don't have that information just yet."

Eyes widening, John opened his mouth to complain, but I spoke before he had the chance. "Just put it under my name for now. After she settles and has a bite to eat, I'll be sure to give you all the information you'll need."

John finalized the room assignment quickly, handing me a key card before marching off to inspect housekeeping's job of cleaning up my mess. Laughing to think they would have another mess to tend once I'd gone to the boutique, I made my way into the store, ignoring the sales woman's surprise at seeing me in such a dreary state of attire.

"Mr. Mercier, how nice to see you."

I didn't know the woman, but her hair was grey and her hand bore a plain gold wedding band. "Madame, I'm hoping you can help me select some clothes for a friend I'd like to take to dinner this evening. As you can see, we were caught in the rain and she needs to change so that her current outfit can be laundered."

"Of course, Mr. Mercier. Do you know her size?"

"Unfortunately, no," I admitted, "although, I'd guess she's at least five foot, ten inches, thin, but curvy. I wish I had more to offer in description, but..."

...but her baggy hoodie hadn't given me an adequate peek to guess much more...

The woman smiled. "In that case, why don't we look at a few sheath dresses? As long as we get the length correct, the fit is loose enough to work for many bodies. We won't need exact measurements to select one."

It took less than thirty minutes to select an emerald green dress that would compliment Penny's hair. Purchase made, I returned to the employee hall to find her crouched against a wall, much like she'd been in the alley when I saw her from the cafe window.

"Are you ready to go to your room?"

Shrugging again, she stood to her full height. "Yeah, I guess. What's in the bag?"

Resisting the need to roll my eyes at her tone of voice, I held the bag out for her to take. "I bought you something to wear to dinner. The saleswoman told me it should fit."

Quickly glancing in the bag, Penny's eyes rounded, a sneer curling her mouth. "This isn't exactly something I would normally wear. Didn't they have anything less...slutty?"

Patience is a virtue. My mother had always reminded me of that before she passed away when I was seven. I repeated the phrase now in an attempt not to snap at Penny's lack of gratitude.

"I'm sure we could have found something to your tastes, but I don't have your size. This should work for now."

"Okay," she mumbled, obviously unconvinced.

Ignoring her, I led her to a service elevator and pressed the button for her floor. We were at her door within a minute. "Here is your keycard. I'll give you time to shower and get dressed. Will a half hour be sufficient?"

Penny shifted her weight from one foot to the other, the shopping bag swinging beneath her elbow where it was hooked. "I guess so."

Forcing another smile, I had to fight not to correct her behavior. Understanding she was young, reminding myself I'd plucked her from the streets specifically for this challenge, I forced a smile. "Very well. Enjoy your shower."

I walked way before could respond, and as I stood at the elevator waiting for the doors to open, I glanced back to find her staring at me. Without bothering to say a word, I walked into the elevator, desperate to take the car up to my suite on the sixth floor and change into clean, dry clothes. It wasn't until the doors had closed that I released a sigh and wondered what it would take to train this particular girl to behave properly.

CHAPTER FOUR

Faiville Prison, 10:08 a.m.

"You're lying already."

Meadow shifted her position in the chair to lean forward and fold her arms over the surface of the table, her eyes locking to Vincent's, daring him to argue. Instead, a wolfish grin split his lips. Imitating her posture, he slipped forward, his shackles rattling as he placed his arms on the table.

"And what makes you so sure of that, Meadow?" The rolling lilt of his voice was heavier, his intention to seduce plain on every syllable, in the depth of his tone.

Refusing to respond to the challenge he'd presented, Meadow answered, "Penny told the story differently. I've read her diary, memorized every word, in fact. I've practically slept with it under my pillow. I know your games, Vincent, and I won't be played by them."

"Is that so?" Like a serpent lingering in the sunlit grass, he wrapped his soothing voice around her, his legs stretching further beneath the table until his foot brushed hers. Meadow pulled her legs tighter to her chair, ignoring the wider grin that graced his features.

"Let's start with what you did to her in that alleyway," she argued, "when you grabbed her ankle. When you hurt her, and *laughed* about it."

Slowly, he blinked, his bedroom eyes heavy, his stare unwavering. "Did she write that? Did she remember the first time I took pleasure in her pain? It was just a small test, so tiny that I wasn't sure she'd noticed it at all. In fact," he proposed, his fingers flaring

26

out in a dramatic sweep, "I would have assumed she didn't notice."

Leaning closer, he lowered his voice impossibly deeper, "What kind of woman would be hurt by a stranger and still follow him to his home?"

When Meadow didn't answer, when her anger was so thick that she couldn't formulate one word in defense, he leaned away, making himself comfortable before guessing, "A woman who enjoys torment. That's who. Penelope had a secret she kept hidden. I would say not even you knew of her need for pain, but then you've already admitted your twin and yourself are one in the same."

The teasing hint of wicked pleasure laced his words. "Tell me, Meadow, would you have followed me as well?"

"No," she answered succinctly, "but Penny was desperate wasn't she? She was homeless, starving, stuck outside in the cold rain with no clothes but those she wore, and no hope of escape from the life she'd fallen into. She was the perfect target for a viper like you, a girl who couldn't say no."

His lips curled. "They can always say no, *Chérie*. The difference in this case is that she didn't want to."

Matching his grin, Meadow said, "My name is Meadow. You can refer to me as such."

"Is it?" He retorted, the question rolling from his lips with affection. "You'll have to excuse me, sometimes terms of endearment tend to slip. You remind me so much of Penelope - like a mirror, really, only without the pain I remember in her eyes."

Her gaze traced the line of his lips, her hands clenching into fists over the surface of the table. Pulling them into her lap so as to keep Vincent from easily

27

spotting the visible signs of what she was feeling, she relaxed in her seat, made it appear as if she were unaffected, even while her heart hammered and her pulse fluttered just beneath her skin. "Let's talk about the second lie you've told. Specifically, Émilie."

Vincent's brows arched just enough for her to know she'd regained his attention.

"You claimed that she merely approached you in the hall when you first walked Penny into the building, but Penny wrote that it occurred differently. What she saw in the greeting between the two of you led her to believe you were involved romantically, that she had nothing to worry about because your sights were set on somebody else. At the time, I'm sure Penny believed the encounter meant nothing, but knowing what I now know, having dissected this story every day of my life since I received her diary, I believe that encounter was calculated, that your behavior with Émilie was intentional. From the beginning, you were attempting to delude my sister into believing you were safe, that you were merely a benevolent employer who wished to help a stray girl off the streets."

He was regal, this man, truly intoxicating, regardless of whether he made the effort. Even at that moment, Meadow found herself looking away as if to break some secretive spell he'd weaved around her, needed to distance herself in order not to feel like she was a moon orbiting his space. She knew women flocked to him, knew that even some men had been unable to deny the lure Vincent cast. Memories like film reels played in her head, the words of the diary whispering across her thoughts.

Taking his time, Vincent ran his eyes along the line of her jaw, dropped them lower to follow the length of

28

her neck, to sweep them over the curve of her shoulder. Tender and provocative, just his gaze was a lover's touch, fingertips teasing the skin, a warm breath drawing goosebumps from her body.

"Émilie was too easy, you see? I'd hired her straight from the Parisian streets, had taken pity on her desire to travel despite her mother's illicit choice of profession and dreary lack of funds. She told me her mother had died and left her nothing except the knowledge of how to seduce a man. I believed she'd be a perfect asset in the lounge, a touch of home that would appeal to the patrons who adored Wishing Well for its flavor."

"As I recall reading, Émilie didn't fair too well either. At least, not for long. What happened to her, Vincent? What became of the buxom blonde that could pull all the money from a man's pocket and have him thank her for the theft?"

His gaze never faltered. "How should I know? As far as I'm aware, she took off once I had a new interest. Jealousy is such an ugly affair. It makes people crazy, does it not?"

"Weren't you convicted of Émilie's murder?"

Vincent grinned, "We'll get to that. You're skipping ahead."

Crooking a brow, Meadow grinned. "So you hire this woman, bring her all the way to your hotel, and what? Sample her before tossing her to the wolves?"

Seconds passed silently between them. "I believe I need to remind you of what little time we have together. While you discuss women of little importance, the clock ticks. We should return to my story with Penelope. I'm curious as to what she wrote of our first encounter. Will you tell me?"

Confused, Meadow scrunched her brow, hated that she'd made the error of dropping her mask of superiority, of having lost being the person with a foot one step farther ahead. Now he knew that he'd surprised her, that he'd caught her off guard. "You didn't read the diary?"

His fingers flared again, a common symptom of his thoughts. "Alas, I was already in jail by the time it was found. I requested it be sent to you immediately. My staff are loyal, Meadow. I doubt even they turned its pages."

It didn't make sense. Vincent was too much of a control freak not to ask what Penny had written about him. He was too much of a collector to allow even one of her thoughts to escape his grasp. If anything, he would want to bask in the confusion he'd created in her head, would want to luxuriate in the spoils of his psychological games. If it were true, if the diary wasn't discovered until after he was arrested, then perhaps he'd neglected to ask about its contents, had feared the recorded calls and conversations in jail would capture some detail in the diary that would ensure his conviction. There was always the possibility, but Meadow doubted it.

"Do we have time to even discuss it?" she asked, "What with your impending death approaching so quickly?"

His grin widened, his perfect, white, straight teeth gleaming like that of a jackal about to bite. "Any good story is well rounded. Perhaps something in her memory will jar something in mine, knock it loose so that I can deliver it to you as a present wrapped in the finest of paper."

Sardonically, she countered, "Or perhaps you simply want to enjoy knowing what you did to her on every level imaginable. Especially now that there is no escape from the executioner."

"Perhaps," he agreed. "But that is your decision to make."

Wondering how he would react to what she knew, from what the diary contained, Meadow relented. "Fine, I'll tell you her side. I'll speak in place of the woman who can not." Leaning closer, she added, "I'll be happy to divulge just how much she hated you in the end."

CHAPTER FIVE

Penny

Life started and ended with Blake Jameson, my boyfriend, my best friend, the soul mate I ate mudpies with in kindergarten and gave my virginity to in the tenth grade. With his wild blond hair, always long and windswept like a surfer, and tan skin that brought out the blue in his eyes, Blake was a constant for me, a puzzle piece that fit, an extension of who I'd always been.

He hung the moon and scattered the stars. He was the sun and I was the Earth absorbing his warmth.

Blake was there when people had attempted to bully me. He'd protected me and knocked a few heads together. He'd loved me even more than my own family. Closer to me than my own identical twin, Blake was the peaceful center in my chaotic storm. He was the island in my turbulent sea, the oasis within my desert. He was my life and my protector, my every dream, and my shelter.

He'd been at my side when my father died, had held me and rocked me when I screamed. His presence soothed me at the funeral when my father was laid to rest, his words had reassured me when my mother met a man across the Atlantic who she believed could replace the man who'd raised me.

And when the time came for my mother to uproot and live in a foreign land, it was Blake who convinced me to stay. Both my mother and Meadow had hated my decision, but they couldn't understand who Blake had been for me.

That's how I'd stayed in the States when my mother and sister left, it's why I'd let my family fly away while I remained rooted. I truly believed Blake would be the man I married, believed I'd have his children, and we'd grow old together, our hair turning silver as the different parts of our bodies shriveled into decay.

It was only a year after my family left me that Blake decided to leave me as well.

He'd met someone else. He'd apologized and cried. But even my tears, my hurtful words, my begging and pleading hadn't been enough to convince him that he was ruining my entire life.

Simple as that.

Blake was the reason I'd stayed in the States in one year. And Blake was the reason I became homeless in the next.

Too ashamed, too hurt, too destroyed, to call my family and beg for help, I'd convinced myself I could make it on my own. But with no job experience, only a high school education and no permanent address I could call my own, finding employment had been impossible. Not that I could have managed much of a job. I was too heartbroken to be anything more than a useless shell, a ghost walking down the sidewalk, a woman who hadn't just lost the love of her life, she'd also lost everything she owned.

The street isn't exactly a welcoming place, and the minute you close your eyes, what little you do have is plucked by the vultures, stolen away and gone.

It's how I'd ended up walking down Stratford Avenue in the pouring rain. It's why I didn't have two dimes to rub together, didn't have a phone, didn't have a hope for salvation beyond the small tattered overhang I found that did nothing to protect me from the storm.

At nineteen years old, I was a failure already.

I'd been so busy freezing my ass off and scowling at well-dressed assholes looking at me like I was the scum that scuffed their pretty, leather loafers, that I hadn't even noticed Vincent Mercier when he'd first approached. It wasn't until his shadow fell over me, blocking the one street light that lit the needles of rain that I glanced up to spy one of the most beautiful examples of the masculine form I'd ever seen in my life. If not for the rain dripping from his thick brown hair and the charcoal grey suit glued to every hard, broad surface of his body, I would have believed he'd walked off the set of some popular television show or perhaps stepped straight from the pages of a fashion magazine.

And when he first spoke - when I first noticed the soft, rolling hint of a foreign tongue - it was music to my ears.

To say I was confused why he was staring down at me was an understatement. It wasn't until he'd propositioned me like a back alley hooker that my anger flared to the surface. I won't lie and say I didn't take pleasure in calling him an old man. I had a gift for pinpointing a person's weak spot, and vanity was his.

I must have struck a nerve because he went from calling me a name straight out of a seventeenth century French romance to calling me a *Dirty Girl*, as if the implied meaning would be lost within the rain.

Fucking pervert.

I'd called him out on it, had accused him of only wanting to get me in bed, and then he'd done something so out of character that I'd vacillated between whether to knock out his teeth or accept the offer he'd quickly rattled off instead.

I won't lie, there's no point when the only audience for this confession is myself. Vincent had startled me from the minute my eyes first met his handsome face. His eyes were the color of glimmering emeralds, a treasure stumbled upon in the depths of some hidden cave, a solitary beam of stubborn sunlight finding its way along the wall to touch those enormous gems and divulge their beauty and secrets.

Framing his face was dark hair I was sure was careless when dry. Although plastered to his head by the unforgiving rain, I could still see the choppy layers, could still imagine a woman wrapping the soft, silken strands between her fingers. And the rain, oh how I'd felt jealous of the drops that were able to touch his cheeks and trace the contours that were carved from stone, the one brave droplet that tracked the curve of his mocking lips to become one with the salt of his copper skin. If ever temptation were to walk this earthly plane, it was in Vincent's shoes...which made it a shame he was the biggest jerk I'd had the displeasure to encounter.

Choosing to kick out at him, I'd understood my mistake the instant he caught my ankle with his hands, the few seconds he'd enjoyed punishing the bones with the strength of his cruel fingers. Fuck, it hurt, the crushing pain enough to send an electric current shooting up my leg to my hip. I'd looked into his eyes at the moment he'd caused that pain and they were hungry, hard, yet laughing. I should have known then what kind of man he was.

But I was starving. I was cold. I was wet, and not in the good sense of the word. Desperation is such a putrid scent, yet it oozed from my every pore.

He offered me a job. He hurt me. He walked away.

And I was the silly girl that followed him.

I should mention the hotel.

The Wishing Well was one of the most famous hotels in the area. Not as large as the skyscrapers that were steel and glass fingers reaching for the sky, the modest, private, somewhat exclusive property demanded far more coin that even the Hiltons could ask for. Luxury wasn't lost on this walled-in paradise and if ever a castle existed in a city, it was this hotel.

At six stories, I'd only viewed the top floors above the walls that circled it, could only imagine what would be found behind the ivy that clung to stone. It was a small block all on its own with lights that twinkled from the branches of tall trees, soft music often escaping its hold on the weekends when businessman flocked in for some convention at the ridiculously large center down the road.

I didn't even know his name when we approached the hotel, and I'd almost forgotten it when he opened the gate and allowed me inside to see what he'd made of the place after tearing down what was once was here to construct his 'home away from home.'

It was as if I'd stepped out of the States directly into a French garden hidden away from the Paris streets, the lights, the wisteria, the cobblestone walkways all at my fingertips without need for a plane or a boat. Although, we ran to avoid the rain, I still caught a glimpse of the well, a large stone circle set among flowers, beckoning me to look inside.

I never had the opportunity to explore before we'd entered the building and I stood frozen and wet, watching as Vincent's girlfriend came rushing forward. They both spoke French and I couldn't understand any of what they said, but it must have been words of adoration, love perhaps, or longing, because Vincent backed her against a far wall, their husky voices dropping to whispers, his lips tracing the line of her jaw as his fingers gripped her hip.

Awkward, I wrapped my arms around myself, unsure whether I should turn away to give them privacy. Neither seemed to mind the audience and it made me wonder. Yet, for as out of place as I felt, for as confused, scared and alone, I stood staring as his hand trailed up the side of her body to palm her breast from over the skimpy French maid outfit she wore. At first, I made myself a promise to refuse the job if that's what I'd be required to wear, but the thought dissolved as the woman's hips pressed closer to Vincent.

Blake had never made me move like that.

Oh, to be a fly on this man's wall when he made a woman moan. I was dry mouthed just from imagining it.

Laughter filtered from the woman's lips, a few more husky words I couldn't understand whispering out until Vincent abruptly backed away and the woman ran off down a corridor, her shapely legs moving fluidly despite the four inch heels she wore.

When he turned to me, I physically flinched in reaction to the hypnotic heat blazing behind his green eyes.

Straightening his soaked jacket (not that it helped), he grinned, the same type of expression you'd assume a fox would wear while stepping away from henhouse.

Stepping toward me, his voice was a deep vibration against my frozen bones when he explained, "You'll have to excuse the interruption, Émilie is quite...passionate."

Unsure how to respond, I practically mumbled my response. "So it seems."

A glimmer of something flickered behind his eyes. "I'll show you to your room, but first I'll need a key. You can wait here while I go to the lobby."

Merely nodding because I was still in too much shock to think, I waited for what felt like forever, my tired legs finally getting to me as I crouched and huddled against a wall. At first, I'd believed he'd forgotten me, but then he returned with a bag in one hand and a keycard in the other.

"Shall we go up?"

"What's in the bag?" I asked, fearful that he'd chosen a maid outfit for me to wear, much like Émilie's.

"Clothes I purchased from the boutique. We can have what you're wearing now laundered and dried in the meantime."

Vincent held the bag out to me and I clenched my teeth to look inside and discover a mass of green silky material that didn't appear as if it would cover much.

I should have known this man would find something for me to wear that was more akin to a negligee than actual clothes.

As he led me to a service elevator, I grew quiet, unsure. We were silent all the way to room 504 where he deposited me so that I could get a shower and get dressed. I couldn't help but stare as he sauntered off, his soaked clothes, his messy hair, his unkempt state doing nothing to disrupt his seductive swagger.

He peeked back at me once before entering the elevator again, the expression on his handsome face making it all too obvious that my new boss - the stranger who'd hurt me before luring me from the streets - was more trouble than I'd understood I was taking on.

CHAPTER SIX

The room Vincent gave me wasn't merely some dumpy five hundred square foot space with a questionable bed, scratchy sheets and a corner kitchenette complete with dirty microwave and a small refrigerator set in a counter. This place was a full suite, a paradise to a girl who'd slept on the streets, a bastion of hope that I wasn't sure how to interpret.

Staring out at a living room with white carpets, white sofas, and white gossamer curtains that hung to the sides of floor to ceiling windows, I felt like I'd stepped into heaven, as if I'd died and Vincent had been the angel to whisk me from this life and deliver me into paradise without mentioning I was now a ghost. The confusion I felt mixed with elation, my light feet creeping to an open door, a gasp escaping my lungs as I stared wide-eyed at a bed that could comfortably fit three people or more. Much like the living room, the bedroom was all white with touches of pastel colors, the wallpaper a tasteful pattern touched with silver. Remembering my wet clothes, I panicked and glanced behind me, thankful to find I hadn't tracked mud across the pristine floors.

Kicking off my shoes, I hopped on one foot then the other as I peeled the sodden socks from my feet, running again to peek inside a bathroom that would make the designers of Roman baths jealous.

In a matching theme of white and silver, the fixtures gleamed beneath a small crystal chandelier hanging delicately from the ceiling, the large bath and glass encased shower beckoning me forth with the promise of warmth for my frozen bones. Soft rugs covered the tiled floors, thick towels perfectly folded and hung for my use. A vanity with a large mirror and huge bulbs like those in an actor's dressing room sat off to the right, the bathroom itself larger than the small apartment I'd shared with Blake before he left me.

I would have believed I was dreaming if not for the way my body shook from the rain and cold. Outside the windows, the storm raged on, but in here - in this paradise - I was safe from the thunder and rain, from the lightning that cut across the sky.

Dropping the shopping bag on a plush chair as I passed, I struggled out of my soaked clothes, letting them fall in place as I made my way to the shower. Water and steam billowed out of multiple heads, my muscles relaxing the instant I stepped inside. I would have remained beneath the spray if not for my time limit before Vincent returned, and with a promise to take a long bath before falling asleep that night, I reluctantly climbed from the shower, wrapped a large towel around my body and discovered a slight problem I hadn't considered until that moment.

Everything I owned was soaking wet, including my underwear, my bra and shoes. I had nothing but a slinky dress to cover my body, and just the thought of slipping on anything I'd worn prior made my lip curl in disgust.

Pulling the dress over my head, I glanced in the mirror, my breasts bulging against the soft material, the length of the green silk falling to my knees. This was not the impression I wanted to give to a man I barely knew. When I heard a light knock at the door, I knew I had no other choice.

Opening the door, I held an arm across my chest, my knees clinging together for fear Vincent would be able to see I wore nothing underneath. "Hey," I said, my voice soft, my cheeks heated with embarrassment.

His eyes traced down my body, goosebumps erupting over my flesh. "Hello," Vincent answered, his words dark...gritty. "I see the dress fits."

Unlike me, Vincent's appearance was impressive, his hair brushed back, the ends dusting the collar of his black suit jacket. Beneath his suit, he wore a black shirt, the top buttons loose, revealing a triangle of tan skin, a hint of the strong pecs across his broad chest. He appeared larger somehow, the intimidation I felt pervasive and elusive, the tremor of nervousness foreign after having survived several weeks on the streets with nothing but my wit to protect me.

"I have a problem," I confessed sheepishly, unable to raise my voice above a whisper.

Taking the opportunity to lean closer, as if he couldn't hear my teeny tiny voice, his eyes swept down the neckline of my dress, my arm tightening over my breasts in response. I hated that my body reacted, my thighs clenching together as a chill coursed down my spine.

"Perhaps I have a solution," he whispered back. Somehow he sounded even more dangerous when his voice was barely a breath.

My cheeks flamed more. "I don't have anything to wear with the dress, as in *anything*..." Eyes widening, I tried to convey what I meant without actually saying it.

Vincent's eyes scanned down my legs to land on my bare feet.

"I see," he commented, a sly grin stretching his mouth. "Normally, I would find the information alluring, an invitation to find out more, but seeing as we've just met..."

"Stop being a perv," I blurted out, censure thick in my tone.

His grin widened, his hand splaying over his chest as if he'd actually been offended by my words. "I am but a man, *ma chérie*. You can't hold it against me."

Not knowing how to respond to the charm that was like a second skin wrapping this man, I muttered, "Maybe I should order room service and stay in."

"Or," he countered, "you can give me your wet clothes, I can send them to be cleaned, and we can return to the boutique where we can purchase whatever else you need to complete your outfit. Shoes, perhaps."

My eyebrows pulled together. "I'm not as concerned with shoes as the other things."

"And I'm not as concerned with the other things as you are."

Rolling my eyes, I opened the door and waved my hand for him to walk in. "I need to grab my other clothes."

Soft laughter filtered through the room. "Take your time. Our table in the dining room has already been reserved."

Taking a seat on the sofa, his arms spread out over the backrest, his posture that of a man who owned the place. I quickly ran into the bathroom, hating how my breasts shook beneath the dress, grimacing at the tell tale draft whispering between my legs. I'd always been a modest girl, the jeans and T-shirt type that spent more time hiding her figure than showing it off. My twin sister had always been the fashionable one, had enjoyed the attention she received for her looks that

43

were identical to mine. In contrast, I'd felt exposed if my shirt was too tight or if my jeans weren't baggy enough to hide the curve of my hips, the weight of my bottom when I walked within a crowd.

Blowing out a breath in an effort to steady the beat of my racing heart, I shoved my wet clothes into the shopping bag that once held my dress and returned to the living room where Vincent remained seated, his head tilting back, his eyes closed. It was ridiculous to think that he looked like a man receiving a lazy blowjob on a warm, sunlit afternoon.

"I'm ready to go, I guess."

Without bothering to open those stunning green eyes, he spoke slowly, his accent a film coating his words. "You guess? Or you know?"

Despite the laziness of those words, they sounded like an admonishment, a ruler against the knuckles, a reminder that I wasn't as classy or educated as him. I'd only known Vincent for two hours and already I wanted to avoid him as much as possible. Dr. Jekyll and Mr. Hyde seemed better balanced in comparison.

Hot and then cold. Gracious and then cruel. Friendly and then unnerving. Vincent Mercier was a puzzle of opposites, the type of person that constantly kept you on guard. "If it's an issue, we could just call this off for tonight."

His eyes opened, the fan of his dark lashes framing observant green orbs. "Why would you suggest that? I was only asking a question."

"It just seems like..." My voice trailed off.

Canting his head to the side, he stared at me. "Seems like what?"

Like you're judging me...

44

Like I'm worthless to a man like you...
Like I'm some stupid mouse caught in a maze you built
with a deck of cards...

"Like you're tired," I lied.

Sitting up, he stretched his long legs out over the floor in front of him. "I assure you, I have much more endurance than a man needs. Endurance that is often complimented. I won't be tired until late into the evening."

Why did everything he say sound like a reference to the bedroom? Vincent was a natural flirt, and I didn't want to see too much into it. "Okay," was my simple response.

At some point in the conversation, I'd forgotten I wore nothing beneath my dress. Vincent's eyes found the evidence of that slip of mind, appreciation rolling behind the green glimmer before he crooned, "You wear the dress well."

I may as well have been naked for as uncovered as I felt. Glancing down, I realized it was slightly cold in the room, two peaks poking at the material of my dress. Quickly, I attempted to shield my breasts with my arms. If I weren't so desperate for food, shelter and cash, I would call off this agreement I'd made with him. Even now, it felt like I'd sold my soul to the devil.

Thankfully, my stomach grumbled, two days without food causing the complaint to be clearly heard across the room.

"We should go," Vincent said, the heat behind his gaze dying off as he stood from the couch and stepped toward me. Instinctively, I backed away, but he grinned and reached out a hand. "I was only going to offer to carry your bag for you. Chivalry isn't entirely dead."

"I can manage," I answered, hating the squeak in my voice as my fingers tightened over the plastic handle. Shaking myself of the nervousness I felt in Vincent's presence, I rolled my shoulders back (as much as I could while still guarding my breasts) and remembered that I wasn't the type to be intimidated. Maybe he had enough energy to last the night, but I was exhausted. That had to be why I felt so small. After a good night of deep sleep, I'd be back in prime form, ready and willing to cut this man off at the knees if it was necessary.

Without arguing, Vincent moved to the door, opened it and paused in the hall to hold it for me. I approached and was about to walk through when he let it slip from his fingers to close in my face. My nose almost collided against its surface.

Slamming my palm down on the handle, I wrenched the door from its frame and glared at the gorgeous man on the other side.

"You'll have to forgive me. I'd forgotten that you didn't want a man's assistance." His expression was a blank page upon which I could scrawl any emotion or meaning. I could have allowed his taunt to anger me, could have stalked off to the elevator, left the building and returned to the rainy streets, but I wanted the food I knew he would give me. I was desperate for a soft bed and warm sheets. If the job he offered wasn't something I could stomach, I'd at least take his kindness for tonight and leave in the morning.

"It's fine," I answered, turning right to head toward the elevator and leave him standing behind me.

Reaching the doors, I noticed the lack of footsteps at my back and glanced over my shoulder to see Vincent's eyes planted firmly on my butt. With a snappish tone, I asked, "See something you like?"

His responsive grin was deviant. "*Oui. J'ai envie de te croquer, ma belle.*"

Annoyed by his use of French, I resisted asking him what he'd said. I was sure it didn't matter...or that I didn't want to know.

If I did accept his job offer, I was positive that working for a man like Vincent would be a lesson in patience.

CHAPTER SEVEN
(Faiville Prison, 11:15 a.m.)

Vincent locked his eyes on Meadow, his stare unwavering, his lips crooked at the corners as if he harbored some secret he would never tell. "Why would you do that, Meadow? And just as we were beginning this dance?"

Humor edged his voice, silk and fur a caress against Meadows skin in the indolent pace of his tone. Unsurprised at how this man used every tool at his disposal to lure her in, she resisted the natural temptation, brushed aside the desire she couldn't help but feel.

Vincent was a gold medalist in attraction, temptation personified, a weapon of cruel seduction that had been honed until wickedly sharp. It was through desire that he distracted and addled the mind, unrepentant for the cheap use of human instinct.

"Why would I do what?" She finally managed to utter.

"Give away a portion of the story I hadn't yet told," he answered, his brows rising ever so slightly in challenge. "I assumed you came here to learn what I believed happened, to dissect the details you didn't discover in your sister's private thoughts."

Letting out a breath over barely parted lips, Meadow noted how his gaze traced the line of her mouth. Two could play at seduction, the truth of Vincent's longings recorded within the hastily written diary. Penny had become his obsession as much as he had become hers.

Purposely rolling back her shoulders, Meadow allowed her eyes to become heavy, enjoyed they way he couldn't resist studying the hint of her breasts where they peeked above the neckline of her shirt. "I didn't think the part I told was of much importance. You picked her up from her room, challenged her independence by showing her how a man could choose to be gracious or rude."

His eyes never left her chest, the tip of his tongue peeking out ever so slightly from between his full lips. How long had it been since he'd sat in the same room as a woman? Meadow would use that to her advantage.

Distracted, he asked, "She remembered what I said to her in the hall?" His gaze lifted. "Enough to write it down? She never did learn to speak my language." A bark of soft laughter shook his shoulders. "Well, at least that particular language of mine. She was a better student in others later on."

"So I read," Meadow answered as she leaned forward, her voice soft, her shoulders dropping forward, intentionally allowing the material of her shirt to fall lower and give Vincent a better view. "Penny wrote all about that *particular* language in her diary."

Masculine pride flashed behind his eyes. "Did she?"

Rounding her lips, pulling her arms tighter together to force her cleavage higher, she answered, "Oh, yeah. In exquisite detail."

Tense seconds passed, his eyes sweeping down to accept the visual offer Meadow had made him. By the time he met her stare again, he was practically laughing. "Nice try, Meadow, but you'll have to be far more convincing than that."

49

She straightened her posture. "Fine. It was worth a shot. And no, in answer to your question, Penny never did learn French while living at Wishing Well. Anything she recorded in her diary, she spelled out phonetically. I was able to interpret what the words meant after pouring over the pages in the past few months. It wasn't easy."

"I'd assume not," he agreed, his response uncommitted, his thoughts elsewhere. "It amuses me that Penelope fought so hard at first. No," he said, reconsidering, "Perhaps fought is the wrong word. Penelope didn't fight, she dodged. She hopped around, making so much racket that it disguised what she was feeling. In one second she'd accuse me of being a pervert - a word she used liberally, I might add - and within the next, she'd smile, almost to the point where I suspected she genuinely appreciated and believed the offer I'd made to her. By the time I'd picked her up from the hotel room, I'd assumed she'd forgotten about the *catch*, assumed that I could lead her down whatever path I chose without her being suspicious. Penelope was good at hiding her thoughts, at first at least. But she wasn't a dumb girl, was she? From what you just told me, she knew what type of man I was from the beginning, the degree of danger she'd been in since the moment I'd approached her in the rain."

Surprised by his rare honesty, Meadow admitted, "No, Penny wasn't dumb in the slightest. Naive maybe. Young and inexperienced. But not dumb."

Vincent grinned. "And yet, she still followed me home."

"A mistake that cost Penny her life," Meadow reminded him.

"I regret that. Beauty such as hers should never be so carelessly lost," he mused, a hint of emotion playing across his softly spoken words. Of course, he ruined it with what he said next. "I guess it's a good thing for this world that there is an exact duplicate...you."

Anger was a tidal wave crashing through her. "That doesn't minimize my loss. I still lost my sister. I still feel the pain of her no longer being in this world."

He leaned toward her. "And you will carry that pain for a lifetime. My name, my face, etched within the memory of it, alive and well, even if I'm no longer breathing." It was a stab straight to the heart, his words twisting the knife to force the full impact of agony.

Meadow refused to release the tears that threatened her eyes. "Is that truly all she was to you? A game? A chess piece you tossed aside like garbage?"

A negligent shrug was his answer, a wave of his hand as if that would brush away the memory of a human life. "Life has no meaning without death. And although Penelope lived a short one, she burned bright. Not many people can claim that. She was like fire, that one."

"And you were the water that doused her," Meadow chided, "That's nothing to be proud of. But then again, in a way, she was the water that doused you. In three days, you'll take a needle in the arm for killing her. It's a pity the person sticking you can't wear a mask that looks just like her."

His eyes tipped up to capture hers. "But you are an exact copy. Perhaps they'll allow you to prick me in the vein. You'd like that, wouldn't you?"

Clearing her throat of the ball of emotion she didn't want to admit choked her, Meadow suggested, "We should move on Vincent. Already three hours have passed and we've barely scratched the surface."

His face was an inscrutable mask, regal, godlike, wistful as he remembered back to the pawn he'd made of Meadow's sister. "Shall I begin where you left off?"

Weaving his fingers together over the surface of the table, he blinked slowly, the fan of his lashes dusting his skin, the curve of his mouth drawing Meadow's attention. She knew he was fighting a smile, knew he enjoyed tormenting her with the slow crawl of his memory. He wasn't just telling a story, he was reliving it, experiencing it again in order to claw at the superiority he'd gained while playing Penny.

As much as that bothered Meadow, her curiosity was too much. There were still so many questions left unanswered, too many layers that needed to be peeled away so she fully understood what had been done.

She refused to believe he felt nothing for the woman he'd so callously destroyed.

"No," Meadow answered, "from what I know, nothing more happened that night beyond you buying her buy some additional clothes, getting her personal information for the job and taking her to dinner. I'm not sure that's important. We should move on to the next morning, when you introduced her to Barron for the first time."

Lifting her eyes to Vincent, Meadow noticed his smile stretch, saw the flicker of humor in a green gaze that missed nothing.

"What?" she asked, knowing that when his mouth took that curve, there was something he'd buried coming to the surface, some secret, some joke that nobody but him had known. Everything about this man was recorded in the diary, almost as if Penny, by writing it, had attempted to decipher all the peculiarities, all the body language, expressions and rolling words of Vincent Mercier in order to pin him down and reveal that he wasn't as elusive as everyone believed.

For as many times as she'd read the pages of the diary, for as tattered as those pages had become, Meadow still couldn't shake the mystery that hovered around this man like a cloud.

Speaking slowly so that each syllable of his words could be caught and examined as they fell effortlessly from his lips, Vincent mused, "Perhaps the diary is not as complete as you believe." Pausing, he toyed with the cuff that locked his wrist, ran the tip of his finger along the edge. "Something did happen that night, but you would need my perspective to discover it."

Her heart lurched with a painful, powerful beat, the click of the recorder stopping adding the perfectly timed sound to her physical reaction. Her eyes blinked once before she regained the ability to think, to act, to push up from her seat and turn to switch the tape.

Pressing record, she wondered why Vincent was so silent behind her. Balancing herself with her palms against the surface of the table, she took a moment where he couldn't see her face to get her emotions under control. What had he done that hadn't been recorded in the diary? What detail had been lost?

"Fine," she breathed, feeling his gaze trace the contours of her bottom, knowing he stared at every asset he could find in a woman that was the same as the one he'd destroyed. "Tell me what happened that night."

Seconds passed silently, the clock ticking, time moving forward toward the ultimate of endings, and then, "Are you sure you want to know? We've barely begun and already you can't look at me, *ma belle.*"

The gritty quality of his voice didn't help, the loss of fluidity of language, the ease of the endearments that would normally roll from his hot tongue gone as he asked his question.

"I wouldn't have come here if I didn't want to know," she answered, struggling, fighting desperately to keep from sounding affected.

"Then I will tell you," he paused, "but only if you retake your seat, only if I can watch your face as you hear the truth, the intimate details, the mastery of a game designed to transform a girl into a woman."

Gritting her teeth, Meadow's fingers clenched into fists, her posture straightening, her head turning just enough that she could see Vincent in her peripheral vision. "She wasn't a girl. She was already an adult when you met her."

"*Oui*, you are correct...but she was not a woman. In that one word lies the distinction."

Icy fingers traced her spine, the chill spreading like that of a spider's web wrapping her, capturing her, making her regret ever agreeing to this interview in the first place.

Meadow wondered if she was strong enough to continue forward, if she could handle the intricate details...if she could swallow the truth and not choke on the thickness of his lies.

Clenching her eyes shut, she fought the desire to run, to leave, to flee the room and board a plane to return to Germany and never look back. She had her career, her home, her life that didn't include Vincent Mercier.

But then, the story would be incomplete, wouldn't it? The reasons lost, the death without meaning.

Meadow couldn't allow that. She needed to know. Turning, she refused to meet his gaze as she took her seat, refused to relinquish the small amount of control, of independence, she had. He'd told her to sit, and she would comply, but not because she was a woman following his demands. She was here to dissect him, to tear him apart, to make him feel the same pain she had felt since the day her sister died.

She would play his games, and she would walk away the victor.

"Tell me, Vincent," her gaze finally locked to his. "Tell me what happened that night that you think I don't already know."

CHAPTER EIGHT

Vincent

Every so often, fate has a hand in opportunity. With a flourish of delicate fingers, it swirls the air around your existence, creating temptations that are too great, challenges that appear to be insurmountable. But within those moments when you doubt how simple coincidence could have led you to clear waters when you are thirsty, to a banquet when you starve, to the heat of fire when your bones scream for warmth and your heart beats weakly beneath the ice that encases it, you understand that certain events were meant to be, were written in the stars, were deemed by the Gods to be worthy for your life even before you were a twinkle amongst mankind.

I was experiencing that moment as I watched Penny walk down the hall, her bare legs strong and shapely, her heart shaped ass bouncing with each step, teasing me and inviting me to touch. My fingers curled into my palm, the inside of my cheek caught between my teeth, my body tensing as she glanced back with anger in her gaze to ask me if I'd appreciated the view as she'd walked away.

And I'd answered her in a language I knew she couldn't understand, because if she'd been able to interpret the words for what they were, she would have entered that elevator, left the building on rushed steps, and permanently stepped out of my life.

Desire is a slippery thing, easing inside a person's skin to capture, to taunt, to strengthen and spread out until your mind becomes mud and your heart races in an effort to escape your chest. From one moment to the next, I was man and I was beast, this rude, inelegant girl that I'd pulled from the streets revealing to me her full potential.

How had I known from one simple glance out a cafe window that a lonely girl walking in the rain would be exactly the woman who would fulfill my every need? Her face had been covered, her hair had been disguised, her body had been hidden beneath clothes that gave no hint of what was to be discovered, yet now, in this moment, I understood that instinct, that fate, had led me to the woman I most desired.

Thrill whispered in to mix with the heat pouring through my veins.

Her head peeked out of the elevator. "Are we going or what?"

Smiling at her question, I tucked my hands into the pockets of my slacks and approached her, taking pleasure in the way she backed to the far left of the elevator while I stood to the right. It wasn't just my instinct screaming at this moment, it was hers, but she was barely listening.

Reaching the first floor, I led her through the lobby, ignoring the pointed glances people made at her lack of shoes or much else. Their eyes had drifted to me as we passed, questions remaining silent as to why the owner of the hotel was with a woman who hadn't bothered to put on shoes.

Knowing Penny felt insecure, exposed, naked to the eyes of the hotel's guests as we walked toward the boutique, I slowed my pace to stretch out the seconds, took pleasure in the way she groaned to realize she wouldn't hurry me along. Disgrace has its advantages, and humiliation can wear down even the most forceful of rebellions.

Penny must have believed I was simply tired or preferred a lazy stride, but in that assumption she was mistaken. The *catch*, as she had so hastily phrased it, began the second she agreed to follow me home, its name that of *domination*.

Every decision, every expression, every word, gesture and deliberate aberration were only tiny pieces of a skilled contraption, one action triggering the next, one result and reaction determining what would be the following step, the choice of direction. The *catch* had already begun, but Penny was none the wiser.

While she tried to hurry me along, I lingered. Her discontent was obvious.

Finally reaching the boutique, she scuttled inside, casting one last look into the lobby before hiding herself behind a rack of clothing. The woman who'd helped me earlier missed the barely dressed girl who'd run in, but lifted her head when I strolled through the doors.

"Mr. Mercier, you've returned!" Hurrying out from behind the checkout desk, she approached me. "Did the dress not fit your lady friend? Perhaps it wasn't to her taste?"

Graciously, I smiled. "That's not the case, at all. The dress fit perfectly and was to her taste. In fact, it looks much better on her than the hanger. But, she has another problem which needs to be addressed. Unfortunately, the dress was all she had to wear, and it left her feeling far more exposed than she liked."

Understanding my meaning, the woman's eyes flared wide, a small smile gracing her thin lips before she could hide it behind a hand. "Well," she finally answered, "I guess we hadn't considered modesty while picking out a dress. Did she tell you her size? I can find some underthings that may suit her."

"I brought her along, actually." Turning, I could barely contain my laughter to see Penny's eyes peeking over the rack of clothes. The sales woman had hit the nail on the head by mentioning modesty. Apparently, Penny preferred to hide. Which meant I would challenge that insecurity every chance I got, just for the fun of it.

"Come over here, Penny," I called out, my voice amused and vindictive. "There's no need to be shy."

If looks could kill, I'd just died three times over. Without moving for fear of chasing her off into the storm that continued to blister the night, I waited for her to make up her mind and come out from behind the rack. The saleswoman gasped from where she stood beside me, no doubt noticing that Penny's assets were far too noticeable in the dress we'd chosen. The material left nothing to the imagination.

"Oh dear," the woman said, "it seems we did forget a few things." Approaching Penny, she touched her shoulder and turned her in the direction of the back room, "We'll get you some underthings, and some shoes. Mr. Mercier hadn't mentioned how...shapely...you are."

I hadn't known at the time I'd bought the dress. Penny's figure had been a welcome surprise. "I'll just wait out here," I called before selecting a seat that was conveniently positioned to give me an unobstructed view of the mirrors in the back room.

The two women hurried back and I watched from my chair, choosing not to turn my head when the woman handed Penny some underwear. Penny hesitated to put them on, the other woman chuckling before turning to give Penny the privacy she believed she had.

As soon as she moved to pull the underwear up her thighs, her fingers dragging the dress up her skin to reveal more of her body to my eyes, a breath hissed over my lips, my pants becoming uncomfortably tight. Her skin was pale, but unmarked in its perfection, the cheeks of her ass firm, yet round. Clenching my hands, I could imagine what they would feel like against my palms, could taste the salt of her skin on my tongue if I were to bite, could see the pink outline of my hand if I were to punish.

Glancing over her shoulder to ensure the sales woman still had her back turned, Penny slipped the straps of the dress from her shoulders, and I wondered how many times could one man die and come back to life. Stifling a growl that threatened to rattle my chest, I watched as she held the dress in place with her elbows, as she bent over to catch the weight of her breasts with the bra, as she straightened to clasp it behind her back, the fullness of her breasts pushed up and into place...not that they needed the help. There is something to be said about youth, especially in the female body. My tongue traced over my teeth, the sharp edges welcome against the soft muscle.

After replacing the straps of the dress over her shoulders, Penny spoke to the saleswomen, and together they moved out of the dressing area and into the back portion of the store. I was quick to turn my head, to make it appear as if something outside the boutique doors held my interest. In truth, I was biting my tongue not to demand an encore.

Selecting shoes took little time, and Penny returned to me with more color gracing her cheeks, her body exquisite beneath the dress, her confidence boosted. "I feel better now," she admitted.

Inclining my head, I cleared my throat. "It's a pleasure to do you the favor."

A crooked smile graced her lips, there and then gone. "You say that like I'll have to return the favor some day."

Oh, you will...

"I already told you that you could pay me back from your checks. Why would you assume any differently?"

She shrugged. "It was just the tone of your voice, I guess."

I didn't bother to answer. "Shall we go get dinner? Our table awaits, and I'm sure we'll want to get there before the kitchen runs out of certain selections. The dining room is open not only to the hotel, but also to any person who passes by. It's quite popular in the city."

Penny nodded, her hair still damp from the shower, the length trailing down her back. "Definitely. After the evening I've had, I'm actually starving."

My eyes closed and opened again. "Then we are one in the same, *ma belle*, because after the evening I've had, so am I."

Her responsive laugh was unsure. "I guess getting caught in a massive thunderstorm has that effect on a person, huh?"

My laughter was anything but unsure. "We can blame the rain," I answered standing from my seat.

But, it's not exactly food I'm starving for...

CHAPTER NINE

Walking into the dining hall, I chanced placing my hand on the small of Penny's back, my efforts to appear the gentleman as I escorted her to hostess desk thwarted when she silently stepped to the side, allowing my fingertips to graze her hip until my hand fell away entirely. She didn't complain openly or bother to glance in my direction, but I didn't fail to notice the distance she kept, the refusal on her part to allow even that small part of a physical connection.

Penny didn't just have walls that closed her in, she'd constructed a moat as well. My thoughts drifted over the possible reasons why.

"Mr. Mercier, you're just in time. We have your table ready for you."

Genevieve was a sweet woman, if not a little slow in the thoughts department. I knew for a fact my table had been ready for over two hours, but still the blond woman with a button nose and blue eyes that were far too round for her face had used a greeting on me that was intended for patrons to the restaurant that didn't actually own the establishment.

The first several times she'd greeted me in such a way, I assumed she was practicing the expected behavior, ensuring she made it a habit to greet the other guests in such a way, but after months of the continued use of the polite phrase, I'd determined she truly didn't understand it was a ruse we used with our patrons, a formality that was lost on an employer who had agreed to the custom with the Maître D'.

Breathing out, I grinned politely, inclining my head as she plucked two menus from the desk and walked both Penny and me to our seats.

Like the gentleman I wanted Penny to believe I was, I pulled her seat out for her, refusing to take mine until she was settled and comfortable. Most women would have thanked me, perhaps batted a lash, or given me some demure grin that told me exactly how she'd show me her appreciation later. Penny merely scowled.

If I had to beat some manners into this young woman to drag her into compliance, I would do so with the utmost of pleasure and enthusiasm.

Stepping away from the chair, I ignored how Penny took her seat as soon as I was outside of reaching distance. Genevieve watched the scene with barely hidden dismay, her eyes darting to me in question as I settled into my chair and slipped the cloth napkin from the table to settle over my lap.

"Matthew himself will be serving you this evening. I'll let him know you've arrived," Genevieve explained before scurrying off, no doubt to tell whoever would listen that I was dining with a woman who had all but told me to take a hike.

"I'm sorry about the chair thing," Penny muttered as she retrieved her menu from where Genevieve had left them on the table. I didn't bother grabbing mine, I knew by memory what the restaurant offered. "It's just weird. I'm not used to all this fancy stuff."

"Fancy stuff," I repeated, disbelief coating my voice. She stared at me sheepishly, shrugged, and hid her face behind her menu. I couldn't help my curiosity.

"How long, exactly, have you lived on the streets?"

"Two weeks," she answered without bothering to lower her menu.

My theory that it had been the streets that raised her went flying out the window. What had caused this girl to be so ill-mannered? Before I could consider the question further, Matthew approached the table, his uniform perfectly pressed, his apron a blinding white.

"*Bonsoir*, Monsieur Mercier," his eyes darted to Penny. "And to you *Mademoiselle*."

Penny ignored him and he returned his attention to me. I simply cocked a brow and skipped the typical formalities. "I'll take my usual evening drink, Matthew, and Penny here would like a -"

Allowing my voice to trail off, I waited for her response. Dropping her menu to the table, she eyed Matthew and answered, "I'll have a coke, and do you all have regular cheeseburgers here? I can't read anything on this menu."

Poor Matthew had to cough just to regain the ability to breathe. My shoulders shook with barely restrained laughter. When he looked to me in question, I waved my hand in the air and said, "You heard the lady. A Coke and a cheeseburger. I'll have my usual meal as well."

His professionalism not lost on the odd scene, Matthew turned and walked away. Penny stared at me expectantly. I waited for her to say whatever was on her mind.

"So what is the job you're offering?"

Straight and to the point. I couldn't blame her there. "That depends," I answered, "on your education and skills." Intentionally lowering my voice to a sultry tone, I asked, "What is it you enjoy doing? Do you have any special talents of which I should be aware?"

Grinning in response to my question, she leaned forward and answered, "I can tie a cherry stem into a bow with my tongue, and I'm a pretty decent pole dancer."

My throat worked to swallow the blistering censure I wanted to deliver to this rebellious girl. Reminding myself that all good things come with time, I asked, "Are you lying to me?"

"Yes," she answered, but I wanted to make sure you didn't get too excited, because if you did, I'd be out of here faster than they could cook the burger you're buying me."

Message delivered and received. It was too bad for her I was a lot more discreet in my plans. "Any real skills?" I asked.

Her expression fell. "No. Does that mean the deal is off?"

I almost felt sorry for her ... almost. "Not at all. There are two jobs that don't require experience, and Theresa is ready and willing to train you on whatever requirements accompany the job. "I believe you can work in the lounge, or as a maid."

Eyes rounded, she shook her head. "Nope. I'm not wearing that skimpy little maid outfit and walking around this place with a feather duster. You can forget we ever had this deal. I'll just take my clothes, go in the bathroom and change, and I'll be on my way."

Penny moved to stand, but I was faster, my hand gripping down on her wrist, a squeal of pained protest bursting from her lips when I squeezed a touch too hard. Her attempt to jerk away was feeble at best, the dinner setting jostling on the table. And although we'd drawn attention, I wouldn't back down. She'd reached the end of the line on my patience. "Sit down," I bit out, the razor edge to my command cutting, "and behave like a respectable woman for once in your miserable young life."

What the hell had I been thinking to choose a girl from the streets? I'd wanted a challenge. I understood that, but Penny was proving to be a touch too rebellious, which only drew the ire of a man like me.

Surprisingly, she sat as I'd demanded, her shoulders folding in over themselves as her eyes scanned the tables nearest ours. Embarrassment colored her cheeks, and once more I saw beneath her bullshit facade to witness the fragility of who she was inside.

Ignoring the stares and whispers of the patrons seated near us, I snapped my fingers to draw her attention to me, my personality leaking out despite my desire to keep it hidden. "Are you trying to destroy your own life? Is that your game? What is it about having a job, food, a place to sleep and some damn class that aggravates you so much? Where were you before the streets? In some dysfunctional home that taught you nothing about how to behave?"

Although I'd kept my voice low enough to be a hiss across the table, tears stung her eyes, the gold flecked brown glimmering beneath the low lighting of the room. Our stares were locked as her lips parted slightly, as her fingers clenched over the napkin she hadn't yet placed on her lap like any decent woman would. Slowly, her brows pulled together, her cheeks deepening in color, a line being drawn between her eyes by the anger boiling inside her, and just as I thought she would attempt to bolt from me once more, Matthew appeared, setting our drinks on the table.

"A Coke for the lady and a red wine for Monsieur Mercier."

Neither of us bothered to glance up toward Matthew, and my hand twitched with the need to slap the rebellious rage from Penny's insolent face. Matthew left without another word, leaving us alone to continue this ridiculous battle.

"You know nothing about me or my life," Penny spat between clenched teeth. "Not a damn thing. And it's obvious you just want me to prance around here dressed like a damn slut for the purpose of putting on a show for your guests. That's beneath me. I won't be amusement for perverts like you."

"You were sleeping on the streets just last night, I'm not sure anything at this point is beneath you."

My smile was finely honed, the line sharp. It was all I could do to keep from reaching across the table to wrap my fingers over her face and hold her in place while I explained, "It was never my intention to make you prance around. I recall offering you a choice of jobs. One inside the lounge where, yes, the clothing choices are risqué, but also in our housekeeping department."

"Where I'll have to wear that stupid black and white dress with sky high heels and fish-nets? No thanks!"

The tension was making it difficult to understand where her refusal was coming from. Thankfully, she reminded me. Canting her head to the side, she gave me a feral smile while saying, "Like the woman you molested in the hall when we first got here? Is that a requirement of the staff? To be ready and available to you?"

My shoulders relaxed. "You mean Émilie."

"Yes," she admitted, Émilie."

Shaking my head, I answered, "You're confused, Penny. Émilie is not a maid, she was wearing one the lounge costumes. And nobody is required to be at my disposal (*except you*). Émilie and I...well..."

"Are dating?"

"More like fucking, but if you prefer a term that's more polite-" My voice trailed off as I gave her a wan grin.

"Oh," she mumbled, her full lips rounding with her eyes.

"Oh," I repeated, happy that she appeared to be backing down from whatever assumption she'd made.

"Sorry, I thought -" Pausing mid-sentence, she settled in her seat, her cheeks flaring with color. On a softer voice, she explained, "I just couldn't understand why a man like you would approach some random homeless girl in the rain. I assumed it was for reasons like what I saw with Émilie."

Interesting...

She wasn't wrong to assume that was my intent, but her adamancy, her anger, at the thought of a man using her that way piqued my interest. I knew nothing about her, knew nothing of her experiences, but I would leave those questions alone for tonight. "The housekeeping uniform is a grey dress, if I'm not mistaken, one that falls to the knees and comes with a white apron. It's in keeping with the theme of this hotel, but I believe most of the female staff wear shorts beneath them, given their duties. What you saw Émilie wearing is one of the costumes used in the lounge, and if you're uncomfortable dressing as such, then you don't have to."

Her expression was apologetic. "I'm sure housekeeping will be fine for me. I don't mind vacuuming, emptying trash cans or stripping sheets."

"Very well. I'll need some information from you before you can begin work."

"Such as?"

"Your full name. Your age."

Pulling the cloth napkin from the table, she settled it over her lap. "Penelope Graham. Nineteen."

This beautiful girl was fifteen years younger than me. "Why did you tell me your name is Penny?"

Shrugging, she refused to look at me. "It's short for Penelope, and I prefer it."

"I prefer Penelope," I confessed as Matthew approached the table to set our meals in front of us. Once he left, I let the conversation go, watching with interest as she practically devoured the food in front of her. Uncaring that ketchup was slipping down her chin or that grease dribbled down her fingers, Penelope had cleaned her plate before I'd taken three bites of my food. Rather than using her napkin, she licked the grease from her fingers, the sight both disturbing for its lack of etiquette and appealing in a way that only a *pervert* such as myself could appreciate.

Rather than calling her out on the faux pas, I stared with keen interest. After barely managing to tidy her hands, she looked up, eyed my food and asked, "Are you going to eat that?"

Without answering, I slid my plate across the table, genuinely amused by this child I'd pulled from the streets.

CHAPTER TEN

(Faiville Prison, 11:57 am)

"She wasn't that bad."

"She was," Vincent answered, disregarding the trivial defense Meadow had made for her sister while laughter whispered on his breath. "Had I not already made plans for Penelope, I would have tossed her from the hotel back out into the storm the instant she first demonstrated just how bad she really was. The girl had no manners." His eyes lifted to pin Meadow. "Is that how the two of you were raised?"

Insulted by the question, she countered, "Because watching a woman get dressed while she has no knowledge of your attention is the best of manners? You don't have a lot of room to talk, Vincent."

His grin was malicious, and inviting. A man with no qualms for the pain he caused, for the games he played, for the lives he manipulated, Vincent took pride in his achievements - if they could be called that. Other people would refer to him as a sadist, a plague, a scourge that should be eradicated from the world for having so thoroughly polluted the men and women he ran across, but he was simply a scoundrel, one who could tantalize with a secretive smile, one who knew how to stroke and kiss, to mold and shape those who had the misfortune of knowing him.

Penny had cared for this man...eventually. And now Meadow watched him with critical eyes, looking for any hint of his humanity. She opened her mouth to ask him a question, but before the words could tumble from her lips, the door to the interview room popped

70

open, a female guard walking in, her eyes drifting to Vincent for only a second before locking on Meadow. "It's noon, which means it's shift change. You'll need to leave the room while we secure Mr. Mercier in an alternate location for the next half hour."

"Am I really that dangerous?" he asked, his voice insidious and flirtatious. "Come now, Lisa, I've never done anything for you to worry about my behavior for the next half hour while you all abandon your posts."

Meadow couldn't believe it when the guard's cheeks tinged pink, her eyes softening. Dear God, had this man managed to seduce the very people who were supposed to keep him locked away and imprisoned from the rest of the world?

"You know the rules, Mercier. I'm not willing to lose my job when you'll be nothing but a memory in three days."

"That's not what you said last-"

"Not funny." Panic edged the guard's voice, her blue eyes darting between Vincent and Meadow as her lips pulled into a razor sharp line. "I'll escort you from the room myself...both of you."

Studying the guard, Meadow took note of her short stature, her figure more akin to a man than a woman, her short hair clipped close to her skull and the lines of age that marred her face. Standing as if to ready herself to leave, Meadow leaned across the table, lowering her voice so that only Vincent could hear, "She's not your usual type."

He grinned. "You do what you can with the selection you're offered." His gaze slid sideways to trap her in his peripheral vision. "I'll see you in a half hour, Meadow."

She chanced another look at the guard to find the woman staring directly at her. Smiling while turning to retrieve her recorder, she was stopped short by the guard. "You can leave your things. We'll be bringing him back here when we're done."

Nodding, Meadow hated having to leave her tapes behind. This was her last opportunity to record his confession, the words he'd already spoken potentially lost if something were to happen to the recordings. Biting her lip, she released a breath, casting one last look in Vincent's direction to realize he was studying her. Did he know how important these interviews were?

Forcing one foot in front of the other, she passed the guard on her way out of the room, flinched when she heard the door shut behind her, and walked in the direction of the hall she remembered from when she'd been led in.

"We'll leave you just outside the first set of gates. There are bathrooms if you need to use one and a vending machine if you're thirsty or hungry."

The guard moved as if to leave, but turned around again, searching Meadow's face. "How can you sit in there and listen to him? Didn't he kill your sister? You should hate him."

"I do," Meadow answered, crossing her arms over her chest.

Scoffing, the guard shook her head. "Doesn't look like it. If you were to ask me, I'd say you have a thing for him."

"I guess it's a good thing I'm not asking you," Meadow snapped. "Perhaps you're just projecting your own feelings onto me?"

The guard chuckled. "Can't blame me. It's not often we get the pretty ones in here."

With that, the guard left and Meadow choose a seat on an utilitarian bench, pulling up her feet so she could wrap her arms over her shins and lay her head on her knees. Skull throbbing with anger, excitement, agony, and questions, she let go of her disgust with the guard to focus on what Vincent had implied about her family home.

He was wrong in his assumption that Meadow and Penny had been raised without etiquette, without having been taught right from wrong, without having it drilled into their heads the merits of gracious manners and proper behavior. But unlike the lives some led when money was never an issue, or when constantly in the public eye, their childhood home had been comfortable, an environment built on a modest income where love had been more valuable than diamonds.

Penny knew how to behave, but whereas she had taken on more of the personality traits of their father - a stern man that still knew how to deliver a well-timed joke and who would often let loose to shirk the stress of responsibility - Meadow had been more like their mother. Refined. Educated. Demure.

They had been identical twins in looks, in strength, in fortitude, but in personality, there were some subtle differences. Penny was the more relaxed of the twins, the one who believed that life could be lived on the cuff, decisions not always carrying permanent results, that fun and relaxation were more important than constantly worrying what the future would hold. She was fun, while Meadow was responsible. She was brash, while Meadow was reserved.

Had Meadow been the one to end up on the streets, she would have suffocated beneath the pressure rather than enduring it long enough to discover a new home.

If Wishing Well could have been considered a home. According to the diary, it was more like a prison. But unlike the one in which Meadow now found herself sitting, Wishing Well had been built with the simple idea of opulence and excessive luxury. In that, Vincent's hotel had been a lie intended to settle the mind of its guests, a dream intended to deceive the mind of a wayward and rebellious girl.

How would Meadow fair against a man that not even Penny had been able to see through?

She didn't know, but she would try. She would bite her tongue each time she wanted to compliment him, would dig her nails into her skin each time she felt herself sliding into his orbit.

Lost in her thoughts, the half hour passed quickly, and Meadow was escorted back to interview room three, and back to a man that followed her with his observant eyes, his posture relaxed, his aura even more alluring now that his hunger had been sated by a female guard.

Meadow didn't have to ask to know what he'd done in the short time he'd been held in an alternate location, his teasing smile and bedroom eyes said it all. She could clearly see him stretched lazily over the white linens of a large, comfortable bed, his tan skin striking against the soft sheets.

Shaking herself of the image, she pressed record on her machine and took her seat. "I want to discuss the following morning, the first time you introduced Penny to your friend, Barron."

Vincent's lazy grin stretched wider. "I knew you would ask about that morning next. That day. That...encounter."

Meadow bit the inside of her cheek to keep from screaming. "Encounter isn't exactly the word I would use. From what I know, it was more like an attack. A lie. A test that Penny didn't know she was taking."

"It was a taste," he said, correcting her. His shackles rattled when he moved just a fraction to stretch the breadth of his strong shoulders. "How is a man to know how far a woman has come along if he doesn't determine who she was before the training?"

Planting her palms on the surface of the table, Meadow had to fight not to stand so that she could be bigger than him as she argued, "You intentionally deceived her into believing you were innocent. That you gave a damn what happened to her. That you would protect her from men just like you!"

A simple shrug, a grin that revealed nothing. "I fail to understand why it upsets you so much, Meadow." Stressing her name, he met her eyes, daring her to reach across for him with shaking arms and fingers that wanted to strangle. "You weren't the woman who was led astray, were you? You hadn't been the one to be deceived."

"She was my sister -"

"That you hadn't spoken to in over a year by the time I found her. When she had her heart broken by her boyfriend, where were you? When she was sleeping on the streets, when she was cold, scared and alone, what had you done to save her?"

Knowing he'd cornered her easily, he folded his hands together over the table, and straightened his posture. "Perhaps you're here to accuse me alone of her death because you're attempting to rid yourself of the role you played in her destruction."

The words stung, a barb settled deeply in her heart as easily as a warm knife slicing through butter. Swallowing down the knot this man so frequently conjured in her throat, she took a breath, willing her pulse to slow down, her muscles to loosen. "I didn't know Blake had left her. I wasn't made aware that Penny was on the streets. As far as I knew-"

"You were happy in the new life you'd created in a foreign country," Vincent said, interrupting her train of thought. "Why threaten that happiness with despair?"

Pausing, he let the words linger, gave her a few quiet moments to gather her composure. "I agree we should discuss what happened that following morning because it's the point where the story becomes more interesting, more unsettling, more divine. Penelope had one night of safety, one night to sleep, and eat, and believe she wasn't being chased through a maze of my design. But when the sun rose the next morning, all semblance of peace was lost to my cravings. The game I set in place had begun."

CHAPTER ELEVEN
Vincent

By seven the next morning, I was sitting behind the large, dark cherry wood desk that took up a sizeable portion of my office. A fire blazed, gently licking at the air in the fireplace with a hand carved oak mantel. Through the windows behind me, the gardens were in full view, the winter blooming flowers still holding court while those that regained life in spring were just budding, their bright green leaves tasting the warmth of the sun-drenched winds, testing and learning whether they could burst forth into full view.

The branch of a small tree tapped against my window with every soft breeze that blew past, classical music lightly playing over my speakers to add a sense of calm and wonder to my morning. And while I was bent over paperwork, scratching my signature onto several pages, I waited for the appearance of a beautiful girl through my door.

The knock came at five after eight, the morning becoming more intriguing when I called for her to come in. Lifting my eyes without straightening in my seat, I bit my lip to keep from complimenting her state of dress.

"I see you received my note," I casually commented, my pen still working ink over the last of my papers.

She took a seat in one of the leather chairs facing my desk, her demeanor quiet and unsure. "Yep. I met with Theresa after I woke up and she gave me the uniform I'm supposed to wear. It's not as bad as I thought it would be," she admitted, shy laughter teasing her voice.

The shapeless frock didn't do much to show off her figure, but I still knew what could be discovered, still craved what was hidden beneath the grey material and white apron that had bunched around her knees when she sat down.

Leaning back in my chair, I toyed the pen through my fingers, watching her with cryptic eyes. "I guess this means you chose to work in housekeeping?"

More soft laughter shook her thin shoulders. "You guess right. Theresa showed me the other costumes used in the lounge, and even though she told me I would make more money working there, I couldn't imagine myself wearing any them. Not in public."

In private, perhaps?

The pen dropped to the surface of my desk. "I'm glad we found something that worked for you. Housekeeping isn't the easiest of occupations, but it will keep you busy."

As will I...

"When does your first shift start?" I asked, wanting to ensure Theresa had followed my instructions and kept Penelope available to me in the morning.

"At noon. I don't need to be in uniform already, but my only other choice in clothing was what you bought me last night. My outfit is still in laundry. I have nothing else to wear."

Cocking a curious brow, I asked, "You have no other clothes besides what you were wearing last night in the rain?"

Shaking her head, her eyes glanced out the windows at my back. "No. I had a bag of clothes when I became homeless, but it was stolen the first night I fell asleep. I guess that's why I saw other homeless people sleeping practically on top of their stuff. Lesson learned."

Tsking my tongue, I flipped the corner of one page with my finger. "That won't do. I can give you some money."

Her eyes darted to mine. "I already owe you too much."

"I have it to give, and I don't mind. You can use it on whatever you need. I'm sure it will stretch further at a store outside of the hotel, the boutique is quite expensive."

"I saw that," she admitted. "While I was hiding behind the rack, I peeked at a few of the price tags. What you spent on the dress, underwear and shoes would have paid a month of rent at my old place. Thank you, by the way. I'm not sure I said that last night."

An errant breeze bustled through an open window, the cool air lifting the papers on my desk until I was forced to slap my palm down on them to keep them from flying away. Penelope laughed.

"A paperweight would help to keep that from happening."

My gaze lifted to hers, noting the easy smile she wore. "I don't happen to have one at the moment."

"Anything heavy would do," she suggested.

Even your ass? While I take the time to spread your legs and explore every nook and cranny?

"Or I could just close the window," I mentioned, standing from my seat to do so, while taking a breath to keep the heat of my excitement from coloring my face. It irked me to realize how husky my voice had been.

Barron was due to arrive at any minute, and following his introduction to Penelope, I would know exactly what type of girl she was. How far she could be pushed. Whether it was a hellcat that lay beneath her skin or a damsel unable to handle the distress.

As I retook my seat, Penelope admitted, "Theresa told me you needed me to fill out some paperwork before I started working. I can give you all my information, but I don't have identification or anything else. It was all stolen with my clothes."

I caught her brown eyes with mine, admired the wisps of gold and green streaked through the light brown. Her dark lashes framed the almond shape, her cheekbones set high and wide. Now that her hair was dry, I could see the natural waves that were soft, the length cascading over her shoulders and down her back. "We'll make due with what we have for now. I'll give you five hundred in cash. That should help you buy some more clothes and have your identification replaced. You can use the hotel's address, if you need to."

"Thank you," she answered softly. Fidgeting in her seat, she added, "I still don't understand why you're doing this for me. It almost feels like you're my father, taking me under your wing and all that."

Her words cut deeper than I was sure she understood. "I'm not old enough to be your father." *And I don't have the same intentions of a man who would look out for what's best...*

Laughter curled her lips, but before she could respond, a knock at the door drew our attention. I rolled my eyes as if I hadn't expected the interruption. "Come in."

Barron walked through the door, his suit perfectly tailored, his blond hair styled back and out of place. Allowing his eyes to land on Penelope for only a short second, he shifted his attention to me, playing his part perfectly without need for my instruction.

"I apologize for interrupting. I didn't know you had someone with you already."

Standing, I extended my hand to shake his. "It's no problem, Barron. I was just going over some information with a new employee."

Releasing his hand, I waited for him to take a seat next to Penelope. "Barron, this is Penelope Graham. Penelope, this is my friend and business associate, Barron Billings."

"Hey," she said, her simple greeting pulling a curious glance from Barron. It didn't take longer than a minute for him to glean that Penelope wasn't the standard type of woman I would endeavor to entertain. A smile tilted his lips.

For the next few minutes we made small talk, discussing subjects as ridiculous as the weather and as boring as our businesses and financial holdings. Penelope shifted in her seat every so often, quiet and obviously wanting an excuse to leave the two of us alone, but that had never been my intention. When she appeared ready to make an excuse to leave the room, I pressed a button on the keypad of my computer and pretended to have noticed a message that never really come through. "It looks like I'm needed elsewhere for a moment. If you two will excuse me, I'll make my departure brief."

I never gave Penelope the chance to complain. I simply slipped from the room and took a stroll through the hotel. It bothered me not to know how Barron would test her. I wouldn't see the attempt, wouldn't know what he said or did to sample her flavor, but he had ten minutes to lay his hands on her, which meant if I timed my arrival just right, I'd witness the results of his game.

Smiling and nodding at the people I passed, I made it appear as if I were simply checking on the ongoings of the hotel, and finding nothing that required my attention or intervention, I returned to my office in time to hear a muted shriek, a few swear words being lobbed from the throat of an angry woman and the unmistakable slap of a hand against skin. Throwing open the door, I narrowed my eyes in anger to see Penelope backed against my desk, Barron's hand wrapping over her shoulder as he cocked an arm to return the slap that left a noticeable mark over his cheek.

"What the hell is going on in here?" I demanded, my voice rising above the commotion, my reaction of surprised anger played well.

Without giving either of them time to answer, I jerked Barron away from Penelope, my anger clear as I shoved him toward the door of my office and growled, "Never return to my hotel again. Do you understand me? My employees aren't here for you to manhandle."

"I didn't do anything," he argued. "She's a fucking tease who got pissed off that I called her out on offering to fuck me and then -"

"Liar!" Penelope yelled from behind me. I turned to see her shifting her skirt back into place, tears leaking from her eyes to drip down her cheeks. "He asked me to hand him a pen and then tried to hold me against the desk and reach beneath my skirt."

Clenching my jaw, I took hold of Barron's arm and made a show of forcing him through my office door. Continuing the display should Penelope peek out to watch me walk him through the lobby, I didn't ease off until we were outside of Wishing Well and fully out of view.

Releasing him, I grinned. "Well, what did you think?"

Rubbing at his cheek that was blistering pink, he shook his head. "Where did you find that girl? She's practically feral."

"The streets. I figured if this were to be an actual challenge, I should make it impressive by starting from scratch."

"Good luck with her. I have a feeling I'll be a richer man by the time you fail with that particular challenge."

Inclining my head, I said, "You've had your first taste. You'll see her again in three months. I fully expect you'll be unpleasantly surprised to discover that you owe me a year's profits from The Castle. Be sure to ice your cheek. We wouldn't want it to swell."

I had to make a concerted effort to erase my smile when I stepped back inside the hotel, had to feign continued anger when I entered my office to find Penelope in her seat, her arms wrapped around her body as she softly cried.

Kneeling in front of her, I rested a hand on her shoulder. "Are you okay? For all the years I've known Barron, he's never acted that way before. I wouldn't have left him alone with you if I'd known."

Swiping at a tear, she sniffled. "It's okay. It's not the first time some asshole thought he could treat me that way. Being homeless tends to make people believe you're less than human."

"I told him he's no longer welcome in Wishing Well. If you see him or if he ever bothers you again, be sure to let me know. I won't tolerate a man treating any woman that way."

Reaching up, I brushed my thumb over a tear that slipped along her jaw, and for the first time since I'd met her, Penelope didn't immediately pull away from my touch.

It was apparent I was on the path of earning her trust, on the path of teaching her why I was the last man she should have let close to her.

"Why don't you wash your face in my adjacent bathroom, and then I'll take you on a tour of the hotel and surrounding gardens before you start your shift? It'll give you time to collect yourself before returning to Theresa."

Flashing me a small smile, Penelope nodded her head and stood to walk to the bathroom. Before stepping through the door, she turned back to me. "Hey, Vincent," she practically whispered.

My eyes locked with hers, but I said nothing.

"Thank you," she breathed out, "for everything."

"It's been my pleasure."

She quietly closed the door of the bathroom, and I stood in place knowing full well that in three months, she wouldn't be thanking me any longer.

CHAPTER TWELVE

The bright sun fought to warm the breeze that blew through the gardens of the hotel, Penelope's hair a waterfall of soft waves that revealed notes of red within the brown, gold hints that matched her eyes where they caught the brilliant light. Strolling beneath a sky that was a breathtaking stretch of clear blue, I folded my hands together behind my back while allowing her to silently discover the different seating areas and fountains, the secretive spaces that allowed privacy to those who desired to be outside but not in plain view.

"The gardens are beautiful, Vincent. Did you design them?"

Smiling, I answered, "I wish I could take credit, but I'm afraid I don't have a green thumb. I hired professionals to create and tend the gardens, showing them pictures from my former home, hoping the climate was right to recreate what I remembered from my childhood."

Her eyes met mine, the sunlight glimmering against the brown, teasing me with what those eyes would look like when filled with passion, with lust, with devotion. "You grew up in a place like this? Was it this peaceful?"

Not always, I thought as I remembered back to my family, to the problems I'd had at home growing up, to my mother's death, to the problems that followed. Choosing to keep those secrets to myself, I decided on a far simpler answer. "Yes. Paris, like many cities, is a busy place full of people, activity, noise. But there are places where one can get away, private havens like the home where I was raised."

"It must have been nice," she mused, her eyes brightening when she saw the well set in the center of the gardens, the feature from which the hotel had gained its name. "Is that real?" Her gaze tipped up to me, "an actual well?"

Nodding, I mentioned, "It's only ten feet deep, the city wouldn't allow it to be dug any lower, and it's supplied by city water rather than a natural aquifer or spring, but it's as close as I could have it. We had a well just like it on a farm my family owned. I used to toss coins inside much to my mother's dismay. She would always tell me that the well was intended as a water source for drinking, and that I shouldn't pollute it, but how else was I supposed to make a wish?"

Her laughter was snatched away by the wind, the current of air as greedy for a part of her as I was. "What would you wish for?" she asked as she moved on hurried steps to the well, peering down once she reached it to see the myriad of glimmering coins other guests had tossed inside. I crept up to stand beside her, my eyes locked on her profile as she watched the dancing display of light over water. There was something far too innocent about this girl despite the time she'd spent on her own. Something so simple and youthful that it wouldn't be difficult to grasp it with skilled hands and rearrange it to suit what I wanted.

"I wished to control my life. To own everything I could ever imagine. To have the world at my fingertips and an existence that was never boring."

Glancing up, she grinned. "Looks like your wish came true."

"Not entirely," I answered, studying her. "There is still one area that has yet to come true. Perhaps I could toss you in the well and make that final wish happen."

Her brows pulled together in confusion. Stepping closer, I leaned over to bring my mouth dangerously close to her ear. "I'm talking about your name. It is traditionally pennies that get tossed in, isn't it?"

"Oh!" Her laughter was like a siren's song. "Yeah," she said, placing distance between us again. I didn't miss the goosebumps that dotted her flesh. She was affected by me already, even if she, herself, didn't recognize it. "Very funny. For a second there, I thought you were going to snatch me up and dunk me just for the fun of it."

"Vincent!"

Right on time...

Penelope's head turned toward the sound, a woman's voice thick with a French accent. Calling out again, Émilie was drawing closer with each second, giving me just enough time to snatch Penelope at the hips, ignoring her surprised squeal as I dragged her backwards into a small, private niche that was bordered by tall camellia hedges, their red flowers still in full bloom. A small swing hung just inside, the chain rattling softly against the breeze, and just before Penelope could ask why I'd stolen her away, I pressed my hand over her mouth, brought my lips to her ear, and whispered, "Shush. I don't want her to find me."

Penelope attempted to turn her head to look in my direction, but I gripped my free hand over her hip, tugging her back against my chest and squeezing just hard enough to force a tiny sound in protest from her lips. My fingers tightened over her cheeks, and before she could panic and struggle, I explained on a voice

87

only she could hear. "Émilie and I had a small falling out last night. I would appreciate it greatly if you'd endure hiding just long enough for her to go away."

I allowed her head to turn just enough so our eyes could meet, one word falling from my mouth that helped her relax against me. "Please."

A single tense second led to some decision in her head. Her body relaxed more in response to my one word of placation. It would be the last time she would hear that particular syllable fall from my lips. But for this moment it was a means to an end, a moment I briefly wondered if Penelope would remember as the beginning of her fall.

From grace.

From independence.

From a life lived with her own thoughts and desires leading her way.

A moment when the heat of our bodies was in opposition to the cold wind. A moment when our shared silence cemented us together, letting her believe that we could be one unbreakable union at odds against the world.

I'd planted a seed that would one day flower, the roots driving deep into the soil as we stared at one another, listening and silently laughing as Émilie continued calling, her voice carrying over the distance as Penelope pressed tighter to my chest. My fingers gripped down on her hip, our shared breath mingling as this interlude took a turn toward the type of heat I was sure she'd never encountered.

The flower budded, Penelope's trust its scent. It was too bad the stem was firmly rooted in a soil of dishonesty and ill-intent.

Where she touched me, I'd become stone, and as my fingers brushed over the curve of her hip, she trembled. Émilie's voice was lost and forgotten, her search for me over, but still I stood in the private space holding a girl I wouldn't allow to run from me much longer.

"Thank you," I breathed out, my breath hot against her skin, the tip of my nose trailing against her hair as I breathed in the scent. Amused by the way she didn't immediately move away, I slipped my hand from her mouth after taking one last second to feel her rasps of breath against my skin. "That was a meeting I wasn't quite prepared for. You saved me."

"That makes us even," she answered, her voice husky with a hint of sex. "You saved me. I saved you." Unmoving, we stood back to chest, a delicate blossom wrapped within the cruel hand that would pluck it from its stem.

When I didn't move, she finally stepped forward, disappointment seeping in to caress the places were her body no longer touched mine. Turning, she asked, "What was the falling out? From what I saw yesterday, Émilie was more than happy to see you."

"It seems I didn't share the same enthusiasm, at least not to her liking. I had quite the evening yesterday and I was tired."

Penelope chuckled. "What happened to that endurance you'd bragged about? A man like you should be able to go all night."

Sucking in a breath, I had to grip the leg of my pants to keep from reaching out and dragging her back to me. Kicking and screaming, if need be. "Perhaps it takes the right woman to draw the endurance out of me. And Émilie has lost my interest."

Penelope's eyes rounded, my comment too close. "I should go," she said quickly, her walls erecting once again in an effort to shove me out. It didn't matter whether she used cement or stone, iron or titanium, I would find the weakness to breach her stronghold, one way or another.

"It's getting late," I agreed. "Your shift will begin soon."

I watched her run off, *un papillon dans le vent*. A smile tugged at my lips as she turned right, taking a path that would lead her farther into the gardens. Noticing her mistake, she paused, turned left and ran off in the opposite direction toward the hotel's entrance.

Her mind was addled, that much was obvious. And I had been the one to swirl my fingers through her calm waters to create that confusion, to disturb the surface just enough that truth was disguised beneath the ripples.

It would have been nice to focus on her entirely, but other matters required my attention, a certain problem that had followed me from home and remained hidden from easy view. Tucking my hands in my pockets, I both loved and regretted that problem. It was my burden to bear.

C'est la vie, I muttered to myself.

Taking the first steps toward a life that chained me, I tilted my face into the sun before pulling a coin from my pocket to toss into the well, a penny that sank as it jostled and turned to land among hundreds of others.

Only time would tell if that wish would come true.

CHAPTER THIRTEEN

Faiville Prison, 1:27 pm

Unable to meet Vincent's cold, cruel eyes, Meadow watched her fingertips tap slowly against the surface of the table. She knew he studied her, knew that behind his brilliant green gaze, satisfaction lurked, the truth of his games bubbling to the surface, the victory of surrender he'd so easily pulled from Penny on a beautiful spring day.

Meadow wanted to believe that Penny had known all the moments that had been staged, that she'd somehow intuited the manipulation Vincent had so easily mastered. But the diary contained no question of his intent, no nascent thought that, perhaps, her encounter with Barron had been intended, that Émilie's arrival in the garden had been planned rather than just mere coincidence. The diary made it clear that Penny had, in truth, been deceived into believing that a man such as Vincent Mercier could see the value of a dirty girl when the grime had been wiped away.

"What if Barron had hurt her?" Meadow asked after clearing her throat. "What if you hadn't returned in time?"

"There was no concern of that." He answered, his voice careful, soft in a way that was unlike him.

"But he was going to hurt her eventually, wasn't he? You shouldn't have believed he could restrain himself then."

Silence, and then, "You're skipping ahead, *Ma belle*. We are not at that point yet. I am simply pointing out what it was in the beginning. Time begins to move quickly now, a few weeks wherein I allowed the seed to germinate, allowed the beginning of her love to push up from the soil." Vincent paused, considering. His voice dropping to a conspiratorial whisper, he asked, "Will you not look at me as we talk?"

"I'm angry with you," Meadow admitted. "So angry I can barely remain sitting across this table from you, can barely remain in the room."

"I have done nothing to you. Not in that sense, at least. Why do you take on the anger, the betrayal, of your sister? It is not worth your time."

Lifting her eyes, she glared across the table. "Maybe because she's not here to feel those emotions. She died before knowing the truth."

"Did she?" he asked, a curious grin tilting the corners of his perfect lips.

"According to her diary, she did. But you're right. We're skipping ahead." Gathering her thoughts, Meadow leaned back in her chair, her gaze dodging about the room, Vincent's presence too much for her to bear. She wouldn't leave. She'd return for the next two days to complete the interview.

And she'd return one day after that to watch this man die for his crimes. A piece of her dying with him to watch the spectacle.

"Let's talk about Émilie. You mentioned her appearance was perfect timing, so you'd intended to have an excuse to drag Penny into that alcove. You'd wanted the excuse to touch her in that way. Was Émilie aware of what you were doing? How many people knew of the game you were playing?"

Mirroring her posture, Vincent relaxed in his seat, his long legs stretching out beneath the table until his foot tapped hers. She pulled her legs tighter to her chair, knowing that even that minimal touch was meant to distract her.

"Émilie did not know what I was doing. Nobody except Barron knew. Every day around that time, Émilie had a habit of coming to my office, sneaking an hour or two with me while I took my time with her on my desk. She'd fallen hard despite my warnings, had believed she could bring to life the heart of a man that had turned cold. Most women want to believe they can change a man, that there is some magic inside them, some trait, that will make him alter his ways. But people don't change, not unless they want to."

"That doesn't answer the question."

Vincent blinked. "I hadn't finished speaking. You should exercise patience. All good things come with time."

Meadow had a visceral reaction to the words. He'd said them many times. Perhaps such a phrase should be chiseled onto his tombstone.

"Knowing that Émilie would arrive around the same time I was giving Penelope the tour of the grounds, I'd emailed my assistant prior to leaving my office asking her to send Émilie to the gardens when she arrived. Her presence was an excuse to drag Penelope into that alcove, but it was also a catalyst to something else. Women, despite their objections and statements to the contrary, enjoy winning what they perceive to be competition. It makes them feel special, preferred, if you will. And by my rejection of Émilie, a woman Penelope had seen and knew was quite beautiful, it made Penelope feel uniquely desirable. It was a boost to her self-esteem."

Leaning forward, he asked, "If something makes you feel good about yourself, especially in a moment where you had been doubting, wouldn't you want to gravitate close to its orbit so you could continue feeling good?"

"What made you think she was doubting herself? You hardly knew anything about her by that point."

He grinned, contentment written into the lazy curve of full lips. "I've spent a lifetime studying women. Their behaviors and mannerisms. Their body language that reveals their secrets without ever having to say a word. Penelope didn't need to tell me why she felt insecure for me to know she did." Flaring his fingers as if this were simple knowledge any person should have, he said, "I gave her a reason to find pride within herself. It was her fault for her inability to let go of the need to continue experiencing the feeling."

When Meadow didn't respond, Vincent canted his head. "Oh, come now, you can't tell me you don't know that men have been doing this for centuries? It's all part of the game."

Clenching her teeth, Meadow asked, "What happened to Émilie?"

His brow wrinkled. "How should I know?"

Proud that she'd cornered him with the question, Meadow thought back on the diary, on the night Penny had first seen the dangers that lurked around Wishing Well. For once, Meadow felt like she had the upper hand. "You were there the night she died, weren't you? According to the diary you were. In addition, you were charged with her death. How do you not know?"

His teasing grin stretched wider, his eyebrows rising in surprise. "Now that, I did not know. Did Penny witness that night?"

Not yet ready to reveal what she knew, Meadow asked, "Is that the reason you had the diary sent to me?

For fear that having it sent to you or even read to you over the phone would give the police more charges to pin on you? To give them more evidence to support your crimes?"

Vincent hesitated, drawing a grin from Meadow's lips. "Oh, come now," she said, repeating his words, "you're already scheduled to die. What's one more lie to admit to? It's not like they can kill you twice."

His shackles rattled, his movement minimal. "I'm beginning to like you. It's a shame I never had the chance to have both you and Penelope at the same time."

"Oh, please. As if that could ever happen. I'm a little too smart for your games."

He laughed, the sound dark, deceptive. "Are you calling Penny stupid?" Tsking, he said, "Your own sister. It's in bad taste to speak ill of the dead."

"Tell me, Vincent, what happened the night Émilie died?"

Breathing out, he stretched his neck from side to side, his eyelids heavy. Meadow knew he wasn't tired, it was simply an illusion he wanted to portray.

"We both have information on that night, apparently. And I'm curious as to what Penelope saw. If you'll tell me what she believed she saw, I'll tell you what actually happened. *Quid pro quo*, Meadow."

"That's Latin," Meadow commented, "has the surprise of what I know forced you to change languages?"

A slow shake of his head. "French may be my first language and English my second, but they are not the only ones I know. Would you like me to tell you what I just said?"

"Something for something," she answered. "You can save your breath, I already know. Fine, I'll tell you what Penny saw, but once I'm done, it's your turn. And I want the truth, Vincent. No painting of pretty pictures to disguise your demons. This is your last chance to confess the truth of your crimes so that the world can know just how cunning and monstrous you were."

His expression was blank, unreadable. "Be careful with the words you choose, Meadow. You may just have to eat them later." Rolling his shoulders, he resettled in his seat. "Now, please, tell me what Penny remembered of that night, and I will tell you what actually happened."

CHAPTER FOURTEEN
PENNY

Housekeeping wasn't so bad, if you didn't mind the monotonous tasks. Vacuuming, sweeping, emptying every tiny trash can, trying not to think what was on the sheets as you pulled them from the beds. One would think businessmen would be a tidy bunch, but judging by the mess they left behind in their rooms, you'd be mistaken to believe it. Every room was the same, papers bunched and tossed haphazardly about, some in the trashcan and others on the floor near it, as if they'd been shooting baskets and their aim became worse as the night wore on. It probably had something to do with the alcohol they were drinking, because that was the other trash you found scattered throughout: tiny bottles of various liquors that I was sure cost a fortune to pull from the mini-bars.

But whereas housekeeping was a strenuous labor, especially as you climbed over the beds to tuck in the sheets and ensure the corners were just right, it didn't do much to occupy the mind. No, that job had been solely Vincent's, my brain running through everything that had occurred that morning both in his office and garden, every expression he'd given me and every word he'd said.

Lying to myself was a waste of time. Every attempt I'd made to convince myself I wasn't attracted to him was met with a skip in the beat of my heart, a breath that it took a fraction more effort to inhale when I remembered how it felt to have his hand wrapped over my mouth and the other gripped possessively on my hip. I was a stupid girl to think that he'd meant anything by it, but I couldn't stop thinking, 'but what if he had?'

He was the total opposite of what I knew in life, a perfect contrast to Blake. Where Blake had lacked in experience, Vincent was an expert in life. And where Blake had been a light in the darkness, Vincent was a shadow that could consume me whole. Just thinking of him thrilled me, and reacting as I did made me feel like the most ridiculous girl around.

I wasn't his type. I was just a pathetic wretch who'd ended up on the streets and had somehow managed to gain the attention of a man who wanted to help. I felt bad for assuming he had bad intentions when first he brought me to Wishing Well. If anything, Vincent had been a perfect gentleman, unlike that asshole friend of his. That slimy leech had wasted no time trying to take advantage as soon as Vincent wasn't around to stop him.

But Vincent had stopped him, hadn't he? An act that earned him brownie points in my book. After giving me time to calm down, and before taking me to the gardens, he'd also given me enough cash to buy myself some new clothes and have my license replaced. I'd offered to pay him back eventually, but he flat out refused and said, *say gra-tees*, whatever that meant. I was going to have to buy a French to English dictionary soon, just so I could understand him. For all I knew, he could be calling me a filthy whore and I would smile like an idiot because it sounded pretty.

My shift ended around six that night and I hurried to my hotel room to find my only set of clothes hanging in a bag on the door, freshly cleaned, dried and folded. I could get used to other people doing my laundry for me, but I assumed that would eventually be my job as well since I was technically an employee instead of a guest.

I showered quickly and got dressed, choosing to twist my hair up in a knot rather than dry it, and within minutes I was heading through the lobby on my way to department stores where I could buy more than just one outfit with the cash that Vincent had given me. I'd practically made it to the doors when a certain deep voice caught my attention, my head spinning to the right to see Vincent standing near the front counter speaking to a group of women who must have been guests.

My heart fluttered like it had tiny wings, and while I cursed at myself for the instant reaction, I watched with interest as Vincent wooed the women, his attitude, his dark looks, his voice that was so smooth it melted on the tongue like the finest of chocolate, easily dragging smiles and soft laughter from the women's lips, two of them daring to reach out and touch him.

I wondered if I was developing a mental problem when jealousy reared its ugly green head, my fingers curling into my palms to see those women flirt so obnoxiously. I wasn't sure what drew Vincent's attention my direction, but as soon as he saw me, he winked and turned his attention back to the women he was escorting from the lobby to the elevators in the back hallway.

Briefly wondering whether he would leave them at the doors, or if he'd follow them to their room to take part in some orgy, I grit my teeth. I knew he'd have no trouble luring them to strip off their expensive clothes, one by one.

There was just something about him that had snuck inside me as easily as I assumed it snuck inside all of his female admirers.

A heavy sigh blew over my lips. I forced myself out the door, and farther out the gate of the large circular wall that guarded the grounds of the hotel from easy view.

Shopping took no time at all, and I'd been careful to save enough for my identification that I'd have to get on a day I had off from work. I bought some toiletries and other odds and ends to hold me over until I would receive my next paycheck, splurging on a leather bound journal I could use to record my thoughts. I had no one I could talk to anymore, so I chose to talk to myself. I made it back to the hotel around ten that night. Picking up another cheeseburger and fries from the dining room (much to the dismay of the chef), I took my dinner up to my room, pigged out and fell asleep by eleven.

It surprised me to wake up that night before the sun was a glow on the horizon, my alarm clock flashing three fifteen when a noise outside caught my attention. At first I'd thought some guests had gotten too rowdy, but then a high pitched voice with a recognizable accent set my eyes wide and my heart racing.

Curiosity dragged me out of my bed, holding my hand as I walked barefoot over the soft white carpet to pull the curtain aside and look down at the wishing well I'd seen that morning when Vincent was giving me the tour. Just as I suspected, I saw Émilie sitting on one of the circular benches, her mouth wide as she spoke to Vincent in French. I couldn't understand a damn word she was saying, but by her tone I knew her words weren't friendly.

Vincent had removed the suit jacket he'd worn earlier that day, and was dressed only in a white button up shirt with the sleeves rolled to his elbows, and dark slacks. He paced angrily in front of her, stopping when she said something else, a smile stretching his face. Feeling like a voyeur, I shifted my weight from foot to foot, not knowing if I should keep watching. But I couldn't help staring down wondering if he was breaking up with her for me. A small smile split my lips, not for the pain she was experiencing, but for the small bit of confidence his attention gave me.

The scene ended as quickly as it had begun when Vincent marched off, leaving Émilie crying on the bench. Seconds passed as I waited for Vincent to return. When he came back into view, he glanced up at the hotel, my heart jumping into my throat for fear I'd been caught spying. Quickly closing the curtain, I pressed myself flat to the wall, my breath heavy in my chest. More soft noises filtered up to my window, and although I fought not to look, I found myself peeking down again from behind a curtain I'd moved just a fraction of an inch.

Confusion filtered in when I noticed that Vincent had changed shirts, the white he'd worn earlier, now blue. It had to be him, I thought. The hair was the same, the build, the color of his skin, but yet there was something different I couldn't put my finger on.

While I narrowed my eyes trying to see his face in the shadows, Émilie wiped the tears from her eyes before standing from the bench. Slowly, she turned around, her shaky hands hiking up her skirt as she presented herself to the man at her back, her skirt pulled up to her waist as her hands moved to brace herself on the bench as he approached her.

My jaw dropped when Vincent, or whoever the man was, opened his pants, grabbed her hips and thrust inside her.

Fighting the urge to scream, or cry, or yell at myself for even caring, I tried, but failed miserably, to ignore the way my body reacted. Moans poured from Émilie's lips, her eyes squeezing tight as Vincent's hand slapped her ass, each hard thrust of his hips knocking her forward while she held on to the bench to keep steady.

I'd been so fucking stupid to believe he would actually leave her for me. I deserved this awkward pain for even wanting a man that would jump from one woman to another. What kind of bitch did that make me?

Letting go of the curtain, I ran to my bed, threw myself on the mattress and gripped the sheets while burying my head in a pillow. I didn't need to see anymore, didn't want to admit to myself that just watching him fuck her was enough to hurt me.

Fuck, I was being stupid. I was being naive. I was being -

A muffled scream from outside drew my attention, a splash forcing me back to my feet. My fingers pulled aside the curtain again. I peered out from behind the partition to see Vincent looking down into the well.

What the fuck was going on?

Leaning over the stone rim, he pulled at something, an arm finally appearing from the water, Émilie's body slowly emerging. After tugging her over the side, he laid her on the ground beside the well, allowing seconds to pass before picking her up and carrying her toward the path leading back to the hotel. Her head was limp against his shoulder and I couldn't tell if she was breathing. But before I could even make a guess,

Vincent shot a look up toward my window, his eyes just barely missing mine. I allowed the curtain to fall back into place.

She couldn't be dead.

She couldn't.

Maybe she'd just tripped and fallen in?

Vincent was walking far too slowly for anything else. It made sense that it had been an accident because if Émilie had died, Vincent would have been running or screaming for help.

My heart raced like it would tear from my chest, my breath coming so fast and hard that I stood frozen in one place not knowing whether to crawl back in bed or call the police.

Taking deep breaths, I attempted to calm my heart, forcing myself to crawl back in bed for fear I'd hear a knock at my door within minutes. Had he seen me watching? Had Émilie just drowned? I didn't fucking know and I slept horribly the rest of the night, every small noise forcing me awake, terrified that he'd known I was spying and would fire me.

The sun had just started rising when I finally gave up on sleep and sat on the edge of the bed, my head cradled in my hands. Within an hour, I'd convinced myself that my imagination was getting the best of me, that maybe the entire thing had been some bad dream. And with those thoughts in mind, I got up and got dressed, not wanting to be late for my second shift.

After taking the elevator down to the first floor employee hall, I weaved through the mazelike corridors, letting myself into the housekeeping department where Theresa stood folding sheets. Glancing at me, she smiled. "You're right on time. It's good to have an employee that cares about her job."

Panic shot through my heart, my pulse like a trapped insect beneath my skin. Walking to the older woman with greying hair and a trim figure, I met her tired blue eyes with my own. "Is there a problem with another employee?"

Maybe Émilie had never shown, not that the lounge opened earlier than six that night. I was being ridiculous, I kept insisting to myself.

"It's Émilie," she breathed out, "one of my cocktail waitresses in the lounge. I guess the love affair she was having with another..." she paused, searching for a word, "...employee didn't work out. She quit early this morning."

Setting the sheet aside, she missed the way my body practically melted with relief. A dead person doesn't quit, they just fail to show up, and if Theresa had heard from Émilie already, it meant she was very much alive. While silently thanking God I hadn't witnessed anything I shouldn't, I leaned against a wall for support.

Turning to me, Theresa asked, "You don't happen to know anybody who needs a job, do you? I need to fill Émilie's position quickly. We're short staffed as it is."

My hand was still over my chest when her inquisitive gaze met mine. Pushing myself up on unsteady legs, I shook my head, attempting not to sound as out of breath as I was. "No. Sorry. But if I run into anybody looking, I'll be sure to send them your way."

Theresa gave me an odd look, but decided against asking a question. "Okay, well, we're waiting on the rest of today's housekeeping staff to arrive. Once they get here, I'll pass out room assignments and we can move forward with our day."

"Sounds good," I answered, studying my feet as I worked to get myself under control. After that particular night, I wondered if I'd be able to look Vincent in the eyes if I saw him, and if he'd seen me watching from behind the curtain.

The best bet, I told myself, was to avoid Vincent altogether, not just because I wanted to avoid getting in trouble for spying, but because my heart skipped a beat to learn that Émilie had been kicked to the curb.

CHAPTER FIFTEEN
Vincent

After leaving the garden, I walked my normal rounds of the hotel, greeting guests as they meandered about, met with the manager to help with any problems that needed to be addressed, and then made my way to the elevators to take the car down to the basement I'd designed to be a practical cage when the hotel was built.

It wasn't a bleak environment by any stretch of the imagination, but for the occupant that lived within its walls, I wanted to ensure there was no chance of an accidental escape at an inopportune time. Wishing Well was built with the idea of luxury and a sense of peace, opulence and a elegant ambience. And if a certain issue were to find his way out of the basement to run loose through the halls, I was fairly certain I would be made to answer numerous questions I never wanted asked.

It wasn't that I didn't love Maurice, in fact, the opposite was true. I loved him too much, which was why I spared no expense to see to his comfort, left no stone unturned when it came to providing him with the best doctors, nurses and counselors the world had to offer, but as I'd known since growing up with a boy of his peculiar problems, there would never be an actual cure.

He'd been normal until age two, except for the temper tantrums that were blamed on age and the inability to communicate. By the time he should have made certain milestones, a problem surfaced that set him apart. The doctors claimed he was slow, at first, some even suggesting he was spoiled. After my mother's constant phone calls, my father's rage, and time spent wherein Maurice could be observed, my baby brother was diagnosed with severe autism.

The signs were there, an inability to communicate, the refusal to meet your eye, the desperate need for a constant routine where just one small change could set him into an explosive panic that was far more violent than my dear Maman could endure. My father was often away, his hotels and other businesses keeping him busy, so it was Maman and I who tended to a boy that, while intelligent, was unable to behave as any normal child would.

It wasn't until he was older that the diagnosis changed.

Slipping a key into the elevator panel and typing in a code that would take me to the basement used only for Maurice, I leaned against the back wall and closed my eyes. My thoughts drifted to my childhood home, to the screaming, the crying, the shattering glass, the whispers of a mother that was losing her own grip on the world. Maman was as delicate as a hollowed eggshell, so easily crushed within the strict grip of panic for her son that not even the nurses and teachers could relieve her pain.

In the end, she'd died of cancer, but I always assumed it was from a broken heart. To say I felt bitter would be an understatement. In all the time she gave to Maurice, she could never spare a moment for me. I would have made her proud had she given me that attention, I would have read to her, behaved for her, showed her that not all young boys were untamed. I could have saved her, I'd believed, as her casket was lowered into the ground, could have provided her sunlight on even her darkest days.

I hated her for dying when I hadn't given her permission, I resented Maurice for wrestling her from my control. I understood that women were just simple flowers that could be cultivated to bloom, or have their petals pulled.

By the time my father moved both Maurice and me to America, I had no respect for a woman's strength, because my mother had none of her own.

The elevator slowed to a stop, the doors slid open as quietly as an exhalation of breath, a large entry room stood open to me as dark and elegant as Maurice had preferred. The walls were painted a deep black with borders of pristine white.

Dark wood furnishings complimented the leather seating, crystal vases shimmering beneath light, a wash of blood red color in the roses that filled them. Breathing in the rich scent, I stepped from the car, made a left and casually strolled to a sitting room I knew Maurice often used. It had been designed to resemble the salón from our childhood home, the color palette bright, just how our mother had wanted it.

Lingering in the doorway, I watched Maurice tap away on his computer, his eyes moving quickly as his fractured mind absorbed whatever information he was studying.

"I thought you had a counseling session today."

This was one of the issues my hotel manager had brought to my attention, a certain counselor racing away, vowing she would never again return to this hotel. Although John knew that something had frightened her, she refused to reveal what, exactly, had occurred.

"The counselor left," Maurice explained, his fingers moving quickly over his keyboard.

In the twenty-seven years since Maman had died, it was discovered that Maurice's affliction was not actually autism, but a severe case of schizophrenia. He'd gained the ability to communicate, he could look any person in the eye, but behind that green eyed gaze that was much like mine, sanity was noticeably absent. The medications kept him partially contained, but only when he was compliant.

"Why did she leave?" I asked, struggling to keep my voice patient.

"I told her I wanted to eat her."

Closing my eyes and opening them again, I remembered telling Penelope the same thing, but in a language that wouldn't send her running. "And did you attempt to eat her?"

His gaze shot up, locking to mine. "I would have if she would have spread her legs. It's been a month."

"Maurice-"

"You have many," he said, interrupting. "Give me one. It's not exactly like I can hunt them down when stuck in this cage."

Sighing, I answered, "It's not exactly like I can steal one away and keep her trapped down here with you. I'm sure your nurses will ask questions about the screaming."

His eyes studied my face, his intelligence so clear while his chaos was pervasive. "One," he barked, "Tonight. Or I'll chase the nurses away."

"We can always keep you chained," I crooned.

"I'm chained already," he retorted, his attention returning to the screen of his computer. Without looking at me again, he demanded, "One, Vincent. Tonight."

Blowing out a breath, I relented. "Fine. I'll see what I can do when I bring you out for your walk through the gardens, but you must promise to behave."

He gave me a clipped nod of agreement and I knew it would be the end of the conversation. Maurice wasn't the type for small talk.

Leaving his space, I made my way back to the elevator while deciding who I would toss to the wolf. By the time I'd reached the lobby floor, my decision was made, a pretty face flashing in my thoughts that I hoped would be amenable to my brother's demands.

The day passed quickly thereafter, the monotonous task of seeing to a hotel that ran like a finely oiled machine within my world. As the sun set behind a glowing horizon, I greeted a group of women who had recently checked in, flirting with them and endearing them to my brand. It was as I turned to escort them to the elevator that would take them to their floor, my attention was drawn to a unique face, my head turning to see Penelope watching me from where she stood near the entrance doors. She was wearing the clothes she wore the night I'd discovered her on the streets, jealousy flashing behind her gold-flecked brown eyes.

Our time in the garden had been well spent, it seemed, the seed I'd planted growing strong. Winking at her, I forced myself to return my attention to the guests because it would be a few days at least before I tested the waters of Penelope's mind to discover if my absence had made her heart beat harder.

I enjoyed dinner alone that night as the guests went about their routine, and after gorging myself on appértifs and fine cuisine, I skipped dessert to stroll to the lounge. As usual at that time of night, the lounge was filled with inebriated men, their eyes tracking the different cocktail waitresses in various costumes and states of dress.

Émilie, however, was the woman who caught my eye. Upon seeing me sitting at a back table only lit by the candle that sat in its center, she smiled wickedly and added a sway to her hips as she approached to discover what I wanted. "*Bonsoir*, Vincent. Are you still tired?"

My eyes lifted to hers. "I'd like to see you tonight. In the gardens, but it will be rather late. I have engagements beforehand and was hoping you'd keep from going to bed early after the lounge closes."

"What time?" she asked, her voice sultry, her lips shining within the candlelight from the liberal gloss she wore.

"Will you meet me at the well around three?"

Her smile stretched, sex written into the passionate curve. "Anything for you, Vincent."

There have never been more unfortunate words spoken. I knew my brother's tastes ran the same line as mine, but whereas I was able to restrain my instincts, Maurice hadn't yet learned self-control.

When I bit down, a drop of blood would spill, but when Maurice did so, skin would rip, tears would run red, women would lose their lives. Unless, of course, the woman knew how to play the game, as long as she was perfectly ready and able. Following instructions to the letter was a necessity when it came to our shared games, but Maurice's form of punishment could be far more permanent.

I hoped that Émilie's training by her whore of a mother would make it easier for my brother to rut with no harm done.

Leaving shortly after she'd agreed, I slipped up to my penthouse on the top floor, settling myself at the keys of a piano I enjoyed playing on nights that stress was a constant pressure in my head. And while the intricate notes floated on air like fireflies on a warm summer night, I allowed my thoughts to escape to a girl whose room was situated below mine.

Émilie had been a distraction for a man like me, a pretty face, a healthy body, a bit of warmth to ease the chill of lonely nights, but Penelope, that dirty, rebellious, hard headed girl, had become a siren's song, *une idée fixe*, an obsession.

The bet meant nothing, the money but a garnish on the meal I would make of her. I imagined my fingertips exploring her body, finding all the right notes, the flats and sharps, that would make her sing like the piano. My body was all tension and crudely cut stone when I remembered her reflection in the boutique's mirror. The day would come when I could resist her no more, my teeth aching to sink into her modest flesh.

Would molding her into the lady I craved chase away the rebellion that drew me like a moth to flame? Could I fashion her to be both hellion and slave?

I hoped so as I became lost between one note and another, the hours ticking past as I planned how to win her heart while watching her grow. I would pluck her beauty from the life of her stem just so that I alone could know her fire.

Émilie was expendable while Penelope was the prize.

Three o'clock came quickly that night, and leaving my suit jacket draped over the back of my couch, I left my room, took the elevator down and retrieved Maurice from the basement.

As we rode up, I mentioned, "I'll need you to remain hidden in the employee hall while I explain to Émilie what she'll be allowing. She'll serve your needs, Maurice, on a regular basis as long as you keep from hurting her too much."

"What does she look like?" he asked, anticipation carved into his tone.

"She's beautiful. Blond hair. Blue eyes -"

A hiss burst from his lips. "Who cares? Her tits?"

"Large," I answered.

"Her ass?"

"Divine."

"You've tasted her," he said, a statement but still a question.

Glancing his direction, I nodded, "I can't toss you a fledgling. We must do this in absolute silence."

"Why not just bring her to my cage?"

Sighing, I admitted. "She doesn't yet know it will be you she's entertaining. That's why I need you to stay in the employee hall until I've had a chance to explain it to her. If it works out, if she's agreeable, we can make alternate arrangements for next time."

"I'll behave," he promised. It was the best that he could say. I should have known better than to set up this meeting in such a public place, but my mind was distracted by a brunette girl that I hadn't had the opportunity to play.

Stepping out of the elevator once the doors pulled apart, I left Maurice in the abandoned hall while I stepped out into the night. Wind tugged at my shirt as I moved down my path, as if nature itself was attempting to stop me. Finding Émilie sitting on a curved bench near the well, I took my place in front of her, moving back when she reached for my pants.

"I have a duty I must assign you," I said, my voice soft within the twinkling night stars, just loud for enough for her to hear me. Blue eyes tipped up to find mine.

"A duty?" she asked in French, the language she preferred when it was just the two of us.

Tucking my hands in my pockets, I reminded her, "When I agreed to hire you and bring you here from France, I told you there would be conditions. You agreed to *anything*," I stressed the word, "a promise you repeated to me tonight."

Her eyes rounded. When she didn't contest, I continued, "Not many people know that my brother lives in the basement of the hotel. It is a secret I keep quiet for many reasons and one I'm trusting with you. If information regarding Maurice's existence were to leak from this point forward, I would know you were the one to leak it, so I suggest you keep in mind that you should always hold your tongue."

"What does this brother have to do with me?"

Pausing before answering, I confessed, "He has needs much like me, and I would like for you to see to them."

Angry tears leaked from her eyes, her voice gaining in volume. "You will share me with other men?"

Locking my narrowed gaze on her face, I demanded, "Whisper, Émilie. Or the guests will hear you. I have no qualms sending you back where you came from."

"You would do that to me?" she hissed, her voice low, her rage heightened.

Inclining my head, I answered, "The arrangements have always been made. All it would take is a push of a button."

More tears leaked, a steady stream over her cheeks. On measured steps, I approached her to lift her chin and tilt her head to mine. Softly, I asked, "What have you always told me, Émilie? Since the moment I first took you to my bed?"

Her shoulders quaked with sobs. "*Je suis ta petite pute.*"

"*Oui,*" I agreed. "You are my little whore, so be that for me now. Maurice is not much different from me. He will satisfy you, if you're perfectly compliant. But you must be careful with him, Émilie. He has a short fuse, he takes even the smallest of insults to heart. He can strike out before you understand you've injured his heart."

"*Tu me fends le cœur!*"

Kneeling in front of her, I caught her red-rimmed eyes with mine. "I have not broken your heart, *ma belle*. I am simply demanding a favor. Never have I told you we would be exclusive, and I know you've slept with men other than me since living at Wishing Well. I know you accept payment. You are more like your mother than you have led me to believe."

Her gaze darted from mine, her cheeks reddening with anger and shame. "Fine. I will make love to your brother is that's what you want from me, but you will pay me like everyone else. It was only for you that my love was free."

A smile tugged at my lips. "Payment can be arranged. Perhaps if you are to Maurice's liking, we can make this a weekly thing. I'll reward you greatly for your time."

She continued to sob, but the agreement had been made. "Stay here. I'll send Maurice out to you, and I'll stand nearby should any issues occur. Stroke his ego, Émilie, he likes that. And for safety reasons, just behave and pretend like you're fucking a starving, feral dog, and you should get through this just fine. Understand?"

Ignoring the way her eyes rounded with apprehension, I retrieved Maurice from where he stood chomping at the bit and reminded him on a soft voice that we are to play nicely with our toys. One wrong move on Émilie's part, one wrong word or facial expression, and it would take a crow bar to pry my brother's violent hands from her throat.

"Play nice, Maurice," I warned one last time as I released his arm to approach Émilie. She was still wiping her tears away when he drew near her, her body tensing from where it was revealed by her skimpy frock. Barely looking at my brother, she stood from the bench, turned around, lifted her skirt and offered herself to his desires.

I wasn't polite enough to turn and not watch, and if I were to be completely honest, it was fascination to see a woman submit so thoroughly. He took no time thrusting inside her, his lips pulled back on a snarl, his huffs of hot breath like white plumes against the cold night air. For a brief moment, I believed Émilie was enjoying herself, but then...

It seemed Maurice was a bit too excited. After taking her in either her cunt or her ass, I wasn't quite sure, he leaned over to taste her flesh. His teeth must have sunk down a bit too hard because she pulled away from him with a scream on her lips and pulled back her hand readying a slap.

Even though I ran from where I stood witnessing the tryst, I wasn't fast enough for my brother. By the time I neared where they had been, Maurice had already lifted Émilie from her feet, walked her the short distance to the well and tossed her in. He stalked away as I ran to the well, his low growls a whisper against the wind as I looked inside the well to see Émilie sinking beneath the water. Reaching, I was barely able to take her hand and pull her up, a wash of red sweeping down into the depths to settle amongst the pennies.

Laying her on the grass beside the well, I felt for a pulse and didn't find one. Blood leaked from her head where it had struck the stone rim of the well from how she'd been tossed inside.

No pulse.
No breath.
No response to anything I said.

Maurice had claimed his latest victim and I was left to clean up his mess.

Picking up Émilie's body, I carried her from the well, my mind racing and my eyes narrowed on my brother who shrugged as if he'd done nothing wrong.

Holding the door open for me, he waited until we were inside before saying, "She called me a dog. She was going to hit me, like Papa."

The breath I'd been holding fell from my lips on a rush. "It's fine, Maurice," I answered, knowing that any harsh words could set him off. "We'll deal with this situation, and perhaps next week, we can find a woman you'll like."

CHAPTER SIXTEEN
Faiville Prison, 2:17 p.m.

"You're not saying anything. I've been silent for a few minutes now."

Meadow attempted to uncurl her fingers from the edge of the table, attempted to silence her thoughts, slow her heart, take a full breath after listening to his sordid confession. "I'm not sure what to say," she admitted on a rushed exhalation.

Vincent was quiet for a short moment before whispering, "Would you like some salt to season those ridiculous words you'll now have to eat?"

Her gaze tipped up and their eyes met. "Ridiculous words?"

The green of his beautiful, mesmerizing eyes glimmered. Softly, he explained, "You accused me of killing Émilie, but as you can now see, it wasn't my hands that led to her death. It was an accident, an unfortunate one at that. I believe she could have fulfilled my brother if she'd just learned to behave."

Without arguing that he had, in fact, been responsible, she chose to instead ask a question that screamed in her head. "Was Penny intended for Maurice? Had that been your ultimate plan for her?"

Seconds ticked past, the quiet hum of the air conditioning the only noise in the room. "There you go skipping ahead again." Vincent's shackles rattled as he sat back in his seat. "We should tell this story in the order that it occurred, and I haven't reached the training of Penelope just yet."

119

"Training," Meadow repeated, the one sickening word echoing in her head. "Training for what?"

"To be the ultimate lady, a woman of such high esteem that even a man like me could never forget her. She was so brash when I found her, wet clay ready for a skilled hand as she was spun around and around on a potter's wheel and given shape."

"She was a human being, Vincent!" Meadow's voice rose in volume, her crushing anger barely contained. "You keep referring to her as a flower, as clay, as a puzzle or some fucked up game, but never what she actually was! She wept tears, she was able to feel love, she could express herself through laughter or smiles or words, but never in this entire interview have you admitted as much."

Cruelty stretched his full lips, the corners lifting with amusement. "She was mine to play with as I wished, Meadow. Penelope gave me that permission eventually. She admitted that without me, she could no longer continue living. She begged to be transformed into what I helped her become." Pausing, he studied her face. "And she did become something truly special, a rarity in a world of facsimiles and replicas, of people who don't have the balls to be who they are. I was, and I'm still, proud of her."

Her heart skipped in rhythm to hear the compliment, rage a tenuous thing. Meadow's recorder clicked loudly behind her in warning to change her tape. After doing so, she retook her seat and stared at a man who watched her far too closely. Could he taste all the feelings she harbored inside? Did he know more than he let on?

"We only have another two hours today, and we've been sidetracked."

Nodding his head once, he commented, "Heightened emotions will do that sometimes."

Clearing her throat, Meadow rolled back her shoulders. "Despite your reluctance to admit as much, Émilie's death was your fault. You knew that Maurice was a danger to any person that got too close to him."

"And I warned her of that," he argued. "It's not my fault she didn't listen. Although, after hearing what you told me of Penelope's recollection of that night, what Maurice said to me when I returned from disposing of her body now has meaning. I couldn't figure it out while sending off the email to Theresa to make it appear as if Émilie herself had quit."

"And that was?"

"That he'd already discovered another toy he wanted to play with. I was so angry with him at the time that I didn't bother to ask what he meant, but if he had spied her watching from the window that night, his words now make sense."

"Would you have given her to him if you'd asked him at that time and found out it was Penny that he'd seen?"

"Stop skipping ahead," he reminded her. "The next part of this story is quite lovely, actually, a fairy tale for both Penelope and me. It was within the next few weeks that her love for me blossomed and I chased her through a maze of deceit." Leaning forward, he added, "I had feelings for her beyond the ordinary, Meadow. The desire wasn't one sided."

Blinking, Meadow fought against the tears that threatened. "Why do you think that matters to me?"

He laughed. "It's just a hunch." Waiting for Meadow to meet his stark gaze, he asked, "Wouldn't any person want to know that their family member was loved?"

"Fine, we'll go in order of events. But first, I want to know why you kept Maurice hidden. There are many people in the world with psychiatric problems, some of which are able to adjust and live perfectly normal lives. Why keep him locked up?"

A shadow darkened Vincent's expression. Meadow knew Maurice was a subject that affected Vincent more than he wanted to admit. It was rare for any person to say something that made Vincent Mercier squirm. "Maurice would never live a normal life. We knew that by the time he was twelve. It wasn't just his disruptive fits, his hallucinations or delusions. There was something else inside him that was never officially diagnosed. I believe my father had a strong hand in that. Whether it was because he didn't want his son to carry another label, or if he believed he could cure the problem himself, my father was the person who first kept Maurice locked down. He was educated like any normal child, given tutors and books and everything else, but he was never allowed to leave the premises of whatever hotel we happened to be living in at the time."

Meadow caught the catch in Vincent's voice, the subtle sneer of his mouth when he mentioned his father. "Was your dad abusive to you and your brother?"

The shadow was gone, there and then no longer an obvious mask over his skin. "Not to me. Possibly to Maurice, but with his fits being as violent as they were, there was never any telling where he got the bruises. He wasn't an easy person to handle. But we loved him.

We cared for him and we kept him as comfortable as possible."

Not wanting to drop the subject, Meadow asked, "Where is Maurice now?"

His jaw ticked. "Shouldn't we be talking about Penelope? That is what you came to discuss, is it not? I'd hate to run out of time over trivial things so that you never discover the full story."

Expertly, Vincent deflected the question, changing the subject as smoothly as night becomes dawn.

"Yes. I guess you're right. What happened next?"

Satisfied that they'd turned back to the story of the wicked game played against Penny, Vincent answered, "For the next two weeks, it was business as usual. I made it a point to remain busy, while managing to always be within sight of Penelope. She'd acted strangely at first, but as the days wore on, she warmed to me again, smiling when she saw me, her cheeks heating with color if our bodies brushed too close. I guess you could say I'd played a game of hard to get until she was chasing me down. It wasn't until that beautiful day in the garden that I finally made a move."

Running the tip of his finger down a scar on the table's surface, he asked, "Did she talk about those weeks in her diary? Did she record what my lack of attention made her feel?" Lifting his gaze, he transfixed Meadow in her place, something raw and naked lingering behind those eyes of startling emerald green.

"Penny did," she managed to say. "While reading the diary for the first time, it was during those pages that I wanted to scream for her to run away. I knew that once you sunk your claws inside her, there would no longer be a chance for escape. I hate those pages most of all."

"Will you tell me about them?"

In truth, Meadow hated giving Vincent Penny's private thoughts, but she couldn't deny she didn't take pleasure in watching his changing expressions as she did so. Some parts obviously touched him, some words surprising him because they revealed the humanity in Penny that Vincent had so obviously avoided or ignored.

When she didn't immediately answer, he offered, "If you'll tell me what was written about that time, I promise to tell you exactly what happened in the days that followed. You should know by now that I am a man that keeps his promises."

Nodding, Meadow worked to swallow the knot in her throat. "Quid pro quo, Vincent?"

His grin was lazy and sincere. "Yes, Meadow, quid pro quo."

CHAPTER SEVENTEEN

Penny

The following days after witnessing Émilie and Vincent at the well were spent actively avoiding my employer as much as possible. When I wasn't cleaning hotel rooms, I was down in the employee office asking Theresa if there were any other chores she needed done. She believed I was one hell of an employee, while I was actually looking for any excuse to stay hidden. Too afraid that Vincent had seen me watching and would corner me with questions, I also took my days off to go to the Department of Motor Vehicles to have my identification replaced, and I managed to catch a movie or two when I didn't actually have the extra money for it.

But after four days of doing what I could to avoid him, the day came where I could no longer stay out of sight.

"Have you been enjoying your job at Wishing Well?" a deeply masculine voice whispered against my ear. Jumping in place, my back met a strong chest, my body spinning to find that Vincent was far too close for me to breath easily. I'd been so caught up in polishing the brass elevator doors on the third floor, that I hadn't heard him approach. A ball of fear lodged in my throat, my answer coming out curt and broken. "Yes. It's great. Pays the bills."

Nervousness was obvious in my voice. Vincent, noticing the reaction, smiled as he stepped back to give me room. "I didn't mean to frighten you. I was passing by and realized I've not spoken to you in several days.

125

I'm happy to hear the job is working out. It would be a shame to lose such a ... diligent ... employee."

I could feel my cheeks flaring red, my thighs squeezing together just a tad too tight. Thanking God this man couldn't read my thoughts, I tried to ignore the way my mind conjured images of what I'd seen that night at the well.

"Diligent?" I asked, swallowing.

Sensuous laughter floated across his lips, the sound deep, dark and heady. Fuck, I was in trouble. There was nothing about this man that didn't attract me and I would have to step up my hiding game just to keep from being in trouble of one kind only to step into trouble of another.

"I spoke with Theresa. She's very impressed with your *dutiful* behavior. As am I. Keep up the good work, Penelope."

He turned to walk off, and I blurted, "Are you going downstairs?"

Not bothering to change course and turn back to me, he merely glanced over his strong, broad shoulder. "I can take the stairs."

"But, the elevator would be easier."

His lips quirked, amusement causing his jeweled eyes to sparkle. "You haven't finished polishing. And it's only three flights down. I'm sure I can manage."

With that, he walked off silently, his powerful stride catching my eye until I found myself leaning back against the elevator doors. I'd failed to remember there was still wet polish on the brass until he disappeared into the stairwell. Spinning, I saw that I'd have to start all over again. "Shit," I muttered, unable to catch the butterflies fluttering around in my stomach so that I could shred their tiny wings.

Three more days went by, each one passing as slow as a disabled turtle crawling through several feet of soft mud. Remaining scarce and out of sight was becoming far more difficult than I imagined. It seemed like every time I turned around, Vincent was nearby. My heart would stutter at the sight of him, then crash down into my feet when he glanced my direction without bothering to say a word in greeting. It especially bothered me when there was a beautiful woman on his arm because I never knew if she was a business associate, a guest, or a special friend that he was entertaining for the evening.

Why did I even care? He was my boss, and I had obviously read way too much into what had occurred between us in the garden.

The next several days I barely saw Vincent at all. Every so often, I found myself peeking outside the window of my room to stare down at the well, wondering if I would catch him again in some romantic liaison. It occurred to me that I missed staring at him as he walked past. I missed those split second opportunities for him to glance at me, even if he didn't acknowledge my existence. Leaving my room to take a walk in the garden on my own, I had to admit to myself that I'd created a fantasy of a man in my head that I had no hope of coming true.

I'd never been so lust-struck while dating Blake, but then again, he had always been so easily accessible. Maybe this was what it meant to be an adult: a life lived with zero chance of having one day, one moment, of knowing how your dreams would turn out. You simply have to shuffle through it, hoping for the best while preparing for the day you eventually fell down.

The moon was holding court as I stepped outside, and it occurred to me that I hadn't checked the time before leaving my room. It didn't much matter how late it was, I wasn't scheduled to work the following morning.

While strolling down the long, winding paths of cobblestone, I noticed smaller pebbled paths that led to out of the way alcoves and seating places set about to be both in view and out. A chorus of night insects was a soft lullaby on the air, and without consciously deciding on a path to follow, I found myself drawing close to the well.

It was there that Vincent and I had shared a private moment, there that I witnessed an event that had frightened me for a few days after, and as I turned to my left to gaze down a darker stretch, I spotted the alcove where Vincent had dragged me, remembered the solitary swing that hung from a tree branch that overhung the tall flowing shrubs providing the alcove privacy.

Making my way to the swing, I sat on the wooden seat, listening to the soft creak of the chains above my head. Unsure how much time passed as I thought about everything that had occurred since my father's death, I found myself with a soft smile on my face, thankful for the direction my life had taken since Blake left my life. I still hadn't contacted my mother or sister to let them know the changes I'd experienced, but perhaps -

Two male voices drifted my direction, one I didn't recognize and one richly exotic and familiar. The rolling beauty of the French they spoke drew me from the swing to stand near the entrance of the alcove. Beneath a million stars and the muted lights that dabbled the gardens to illuminate the paths, Vincent and a man who looked just like him walked side by side, their voices low, their words fast.

From what I could understand by their hand gestures and clipped tones, they were arguing. Squinting my eyes as if that would bring them into better focus, I stared at the man by Vincent's side. He wasn't a mirror image of the man I'd been fantasizing about for over a week, but he was close enough in resemblance for me to assume there was a familial relation. Brothers maybe, or cousins. I wasn't sure, but both were the type to conjure illicit fantasy in a woman's head.

I had to shake myself of the thought.

Daring to step out further from the hedges that concealed me from easy view, I recognized the second man as they stepped closer to sit near the well. He was the man in the blue shirt, the one who'd had sex with Émilie in plain view. Although I couldn't begrudge the woman for wanting either of these men, I had to wonder what type of seedy arrangement the three had between them.

Obviously, whatever happened that night was upsetting enough for Émilie to quit her job. What was it? What had these two men done?

Curiosity pushed me another step forward, my eyes locked to their bodies as they huddled close to talk. I should have paid better attention to where I was standing. As soon as a twig broke beneath my foot, the man with Vincent looked up. His eyes locked to my face, his body going rigid, his words speeding so fast that it forced Vincent's head to snap in my direction. I stood frozen as both men grew quiet and watched me.

Aggravation was written over Vincent's expression, the force of it a pulse in my throat. "Um," I stammered, an unshakable need to fill the silence of the night, "sorry. I was out here on the swing when you came out. I didn't mean to-"

Like that, the aggravation was gone, polite professionalism softening the lines of Vincent's face. The man beside him said something I couldn't understand. Without answering, Vincent stood from the bench seat and walked toward me, shadows from the garden cutting razored edges across his face. "Penelope, we were just surprised is all. Are you having trouble sleeping?"

"I don't have to work tomorrow," I responded, as if that would excuse lurking about in the shadows.

From the bench, the other man spoke harshly, even the beauty of the foreign language lost on his tone. Vincent's head snapped to look at him, his mouth pulling into a line as sharp as a honed blade. "It seems my brother would like to meet you," he explained, his fingers tightening over my shoulder as he pushed me back deeper into the alcove. Lowering his voice to a bare whisper, he leaned into me, the notes of his cologne wafting beneath my nose, "Do me a favor and say very little when I introduce you. After that, you should hurry back to your room."

"Okay," I whispered, an icy finger tracing my spine. Remembering that Vincent's brother had been the man with Émilie before she'd ended up in the well, apprehension choked me.

I took a step, but Vincent wrapped his long fingers around my bicep, tugging me to him. A gasp of breath escaped my lungs the instant my back met his chest. Angling his head so that his lips were dangerously

130

close to my ear, he whispered, "Do not move too quickly around him. I'll keep hold of your arm. Once you say hello, I'll walk you away from him. Be sure to go straight to your room after."

The apprehension tightened into a knot of panic deep inside my chest. "Vincent, what's going on?"

"I'll explain later. Just follow directions, Penelope. Do *exactly* as I say."

Not liking the sound of that, I clenched my teeth, my legs not quite responsive when I attempted to put one foot in front of the other. Vincent's brother stared at me as we moved forward, his eyes shadowed, his body so still that I could imagine a snake perfectly coiled to strike. Only the heat of Vincent's hand on my arm kept me from screaming and running away.

However, as we moved closer, I was able to see his brother's features more clearly, was able to relax just a small amount to discover that the too-still man was just as beautiful as Vincent. The only difference I could plainly see was that the brother had an emptiness behind his eyes that wasn't noticeable in Vincent.

"Maurice," Vincent said as we stepped close enough to speak quietly and be heard, "this is Penelope Graham. Penelope, this is my younger brother, Maurice."

"*Bonsoir...*" Maurice said, his body rigid.

"*Elle ne parle pas français,*" Vincent answered.

I merely swallowed, a lot, finding it impossible to dislodge the trepidation clogging my throat. Holding in a cry of surprise was nearly impossible when the snake finally struck. From one second to the next, he was standing feet from me and he was leaning over me, the heat of his chest colliding with mine as the tip of his

131

nose brushed over my hair. Vincent's hand tightened on my arm.

I trembled to realize Maurice was inhaling my scent, and lowered my eyes to see his hands clenching into fists at his sides. On an amused voice, he whispered, "*Es-tu diabolique ou divine?*"

Clearing his throat, Vincent said, "Penelope was just saying hello before going up to her room. Weren't you, Penelope?"

"Yes," I managed to choke out. "Hello, Maurice."

"Hello," he greeted me in return, his accent thick, his voice penetrating.

Without waiting another second, Vincent directed me away from Maurice, lightly shoving me onto the cobblestone path that would take me to the hotel's back entrance. "I'll explain tomorrow," he promised before turning around to return to his brother. I didn't hesitate, and was practically running by the time I turned a corner to be out of sight.

CHAPTER EIGHTEEN

I woke late the following morning, dreams haunting me with images of two men, both beautiful and so bizarre. Both frightened me for different reasons, both crawling beneath my skin, scratching at my nerves until my body buzzed.

It was confusing how fear tasted like desire, how desire carried the hint of pain, how pain left a woman thrashing over soft white sheets tucked over a comfortable bed.

Crawling out of bed, I took a shower and wrapped myself in one of the plush robes the hotel stocked in the rooms once my skin had turned pink and I could breathe easily again. I craved a cup of coffee from the small cafe in the lobby, but was wary to leave my room for fear of seeing Vincent before I'd had a chance to get my thoughts in order.

Maurice had been an experience, a deep shadow cast over the happiness I found in Wishing Well. I'd only seen him twice now, both times at night, both times in the garden. Where was that man during the day? A tremor coursed through me as I stepped into the living room, a note catching my eye that had been slipped beneath my door.

On heavy vellum paper, a masculine font swirled in black ink told me I wouldn't be hiding like I'd planned.

My office. 11:00 a.m.
~Vincent

It was never a request with him, always an order. Cursing the way my breath caught, the way my heart picked up its pace, I glanced at a clock to see I had fifteen minutes to be in his office on time. I dressed quickly in a pair of jeans and a loose black shirt I'd purchased with the money Vincent had given me to use. Slipping on the Converse I'd worn the night he met me, I made my way to the elevators, my head leaned against the wall as it carried me down to the first floor. My feet dragged as I crossed the lobby, my eyes darting to Vincent's secretary as I approached.

She simply smiled and said, "You can go ahead inside. He's expecting you."

I opened his door to find him standing behind his desk, his hands folded together behind his back, his legs held at shoulder width apart and his attention focused out of the floor to ceiling window. Unable to speak without croaking, I choose to clear my throat. He didn't bother turning to face me.

"Have a seat, Penelope. We need to talk."

"Am I in trouble?" I asked, my voice soft, mousy.

Glancing from over his shoulder, he shook his head just slightly. "There's nothing for you to be in trouble for."

Spinning slowly to face me, he pressed his palms against the surface of his desk, his shoulders wide as his white, pressed shirt stretched to span the breadth of his chest. "I wanted to apologize about Maurice," he explained as I slipped into my seat. "My brother is somewhat of a thorn in my side and I never intended for you to meet him." Pausing, he breathed out. "Now that you have, I must request that you never speak a word of his existence to anyone."

"What's wrong with him?"

134

He didn't answer immediately, and when he finally did open his mouth, it was to ask his own question. "Did he frighten you?"

"Yes," I confessed, the word slipping so easily from my lips that I couldn't have kept from saying it if I'd tried.

His green eyes glittered, drawing me in. "Maurice has some issues, to put it mildly. None that you'll have to concern yourself with. I'm only asking that you stay silent. Not many people know about him and I prefer to keep it that way. It seems, we now share a secret."

"Okay," I agreed, my stomach clenching as Vincent straightened his posture, rounding his large desk, and leaned against it to stand in front of me. His knee brushed mine and a spark shot through me. He was the most beautiful man I'd ever seen.

"I was impressed with your behavior, Penelope. So much so, that -" his voice trailed off before he could finish the thought. For several seconds, we stared at each other, my heart beating erratically.

Breaking the tense silence, Vincent asked, "Why do I get the feeling I frighten you as well?"

He'd caught me off guard with the question, my cheeks heating, the pink color chasing down my neck and chest. "Because you do," I admitted. Attempting to cover up the true reason for my reaction to him, I quickly explained, "You're my boss. You can fire me at any time and I need this job."

"Is that all it is?" Lips pulling into a knowing grin, he watched me, saw through me, touched me without so much as lifting a finger.

If desire itself had a voice to speak, it would sound like this man.

"You should go," he suggested softly. "Before either of us end up making a mistake."

Except, I wasn't sure anything we could possibly do when nobody was looking would be a mistake. I knew deep down, that even if it meant nothing, just having one moment of being with Vincent would be like dying and stepping through Heaven's gates.

"I should go," I breathed out, repeating his words as I pushed from my seat, careful not to touch him as I moved past. Reaching the door, I couldn't help glancing back to see that he was still watching me. My pulse fluttered beneath my skin when our eyes met.

. . .

I wish there was a way to turn off your brain. Like a special switch, or perhaps a drug you could easily access at a corner store that would enable you not to think, not to dream, not to wonder how stupid you are.

While working the morning shift the day after meeting Vincent in his office, I found that even the physical labor wasn't enough to distract my every thought from being homed in and focused on him. Questions lingered in hidden corners, whispering - always whispering - as I told myself that I was a silly girl for even entertaining the thought that I'd seen desire in his eyes when I'd glanced back before leaving his office.

Desire.
Heat.
Regret.
Dismay.

Was he thinking about me as often as I was thinking about him?

Returning my cart to the employee office, I said my goodbyes to Theresa for the day when she informed me there weren't any additional jobs that needed to be done. I didn't feel like going up to my room immediately, so I wandered the employee halls instead, eventually making my way out into the gardens. Still wearing my housekeeping uniform, I wound down the cobblestone path, continuing far past the wishing well that was a centerpiece of the gardens, and after exploring for what felt like an hour, I discovered another small alcove, one large enough to hold a bench swing.

Spring was settling into the air, the sun able to warm the breeze that softly blew past. The vines, bushes and trees were all a bright green with new leaves, and except for the muted sounds of traffic outside the walls, the garden was silent.

For the first time in two weeks, I felt peace settle over my mind, the constant whispers quieting as I approached the bench swing. Lying down, I allowed a leg to drape over the edge, the tip of my foot pushing against the ground so that the swing would rock me like a cradle. A breeze tickled up my legs, but I didn't feel exposed with my unladylike position since the alcove provided privacy and the boy shorts I wore beneath my grey dress kept too much from being seen.

After a while, I wasn't quite sleeping and wasn't quite awake. Instead I was in an in-between, a place where I felt hypnotized, relaxed, drifting over a softly rolling wave that came to a sudden stop as soon as gravel crunched beside me and a heavy weight dropped down onto the seat near my legs.

"Are you enjoying the peace and quiet?" Vincent asked, his voice smooth and rich, fluid and entrancing. I opened my eyes to see him with one arm draped over the back of the bench seat, the corners of his lips tilted up just slightly, the green shirt he wore bringing out the jeweled clarity of his eyes. "Have I ruined it for you?"

Yes...but in good way.

"No," I answered, "Not at all." Moving to sit up, he gripped the ankle of my bent leg that I'd propped on the seat of the bench.

"Don't move on my account. Continue relaxing. I was just out for a stroll looking for a bit of peace and quiet myself."

Sparks chased up my leg from where his fingers wrapped over my skin. Unable to breathe, much less talk, I trembled when he gripped beneath the knee of my other leg and lifted it so that my leg would drape across his lap. The bench continued softly swinging, and I assumed it was his feet that pushed against the ground to keep the slow motion going.

"I was just getting some air after working this morning," I finally said, searching but finding nothing more interesting to say. Vincent watched me with amusement in his eyes, his left hand still gripping the ankle of my right leg. When I realized that he had an unobstructed view down my skirt, a shiver coursed through me. Normally, I hated to be exposed, but for this man, the feeling was far different.

My heart stuttered, a pulse in my throat as his left hand released its hold on my ankle, his fingertips slowly brushing up the side of my calf.

"Does this bother you?"

"Your presence?" I asked, my voice shaky.

"My touch." There was no waver to his voice. Fluid as water, strong as steel, as assured as any man would be, knowing he cornered his prey.

"No." I inhaled. "Yes." Exhaled. "Maybe."

Dark laughter danced along the breeze. "That's not an answer. Or perhaps it's the most accurate answer of all."

When I thought he would continue taunting me as the tips of his fingers stroked up and down, never reaching my knee, never going any place inappropriate, he surprised me with an unexpected question.

"Will you be attending the Masquerade Ball next week?"

"The what?" I squeaked, willing his fingers to go just a little higher, to breach the curve of my knee...to explore down. As usual, he refused to give me what I wanted. I was practically squirming when he finally answered.

"Our annual Masquerade Ball. It is one of the biggest events for the Wishing Well. Every person will be elegantly dressed, their masks concealing their faces. Everybody who is somebody will be there."

His fingers swept up to tickle the back of my knee and I felt heat bloom between my legs. Just as I thought he'd follow the curve to the back of my thigh, he changed direction, a whisper of touch dragging back down along my calf.

I struggled to speak intelligently, my eyes shut, the bench still softly swinging as birdsong crept within the silence of a clear spring day. Opening my eyes as his fingers kept brushing the skin, a touch but not really, I watched white cotton clouds dance along azure skies, the verdant green of fresh leaves rustling across the dainty branches of tall trees. "I'm just a housekeeper. I'm not sure that qualifies me as somebody."

"My interest in you qualifies you as somebody," he answered.

My breath was trapped in my lungs. "Isn't that the mistake you were trying to avoid?"

"What is life without mistakes?"

How the fuck does a question become the perfect answer?

"I don't have a dress."

Silence, and then: "We keep extra gowns and masks for guests who are in the hotel but may not have known about the ball and would like to attend. I've set aside two gowns and two masks that will fit you."

Applying pressure to my skin as he dragged his fingertips up, he said, "You can answer my question with your choice of which gown. If you wear the red, then I will know your answer is no." His fingers swept under the curve of my knee, continuing down along the back of my thigh, so slowly. "And if you wear the green, my favorite color, I'll know your answer is yes."

My mouth went dry. Swallowing was impossible. Down, down, down his fingertips traveled. "What's the question?"

"Will you take me to your bed?"

His fingers were between my legs driving a line down the center of my boy shorts, teasing all the places from top to bottom of what skin against skin would be like.

I opened my mouth to answer, but his hand pulled away, the bench swing shifting as he stood up. A shadow fell over me and I opened my eyes to see him standing tall, looking down, blocking my face from the sunlight. "*Bonne journée*, Penelope. I'll expect your

140

answer at the ball." He stepped away, but then stopping, twisted back to look at me. "I think it's only fair I warn you that in the bedroom I am a man with particular tastes. You should keep that in mind while making your decision."

Tucking his hands inside his pockets, he strolled off, and I was left a quivering mess of damp need while lying on a bench swing in the brilliant afternoon sun.

CHAPTER NINETEEN

Red or green?

Green or red?

Nope. Didn't matter which way I asked it, the question had no clear answer. Was not showing up at all a way to avoid it?

The next week sped by fast, despite my wish for it to crawl. The monotony of my job did nothing to silence my thoughts, the glimpses of Vincent I caught here and there doing nothing to tell me which direction I was going.

Green!

Green!

Green!

No, wait. Red.

My heart, my body, my traitorous soul were warring against my logic. Vincent was my boss. Vincent was the man keeping me from being homeless. Vincent, I was sure, was a man-whore with a slick tongue and powerful swagger. Vincent was the man that had tossed Émilie to Maurice. Yet, Vincent gripped my every thought.

As the hours passed, as the minutes now ticked quickly, I stood barefoot in my bedroom, staring down at my bed wondering which beautiful gown I would be wearing. My weight shifted from one foot to the other, my heart leapt and then dove, pounded and then stopped. I was going to pass out if the rhythm didn't steady.

My hand reached for the red gown, the silky material sliding against my fingers, before I dropped it down to the white sheets and picked up the green instead. I must have repeated the act several times before having a anxiety attack and walking away entirely.

It wasn't that I didn't want Vincent. It was that I wanted him too much. And I was certain that like any drug that was oh so good, but oh so lethal, just one taste would make me an addict.

Red.

No, green.

Red, definitely red. I would be crushed if he took what he wanted and walked away. I would be homeless if he kicked me to the curb after getting what he was after.

I would be an idiot not to jump at the chance to learn what that man would be like in bed.

Walking back to the foot of my bed, I closed my eyes and spun quickly in place until I was dizzy. And like I was playing a children's game, I reached out blindly, deciding I'd let fate decide what would happen to me with whatever gown my hand landed on.

Gripping the silk, I blew out a breath, and opened my eyes to see green.

It appeared fate had chosen to throw me to the wolves. I chose to ignore the way my breath caught at the thought of it.

In a ridiculous rush, I pulled on the slinky gown, taking note of how low the neckline rode, my cleavage on full display above a bodice jeweled with crystal. Sleeveless, the gown hugged my chest and abdomen, green silk cascading down from an empire waist to brush the ground as I walked.

If not for the matching heels that gave me four more inches of height, there would have been no way

143

for me to walk in this. Carefully twisting my hair up into an elegant design, I pinned it all in place and hurried out to the bed to grab the mask and tie it on. Green like the dress, the jeweled mask only covered my nose and eyes, the ribbons long and trailing down my back.

The room spun as I made my way out into the halls, the silence of the elevator ride down the first floor ballroom setting my nerves on edge and twisting my stomach into so many knots, I wasn't sure I'd ever be able to eat again.

But for all the trepidation, for the fear and panic and uncertainty that drowned me, I was still able to stand amazed and mesmerized when I turned a corner and followed the music that filled the hotel to see the glamor and opulence of the ballroom.

They'd spared no expense in its splendor, cut no corners in its design, and now with the room filled from wall to wall with beautiful people, I felt like I'd stepped out of some ordinary life and into a fairy tale. Never had I imagined I would attend an event such as this, never had I felt like I was floating while my feet were planted firmly on the ground.

Stepping inside, I glanced up at the large, crystal chandelier, its light spilling down onto the dancers casting prisms of colored designs. The walls flickered with hundreds of fire sconces, the silver fissures in the black marble floors sparkling beneath the dance of shadow and light. A waiter moved past me dressed in a black on black suit, pausing to bow shallowly and offer one of the flutes of sparkling champagne. After plucking one from the silver tray, I inclined my head to thank him and brought the rim of the glass to my lips.

144

Nobody in this room knew who I was, they had no clue I was simply a housekeeper. And as they passed me in their tailed tuxedos and partial face masks, I smiled back with red glossed lips when they nodded their heads in greeting. If I knew how to dance, I would have done so, but instead, I stood off to the right of the room watching while people laughed and clapped and kissed each other, the center of the room a whirlwind of activity as masked dancers moved in coordination.

My eyes peered about the room wondering which masked man was Vincent, which tuxedo would he wear? Black on white, black on black? Would his mask be gold, or black or red? Who was he the among these glamorous people and would he make himself known to me now or later?

He would recognize me because I wore the dress he selected. He would know my answer was yes.

An hour passed and then another as I drank more champagne and ate the hor d'oeuvres that passed by on silver trays, my head spinning as the alcohol coursed through my veins, my cheeks hurting from smiling so much. Just as I'd given up hope of ever recognizing Vincent, a hush fell over the crowd, people backing away from the center of the room as dancers dressed in jaw dropping costumes took their place beneath the chandelier.

A song lightly played, the crescendo building, the increasing tempo driving my pulse until the room was spinning, the dancers hearing their cue and becoming the music that transfixed me. One man stood facing them from the front of the room, his tailored tuxedo perfectly displaying broad shoulders that tapered down to a strong chest and a trim waist, his face completely covered by a black mask that bore no embellishments except shadow.

It must be him, I thought, but then a pair of strong hands grabbed me, a warm chest pressed against my back as the cool surface of a devil's mask brushed against my cheek. Twisting so that I could see the man that held me, brilliant green eyes stared back.

"Vincent," I whispered, unable to see if he smiled that dangerously devilish grin that fit so perfectly with his green and silver mask. His hand found mine, and before I could utter another word, I was being led from the ballroom by a man whose black tuxedo did nothing to hide the masculine strength of his body.

I was practically running to keep up with him as we wound our way through the halls, and when we were alone together as the elevator climbed, I laughed and reached for his mask.

His grip was bruising when he snatched my wrist to keep me from pulling it off.

The elevator doors opened and he swept me up into his arms, cradling me to his chest as he ate the distance of the hall with his long, powerful stride. He didn't set me down again until we were in the privacy of my room.

He stilled as we stood staring at each other, our masks in place and our chests heaving. It was the motion of his arm that caught my gaze, the length of his fingers slipping into his pocket to extract a long stretch of black silk.

I think it's only fair I warn you that in the bedroom I am a man with particular tastes.

My heart was a trapped bird beating its wings desperately beneath my ribs.

146

Raising a black-gloved hand, he twirled his finger in the air, silently demanding I turn around. I obeyed him without uttering a complaint.

Without making a sound beyond the soft thud of his shoes against the carpet, Vincent stepped behind me, so close that the heat of his chest was a furnace against my back. His hands were gentle as he untied the ribbon holding my mask in place. It fell to the ground as silently as a feather. Soft silk stretched over my eyes, the low light in the room disappearing, and after securing the blindfold in place, his fingertip traced the shape of my mouth, his breath a whisper of sound near my cheek as his other hand gripped my hip and pulled me against him.

I could feel the hard length of his excitement against the cheeks of my bottom, a violent tremor coursing through me. His finger slipped inside my mouth and I suckled the tip without thinking. The responsive growl that rattled his chest was full of male satisfaction. His hand was a bruising pressure on my hip, his body pressing closer, his finger pulling out of my mouth so that he could rip the mask from his face. I felt the skin of his cheek against mine, felt the burn of stubble as his face fell down and his teeth locked on to the tender place where my neck met my shoulder.

All the breath that had been held in my lungs rushed out at once.

My head fell back as his hand splayed over my stomach, slowly moving up until they palmed the weight of my breast over my dress and tore at the bodice of my gown. The material ripped apart, the beauty of the silk shredded as he stripped me bare except for the panties I wore and the heels still holding my feet at four inches above the floor. While his teeth

147

grazed over my shoulder, the tips a sharp line against sensitive skin, one of his hands held me in place by the hip, while the other dove down beneath my panties.

My knees gave out and I would have fallen had he not been holding me up. Circling a fingertip over my aching clit, he'd never bothered to take his gloves off. The cloth was a rough texture against that pulsing place, the movement of his hand tortuous and demanding. His foot moved to kick my legs farther apart and he dipped that finger down to thrust inside me.

A startled moan burst from my lips, my body like putty as his teeth sank down again, his tongue licking over the skin for a taste. It didn't matter the pain he caused, I didn't care if he broke the skin to lick the blood away, all that held my attention in that moment was the way his finger played me. Every muscle beneath my skin tensed as a storm sparked to life in my body, the whispers of an orgasm licking at my brain until my hips moved to beg him to drive deeper.

I was so close to coming apart when he released the hold his teeth had on my shoulder, pressed his mouth to my ear and whispered in the most haunting voice I'd ever heard, *"Du sang pour le plaisir, ma chérie. Je suis à genoux mais je te possède."*

It didn't matter what he'd said. I would agree to anything just to feel the pulse of him inside me.

His hand pulled away as his arm swept around to lock over my abdomen and lift me from the floor. From one second to the next I was standing in my living room and being tossed down onto my stomach over the bed. I tried to turn, my his hand slammed down on my back until I gave in, the tips of his fingers dragging down to cup me between the legs until he took both my legs in his grip, pulled my body to the edge and forced my knees apart.

His hot breath was a wash between my thighs, sending a violent tremor up my body. Slowly, oh so fucking slowly, he ran his lips up the inside of my thigh, his teeth softly biting on the soaked skin when he reached the apex, his tongue flicking out to taste me. A cry of desperation tore from my lips, his palm slapping my ass to silence me. I bit my lip to keep from crying out again, the skin of my cheek blistering hot from how hard he'd struck me.

His tongue sunk inside my body, his thumb finding the entrance to my ass and as he worked me into a whimpering plaything, I came apart over the bed. Unable to stop from releasing the force of violent, implacable pleasure, a moan tore from my lips and filled the room despite pressing my face to the bed to silence it.

He stopped as suddenly as he'd began...until his teeth sank into the inside of my thigh, another cry forced from my lips to be met by the sound of his dark laughter.

A rush of cool air swept in when he pulled away, the room silent and still until the sound of rustling cloth was a whisper to my senses, another slap against my bottom splitting the air. Before I could move away, Vincent had trapped my thighs in his grip, shoving my legs up until my chest was pressed to the bed and I was presented for his pleasure.

With a long, hard thrust, he took what was his, possessing me, claiming me, marking me as his toy that could be wound up to dance for his amusement. There was no care or concern for the pain and pleasure I felt, no words spoken with love, no questions asked as to whether or not I could handle him. This was violence. This was cruelty. This was primal and raw. This was a man showing a woman who owned her.

Not one complaint fell from my lips. Not one argument or protest. And as tears leaked from my eyes to mingle with the moans from my lips, his pace sped, his hips pounding until he was deep inside, spilling his approval of my submission inside me.

Releasing me, he left me sated and spent over white sheets that covered the bed, and when I thought he'd gone to the bathroom so that he could clean up, I closed my eyes and waited for his return.

A return that never happened.

A return that had never been planned.

When I found the strength to push myself up and off the bed, I whispered Vincent's name and crept through the rooms to find that his mask was gone and that the soft click of a door hadn't been Vincent going into the bathroom like I thought, it had been the sound of him quietly leaving.

CHAPTER TWENTY

Faiville Prison, 4:57 pm

For the first time since Meadow had started the interview with Vincent Mercier - the last confession he would give before his death by lethal injection - the man who had so easily led the dance she'd entered, sat silent and remorseful.

It wasn't that he'd said a word to her to express what he felt, it was that she could see a subtle shift in his expression, a soft bruising beneath his normally cutting stare that betrayed his exhaustion. Something she'd said when offering him Penny's recollection of events had reached inside that cold, cruel body and touched the careless heart inside to set it beating again.

"I guess it's my turn to tell you I've stopped talking and yet you've remained quiet. A promise is a promise, Vincent. It's your turn to tell me what happened."

Without lifting his gaze to meet hers, he attempted a smile, the effort lost when his eyes failed to reclaim their ever-present glimmer. "I'm wondering why you continued forward," he admitted, his voice empty, without inflection. "The deal we'd made was for you to tell me her perspective up until that afternoon in the garden, yet you took us past the ball, to the moment -"

Voice trailing away, he shook his head, tracing his finger against the edge of the table. The silence of the room was cut through by the soft rattle of his chains. "Is that all she wrote about that night?" Eyes finally tipping up to capture hers, he asked, "Did she mention what she felt in her heart?"

No. Meadow hadn't told him what she knew about that. She'd purposely avoided describing the adoration, the odd safety, the hopelessness of falling for a man Penny knew she could never have.

Penny's entire being has been changed that night, an independent girl who'd accepted a master's glass, drinking the poison offered to her in order to become a slave that would give him everything. Her heart. Her soul. Her life. So easily stolen by a man who'd been playing games. All for a bet, it seemed, which was why Meadow refrained from telling Vincent that, on the night he'd brought Penny Graham to life, he'd also destroyed her by quietly leaving.

"I think you know how she felt that night. You were there with her. You'd led her away from that ballroom in order to take the first bite...literally." Pausing, Meadow wished she had a pen she could use to busy her hands, something she could spin or click, a distraction from the pain she was feeling. "Not to skip ahead, but you'd left your mark. The bruises you'd left behind disappeared before you felt the need to taste her again."

It was that particular visual that changed Vincent's expression, life bleeding back into the eyes of a sadist and murderer. Lips tipping up at the corners, he crooned, "I've left many marks, Meadow. Not just on Penelope, but on any woman that came to my bed. Nobody has ever complained." When she didn't answer, when her anger was plain on her face, Vincent leaned forward to whisper, "I'd leave them on you, too, *ma belle*, if my present situation didn't prevent that from happening."

"I would never let you touch me!"

His sly grin widened. "Wouldn't you?"

Meadow wanted to rip the teasing note from his voice and shove it up his arrogant ass.

Smirking, he tsked his tongue and reminded her of her earlier question. "What did Penelope feel that night? Was it love?"

Irritated by his refusal to drop the subject, Meadow asked, "Why do you want to know? Won't it just be another notch on your bedpost, another victory you so easily sweep aside along with the rest of the shattered hearts you've left in your wake?"

"It's important to me," he admitted, saying nothing more as to why Penny's feelings that night mattered.

Giving in, only because she was curious about the reason Vincent cared, Meadow confessed, "It was the first stirring of love, at least until you left quietly without telling her, until you tortured her by keeping your distance for the weeks that followed." Blinking away tears that threatened, ignoring the whispers of Penny's pain, Meadow asked, "Were those weeks all part of your game?"

His jaw ticked just as the door to the interview room burst open, a male guard walking inside to announce, "It's after five. You'll need to conclude the interview for today."

Irritation at the interruption felt like claws scraping down Meadow's spine. Vincent said nothing as Meadow struggled to push to her feet, as she turned to stop the tape and gather her things. It wasn't until she was walking to the door to be escorted from the room that Vincent spoke again.

"Tell me, Meadow, why did you go past the point of the story we agreed to? Why did you feel the need to tell me Penny's perspective from the night of the ball?"

Standing in the doorway of the room, the guard waiting not-so-patiently in the hall, it was Meadow's turn for a wry grin. "Because I knew that night was the first time you had her, it was the first time you conquered Penny and pierced her heart. I didn't want to hear it from you at first. Didn't want to listen to you brag. I plucked the moment from your hands, Vincent." Meadow locked her stare with his. "I kept going so that I could steal your thunder."

Vincent's responsive smile matched hers, the guard's hand wrapping over her bicep to lead her away.

"It's a shame you see it that way, Meadow, because it wasn't my thunder you stole, it was somebody else's."

Eyes widening, Meadow only had time to shout, "What are you talking about?" before the guard yanked on her arm and raised his voice in warning.

"It's time to leave. Continue resisting and we won't allow you to return for the next two days."

Bringing his fingers to his lips, Vincent blew Meadow a kiss, the last thing she saw before she was dragged down the hall.

The last thing she heard was Vincent's voice chasing her through the prison. "I'll see you tomorrow, Meadow. Sleep well tonight."

. . .

Meadow barely slept at all that night, her thoughts scattered, her body moving between the bed where she attempted to lie down and the table upon which sat the recorder she kept incessantly playing. Vincent's voice

154

haunted her, the secrets he had yet to reveal cutting scars into her mind, taunting.

It's a shame you see it that way, Meadow, because it wasn't my thunder you stole, it was somebody else's...

His last statement was forcing her jaw to clench, punishing her teeth, as questions wouldn't stop screaming, as puzzle pieces fell into place.

Was he toying with her as he had all the others? Or had there been more lies and secrets that blinded Penny despite her presence within the game?

Meadow didn't know, her heart tearing open, her own secrets boiling to the surface, spilling over because they were too painful to contain.

By the time the first fingers of sunlight were scrabbling up the horizon to scratch at a midnight sky, Meadow remained seated at the table listening to a sadist weave his tangled web. She had to be at the prison in less than two hours, she had to force herself from her seat to get ready to begin the second day.

She showered and dried her long hair, putting it up per prison protocol even though she wanted to let it fall down her back in cascading, soft waves. Dressing with extraordinary care, she intended to seduce Vincent while staying within guidelines of what the prison would allow her to wear. They didn't make it easy. No skirts, no embellishments, only shirts that weren't revealing and pants that hid her legs. And while buttoning into place her white, long sleeved top, she knew she would loosen those closures once it was Vincent's eyes that looked her way.

He spoke easier when beauty faced him, lost his tongue while luring a woman into his sordid games. She should have worn a sturdy bra beneath the top, but had chosen a loose, lacy camisole instead.

155

The drive to Faiville Prison was made in silence, the sky as dreary as it had been when she'd first arrived the prior day. Armed with the same recorder with fresh batteries and tapes, she walked the same scarred sidewalks from the parking lot to the front gates, flashing a professional smile at the guard who stood waiting to escort her in.

"Good morning," she said, approaching the same exhausted guard she remembered.

"You came back," he answered, somewhat surprised if his expression were any indication of his thoughts. "And here I thought Vincent would have chased you off on day one. You must be tougher than you look."

Laughing softly, she allowed him to go through her things, to check her identification and papers although he knew her already. "Vincent's not so bad," she mentioned, desperate for something to say.

The guard shook his head, his lips a line of disapproval. "Yeah, tell that to his victims." With a wave of his hand, he said, "This way. You should already know where we're going. Vincent will be waiting in interview room three."

After being escorted through to interview room three, Meadow discreetly unfastened a button, revealing more of her body so as to addle the mind of a man who wouldn't be able to look away. If there was one thing she knew about Vincent, it was that a pair of shapely breasts could loosen his tongue before he realized what he was saying.

His gaze trapped hers as soon as she stepped into the room, his green eyes beaming above an white jumpsuit, his shackles rattling as he settled himself into

156

his seat and allowed himself a few moments to survey her body with unhidden approval.

The door slammed shut behind her.

"Good morning, Meadow." Canting his head to the side, Vincent ran the tip of his lying tongue along his lower lip. "Are you going to set up your recorder and take a seat, or are we going to spend the day simply staring at one another?"

Meadow's heels clicked across the scuffed, concrete floors as she approached the table. After setting up her recorder, she took her seat opposite Vincent, her hands folding demurely over the surface of the table. "What did you mean it was somebody else's thunder?"

Laughter burst from his lips, the sound rolling and expanding until it had filled every tiny nook and cranny of the room where they sat. "Did that keep you up last night?" He paused, his smile triumphant. "Meanwhile, I slept like a baby."

"Quid pro quo, Vincent. I told you Penny's perspective, now you owe me yours. I want to know what happened the night of the masquerade ball, whose thunder it was that I stole."

Tsking, he rolled his shoulders. "Such a demanding voice from such a small woman. That turns me on, you know?"

She scoffed, "And here I thought it was a helpless woman that turned you on the most."

"Not helpless," he corrected her, "submissive. There's a difference."

She wouldn't take the bait, so he explained his meaning without Meadow bothering to ask. "A helpless woman has no say in how I treat her. She can't fight or bargain her way out of the pain. A submissive woman on the other hand..."

157

He flared his fingers adding emphasis to his words. "A submissive woman simply accepts the treatment she's given. She thanks her master for every strike, every bite, every punishment and every slap. She begs for more of the rough treatment, much like Penelope did when she learned to behave."

His words couldn't have cut deeper, even if he'd used a hatchet instead of a scalpel.

Palm slapping down on the surface of the table, Meadow answered, "Your perspective of that night, Vincent. You owe it to me."

"And I'll give it to you. All good things come to those who wait."

Leaning forward, she spoke through clenched teeth. "I've waited long enough and we're running out of time."

Smiling, he leaned toward her, closing the distance. "Actually, Meadow, our time has just started, but I'll give in to this demand of yours because I already had my fun yesterday when you left. I knew my words would keep you up all night."

CHAPTER TWENTY-ONE

Vincent

Staying away from Penelope following our meeting in the garden was far more difficult than it should have been. I was a man acclimated to handling women, a seducer who had grown tired of the easy games, yet with that particular woman I couldn't quite rid myself of a constant question of whether or not she'd accept my invitation and take me to her bed.

Seeing her in the halls of Wishing Well wasn't easy, watching her as she pushed her housekeeping cart, and spent her time polishing and sweeping, her heart shaped ass bouncing with every step and every swipe of cloth on some soiled surface. It amused me far too much when I'd pass by and see her eyes tracking my path, the shy smiles she gave me that I never returned. It was always more fun to keep a woman guessing.

To pass those days without giving in to my need to taste her, I spent some time visiting my other hotels and properties that would never bring me as much joy as Wishing Well. Several nights, I'd taken different women to bed when I wasn't within easy view of a young woman still making up her mind. None of those women could please me. They were too easy. Too greedy. Too experienced for what I had in mind.

Only Penelope would satisfy that craving inside me, only her wide eyes, her startled gasps, her introduction into a lifestyle that would test her every boundary and make her mine.

One day remained before the night of the ball and I was seated at my desk in my office at Wishing Well when my door popped open and John peeked his head inside. "Do you have a minute to talk?"

"Is there a problem?" I asked, my eyes focused on financial documents that were giving me a massive headache.

"It's Maurice," he stated calmly as he shut the door behind him. "He's chased off another counselor."

Sitting back in my seat, I released a heavy sigh. "Is the counselor injured in any way?"

John shook his head, "No. This one didn't get close enough for Maurice to touch, but before leaving the hotel, she told me that Maurice was demanding to speak to you. She claimed he was complaining that he hasn't been let out of the basement for over a week. He's refused to work with anybody until you go down to see him."

Pinching the skin between my eyes, I clenched my teeth. After the night in the garden when Penelope found both Maurice and I near the well, I'd been avoiding my brother. He was adamant that I give him Penelope as if she were some gift, but I refused to surrender the girl just so he could destroy her as easily as he had others. "I'll go see him, John. Thank you for letting me know."

Inclining his head, John left without saying another word. I spent several minutes in the silence of my office before finding the strength to leave my seat and head down to the basement to face my brother.

Stepping into the entryway that was as dark and elegant as a rich man's tomb, I noticed the lights had been turned off for the sake of the flame sconces, the dancing shadows cutting across Maurice's face where he sat on the brown leather sofa waiting for me.

"I want her," he barked, taking no time to jump back to the last argument we'd had following that night in the garden.

Patiently, I responded, "I've already told you, she's not that type of girl. You'll end up killing her when she fights back. I can't afford to lose another employee, Maurice. The bodies are stacking up."

Rage twisted his expression. "Her," he said simply, refusing to listen to anything I was saying.

Leaning a shoulder against the wall, I stared at him, careful not to show my frustration. He took what he considered to be rejection too close to heart and could react without thinking. "This is why I haven't taken you up to the garden for a week. You'll need to let her go. How can I trust you not to make a scene if you won't even calm down while in your cage? You chased another counselor away."

"And I'll keep doing it until you let me have her. I won't kill her." His voice lowered in volume as if he were speaking to himself and not me. "I won't."

Lifting his green eyes to mine, he argued, "The others were an accident."

My heart squeezed at the sorrow of his tone. Maurice never could control himself. It wasn't his fault those accidents happened. For as intelligent as he was with formal education, he was terrible when it came to emotion or social norms. It's why we had to keep him locked up like an animal. He didn't know any better. "I know," I answered. "Which is why you have to trust me that Penelope is the wrong woman for you."

What I didn't tell him was that a large part of my refusal was the fact that I wanted Penelope for myself. I could never reveal that particular truth. It would drive him to violence.

161

It broke my heart to see his expression fall, to see the shame Maurice felt. Regardless of how difficult a problem he had been in my life, I truly loved my brother.

"I'm sorry," I whispered, moving across the room to take a seat next to him. He trained his eyes on the elevator doors, refusing to meet mine. Filling the silence, I offered, "I can find someone else. You just need to give me a few days. The annual masquerade ball is tomorrow and it's taking up most of my time, but after it's over, I'll find you another woman. Okay?"

"*D'accord*," he answered, switching back to our native language.

With pure truth in my heart, I said, "*Je t'aime, mon frere.*"

He nodded his head, still refusing to meet my gaze, and also refusing to tell me he loved me back.

. . .

The night passed uneventfully, my thoughts trapped by a certain brunette that had made herself as scarce as I had over the past few days. Like a rabbit avoiding a hungry wolf, she'd scattered each time she caught a glimpse of me inside the hotel, my desire deepening because it was the frightened ones that drew my notice, the shy women that would fully bloom beneath the direction of a skilled hand. I knew in my heart that by the time I was finished with Penelope Graham, her body would sing and she'd lose her inhibitions to become exactly what any sensual man would want in a slave.

The ball had already started on the first floor by the time I dragged myself away from my piano to dress in

162

my tuxedo and mask to make an appearance among the wealthy crowd that could afford the cost of entrance. I had no intentions of staying at the ball for long, but looked forward to the time I could remain incognito watching a woman find her way within an event unlike anything I assumed she'd experienced before. From what I knew of Penelope, from the behavior I'd seen, she was not raised among the privileged and elite; she'd gone from humble beginnings to the streets. Observing her when she didn't know which man was me would be a pleasure because she wouldn't tuck tail and run away.

The only question was: Would she wear red, or would she wear green? I wasn't worried that she'd choose the wrong color. Her behavior over the last few days had been telling.

Tugging my black jacket into place over my black shirt and black bow tie, I settled my mask over my face, tying my hair back at the nape of my neck to keep it carefully out of place. The ends brushed my collar and I considered trimming the length as I left my suite and made my way to the elevator, admiring my reflection in the polished bronze doors as I was taken to the lobby and to the ball.

Music reached out to whisper against my ears and draw me in its direction, the sound growing louder with each step I took toward the large ballroom. I didn't see Penelope immediately once joining the party, but after circling the event a few times to make sure everything was moving along as expected, I spotted her within a small crowd to the right of the dance floor, a broad smile stretching her beautiful face.

My breath caught in my chest to see the color dress she'd chosen, my body rigid and tense to know that tonight would be my first taste. I couldn't wait to strip the dress from her perfect body, could barely contain the urge I had to bend her over and spank her perfect ass until all the rebellion had deserted her mind. She'd calmed down some since I first brought her to Wishing Well, but there was still that streak of defiance and disobedience I knew she carried inside.

But first, I would watch her, I would study her and observe her to see if she blended well within a crowd of people who were nothing like her. I would see how often she glanced about attempting to find me. And then, after the show was done, the dancing over, the night winding down as the guests continued to drink champagne, I would lead Penelope to her room on the fifth floor and show her what to expect from a man with my tastes.

Two hours wasn't too long a time to wait.

Taking a woman by the hand, I invited her to dance, and as I led her through each spin and dip, I kept Penelope within my peripheral vision, enjoying how she sipped from her champagne flute watching the event. I was wrong to think her humble beginnings would keep her from blending in ... it was her striking beauty that drew every man's eye that accomplished her inability to go unnoticed. Let them look, let their eyes take their fill. Penelope would be guided by my hand tonight.

The music in the ballroom grew silent as the lights of the chandelier dimmed. Professional dancers dressed in their finest costumes took their place on the floor as the crowd parted to give them adequate space. After this show, after allowing Penelope to watch a dance that would awaken the desire inside her, I planned to lead her from the ballroom up to her room and show her how pleasure could mix with pain.

Standing back, I watched the dancers move into place, I felt my heart kick beneath my ribs, felt the music flow through me as the lighting in the room shifted to focus on the dance routine. Their bodies moved in a perfect beat, their costumes provocative and appealing, but by the time they ended their coordinated moves, Penelope was nowhere to be seen.

Glancing around, I wondered where my beautiful girl had run off to, thought that perhaps she'd gone to use the restroom or to find another drink. When she didn't return for another half hour, suspicion gripped my thoughts. Had she gone to her room alone? Had I spent too much time enjoying watching her when she didn't know it was me?

I needed to find her. Needed to tell her that she wasn't a mistake at all, but a sadistic man's dream.

Leaving the ballroom, I walked the halls to the restrooms, and not finding her, I took an elevator to the fifth floor. Rage tore through me, blinding anger, as I turned a corner.

Tuxedo in place, mask in hand, a man walked down the hallway from the direction of Penelope's room - a man that should never have left his cage. Beneath the burning heat of my fury, ran a cold line of fear.

"Maurice," I said, my voice soft, my mind unwilling to believe I was watching my brother walking around without me there to control him. My heart stumbled, skipped, images flashing through my head of broken women and the blood that spilled. "Is she?" I couldn't finish the question, my terror too intense.

165

"I didn't kill her," he said, approaching me, his green eyes locking to mine, his broad shoulders rolled back, his demeanor triumphant, daring me to say something.

"How did you get out of the basement?"

I was so shocked by his appearance, I could barely formulate a logical thought. Concern trickled down my spine followed by disappointment. Had he killed Penelope and lied to me just now? Had he torn apart a beautiful girl that was showing so much potential?

"Same way you get in," he answered, a challenge in his grin. "I also didn't kill the man you sent with my dinner. But he has been bound for an hour by now. I had to make sure he didn't come running to tell you I'd escaped my prison."

"We need to get downstairs, Maurice. Before anybody sees you."

There was no strength to my voice, my shoulders withering with the weight of my anxiety, my fear that Penelope Graham breathed no longer.

As if intuiting my thoughts, he repeated, "I didn't kill her."

I blinked slowly and swallowed down the knot clogging my throat. "Did she behave for you? Was she scared?"

Anger flashed behind his eyes, shame, satisfaction and something else. "She called me Vincent. I didn't like that. But it was *my* cock she came on, wasn't it? *My* tongue, *my* words, *my* hands, *my* teeth."

Grin stretching wider with the knowledge of having beat me to her, he moved past me toward the elevator, not fighting to remain free of his cage.

I turned and watched my brother stalk off, and I realized as he moved smoothly down the long hall that this was the first time I'd ever seen him so calm.

CHAPTER TWENTY-TWO

I spent two weeks avoiding Penelope after the night of the ball, two weeks avoiding Maurice, two weeks staying away from Wishing Well as much as possible so that I wouldn't have to face what had occurred. The morning after the ball, I'd checked in with Theresa to ensure Penelope showed up to work, and after discovering she was alive and well, I'd taken off to stay at one of my other properties, avoiding everything but emails from work.

Taking my anger out on women in bed had done nothing to soothe my rage, and no matter how I busied myself, how I gorged on food, on alcohol, on sex and on entertainment, I couldn't shake Penelope from my thoughts.

That night was supposed to be mine. The first taste of her should have been by my mouth and not my brother's, yet Maurice had proven to me that his prison wasn't as secure as I'd always thought it was.

Why that night? Why her? Why hadn't Maurice broken free before that moment and alerted me to his ability to escape? It was my own arrogance that I'd locked him down sufficiently that led to a night where he gnashed his teeth and broke free of his chains.

I'd wanted to give him as much freedom as possible by having the basement of Wishing Well modified for his use, and in doing so, I'd put lives at risk. I'd put my business at risk. And I'd put my own welfare at risk.

After three weeks, however, I couldn't stand being away any longer, and from what I'd been told by my hotel manager, Maurice hadn't again attempted escape. I wondered about his sudden good behavior after discovering there were ways to breach his cage.

Returning to the hotel, I'd worked for most of the day before deciding to take a walk through the garden. While wandering down the path, I wasn't surprised to find Penelope standing over the well, her hand opening to drop a penny to the bottom, the copper coin flashing in the afternoon sunlight as it fell from her palm. Unable to resist the siren's song, I stepped up behind her silently, leaning down so I could whisper against her ear, "If you could wish for anything in the world, Penelope, what would you wish for?"

Tears slipped down her cheeks. She reached up to swipe the tears away, but I caught her wrist with one hand while using a fingertip of the other to catch the tear for myself. "Why are you crying?"

Penelope sniffled, the sound wrecking the silence. "No reason," she answered, her voice curt, defensive. "Just had a bad day, is all. It's nothing important."

Attempting to step away from me, she gasped when I refused to release her wrist, snatched her close and spun her to face me. I knew why she was crying. I knew it had to do with me. But I wanted to hear the words fall from her lips. Despite everything, I was still a cruel, greedy bastard.

"Tell me why you're crying."

"Why do you care?" she hissed, wanting to scream but keeping her voice quiet so as not to disturb the other people who were wandering down the paths. More tears spilled over cheeks that were stained pink, and like the first time I'd given her a tour of the gardens, I dragged her away from the well and into the private alcove.

I wouldn't lie and claim her anger didn't turn me on, it was just another example of the rebellious nature she harbored inside her beautiful body.

"Why wouldn't I care?" I asked, my hand still wrapped firmly over her wrist. When she scowled up at me, I had to fight not to spin her around and bend her over my knee. Three weeks hadn't been enough to rid the obsession I had for her. If anything, it had only dug the obsession deeper.

What had she been like when Maurice deceived her? What had he taken that was mine?

After several failed attempts to yank her arm free, Penelope gave in, gave up, practically withered beneath the understanding that she was battling a far stronger opponent. I admired her for the fight, and wanted her for the ability to acquiesce and submit. "You used me," she finally admitted, a rough edge to every word doused with sorrow, anger, and insecurity. So confused as to my behavior, she was lost, and I wouldn't be the one to chase away the shadows that held her - not yet. Not until I knew exactly what had occurred the night of the ball.

"I never promised you anything. Only a mistake, only one night."

Tears slipped from her face to fall to the ground, watering the grass, drenching the soil, her pain nourishing the life of the earth beneath us. Much as it nourished me. "I know, and that's why I should go before I say or do something that gets me fired. I need this job."

"What were you wishing for when I found you just now? What did the coin you dropped represent?"

"What does it matter?" She asked, her voice broken, defeated.

"It matters to me. Perhaps I can help you achieve whatever is you desire."

Flinching at the words, she shook her head. "No. I won't go through that again. I won't." Finally succeeding in pulling her wrist from my grasp, she crossed her arms over her chest, her walls resurrecting. And with an honesty that dragged breath from my lungs, she locked her glistening brown eyes to mine, the gold flecks brilliant in small streams of light. "You made my body sing. I won't deny that. But then to walk away without a word? Without a thank you or a goodbye - with nothing! I can't, I won't, I-"

Catching her chin with my fingers, I stilled her head, moving closer as her eyes widened, her nostrils flaring just slightly from fear, from need, from uncertainty.

My voice was a bare whisper as my lips hovered a teasing inch above hers. "Did I kiss you that night? Do you remember?"

"No," she answered, the one word drawing more anger, slicing deeper into her heart.

At least this first, this taste, will be mine. For what my brother stole from me, he didn't take this...

Softly, I pressed my mouth to hers, stood unmoving, undemanding, as a shudder coursed through her body, the tremble easing as she relaxed into the kiss, a pitiful sigh escaping her lungs for me to swallow.

Maurice may have stolen this angel's body, but her soul belonged to me.

Myths. Legends. Fairytales. They all betray the truth about a person's lips, that their kiss is the means

171

by which life can be given or taken away. It's never in the physical act of dominance and decimation, it's in the submission to whim, the simple caress of one mouth against another, the slide of a tongue, the passion that ignites when two people share that single moment of pure bliss.

Even a whore will spread her legs for whatever a customer offers, but she won't give her mouth to him, only because a person's secrets, their hopes, their dreams, their heart can be found in a kiss.

I'd taken that from Penelope as she pressed her body to mine, as her lips parted to grant me entrance, as my fist tightened within her hair and I delivered the promise of pain. She trembled again, but not from fear, and that's when I knew she was mine.

I could forgive Maurice for what he'd stolen because, in truth, Penelope's heart was still firmly held within my hands.

Breaking away, I left her breathless, I watched as her eyes fluttered opened, noticed the hint of pink that colored her skin, the distance she'd placed between us now gone.

"I want you to come to my suite tonight." My voice was huskier than I liked, the truth of my feelings coming out in the rough texture, the loss of fluidity in speech.

"Okay," was her simple answer, her eyes closing again, her lips slightly parted, inviting me to taste again. I grinned, always amused by this puzzling beauty.

"Ten o'clock. I have work to accomplish beforehand. The entire sixth floor is mine. The elevator takes you directly to my door."

Stepping away, I stopped, turning just enough to glance at her from over my shoulder. She stood entranced, slightly drunk, bewitched. "You never told me what you wished for."

Heat colored her cheeks, a sheepish expression changing her face. "I wished for happiness."

Penelope was a horrible liar. My lips curled at the corners. "Is that all?"

A few seconds passed before she released a heavy breath. "I wished for love."

Inclining my head, I flashed her one last smile before walking away. I wished I could be going somewhere peaceful, somewhere quiet where I could enjoy the moment I'd shared with a woman that had expertly trapped my thoughts. But instead, I was in route to the basement to face Maurice for the first time since the night of the ball. I already knew what he would demand from me, and after my time with Penelope in the garden, I already knew how I would answer. This meeting would not be pleasant.

Not at all.

CHAPTER TWENTY-THREE

Faiville Prison, 10:37 am

"You look tired."

Meadow sat back in her chair, her intent to seduce Vincent choked out by her vehemence and anger. Losing the battle she'd intended to wage against a man used to the emotional fray, she did something he wouldn't expect: She answered him honestly.

"I am tired. But I'm also angry with you. I'm sad for Penny. I feel lost, which I assume is how she must have felt her entire time at your hotel." Another question nagged at her mind, but it wasn't one she would state aloud, not yet anyway.

Vincent watched her carefully, his focused attention unsettling because Meadow knew he could see every emotion that battered her defenses. She'd wanted to win against him, to do what Penny could not, but even now she felt herself sinking beneath the surface of turbulent waves.

Vincent had created a storm, and like Penny, Meadow was caught in its violence, in its hopelessness, in its drenching rains. Despite the secrets she had yet to uncover, the weapons she planned to use against a man who was tearing her heart in two, Meadow couldn't help but understand that, in this game, there were no winners or losers. "You never told her it was Maurice that night of the ball. She never knew."

Eyes searching her face, his expression was blank, unreadable. "How do you know?"

Daring to lock eyes with Vincent, Meadow curled her fingers into her palm, her nails cutting half-moon circles into the skin, just barely drawing blood. She needed the physical pain to divest herself of the emotions that gripped her in a sadistic hold. How can emotions make you hurt everywhere? How can they choke the life out of you from inside? They were nothing but chemicals being dumped in your veins, but still they froze you faster than even the depraved stare of a man who knew he held you in place. Penny had blamed herself at times for the torment she'd endured, and like Penny, Meadow blamed herself now.

"She never wrote it in the diary. I have to assume it was because she didn't know." Bitter laughter fell from her lips. "Maybe if she had, she would have left that damn hotel. Would have realized that she'd become the sole focus of a monster you so expertly created."

It was Vincent's turn to flinch. Maurice was the only weakness in his armor, the only regret he carried. Meadow could see, plain as day, how true Vincent's love was for his brother. And now that the weak spot had been exposed, Meadow reached in with greedy fingers to rip out the heart of a bastard who'd enjoyed destroying the lives of others.

Canting her head, much like Vincent would do when he knew he had you cornered, Meadow grinned. "What's wrong, Vincent? Does it hurt to know what you did to Maurice? How you tortured him and made him worse by keeping him separate from the world? By keeping him caged?" Vincent simply smiled back, but Meadow knew she'd sunk the blade deep, and she wanted to twist it around and around and around until this son of a bitch was screaming.

"You created a monster. You took a person who could have succeeded despite his problems, and you only managed to make them worse." Tsking, Meadow admired the razored edge to Vincent's grin. For fucking once *she* had *him* cornered.

But it wouldn't be the last time, and for that reason alone she would continue this fight. For Penny. For her twin sister. For every person Vincent had hurt and destroyed.

"We're not here to talk about Maurice," Vincent answered, his voice calm, assured, so practiced that Meadow knew he was fighting to keep it controlled. There was no humor touching his tone, no satisfaction now that it was his destruction of Maurice that came into focus.

After Penny's death, and after receiving the diary that had been left in Vincent's wake, Meadow had locked on to the task of finding the mysterious brother kept in a basement cage.

Refusing to drop the subject, Meadow commented, "Actually I think we are here to talk about Maurice. He was another one of your victims. You may not have been the one to kill him, but you were certainly the cause." Pausing, she enjoyed seeing pain flash behind his green eyes. "And let's not forget what you did to Penny. Tossing her to him like a scrap of meat." Leaning forward, she lowered her voice, "Did you watch?"

Taking the bait, Vincent leaned forward as well, his lips only inches from her own. She would have felt frightened if not for his chains.

His voice was equally as soft. "You're skipping ahead again. And just as we were getting to the true tests of Penelope's strength."

176

Rolling her eyes, Meadow sat back in her chair. Vincent would give her nothing, his mask back in place, his eagerness to gloat apparent. She wouldn't give him that chance. Sure, he would enjoy knowing exactly how Penny had felt during the next week of their games, but she wouldn't let him brag. And when she was done filling him in on this small portion of the story, this heart-wrenching perspective, she would enjoy seeing his smile falter when she drove the knife into his chest deeper with things she knew but he didn't.

Vincent may have had his secrets, but so did Penny. So did Meadow.

"I know this is the point in the story where you finally have sex with Penny. And I know you've been chomping at the bit to tell me all the sordid details of what you did to her in the privacy of your suite. How she liked it. How she asked for more. How you eventually tossed her away once you'd grown tired of your games, only to drag her back for more of your intimate *training*. You've been hinting to it during this entire interview."

Relaxing against the back of his seat, Vincent asked, "And your point is?"

"I won't let you brag to me, Vincent. And while I know hearing about how you made Penny feel during the nights and days you trained her, used her, fucked her and, well, showed her just how well you could torment her, I'm going to take control at this point in the story to deliver Penny's perspective. It might be eye opening."

Laughter, dark and sultry, rolled over his lips. "*Chapeau*, Meadow. It's about time you wrestle me

177

under control. I was beginning to think you are as weak as Penelope."

Stretching his legs out beneath the table, he rested the tip of his boot against Meadow's shoe, except this time, Meadow refused to yank her foot away, refused to give him the slightest indication that he affected her. Vincent smiled knowingly, his shackles rattled.

"Let's begin, shall we? Or rather, I should say it's time for *you* to begin. Please, Meadow, school me on all the horrible details that will make me rethink my evil ways. I'm quite curious as to what direction this is going."

"You know what they say about curiosity," Meadow quipped.

"Ah," he answered, his voice slick, "but then Penelope also found that out, didn't she?"

Bastard. The fucking bastard. He was toying with her even now.

Vengeful for the ease with which he smeared Penny's fate into her face, Meadow struck out with a cheap blow. "Before I start, I'd like to take stock of all the players for this part of the story."

Vincent cocked a single brow, waiting.

"Where is Maurice right now?"

Meadow was desperate for the answer to that question. She had her suspicions, but she wanted Vincent to say it, to admit how he'd fucked up and left his brother to wither and rot, she wanted him to feel the same agony that she felt at that moment. She wanted confirmation that Maurice was dead.

His jaw ticked once, fury and annoyance written into that subtle tell she didn't think he realized he had. "Are we back to him again? I'm not sure why Maurice matters," his grin stretched, "unless of course you're

178

just trying to upset me." Exaggerated censure was the line of his brow. "Come now, Meadow, aren't we more mature than that? I'd expect more from a woman who's had time to prepare for facing me down. You came here to find out about Penny, and yet you're taking cheap shots-"

"Where is he?" She shrieked, interrupting him. "I want to know what happened to your brother."

His shoulders shook with silent laughter. "Oh, I'm sure you do, but I won't give you that information. Not now. Perhaps I can be convinced to tell you after you tell me Penelope's version of events. Give me something to take to bed with me tonight, and I'll give you what you're after."

She sighed, knowing he'd issued his demand and wouldn't budge until she'd given him what he wanted. "Fine. But after I tell you this, you tell me what happened to Maurice. Deal?"

His tongue traced his bottom lip. "Deal."

CHAPTER TWENTY-FOUR

Penny

Sick to my stomach, I paced my room on the fifth floor, my nails bitten down to the tips of my fingers, my thoughts racing, my heart beating out a frenetic rhythm of self-loathing and warning.

I knew better than to trust Vincent after what he'd done before, but despite all the questions screaming in my head, and all the haunting whispers, I still couldn't shake the need I had to feel alive again.

I'd been crushed the night of the ball after having flown so high, had felt like I'd crash landed back to the ground when Vincent left without saying goodbye, but then to be dragged through the mud, to have my face shoved into the ugly truth that he didn't give a damn about me, I'd sworn off every desire I had for the man, choosing to swear off my hopes there could be *something*.

And yet, he'd returned and he'd found me at the exact moment I'd made a wish while tossing a penny to the bottom of a well. I may as well have tossed myself for as conveniently timed his arrival had been.

It was as if fate had stepped in and shoved all my instincts away to take a seat, front and center, while flashing a sign saying 'maybe'.

Maybe is such a fucked up word.

No matter how I tried to convince myself that I shouldn't go up to Vincent's suite, there was a small part of me lingering in that alcove where he'd dragged me, still melting from the way we'd kissed. It was that part that forced me to get dressed. That part that led me to carefully comb my hair and leave it loose down my back. That part that forced me out the door of my room, down the hall, inside the elevator. It was that part that hit the button marked six.

Like Vincent had said, the elevator doors slid open revealing another set of dark wood doors, intricately carved until the pattern itself was enough to hypnotize. Those doors spoke of money, they spoke of masculine taste, they spoke of the man that would be waiting on the other side for a stupid little girl who hadn't learned the first time that his interest was mercurial at best.

My choice was to step forward or step back, choosing which side of the elevators doors to be on when they slid closed with a quiet, electronic hiss.

I stepped forward and lifted my hand to knock on the dark wood door, my heart thudding within my chest. Vincent opened the door, his suit jacket missing, his cream colored shirt unbuttoned at the collar, the sleeves rolled up to reveal strong forearms. "I'm glad you came," he greeted me, the rolling lilt of his voice creating small tremors in my core.

Mouth dry, heart pounding, I didn't know what to say. Thankfully, he filled the awkward silence. "You should come in. Would you like a drink?"

"I think so," I muttered, following him on shaky legs. Although we'd spent time together after the ball, it hadn't felt so professional - so planned. There was no telling what I was walking into now and why Vincent felt so cold.

His suite was exactly how I'd envisioned it would be: opulent, elegant, as breathtaking as the man who owned it. A color scheme of dark red curtains and other

181

accessories, rich brown leather and cream carpets and walls, he had fine art hung to accentuate the setting, and crystal and silver fixtures that glimmered beneath soft lighting. Bookshelves lined one wall while floor to ceiling windows lined another, and in the center of the room with lit candles glowing against its surface was a black, grand piano.

"You think so?" he repeated, not waiting for my answer before crossing the room on his powerful swagger to start mixing drinks at a sidebar.

"I don't know what to expect," I admitted, the honesty spilling out of me no matter how badly I wanted it to stop.

Glancing over his shoulder, he cocked a brow. "I assume you've had sex before. Once already with me. The mechanics are pretty much the same, although the experience can be dramatically different."

"Maybe it's the experience I'm worried about. Last time was..." My cheeks flushed red. "...it was memorable, but the ending left me hanging."

Turning with two drinks in hand, he pinned me in his stare as he approached. Handing one to me, he asked, "You didn't get off?"

"It was more about the abrupt exit," I admitted.

My cheeks flared brighter and I brought the glass to my lips not caring what the hell he'd poured in it. Vincent grinned to see I'd polished it off. Eyeing his glass, I asked, "Are you going to drink that?"

He handed it over. "You may want to pace yourself. I can't have you passing out during the best parts." Correcting himself, he added, "Well, not from the alcohol anyway."

I chugged the glass down, the alcohol seeping quickly into my veins. Feeling a touch more relaxed, I

182

licked my lips and asked, "So, how will all this work? Are you going to blindfold me like last time?"

His green eyes flashed with some unspoken thought. Taking the glass from my hand, he was walking it back to the sidebar when he said, "Take off your clothes, Penelope."

What? Somehow the sentiment wasn't as romantic as him ripping the clothes from body. When I'd been with him after the ball, it had been naked, raw, stifling heat. Now? It was distant, calculated, cold.

Setting the glass on the bar, he glanced over, ice clattering within a new glass he was whipping up. "I wasn't joking. If you're here to learn what it's like being my lover, I suggest you learn to follow directions. You won't like the punishments I have to offer."

Punishment?! My eyes rounded. "You didn't do this last time," I stammered, accepting the drink from his hand after he'd crossed the room on smooth steps to stand in front of me.

Taking a sip from his glass, he answered, "Last time was an introduction. Tonight is the real thing."

His smile was lascivious. "I warned you I'm a man with particular tastes. Don't act so surprised." Jutting his chin, he commanded, "Finish your drink, Penelope, and strip down. If you don't like the terms of this arrangement, you know where you can find the door."

My first instinct was to toss the drink in his face and storm off. My second, however...

I couldn't forget how he'd made my body sing. Memories of it had kept me up every night for the past three weeks. This? This felt more like a business deal.

Breathing out, I slammed the drink, placed the glass on a nearby table and looked over to see Vincent settling himself on the piano bench. His nimble fingers softy played over the keys while I made my decision as to what I would do.

It wasn't like I had to do this again if I didn't like it. Maybe the raw heat I remembered would come back once my clothing was off and my body was bare. Slowly, I peeled off the clothes I'd carefully selected earlier, insecurity roaring through me as Vincent quietly played piano. The floating notes did nothing to ease my anxiety. He didn't bother to look up until I'd walked over to stand at his side.

Even then, it took him another minute or two to give me his attention, and when he did, his gaze slowly traveled up my body, starting from my toes and ending with my eyes. "You're beautiful," he said, his voice soft, husky. "I hope you know that."

A rush of self-consciousness made me dizzy. I felt exposed. Studied. A lab rat waiting for the hot as hell scientist to poke me with one tortuous instrument or another. Ignoring the shiver coursing down my spine, I answered, "Thank you."

"You're welcome." His head tilted to the left. "Second door from the window. Enter the room, stand in front of the Saint Andrews Cross, and wait there until I come to you."

My heart skipped, then sputtered, jolting back to life with a ragged rhythm. "The what?"

Lifting a hand, he caught my chin between his fingers and angled my face down to look at him. "The point to these exercises is to learn total submission. You must do as you're told without question. You must accept pain. You must keep from screaming and crying unless I ask you to do so." Pausing he let those thoughts sink in before: "You must *trust* me, Penelope, and know that you'll thank me in the end."

"I'm scared," I whispered.

He was faced me fully and stood to his full height, his proximity reminding me just how small I was compared to him. It didn't make me feel any better.

However, his demeanor softened as he reached to cup my cheek with his palm, his thumb sweeping across my lips with a staggering gentleness I hadn't expected from him. Warmth returned into a dynamic that, until that moment, had been devoid of feeling. "I know you're scared. You should be scared. And that's not how I want you to feel. But in this, you have no idea how important it is that you trust me no matter what you're feeling. I only have your best interests at heart. But you must submit, and you must obey."

Leaning down, he kissed me, the warmth of his lips causing my body to melt against him, the warmth of his hands carefully sliding up my sides, never touching my breasts, but stopping just below them. A pervasive need was a tidal wave crashing through me, memories of the first time we'd been together becoming liquid heat between my thighs.

"*Tu es ma seule chagrin,*" he whispered pulling away from a kiss that left me breathless, the meaning of the words lost on me, but not the sad tone.

"What did you say?"

Eyes tracing down my body, he answered, "Trust me, Penelope. And do as I say. Go in the room and wait for me."

Wavering in my decision, scared by how strange it all was, I focused on the kiss, on the way my body felt when he touched me, on the release he'd given me the last time I trusted him to show me that he could make me melt. And for those reasons, despite how ridiculous they were, despite the logic inside me screaming to get

185

dressed, get out, keep running as far from Wishing Well as I could, I put one foot in front of the other and obeyed him.

Opening the door, I stood confused for a moment, because despite there being a bed, this was not what I'd expected of a bedroom.

The carpets were a plush, thick black, the fibers soft against my feet as I stepped forward. On the right side of the room, a large bed was dressed in blood red silk sheets, small chains hanging above it on the wall, the silver metal glinting against the dark paint. At its base were ropes attached to the two tall posts, the loops at their ends casually lying over the mattress as if they'd been left in place following their last use.

I wanted to run, but I didn't. I don't know why I didn't, the leather bench on the left side of the room should have chased me off, especially the array of straps, whips and paddles that hung on the wall above it. Carefully creeping forward, I eyed the large wood and leather cross that was attached to the wall in front of me. Not really a cross as Vincent had called it, more of an X with cuffs attached at the top and bottom. Stepping up to it, I could smell the wood polish, the leather - I could imagine the helplessness one would feel when fastened to it, the absolute relinquishing of control.

I was turning to leave by the time the door opened again, Vincent stopping to lean a shoulder against the frame and watch me. "Are you reconsidering your decision now that you see the truth of what this can become?"

My voice shook as I stood naked, exposed. "Will you hurt me?"

His eyes caught mine, the low lighting of the room casting a shadow over the jewel green, cutting sharp, ominous edges over his cheekbones and jaw. "I will."

The depth of his honesty startled me. "Will I die?"

"No," he promised, "Not by my hand. This is about pleasure, not death. Control, not destruction. Fear, but not terror."

Scrabbling for a way to understand it, I asked, "So more like a horror movie than a slasher film?"

His eyebrows tugged together. "What?"

"Nothing," I breathed out, every muscle in my body tense with anxiety. "Never mind."

Silence had a beat, a chorus, the white noise of the air conditioning punctuated by the soft fall of his steps over the carpet. "Will it be easier for you to be blindfolded...like last time?"

Strangely, I thought, *it would.*

I was learning rather quickly that I wasn't the type of woman who would face down monsters, I was the type who would hide in the closet, peeking through clothes, hoping like hell they'd pass by. "Maybe."

Vincent nodded and changed direction to pull open the doors of the large dresser that stood near the bench. I only caught site of a few odd, (what-the-fuck-are-those?) objects before he slipped a red stretch of silk from a hook, closed the doors and faced me again. "Turn around, Penelope."

Memories of last night were a wash of flutters in my stomach, a tightening in my core, a force so utterly inescapable that I found myself obeying him without thought or question. The silk was soft over my eyes, the knot he tied at the back of my head pulling at the individual strands of my hair that it caught. His

187

fingertips were a whisper down my spine, slowly grazing the skin and stopping just above my behind.

His breath collided with my cheek, his mouth close to my ear when he whispered, "I'm going to direct you in place. I'm going to restrain you. And then I'm going to leave you to think about the loss of control, the loss of opinion, the loss of the ability to fight."

My teeth chattered, my fear a noxious thing.

"And then I'm going to show you how pleasure comes with pain."

The warmth of his hand caressed my shoulder, and I was led to stand with the cross at my back, my arms lifted in locked in place, my legs parted as cuffs were locked over my ankles as well.

His mouth covered mine, his tongue sweeping in, his taste filling me as my body relaxed despite being restrained. Vincent must have felt it the second I'd given in. Trailing light kisses up my cheek until his mouth pressed against my ear, he said, "*C'est à regret que je te le donne...*"

I was beginning to despise French. But I didn't have the strength to ask what he'd said, didn't have the ability to conjure thought when my words were lost to fear, to want, to oblivion.

The room went silent around me, the constant hush of cool air rushing through the air conditioning vents growing louder with nothing to compete against it. I would have settled for anything to pull me from the trance brought on by my inability to see, my inability to move, the fear that I'd made a huge mistake by trusting a man who'd already hurt me.

It was the door opening that drew my attention, my head turning toward the sound, my lips parting to say something - anything - but in the silence, I'd lost my voice.

Footsteps softly fell over soft carpets I knew were dark, the cuffs that bound my wrists and ankles gently rattling as I braced for what would come. I stood trembling, locked in helplessness, locked in a state of deprivation, locked in place without knowing if it was pain I'd suffer, or pleasure.

A masculine growl of satisfaction filtered through the air. Feral, primal, intimately possessive, as a hand closed over my breast. A gasp burst from my lips, every muscle locking as the hand released me to be replaced by his mouth. I cried out when the soft, wet heat of a tongue transitioned to the sting of teeth.

Tear slipping from my eye, pain spreading like a spider's web, I cried, "Stop, it hurts."

"*Shhhhhhhh...*" was all he said before biting down again, a finger slipping between my legs. Every sensation was heightened, my body a taut string to be played as pleasure collided with pain.

I couldn't be sure, but as my body trembled against the rush of opposite sensation, I intuited the careful struggle, the barely discernible battle, of a man trying not to lose control. It was a vibration that surrounded me, an energy that reminded me to be afraid.

The finger slipped inside me, his teeth biting down harder on the center of my breast before his tongue licked the pain away.

More tears spilled over my cheeks as his finger moved inside me.

My fear...
His fear...
Our fear...

It was hypnotic and intoxicating.

Mouth pulling away, the crushing grip of his hand took possession of my other breast, his finger still moving inside me - faster, harder, deeper - until this powerful man lost control.

Don't be afraid...

A voice slipping through the silence. Vincent's voice.

Obey...

I was being studied. I could feel his eyes watching me with greedy hunger. I knew that with one wrong move, the gentleness he was fighting to give me would be lost with his restraint.

Why did the thought of him losing control make my body beg for more?

His touch was gone so suddenly...until both hands locked down on my wrists over the cross, locking me in place. Unable to keep from crying out, I swallowed the fear, shaking as those punishing hands trailed along my arms, over my breasts, down my waist to grasp my hips, and then his mouth was between my legs.

Tongue, teeth, virile hunger, he owned me while he was on his knees. My head fell back, his hands releasing my hips to palm my ass, his fingers gripping down until I flinched from the pain. Like a starving man, he tasted me, gorged himself on me, driving his tongue inside to swallow my release. And when he softly, slowly, regretfully pulled away from me, I felt a distinct change in the air.

Where there had been restraint, none now existed. Where there had been care, cruelty now reigned. I wasn't given the slightest hint of warning before he thrust himself inside me, the cuffs over my ankles cutting into my skin. His fingernails dragged down the backs of my thighs with each driving beat of body, gripping me behind the knees to spread my legs apart despite the shackles that bound me.

Lost to the predatory rhythm, the viciousness of his thrusts, I moaned out the wicked pleasure, relieving the pressure building inside. My back slammed against the padded cross, my heart hammering, my muscles gripping as he drove himself impossibly deeper, as his feral nature devoured me.

I'd been a stupid girl to give myself away so easily, but if this was the punishment I would receive, I would do it again and again.

A switch was thrown, the pleasure relentless, an orgasm surging through me so violently that I screamed out in release.

It only drove him harder. Only forced him to pull away, to rip at the shackles of my wrists and ankles, to break the hold they'd held. I fell forward, unable to keep myself standing, but I was caught over a strong shoulder, I was lifted and carried before being lowered down and positioned with my stomach over a padded bench.

With one strong hand, he pinned my wrists to the wall in front of me and he thrust inside me again. He owned me as he forced himself deeper, he tormented me as his teeth dragged down my back, and as his palm closed over the weight of my ass, he slipped his thumb between the cheeks and pushed the width within the tight opening and claimed possession of me entirely.

Another orgasm as his chest vibrated against my back, another scream as his teeth locked down at the junction of my shoulder and neck, a rush of his power crashing through me when I clenched my eyes shut and passed out.

Perhaps the alcohol had been too much, or perhaps it was simply him. But when my eyes fluttered open to find the blindfold gone, I was resting atop a soft, silky bed, the room empty, the walls silent, my exhaustion so cumbersome that I smiled and fell asleep again.

CHAPTER TWENTY-FIVE

You don't know fear until you've traipsed through darkness. You don't know desolation until you've been tossed to the wolves.

You don't know pain until you're shown just how disposable you are...

I never knew where those words had come from, those warnings, those whispers, during the three weeks that Vincent claimed me as his. I was learning that I should have listened to them. I was learning that I should have run.

"I'm going to need makeup for the bruises. Theresa keeps asking questions."

Sitting in one of the leather seats that faced Vincent's desk, I stared at the profile of his face as he read over paperwork. He didn't bother to look up at me, instead holding up a finger to ask for another few moments of silence as he read over whatever document he was studying.

Weeks had passed, each night bringing more pain, each day bringing heartache and humiliation as he exposed me more to his tastes. I was beginning to believe he was attempting to discover just how far he could push me before I gave in and fled. Silly man, he never considered I would become addicted to his peculiar flavor.

Being owned had become a drug.

What would my mother think? My sister? In the two months I'd spent at Wishing Well, I still hadn't contacted them. I was ashamed, but they kept writing me, kept begging for some information through an email address I'd always kept since before my mother remarried and moved away. I would have to answer eventually. I just didn't know what I would say.

Help?

Everything's great?

I'm enduring whips and floggers and naked tours of a garden at night while my boss and lover follows me, his body fully dressed?

Only the blindfold he loved to use with me kept me from knowing if guests had passed while the grass tickled my bare feet and I was led to benches and swings.

Somehow I didn't think they'd approve, so I hadn't brought myself to respond despite my sister contacting Blake to learn I was no longer with him.

Yet, here I was, knowing how they would react to this lifestyle I'd chosen, staring at a man who didn't bother to lift his eyes to me after I'd spoken. As usual, I waited until he was ready to acknowledge my presence in the room. I waited until he deemed me important enough to greet. I wondered when the day would come where he didn't wait for the dead of night to parade me through the garden, to display for all the guests' approving eyes how well I'd learned to obey.

Was it wrong the thought caused my thighs to clench tighter? In the months I'd been here, being exposed had taken on an entirely new meaning.

Dragging pen across paper in a flourish of dramatic and masculine script, he signed whatever it was he'd been studying and sat back in his seat, steepling his fingers at his chin as he studied me.

"What have you told Theresa about the bruises?"

Fidgeting in my seat to be pinned by his stare of fathomless, unrelenting green, I answered, "I can cover most of them, it's just the ones on my wrists that are a problem."

Some unspoken decision was obvious in his gaze. "Then I'll find you a new position in the hotel. A new job with better pay. I'll explain to Theresa that you've adequately proven your worth and as a reward I've switched you to a new department."

"Really?" Surprise tugged my eyebrows up my head. "More money?"

"Yes," he said, opening a drawer at his side and extracting a small ring, attached to which was a single key. "I recently had an abrupt departure and need to fill the position. There's no reason I shouldn't give it to you." Tossing the key in my direction, he grinned when I caught it.

"What's the new job?"

"We'll discuss that in a minute." Pushing his seat away from his desk, he ordered, "Come here."

Standing from my seat, I rounded his large desk knowing he wanted me to take seat on the surface in front of him. Dutifully, I did so, knowing that one complaint would lead to his palm slapping my ass. It wasn't that I minded the pain, he had ways of soothing it away.

Voice dark, deep, rough, he commanded. "Take off your shirt, Penelope."

Although the windows behind him had no covers, and although in the gardens beyond I could see guests walking about, I did exactly as he'd said. My breasts tightened as soon as they were exposed to his eyes, needy, throbbing, desperate for his touch. He stared at me instead. "On your knees."

195

Slipping off the desk, I lowered myself to the floor. "Take me into your mouth."

The corner of my mouth quirked up, a wicked grin meant just for him. Unbuckling his belt and the button that fastened his pants, I freed his erection, locked my lips and took him in. The fingers of both his hands fisted in my hair as he directed me down and set the rhythm he wanted.

Only a few seconds had passed as I suckled and licked and tasted the salt of his skin before he started talking.

"I wanted your mouth occupied while I tell you this. You're not going to like it, and I don't want you talking back, not until you've had time to consider your decision."

As fear traced up my spine, pricking tears in my eyes, I had to fight not to clench my teeth. Any scrape would anger him, and he had ways of returning that displeasure, ways of showing me that for as graciously as he can bestow his attention, he can just as easily strip it away.

"When you're finished sucking my cock, and when you've swallowed down the release you give me, I want you to put your shirt back on, take the key I've given you, and go to the kitchens to retrieve a meal that will be waiting."

My teeth brushed his skin, tears falling faster when his hand fisted my hair harder. "I wouldn't do that again, Penelope. I'm trying to save your job."

What?! Anger filtered in to mix with the pain, terror that I would be homeless again, and for what reason? Because he'd bruised me and someone noticed?

Heart hammering beneath my ribs, I pulled my lips down to guard my teeth.

Dark laughter floated above my head, his hands driving my mouth faster. "That's better. For a second there I thought I' regret having to fire you."

I'd never cried before while sucking his cock, never hated him while I obeyed him. But now, I wanted to do was reach up and gouge his eyes out. He didn't need to say another word to prove how easily he'd cornered me. I needed this job. I had nowhere else to go, and now he would give and take whatever he felt like.

His grip loosened on my hair just a touch, the blister of fire across my skull easing. "Once you've picked up the covered dish that will be set aside for you, you'll need to take the elevator down to the basement using the key I've given you and the numerical code that's taped to its side."

Without warning his hips bucked and he shot his release down my throat. "Swallow, Penelope. You won't like the results of angering me."

Doing as he said, I could still taste him on my tongue when I asked, "What's in the basement?"

He didn't need to answer for me to know. Thoughts of Émilie at the well flashed through my head, the vacant eyes of a man I'd met before staring at me in my thoughts. Is this what Vincent had done to Émilie back then? What he was doing to me now?

My chest shuddered with a wrenching sob. What a stupid girl I'd been.

"My brother, Maurice. It seems his last caretaker has quit suddenly, and I need a new person to bring his meals to him."

Terror tightened my muscles over every bone. Still kneeling on the ground, I couldn't look up at Vincent while he fastened his pants. "Why are you doing this to me? I thought he was dangerous."

"He is," he answered softly, "which is why you need to follow my directions exactly."

"And if I refuse?"

Pressing a finger beneath my chin, he tilted my head to force me to look at him. There wasn't a hint of regret or concern on his beautiful face. "Then I regret to inform you your time at the Wishing Well is over."

Tears slid down my cheeks, pain so pervasive in my heart that I thought it would split apart in my chest. Vincent tsked his tongue and shook his head. With a silky voice, he said, "You couldn't have honestly believed I'd keep you forever, or that I would love you? How silly is that, Penelope? You were a dirty girl I pulled from the streets and gave a job. You have no say in what that job will continue being and if you refuse what I offer, I'll replace you. It's that simple."

Why hadn't I saved money? Why had I believed the fairy tale he'd given me? Why had I crawled into the spider's web when he'd done nothing but crook his cruel finger to invite me?

It was as if the last several weeks had killed the girl I used to be. I become weak in the lap of luxury. And now, too afraid to return to what I'd been before he found me, I nodded my head. "What are the directions?"

Smiling, he answered, "Don't make any sudden moves around him. Don't scream or say anything. Don't resist if he scares you. And if you want to walk out of the basement unscathed, just do whatever he wants."

"Anything?" I breathed out.

He nodded his head. "I'll triple your salary. And instead of scrubbing and polishing and running yourself ragged, you can spend your days relaxing when you're not in my suite. You'll be pampered for delivering three meals a day."

The money was difficult to turn down. And in a month's time I could save enough to get away, now that I knew my job here and my affair with Vincent weren't reliable.

"Fine," I answered as hatred rolled through me. But despite the ugly feeling, the betrayal, I only thought of the reward I would receive when Vincent took me to his suite again.

What the fuck was wrong with me?

Pushing to my feet, I pulled the shirt over my head and snatched the key from where I'd set it on the desk. I didn't bother glancing back as I left his office and headed to the kitchens to find a silver domed dish as he'd said. My legs barely held me up as I made my way to the elevator, inserted the key and punched in the six digit code.

I wanted to vomit from the consuming fear, wanted to scream at the way I was letting Vincent use me.

Why hadn't I seen this coming?

The elevator slid smoothly down to the basement floor, the polished doors opening to reveal an entry lobby with black walls, black floors, leather seating and crystal vases full of roses. Stepping through, I could barely see by the flickering light of the flame wall sconces.

My fear consumed me and I had to take a breath to keep from dropping the plate and running away.

"Hello?" I called out, not sure where to leave the meal, not sure about anything anymore.

A noise down a side hall drew my attention, the pathway lit only by flickering candlelight. I would have

199

thought the scene to be romantic if I didn't fear the monster lingering out of sight.

Maybe nothing would happen. The thought occurred to me that like all the games Vincent had played with me over the past few weeks, this was just another one, a test to see how truly obedient I could be. I must have been truly sick in the head when the thought of the reward that would come thrilled me.

Breathing out a heavy breath, I turned left to walk down the hall, pacing my steps as I peeked inside dark rooms waiting for something to jump out at me. Reaching the last door, I looked inside expecting to see a torture chamber or some kind of dungeon, but instead I found a brightly colored living room with yellow walls and brilliant, electric light. It was the tapping of fingers against a keyboard the drew my gaze to the right, the man sitting behind a computer staring back at me as surprised as I stared at him.

This was not what I was expecting. Maurice appeared...normal.

The relief was like a deflating balloon inside me.

I wanted to laugh at how stupid I'd been to think Vincent would actually toss me to a rabid dog. That extra salary he'd promised me looked much better now that I understood the lie he'd told.

"Lunch is here," I announced with a smile. Where would you like me to leave it?"

Maurice blinked, his lips pulling into an unsure grin. There was something off about him, but it wasn't scary, not like I'd imagined it would be after meeting him in the garden. It was like he wanted to express emotion, but couldn't. "Table," he said with a voice as deep as Vincent's. "To your left."

Glancing over, I spotted the small round table I hadn't seen when first walking into the room. Maurice didn't say another word as I made my way across the room to set the domed plate down. A scream tore from my lips when I spun again to find Maurice standing behind me. His hand flew up to cover my mouth as mine flew to my chest to keep my heart from busting out. The visceral terror had returned in a split second to see how silently Maurice had moved, to understand that, perhaps, Vincent hadn't been lying.

My body shook as Maurice pushed me back, his fingertips digging into my cheeks as he locked his eyes to mine with lethal curiosity. It felt like being stared down by a predator deciding whether to eat you quickly or take their time. My butt scooted across the table and I couldn't stop the tears that welled in my eyes.

Vincent's words were a whisper in my head.

Don't make any sudden moves around him. Don't scream or say anything. Don't resist if he scares you. And if you want to walk out of the basement unscathed, just do whatever he wants.

Remembering his instructions, I froze in place. Maurice leaned forward, his nose to my hair as he dragged in a breath to smell me. I trembled beneath his hand, my eyes wide, my muscles so rigid that pain blistered over my bones. Barely able to drag in a breath, I fought to keep from screaming.

Maurice's eyes met mine, his expression unreadable. It wasn't until he spoke again that I realized how he fought to control himself. "Thank you," he said, as if the words were foreign on his tongue. "For the food."

It was like watching a wild creature attempt to wear the skin of civility. He wasn't used to behaving so cautiously.

I occurred to me just then that for as frightening as this man was, he was also beautiful. He had the same green eyes and tan skin as his brother, the same broad shoulders and dark, unruly hair, but there was also a vulnerability in him that I'd never seen in Vincent. It didn't help ease the racing of my heart, the tightness of my body or the fear that drowned me, but it was there.

"You're welcome," I mumbled beneath his hand, thinking that, maybe, he would release me.

Our eyes remained locked for what felt like hours, my pulse fluttering beneath my skin, his gaze finally tracing down my face to watch the beat of it on the soft spot of my neck.

"You're scared."

Slowly, I nodded my head, trapping the inside of my cheek between my teeth to keep from screaming.

"*Je suis désolé.*"

My mouth still trapped by his hand, I mumbled. "I don't know what you said."

"I'm sorry," he answered, English not as fluid on his lips as French had been. This man was struggling to behave and communicate.

I jumped when the fingers of his other hand clamped down on my knee, when his arm flexed to force my legs apart slowly.

The tears in my eyes fell down my cheeks. He watched them, his head tilting to the side in confusion. "I don't want to force you."

"But you will?" I mumbled from beneath his hand.

The nod of his head was jerky, as barely controlled as him. Remorse flashed in his eyes, a sorrow so deep that I felt it in my chest.

"*J'aime quand tu me regardes comme ça.*" He shook his head as if banishing the language. "I can't help it. I'm not-" his voice trailed off, ashamed.

Taking a risk I knew could potentially endanger my life, I reached up to touch the hand he had pressed over my mouth. Curling my fingers over it, I attempted to pull it away. His brows tugged together in question, but he let me.

I'd gone from frightened, to feeling foolish for that fear, to bargaining for my life. The sequence of emotions had made me dizzy.

My voice quivering, the volume barely a whisper, I asked, "Will it be less violent if I cooperate?"

No wonder his last caretaker had fled, the man was devastating and terrifying at the same time. The shame alone was a cloak he wore, as obvious to the eye as his fight to remain civilized. I feared for my life to be alone with him, yet I had this compulsive need to reach out and tell him it would be okay. And while enduring the clash of those emotions, I cursed the odd heat between my legs. Something about him was so familiar, but I didn't understand why.

"*Oui.*"

In my time with Vincent, I'd learned the meaning of that simple word. Swallowing down the knot that clogged my throat, I said, "Promise not to hurt me too badly, and I'll give you what you want."

Surprise. Frustration. Elation. Sorrow and shame. They all could be seen clearly in the shadows behind his gorgeous eyes. My heart hurt for him, despite only meeting him for the second time.

Nodding his head, he released my knee, stepping back just far enough for me to slide down off the table and stand on my feet. My legs could barely hold me up.

I didn't have to ask what he wanted me to do, Vincent's training came to mind, the rules he had set in place for me to follow every time I went to his suite. I could only hope they were the same for the beast that stared at me now.

Slowly, so as not to move too suddenly, I gripped the hem of my shirt to pull it over my head. As soon as my breasts were exposed to his eyes, his hands clenched into fists, a rigidness moving across his shoulders as his eyes locked on my chest. When his jaw ticked, my heart beat like a war drum beneath my ribs.

My hands were shaking as I unbuttoned my pants and slid them over my hips. The material bunched at my ankles over the floor, and as gently as I could manage I kicked it off my feet. I hadn't worn underwear beneath my clothes because I thought it would be Vincent I'd entertain.

Maurice's chest beat heavy, a feral sound emanating that shook me in places I didn't know existed. He stepped toward me and I flinched, insecurity flooding his eyes as if the tiny reaction had been a slap across his face. It was that fear of rejection inside him that made me regret my terror of him.

"Remember not to hurt me, okay?"

Surprised he could hear the words for how quietly I'd spoken them, I tried to smile and reassure him. But before he could lay a hand on me, I reached out, noticed the way he winced before forcing himself to become still and let me palm his cheek. The stubble of his skin was rough against my hand, the vulnerability in him staggering. I could have been touching a hungry tiger and would have felt less scared.

"You're beautiful," I confessed. "Do you know that?"

"I'm not," he said, the truth of his belief sinking deep inside my heart. "I'm -"

Shaking his head again, he snatched my wrist in his grip to yank my hand from his face, stepping forward to force me back onto the table, the surface cold against my skin, as he released my wrist to wrap his hand over my throat and forced me to lie down. I froze in place, refusing to move, to speak, to breathe, as he held me in place while lifting my legs to place my feet on the edge of the table. Shoving my legs apart, his chest beat with excited breath to stare down at my body so exposed.

I couldn't stop my shaking. Couldn't help but feel like he would kill me without meaning to do it. Vincent kept this man caged for a reason and I was discovering that reason now. Maurice didn't behave like an ordinary man. He behaved like an animal - an animal that had lost his restraint.

Releasing my throat, he dropped to his knees, grabbed my waist and pulled me to the edge of the table. And before I could process what he was doing, he grabbed my ankles and forced my feet to his shoulders, holding my legs in place as his teeth nipped at the inside of my thigh, biting down one rough time before his mouth bore down at the apex, his tongue licking inside my body.

The pleasure was instantaneous, the force of it divine. It was as if fear had left me stumbling and over-sensitized and that his mouth would drive me too high. My fear of pain was now a fear of the climax that was building so fucking quickly that I knew it would fracture me once the force of it exploded in my core. I was right to fear that release, the crashing wave of it sweeping me beneath the violence of its storm, dragging me up so high that I floated for only a moment before crashing down again.

As if knowing what he'd done to me, Maurice shook off the last bit of control he had, stood to his feet, ripped his pants open, and with my legs still locked over his shoulders, he gripped his hands on my hips and drove his cock inside me.

The rhythm was brutal, the force without apology, the claiming of me accomplished as his teeth gnashed with each violent thrust, as I looked up into a face that refused to look back at me. Moans poured from my lips as loud as the slap of his hips against the back of my legs, but despite the build of my next release I could see that he felt bad for what he was doing.

Is it wrong that if I wasn't gripping the edge of the table to hold myself in place, I would have reached up to touch his face again and tell him he wasn't to blame?

Someone had broken this man, had fractured him while keeping him caged, and I knew that someone was upstairs right now enjoying what he had done to me. It hadn't been love I'd felt for Vincent before, I could see that now because of the depths of my emerging hatred.

All those thoughts were blown apart when my body quaked with the rush of an orgasm, when I opened my mouth to release a scream as feral as the one from Maurice. We both found ourselves gripped in the cruel but loving hand of a release that was a terrifying as it was natural. And as I slipped back to an earthly plane, I opened my eyes to find Maurice watching me with sweat dripping down his strong chest.

He moved away from me quickly, buttoning his pants and not even bothering to help me up before leaving the room entirely.

A feeling of regret and shame had been left in his wake as a thought occurred, a whisper in my mind. However, as shocked and as breathless as I felt in that moment, I couldn't put my finger on what my mind was trying to tell me.

The aftershocks wore off after a minute or two, my anger surging to the surface. Not at Maurice, not at a man who was obviously so tortured and broken, but at the arrogant bastard I knew would be waiting for me just as soon as I returned upstairs.

Climbing down from the table, I took a breath and got dressed, a million thoughts racing inside me, crashing against the wave of emotions I felt.

Maurice was nowhere in sight as I made my way back to the elevator, inserted the key, typed in the code and pushed the button for the lobby floor. And just as I'd known he would be, Vincent stood waiting outside the doors.

Except, instead of a slimy smile, he looked at me with concern. "Did he hurt you?"

"No," I spat, taking a left down the employee hall. I should have just gone to my room but I needed to go outside, to take a walk in the garden and calm down.

"So you submitted?" Vincent followed behind me. If I weren't so afraid of being fired, I would have turned around and launched myself at him to beat his face in. Instead, I ignored his question.

"Are you quitting?"

"I don't know," I answered, still storming off.

"Will you come up to my suite tonight."

Stopping suddenly, I spun on my heel to face him. "Fuck you. I'll let you know tomorrow if I'm still working here. Until then, leave me the fuck alone."

Surprisingly, he stopped following me, and slamming my hands against the back door, I walked out into the garden alone.

CHAPTER TWENTY-SIX

I spent several hours of that late afternoon deciding what I would do with the cards I'd been dealt. An hour in the garden, and then leaving through a back, employee gate, I spent more time walking the streets of the city, eventually stopping inside a small cafe to grab some food. Choosing a quiet table by the window, I wrapped my hands around a cup of coffee, my head hung as I contemplated the sudden change in Vincent, the heartless way he'd told me that if I didn't take on this new job he'd offered, I wouldn't have a place to sleep.

Lifting my eyes to watch the traffic on the streets and the crowds moving down the sidewalks, I realized that during my wanderings I'd returned to the place where it all began, to a cafe facing a particular alley where I'd taken shelter from the rain. Had Vincent been sitting in this very spot when he first saw me?

A shiver of disgust rolled through me, but while staring at the small overhang that had done nothing to shelter me from the freezing rain, I realized I could never return to the streets. For a moment I was crushed beneath the hard truth that I was out of options...until I remembered one.

It would be an admission of defeat, a figurative crawling, but there was one door left that I could open, I just didn't want to make that step, to choose to admit that I'd been wrong.

God, how we'd fought when I told my mom and Meadow that I wouldn't move with them to Germany. In her anger, my mother had screamed that I was a stupid girl, a teenager caught up in what she foolishly believed was love. And while she'd been right to point out that Blake and I were too young to use words like 'forever', she hadn't been right to call me every horrible name in the book.

Only Meadow had been strong enough to stay silent, had refused to judge me for my decision, and had wished me luck the day I hugged her before walking her to the airport gate. If I had to open that door, if I had to test the waters, it was Meadow I should contact.

Standing from my seat, I left my coffee half full on the table, dropped some money for the waitress and headed for the door. A hand gripped my bicep as I attempted to pass through, a familiar voice that said, "I owe you for the slap, you know?" His voice dropped to a whisper, "And I'll pay you back before too long."

Glancing up into Barron's face, I scowled. "If you don't take your filthy fucking hand off me, I'll scream as I rake my fingernails down your pretty face."

Barron laughed and shook his head as he let me go. "You haven't changed at all. Vincent is going to owe me so much fucking money."

He walked off as if the exchange hadn't happened, his expensive suit perfectly tailored to his body. Glancing back, I watched him take a seat, my disgust so thorough that I didn't pay attention to what he'd said. Storming off down the sidewalk, I resisted the urge to return to the hotel and cry into my pillow. Instead, I forced myself down another three blocks to an internet cafe where I could use their computers. After paying the cashier for a half hour, I selected an empty desk and pulled up the email I'd kept active since before Meadow and my mother had moved away.

Pulling up the last email Meadow had sent - the one that used all capitals to tell me she knew I was no longer with Blake - I clicked the button to reply and paused because I had no idea what I wanted to say. At that point I wasn't sure I wanted to leave Wishing Well just yet. I had too many thoughts to sort out before I could make a decision as important as that.

Reminding myself I was merely opening a door through which I could escape, I typed a non-committal response apologizing for staying out of touch and informing her that I'd found a job at a wonderful hotel which also provided me a place to stay. At first, I was hesitant to name the hotel, but with a shrug I decided avoiding the name would only draw Meadow's suspicion. It wasn't like she was going to leave college in Germany to come rushing to investigate. At most, she would be relieved to know I was okay and we would correspond back and forth until a time I made my decision.

Sending the email, I felt slightly better about my situation and I returned to the hotel to think about what I wanted to do given the direction my job had taken.

Lying in bed, I couldn't silence my anger toward Vincent, but even more unsettling was that I couldn't stop thinking about how broken I'd felt to look at Maurice. There was something so deeply sad about him that it kept drawing my attention back to thoughts of him. And I wouldn't even try to lie and claim that what we'd done together hadn't been amazing. A nagging whisper kept filtering through my head, a familiarity that I couldn't quite pinpoint no matter how I focused on it.

Perhaps it was that mysterious thought that helped me make the decision to stay. I needed to know *why* I felt what I did around Maurice. Not the fear. Not the sorrow. Not the understanding that there was something broken in him that may never be fixed.

No. I wanted to know why I felt so attached to him every time our eyes met.

I would go to Vincent in the morning and let him know I was keeping the job, and I would spend enough time with Maurice to unravel the mystery of why he was affecting me in such an indelible way.

. . .

The next morning found me standing in Vincent's office, the new distance between us palpable.

"I'll keep the job," I informed him, careful to hide what I was feeling. I knew him well enough to know that he could pick apart a person's thoughts through body language or the tone of their voice. He'd always seemed psychic to me at first, but it wasn't that Vincent could hear what was screaming in a person's head, it was simply that he studied the people around him and paid close attention.

The leather of his chair creaked as he relaxed back to stare at me. "It's good to see you've calmed down. And here I was thinking we'd find your room empty this morning. Why the change of heart?"

"I need the money. And since you've made it perfectly clear where my job security stands, I've decided having a roof over my head is better than life on the streets."

"You've grown since coming here. The girl I remember meeting on the streets would have left,

212

despite shooting herself in the foot for doing so." A grin stretched his full lips. "And what of our arrangement?"

"That's off."

The light streaming in through the window must have flared funny, because for a moment I could have sworn I saw regret flicker across his face. He didn't answer immediately, choosing instead to let my statement linger much longer than it should. "We'll discuss that decision later."

Eyes darting to the screen of his computer, he tapped a few keys. "You should go, Penelope. Maurice will be expecting his breakfast. He gets moody if he's kept waiting."

Unable to contain my anger at his simple brush off, his arrogant response that my decision could be discussed, I crossed my arms over my chest. "I mean it, Vincent. If I take this new job, our other arrangement is off."

He didn't bother to look at me. "That's funny, because just yesterday you were on your knees sucking my cock. Women are fickle creatures, but their hearts don't change so easily."

If I'd been in reach of him, I would have slapped his handsome face. "What is that supposed to mean?"

"I'll talk to you at another time. For now, you have a job to do. I suggest you do it."

Dismissed, I left his office, angry at him but not angry for having an excuse to leave. Vincent thought he was waving off an annoying fly without understanding that the fly wanted nothing to do with him. Any discussions he thought we might have were off limits to the fly.

For the first time since coming to Wishing Well, the fly had pulled out her pretty silver scissors and snipped herself free of his tangled web.

Damn, it felt good to be a fly.

After grabbing Maurice's breakfast from the kitchen, I slipped the elevator key from my pocket, tapped in the code and was on my way down to the basement. The doors slid open revealing the small entry lobby I remembered from the day before, except instead of fire sconces lighting my way, the small crystal chandeliers above my head were casting brilliant light, the black on black texture of the walls coming into focus. Turning left, I returned to the room where I'd found Maurice, only to discover it empty.

Not knowing what to do, I set the covered dish on the table, a jagged pulse beneath my skin to remember what had occurred there. Shaking off the memory, I left the room calling Maurice's name as I explored.

Except for that one room, the rest of the basement was dark: the walls, the floors, the furniture, even the flowers. Dracula's tomb would have been considered more festive in comparison to this depressing place. But for unrelenting darkness, there was also an odd tranquility, a respite from the bright opulence of Wishing Well, a taste of truth hidden beneath the ground.

Passing the entryway and the elevators I continued down the hall, my fingertips dragging along the textured walls, my voice becoming softer to enter an area I hadn't seen before.

"Maurice?"

"*Derrière toi.*"

My heart leapt into my throat as I spun toward the low voice, Maurice's palm slamming against my chest, pinning me to the hallway wall. Remaining still, I didn't dare breathe as he leaned down, the tip of his nose sliding up the side of my neck. While my pulse was frenetic beneath my skin, his beat slow and sure, the sound of it a whisper against my ear from where my head reached his chest. I let several seconds pass before swallowing down my surprise and fear to speak to him as calmly as possible.

"It's me, Maurice. Penny. From yesterday."

His voice was smooth and deep. "I know who you are." Fingers curling, he clutched my shirt.

"I-" *Breathe, Penny...just breathe.* "I brought you breakfast."

Maurice didn't answer, the slide of his teeth sharp against the line of my jaw. It was impossible not to tremble, not to part my lips in an attempt to breathe deeper, to calm my racing heart. "It's in the other room," I whispered, "on the table where you had me leave it yesterday."

His voice a honed blade beneath the softest of satin, he said, "You didn't bring me dinner."

"No," I admitted, "I didn't. I was angry and I left the hotel."

His fingers eased their grip on my shirt, a tremor in his body obvious against mine. "I'm sorry," he whispered.

Closing my eyes, I counted in my head, gathering whatever strength I could find in an overwhelming crush of emotion. "I wasn't angry at you."

Letting me go entirely, he backed away, his eyes meeting mine. Confusion muddied the beautiful green, sorrow, and regret. "I hurt you," he said simply, accusing himself of being a monster.

215

Unable to bear adding to the self-hatred that was so obvious inside him, I shook my head, careful for the movement not to be too fast or too sudden. "No, you didn't. You didn't force me."

"I would have. I'm a -" His jaw ticked as he cut the sentence off.

A monster...
A beast...
A man too dangerous for the world...

I could clearly see all those labels rush behind his pained gaze. It only made me angrier. I didn't know Maurice's problems, but I knew trapping any person in a basement by themselves wouldn't help them. You make animals of people when keeping them caged, much like this man was. But I couldn't show that anger, not when he'd assume it was meant toward him. The eggshells beneath my feet cracked with every thought, every decision, every step I took to discover why Vincent treated his own brother so poorly.

"Are you hungry?" I asked.

Without answering, he stormed off in the direction of the room where I'd left his food. I didn't follow him immediately, not with my legs feeling like rubber. Sliding down the wall to sit on the floor, I held my face in my hands. We were going to have to come up with a new way of greeting one another. The sneak attack would stop my heart eventually. Once my vitals felt like they could sustain life again, I pushed to my feet and crept down the hall to the oddly cheerful room hidden within a dreary, dark basement.

I'd expected to find Maurice eating, but instead he was sitting at his computer busily typing. Not knowing whether he wanted me there or not, I stepped in, wringing my hands as I approached his desk.

"Should I leave?" I asked, my voice barely a whisper.

There was no reason for me to stay. I'd done my job of delivering his meal and I didn't have to do another thing until noon when I brought him lunch.

His eyes tipped up to meet mine. "The counselor will be here in an hour. If I don't talk to her, Vincent won't take me outside."

Fuck Vincent, I thought. Maurice wasn't so bad that he had to be trapped. Remembering back to the night I first met Maurice, I realized that Vincent had spoken of him like he was out of control, but I wasn't seeing it. To me, Maurice wasn't definitely odd, he was unsettling, but it was more that he lacked social skills than being a monster.

"I could take you outside," I suggested. "We wouldn't have to tell Vincent."

He was out of his seat and practically on top of me before I could take a breath, my heart screeching to a stop for just a second. "We need to set rules, Maurice. The first one being that you need to stop sneaking up on me or rushing toward me. I don't like it."

He must have taken my words as a type of rejection. Between one second and the next, he was calm and he was violent. By the time he'd broken several objects in the room, he backed me against a wall again, his chest beating with furious breath. Vincent had warned me of this this, but I hadn't listened, and despite being terrified, I wouldn't listen now.

"I still like you," I whispered, his face so close to mine that I could feel the warmth of his breath against my skin. "I just don't like being scared by you."

Trying and failing to break through the wall around his thoughts, I flinched when he palmed my breast, a possessive hold over my shirt, his grip painful. Snatching my wrist with his other hand, he pulled me away from the wall and used my arm to force me over his desk. Bent over me, he breathed against my ear. My first instinct was to fight, to thrash, to scream, but I knew it was the wrong way to handle this man.

His excitement was a hard ridge against my ass. Ignoring the shiver that coursed over my body, I kept my voice calm. "Maurice, please. You're hurting me."

It surprised me again when he released me as suddenly as he'd pinned me down. Behind me a race of words - all in French - were spoken, and as I slowly straightened my body, I turned to see a very agitated, confused man.

"I don't know what you're saying."

"Get out!" he roared.

He didn't have to tell me twice. Slowly, and with absolutely *zero* sudden movements, I crept past him, knowing his head turned so that his eyes could follow me, hearing his heavy steps behind me as I forced myself to walk calmly down the hall. And with the feeling of a stalking tiger at my back, I extracted the elevator key from my pocket, waited for the doors to open, and stepped inside.

Maurice stood staring at me as the doors closed, self-loathing and sorrow obvious in his eyes.

Like last time, Vincent stood waiting for me when I reached the lobby floor, but before he could speak, I barked, "I'm not hurt," as I turned left and stormed down the hall.

CHAPTER TWENTY-SEVEN

Faiville Prison, 12:03 pm

"It's noon," a guard said as he walked through the interview room door. "We'll need you to wait outside the room while the guards change shifts."

Despite the guard's words, Meadow and Vincent stared at each other, both locked in a moment where truth had been revealed, where secrets were beginning to emerge.

Before Meadow could respond to the guard, and while she sat confident that she knew more to this story than even Vincent knew, Vincent shook his head and laughed.

"You should listen to the guard, Meadow. There's no telling what could happen if we're left together, *alone*, for a shift change."

Regardless of the idle threat, Meadow smiled, believing she'd cornered Vincent with details from Penny's diary she was certain Vincent had no way of knowing. There had been moments when his expression shifted, surprise drawing lines across his brow. Anger drawing a line between his eyes.

Reluctant to leave, she convinced herself that it was as good a moment as any to take a break. Letting Vincent absorb his part in the destruction of several lives would weaken him, she hoped.

Or, it would give him time to strengthen his lies.

In the end, it didn't much matter. Penny was dead. Maurice was dead. Émilie was dead, together with several other women who'd had the misfortune of meeting the monster Vincent created.

Because, what Meadow knew that even the police and prosecutors hadn't, was that although Vincent had been responsible for all the lives lost, he hadn't been the one to kill them. Some, perhaps. But not all. And that fact drew Meadow's notice more than she'd yet had a chance to admit.

The question now became: Why hadn't Vincent told the truth and thrown his brother behind bars?

"I'll see you when I get back," Meadow said, standing from her seat and enjoying the metallic screech of the chair legs against the floor. Vincent merely watched her stand, ignoring the jarring noise as he held his expression carefully in place.

Allowing the guard to lead her out, Meadow spent the half hour she had to wait worrying her fingernails between her teeth, gnawing at the edges while considering her next step. A day and a half remained, and there was still more to this story she hadn't revealed.

More importantly, there was more that Vincent hadn't yet confessed. Wanting to save the best parts for the last day of the interview, Meadow formulated questions she would ask, prepared herself for answers she wasn't sure she could bear to hear.

Her heart shattered each time she thought about the man Penny had written about in her diary, the confused, sorrowful creature that hadn't been given a chance. Meadow wanted to hate Maurice for killing Penny, wanted to curse his soul after discovering he'd died after Vincent went to jail. But the images in her head that Penny had painted of him, the whispers and memories that came to Meadow in dreams, made it impossible not to feel pity for the man.

Vincent was one thing entirely. A scoundrel that enjoyed the games he played. But Maurice? Wasn't he just another victim, another pawn caught in Vincent's tangled web?

"You ready?"

Meadow's head snapped up to see a new guard waiting at the gates. Forcing a polite smile, she pushed herself to her feet and followed him to interview room three where Vincent sat waiting.

Patient as ever, Vincent said nothing while Meadow readied her recorder and turned to take her seat. "So, about Maurice, I think you owe me an explanation as to how he died."

"Not just yet," Vincent responded, the note of humor she'd always heard in his voice absent. "I want to ask you about what Penny wrote regarding her first meeting with my brother. Not that night in the garden, but when I sent her down with his lunch. No..." his voice trailed off, his eyes refusing to meet hers as he studied a scratch that ran across the table where they sat. "Not then, either. I want to talk about when she brought him breakfast the next morning."

Gaze lifting, he asked, "Did she write anything beyond what you told me? Beyond being frightened? Beyond feeling sorry for Maurice?"

Straightening her posture, Meadow gave the question some thought. Revealing too much would betray the secret she'd been guarding, and she wanted to save the sting of that for the last day of the interview. "I'm not sure what else she would have written. Your brother was a frightening man, but Penny saw him

221

differently. She saw a man unaccustomed to social graces, to the rules of interaction between two people."

"So, she didn't view him as a monster?"

"No," Meadow answered confidently, "she never did."

Vincent nodded his head, his throat working to swallow down the acrid flavor of Meadow's admission. It must have burned him to know that his attempt at torturing Penny by forcing her to serve Maurice hadn't scarred her as deeply as he'd assumed.

"How did Maurice die, Vincent?"

Trailing a fingertip across the scratch he'd studied earlier, Vincent answered, true remorse in his tone. "After I was arrested, I hired a management company to maintain my properties, including Wishing Well. I also hired an attorney I believed I could trust to look after Maurice's continued care. The company and attorney were intended to work together to see that nothing changed for Maurice."

"Why did that matter?"

"I was saving lives," Vincent admitted, his voice hollow, empty. "After Penny's death, Maurice was devastated-"

"Because he killed the woman he loved?"

Meeting her stare once again, Vincent grinned, the expression tight. Meadow believed he'd forced the stretch of his lips, that it was a poor attempt to disguise his true feelings. "Why would you say he killed her when I'm the one being put to death for it?" The corner of his mouth crooked, a challenge issued in the slight grin.

Cornered by the question, Meadow dropped the subject, "So, you had an attorney seeing to Maurice's care. What happened? He was young. Healthy in a physical sense. Was it an illness that killed him?"

A flash of guilt, of secrets and regrets, his eyes shadowing over before he admitted, "Maurice killed himself. He was found swinging from a noose he'd fashioned and hung in the room he'd demanded be designed to look like our childhood home."

True pain shot through Meadow's chest, the heart-wrenching impact of it stunning her into silence. Vincent watched her reaction with curious eyes before clearing his throat and changing the subject. "We should get back to the story. Time continues to tick by."

Shaking herself of the agony she felt to learn Maurice's fate, fighting the tears that threatened her eyes, she could barely speak with a steady voice. "Yes, we should. I guess at this point I'd like you to explain why, even after tossing Penny to Maurice, you continued to pursue her. I've given it some thought since what you admitted to me yesterday and the only reason I can fathom is that it had to do with the bet."

Canting his head from side to side, Vincent stretched the muscles of his neck. "Do you honestly believe money is my only concern? Even after what I've already told you?"

"What else could it be? You obviously cared very little for Penny. She was a woman you were toying with since the beginning. And although I believe you truly loved your brother, I don't think you loved him enough to stay away from a woman he wanted to be his. Unless of course," she surmised, tapping her fingers against the table, "you really did have feelings for Penny. Did it bother you that she cut of the sexual relationship she had with you after you demanded she

223

have the same type of relationship with Maurice? Is that why you forced her?"

Soft laughter shook his broad shoulders. "I never told her to fuck Maurice."

"You implied it. By sending her down there - alone - you knew he would take what he wanted."

Vincent relaxed back into his seat. "You've neglected to focus on an important detail in what we've explored so far."

"And that is?" Her fingers stopped their rhythm, the room growing quiet.

Giving her question time to linger, Vincent finally parted his lips to answer, "Whereas Maurice had sex with Penelope as soon as he had the opportunity, there was one part of her that was mine."

It was Meadow's turn to laugh. "Please tell me you don't mean her heart."

His snide grin returned. "No, of course not. I'm not sure that belonged to anybody but herself. Penelope was rather fickle. The part of her that belonged to me was her mouth. I'm the one who kissed her. It was my cock she wrapped those pretty lips around. In that way, I took the most intimate part of her, despite what Maurice had done. No matter how many times she spread her legs for my brother, those lips would always be mine."

Oh, how Meadow wanted to skip ahead, wanted to strike out at him to leave a deep scar, but with a calm professionalism, she took a breath and held those secrets to herself. Reminding herself less than twenty-four hours remained for her to crush the arrogance of this evil man, she threaded her fingers together over the surface of the table.

Leaning forward, Vincent stared at Meadow as if he were holding her feet over a fire. She didn't like the feeling that all he had to do was loosen his fingers and drop her down to burn.

"And how curious is that? Don't you think? Penelope was a rebellious girl. She had you and your mother she could run to and avoid ending up back on the streets, but she stayed at Wishing Well even when demands were made of her that she didn't like. Even when she was forced to participate. Perhaps the answer to that odd question was written in the diary you have? Perhaps it's trapped inside your head? For once, you might know something that I don't, so as usual in this game we're playing, I'll give you my perspective if you'll give me hers."

"Fine," Meadow agreed. "We'll continue this dance. Now, start talking."

CHAPTER TWENTY-EIGHT

Vincent

"I'm not hurt," Penelope spat as she moved past me, her body moving quickly to escape down the employee hall. Cocking a brow, I watched her until she'd rounded a corner, and then I let myself into the elevator, typing in the code to ride down to the basement and speak with my brother.

While Penelope had been away cooling off the prior evening, I'd taken Maurice his dinner. It was a surprise to find him in a good mood, his demeanor not quite, but almost normal. We'd talked of what occurred when Penelope brought him lunch, and oddly he'd left out most of the sordid details. I'd found the exclusion of pertinent information strange for a man who normally treated women like objects used to get off.

Tits. Ass. And a cunt. That's all he cared about, all that interested him. But with Penelope, a curious shift had occurred in his thinking.

First noticing the change on the evening of the masquerade ball, I'd neglected to pay better attention during the weeks after that I'd stayed away, but after returning, and in the weeks that followed, I'd breathed easier with how even-tempered he'd become. I'd thought that, maybe, he would improve even more if he could admire Penelope's face during the encounters he had with her.

But what I found when taking the elevator down to his cage was a complete reversal in a man who, until now, had struggled to behave.

The sound of breaking glass drew me left down the long hall. Entering the only cheerful room that could be found in this dark maze, I stood watching as Maurice destroyed a large part of it. Interestingly, I noted, he hadn't destroyed his breakfast or the table it was set on.

"Is there a problem?" I asked, intentionally keeping my voice calm.

He spun to look at me, a vacancy in his eyes I hadn't seen in weeks. The regression scared me. What had Penelope done?

"She won't come back," he growled, the sentence a mix of French and English I was unaccustomed to hearing.

"One language, Maurice." Although I'd tucked my hands inside my pockets, and although I'd made my request as if his choice in words hadn't stunned me, I was frightened for my brother. Somewhere in that twisted mind of his, Penelope had managed to clutter his thoughts further.

Slamming his palms down on the surface of his desk, he ignored the wreck he'd made of the room. It wasn't like this was the first time, and as usual, I'd clean up the mess and recreate the memory of our childhood home. When he said nothing, I asked, "What do you mean she won't come back? Did she tell you that?"

"No." His bark of a response was followed by the slide of his hand, knocking the keyboard away from his computer. "I hurt her."

My brows pulled together. "I just spoke with her in the lobby. She told me she wasn't hurt."

"I tried," he admitted through clenched teeth before stalking away from his desk to drop his body down onto the leather sofa.

"Did she submit?" I asked calmly.

One harsh shake of his head. "I didn't want her to."

My eyes rounded to hear it. For the first time I realized my brother might actually love the woman for whom he'd developed an obsession. Heart pounding, I attempted to convince myself that it was possible for him to feel such an emotion, despite what all his doctors and counselors had told me.

Psychopaths don't love.

Sociopaths care only for what they can toy with as long as it amuses them.

Schizophrenics develop delusions that can, sometimes, make it impossible for them to believe that another person might love them in return.

He wore all of those labels, or just one - depending on the person diagnosing him.

But despite the labels, all I'd ever seen in my brother was a man with limited communication regardless of his intelligence, and a man who was so out of touch with emotion that feeling anything beyond anger and rejection were impossible. He was never compliant with medications. Never.

It wasn't until Penelope that I'd believed in the possibility of something else. I wouldn't let her ruin that.

"She'll be back at lunch, Maurice, and I promise you that she'll be in a better mood, but I need you to promise me that you'll clean up this mess and calm down before your counselor arrives."

Doubt lingered behind his eyes, but he nodded his head regardless. "I'll do it, for her."

My shoulders relaxed. "I know you will, brother. I have business to attend, so I need to go upstairs. If you behave for the rest of the day, I'll take you out into the garden tonight. It's been a few days since you've left your cage.

Another nod was all he gave me, and knowing that he was done with communicating with me for the morning, I slipped away from the basement, reached the lobby and went in search for Penelope.

Finding her at the well, I watched her silently for several minutes, noticing the way her shoulders shook with tears, the way her arms crossed over her chest protectively. In truth, I should have left her alone to her quiet moment, but I was more of a bastard than that. She'd angered me. She'd upset Maurice. She deserved what was coming to her.

Stepping up to the other side of the well, I waited for her to lift her eyes, to lock the gold-flecked brown with mine, to show me her rebellion peeking out from her sorrow.

In the weeks I'd spent toying with her, I hadn't broken her completely. That fact pleased me.

"Have you given any consideration to what we discussed in my office this morning?"

She rolled those pretty eyes, and if she'd been any other woman I would have made her regret such an act. However, in this moment, I needed Penelope's refusal to surrender. I needed her to fight.

"I take that as a no."

"You take it right," she said, her hand brushing away a tear. "You and me, we're done. I'm not some fucking whore you can pass around in the hotel. I'm not Émilie."

Pinning me with a stare that dared me to ask, I had to fight not to show my confusion. What did she know of Émilie, and why use that particular woman in this fight?

It didn't matter enough to ask.

"Fine," I relented, shoving my hands in the pockets of my slacks, "I won't pass you around. I've decided I want you all to myself. What you've done already is enough. You gave Maurice a taste, and as I just informed him, he won't get another. You're mine, Penelope."

Narrowing her eyes, she glared at me as a pink film of hatred colored her skin.

Grinning to see the color, I said, "Let's face it, Maurice is just a pathetic mess that has no hope of a future. The man can barely communicate, much less control his emotions. I've been telling him that for years, but the idiot won't listen. I apologize for using you to prove my point to him, but you did it quite well. I bet the man thinks he's in love. How ridiculous is that? He'll spend the rest of his life in that cage while I enjoy all that life has to offer."

The pink transitioned to a brilliant red. Hatred was woven into that color. Pain, anger, and a loathing so deep, I would have felt the sting of it if it could reach out and slap me. Daggers were her eyes, her mouth pulled in such a tight line that holding the expression must have been painful for her.

"Why do you treat him so badly?" she hissed, her voice barely controlled. "Sure, Maurice doesn't know how to communicate very well, and yes, he has no clue how to behave around other people, but keeping him down in that fucking basement doesn't help him! What you're doing to him is evil and it's your fault he is the way he is!"

Shrugging my shoulders as if her words hadn't cut deep, I ignored the confirmation – the perfect reflection - of a fear I'd held for many years. My feelings, my thoughts, were not for her to know.

Shoulders rigid, she tipped her chin. "Are you telling me my new job is over? What's the next one you plan to assign to me? Making me strut around in one of those bullshit costumes in the lounge?"

Although, the idea of watching her strut around in costume aroused me, I glanced out over the garden, silently telling her that the anger she felt had no effect on me. It wasn't even worth looking her in the eye, wasn't worth acknowledgment. "No. I still want you to take Maurice his meals. But I expect you to treat him as all the other professionals I hire for him do. Keep your distance. Give him nothing. And make it clear that he'll never be good enough for a woman's love. That's what I want. That's what I intended. And if you won't do it, I'll find someone who will." My eyes finally met hers. "It's that simple."

I worried she'd break apart if she didn't let the anger out. But somehow, she remained in place, she managed to keep from exploding. A decision filtered behind her gaze. I could only hope it was the right one.

Smiling, I inclined my head. "Have a good day, Penelope. I expect to see you in my suite at ten tonight. Because, regardless of what I've led you to believe, you don't have a choice as to whether you are Maurice's lover or mine."

It took everything I had to stroll off calmly without looking back, and I could only hope that by pushing the buttons that were so plainly obvious in her, I'd shoved her in the direction I wanted her to go.

CHAPTER TWENTY-NINE

Faiville Prison, 1:37 pm

"Stop."

Vincent's gaze shifted to brush Meadow's, not giving her his full attention, just a tease that he was concerned with what she would have to say. Arrogance lined his face, the knowledge that he knew something she did not, that in his games, he'd led her to believe she could hurt him.

"Is it something I said?" he asked, humor having returned to his voice, victory infecting his tone. "And here I thought you would continue this discussion as we'd agreed. I gave you my portion of the story, now you owe me Penelope's."

Meadow was mere inches away from scraping her fingernails down his handsome face. If what he'd just told her was true...

"You intentionally shoved her to Maurice. You know goddamned well that what you said to her, that making her hate you and then stripping her of a choice, would make her rebel against you by choosing Maurice. Why would you do that?"

Tilting his head this way and that, he considered her question. "You have it half right." Pausing, he splayed his hands over the surface of the table, his mouth puckering with thought, his eyes directed at anything but her.

Meadow knew he was intentional in the direction of his gaze. There was nothing of interest in the room, only plain white walls and two tables. He was making it clear that, she too, carried little interest.

Finally locking his eyes on hers, he commented, "People are so easy, aren't they? It takes practice and control to be able to see through one's anger, patience that not many people possess. So muddied by their own emotions, most people don't stop to think - to plot - before they react. They're like a bull charging the red cape of a matador, their hoof scraping the ground before they lunge. But it's the matador who has the advantage, the weapons hidden that will stop the bull in its tracks."

He blinked slowly, smiled a lazy grin. "If Penelope had taken the time to think about what I was doing, she might have seen how easily she was being led. But she was too angry, wasn't she? And with that streak of rebellion she carried inside, it was too easy to guess what her next move would be."

Meadow refused to respond, she was too locked in frustration that Vincent had managed to pull the rug out from beneath her on this one subject - this one secret. It wasn't the best card she'd intended to play, the biggest card, but it was one she'd hoped to slash across his twisted heart to cut deep. Wanting to slap the amusement from his face, Meadow clenched her hands in her lap.

Vincent stared at her for several seconds before laughter burst from his lips. "Oh, come now, Meadow, you couldn't possibly have believed I didn't know what was going on in my own hotel, with my own brother." His shoulders shook as the laughter faded, his eyes flicking to hers before he canted his head. "Did you think you were going to surprise me with the fact that Penny loved Maurice more than she loved me?"

Sighing, Vincent shook his head. "I'd say I'm sorry for having stolen that moment from you - that revelation - but I'm not. If anything, it's rather funny to see the anger on your face. You can't hurt a man who made puppets dance by pulling their strings. Of course, Penny cared for Maurice more, I'd made sure of that."

Meadow ground her teeth, hating the satisfaction behind his glimmering, green eyes.

When she remained silent, Vincent resettled in his seat, his shackles rattling. "It's your turn to tell me Penelope's perspective."

Finally, Meadow snapped, "Why do you care or want to know? It's not like the information will be new for you."

He grinned. "That's not entirely true. Whereas I knew Penny continued in her relationship with Maurice, I never knew how either of them felt for each other. In a small way, you've already answered that question with the anger you're showing me now, the fact you'd hoped to surprise or hurt me with the depth of feelings between the two. But, I'd like to know."

"Why?" Meadow asked again.

Resignation smoothed the laugh lines of his face, a soft breath whispering out from between parted lips. "Because Maurice was my brother, the only person I cared about in this world-"

"He's dead because of you," she spat, interrupting him, doing her best to drive a knife into his rotten heart.

Holding up a finger, he said, "We'll get to that. But first, you owe me a story, and I would like to hear that, in Maurice's life, he found some light within the darkness, some small bit of hope that he could be a normal man for once. It would make his death less

235

tragic to know that he'd experienced actual joy just once. He had such a difficult life, was so walled off and out of control. It would be a shame if he'd never had one day, one hour, of peace and contentment."

"I still don't understand why you care."

Vincent sighed loudly, his voice soft as he confessed, "Because if you haven't realized it by now, Meadow, then you must be blind. If ever I had a weakness, a soft spot that could have been used to strike me down, it was Maurice. I may have resented my brother for the problem he'd been in my life, but that doesn't mean I didn't love him."

"And yet you treated him like garbage," she posited.

Nodding his head, his smile turned into a frown. "I thought what I did to keep him out of trouble was best for him. Looking back, I regret those decisions. I regret the cage I'd built for him, and for having kept him alone and apart from society."

The honesty of that statement - the admission - stunned Meadow. "Are you telling me you know that you helped create the problems Maurice had?"

Vincent swallowed down whatever guilt he was feeling. "I wouldn't say I created the problems, that was a matter of nature and brain chemistry. But I didn't help make the situation any better, and for that, I blame myself. In my haste to protect him, I never gave him the chance to grow."

Meadow considered how to approach a topic she wasn't sure Vincent would answer honestly, but she had a day and a half left to ask it, to confirm what she'd known all along. Knowing she'd made the demand that the prison not record the interview, telling them they could watch the security cameras, but not listen, she leaned forward with little worry that if Vincent admitted the truth, it would save his life.

"I want you to be honest with me for once. This information won't be written into my article about you, Vincent. It's only for me to know."

He stared at her, curious.

"You didn't kill Penny, did you? It was Maurice."

Shifting, he leaned forward so that their faces were close together, his voice lowering to a whisper as he spoke. "Why would I give up my life for a murder I didn't commit?"

Meadow's brows pulled together. "That doesn't answer my question, Vincent."

"It's not my turn to answer questions," he responded calmly. "Tell me what I want to know, and perhaps we can revisit your question when you're finished."

Knowing she'd hit a wall, Meadow leaned back in her seat, happy for the distance it put between them. This part of the story had become more depressing for her to tell now that she knew it wouldn't have the effect she'd hoped for.

Once Vincent, too, had sat back in his chair, Meadow breathed deeply before admitting what she knew of the love Penny and Maurice shared.

CHAPTER THIRTY

Penny

I spent the remainder of the morning furious with Vincent, so fucking outraged that I couldn't sit still, couldn't keep from pacing around the paths of the garden considering my next move.

It broke my heart to think of how he treated Maurice, to remember the pain I saw in that man's eyes every time he felt rejected or lost control. What kind of life could a person lead when constantly drowning in embarrassment, in doubt, in sorrow? Not that my life was any better at the moment, but at least I'd experienced happy times I could think back on.

I'd had a family that loved me even if my father died and I hadn't kept in contact with my mother and sister. And although Blake had eventually broken my heart and left me with nothing, I would never lose the years we'd shared together.

I'd experienced moments lying in the warmth of sunshine. I'd been allowed to laugh, to be silly, to dance and sing. I'd felt love expand my heart with both joy and sorrow, and I'd clung to friendships at times that had meant more to me than the world.

Even in the darkest moments, I could remind myself that there had once been light, and even when nightmares chased and it felt like I would break, I could escape into memories of happier times.

What did Maurice have to remember except a brother who kept him confined to a cage? When had he ever walked beneath the warmth of the sunlight? When had he ever looked a person directly in the eye and known that he was loved?

Suspecting Maurice had never experienced the best parts of life, I made a decision in my heart before it was ever an obvious thought in my mind. And when noon rolled around, the sundials hidden along the paths of the garden shaded just right, I found my way back to the hotel and retrieved Maurice's lunch.

To say I was excited to return to the basement was a lie. In truth, I was once again terrified. Not because I thought Maurice would hurt me - although that act was always a possibility - but because I worried that I would hurt him. I'd never dealt with a person so sensitive, so distraught. I'd never had to walk on eggshells for fear that one wrong look, or a word spoken that could be taken the wrong way would break apart every bit of self-control a person fought to have.

Being a catalyst for Maurice's rage, for his sorrow, and his lack of restraint, wasn't what I wanted to become. But as I'd already discovered that morning, he had made me exactly that.

The elevator doors swung open to an entryway lit by candles alone, and it occurred to me that when his mind was mired in darkness, so too was his surrounding space.

Tapping drew my attention to the left hall, the sound pulling me to a room that was in perfect opposition to the rest of the basement where Maurice was trapped. And like yesterday at this time, I found him seated at his desk. Although not messy, the room was practically empty of many of the decorations and furnishings that had been here this morning. Sorry for having pushed him to a point of destroying a room it was obvious he preferred, I cleared my throat and forced a smile.

"Lunch is here. Where would you like it?"

His beautiful face tipped up to look at me, embarrassment staining his cheeks. "The table, as usual," he answered, restraint obvious in his clipped words.

Crossing the room, my eyes caught sight of a few shards of glass he'd missed when cleaning the room. I simply stepped around them and said nothing. Setting the covered dish down on the table, I shifted my weight between my feet, not knowing what to do next. But rather than running away like my instincts were screaming for me to do, I turned and walked to stand in front of his desk.

Tap, tap tap...

His fingers over the keys moved quickly, and I wondered briefly what he did on his computer all day. Refusing to ask the question, I stood and waited for him to look at me again. When he did, I had to grip the side of my pants to keep from reaching out to wipe the lines of sorrow away.

"Did you enjoy your breakfast?" I asked, deciding that keeping our conversation contained to safe subjects was the best way to communicate with Maurice.

He nodded slowly, one small movement while his eyes watched me with suspicion.

"What did they send you? I never look beneath the cover, so-"

My voice trailed off, and suddenly I felt stupid for the ridiculously boring question.

"The usual," he answered softly. Shaking his head, he added, "Bacon, pancakes, eggs."

My stomach growled just hearing about food. With the anger I'd felt toward Vincent, I'd neglected to eat anything.

Maurice's brows lifted above his eyes. "Are you hungry?"

"I'm fine," I answered a bit too quickly. He cocked a brow and I laughed. The sound from my lips caused his mouth to crook with an unsure smile.

Realizing I liked being around him when he was calm, I scoured my thoughts for more safe subjects to discuss. "I was walking in the garden this morning after bringing breakfast to you. I like to lie on the swings and watch the birds fly overhead. It's peaceful."

The words were a lie. In truth I'd been storming around burning off the anger Vincent had driven deep inside me. But I wouldn't admit that to Maurice.

"I don't see many birds at night. I guess they're all sleeping," he responded, his words crushing my heart. This man deserved to explore outside while the sun was high and shining.

Turning to glance at his waiting food, I asked, "Did you want me to leave so you can eat?"

He shook his head. "No." His expression tightened, as if he were attempting to conjure words he wasn't used to speaking. "I'd like it if you eat with me." A flash of embarrassment rolled across his expression, his head tilted down as his eyes tipped up, like a dog waiting to be hit. I wouldn't be the one to slap him.

"Do you think there's enough?"

Maurice nodded his head.

Not sure what to do now that we'd gotten this far, I made a decision to be the first to make physical contact with a man who was obviously afraid he'd hurt me. Slowly, so as not to startle him or give the wrong indication that I was leaving, I inched around the edge of his desk, stepping as close as I could to him while extending my hand. He stared at it as if not knowing what to do next.

"I'm offering to lead you to the table," I explained, "by holding your hand. All you have to do is reach up and take it."

His eyes remained fixed to my palm as if it would snap out and smack him. Eventually, though, he lifted those gorgeous green eyes to mine, insecurity written behind them as he lifted his hand and wrapped it with mine. His skin felt like it was on fire, the heat of him helping drive the cold anger from my bones.

Tugging softly so that he would stand from his seat, I led him across the room to where his food sat waiting. Taking a chair, I let go of his hand and patiently waited for him to sit. Neither of us reached to remove the dome from his plate immediately, we just sat staring at one another as thoughts raced through our heads. After a few seconds, he finally broke our stare to lift the dome from the plate and released a scent that sent my stomach tumbling through another loud growl.

Maurice chuckled, the sound not loud or boisterous enough to be called a true laugh, but I smiled regardless because it was a start. It was the first time I saw even the bare hint of happiness in his eyes.

The only problem we faced was that there was one plate and one silverware setting. We would have to find a way to share and Maurice appeared confused as to what to do.

Deciding to make this fun, I joked, "You can feed me if you want."

His eyes lifted to meet mine. "What do you mean?"

Taking the fork and unwrapping it from the cloth napkin, I slid it over to him. "You take a bite, and then you can give me a bite. Back and forth, so it's fair."

"Fair," he repeated, more to himself than to me. It didn't take a genius to figure out this beautiful, lonely man had no idea how to handle himself around company. Sure, he may have been used to doctors and counselors, Vincent, and other people that studied him like an animal in a zoo, but he didn't understand what to do when a person sat beside him with the intention of being a friend.

The realization only cemented my decision to become anything he needed. If Vincent wouldn't let Maurice upstairs to see the sunshine, I'd bring the sunshine to him.

"Want me to show you?"

He nodded, his cheeks flaring red. It was so intriguing watching a man who had the strength and aggression to rip my head from my body fighting to behave like an ordinary person. Like watching a lion tuck a napkin into his collar while sitting at a table sharing lunch with the gazelle instead of eating them.

"Okay." Sliding the fork back to my side of the table, I picked it up, scooped up a bit of the chopped steak and sautéed onions before carefully reaching across to offer it to Maurice. He stared at it for a few seconds, his eyes flicking to mine before he opened his mouth, and used his teeth to slide the food off the tines.

Smiling, I scooped up another bite and ate it myself. After moaning softly from how amazing the food tasted, I chewed, swallowed, and then slid to the fork back over to him. "Now you try."

Maurice picked up the fork, carefully loading it with food while I tried not to think that this could go very wrong. What if the food fell off before he could get it to me? What if I didn't take the bite fast enough to reassure him that I was still his friend? What if he stabbed the fork in my eye to teach me a painful lesson that he was more of a wild animal than a civilized man?

It could go either way, I realized, but still I sat and waited for him to reach to me and offer me a bite of food.

Locking my gaze with his, I smiled shyly before opening my mouth to take the bite. The way his eyes dipped down to study my mouth, the way his nostrils flared slightly, the heat I saw beaming from his face, it did funny things to my body while I slid the food from the fork.

After chewing, I had to fight to swallow, the food colliding with the frantic storm of butterfly wings in my stomach.

The remainder of the meal was spent much in the same way, Maurice's shoulders relaxing with each minute that passed, with each shy smile shared between us. Once the plate was clean, Maurice looked at me, unsure what to do next. Fighting not to sigh when I realized how long a distance he had to walk to act normal around another person, I stepped up my game by making another suggestion.

"Would you like to sit on the couch with me?"

His brows pulled together in confusion. "Why?"

Shrugging, I answered, "To talk?"

"Talk?"

I nodded.

"About what?"

"I don't know. About anything."

He considered it for a second and shook his head. "I'd rather fuck."

Opening my mouth to immediately dismiss that idea - or at least the way he'd suggested it - I closed it and remembered that Maurice was unaccustomed to how that particular part of a relationship was handled.

How the hell was I going to wiggle my way out of this one without setting him off?

"We should go to the couch first and then figure out what to do."

"*D'accord.*"

I blinked, smiling when I reminded him, "I don't speak French."

His eyes rolled. "It means okay."

Before I could push out of my seat he stood from his and rounded the table. I won't lie and claim I didn't brace myself for a sudden attack. But instead of forcing himself on me, or lifting me from my seat to sit me on the table to fuck me silly, Maurice simply offered me his hand. My eyes widened at the gesture.

Taking it, I let him help me from my seat and lead me to the couch where he sat on one end and I took the other.

This is going well, I thought.

Famous last words.

Before I could come up with a subject for us to talk about, Maurice grabbed me by the ankles and tugged me across the couch. Wrapping my legs around his waist, he deftly maneuvered his body on top of mine, his hands pinning my shoulders to the cushions as his mouth came down to bite the tip of my breast from over my shirt and bra.

"Maurice!" I cried out, but softened my voice to remember how he'd reacted this morning when I'd yelled at him. "I thought we were going to talk."

The tip of his nose was tracing the line of my neck. "Then talk, if that's what you want to do. But it's not what I want to do."

Teeth sank down on the lobe of my ear and my body arched against his. There was no mistaking how excited he was, the ridge of his erection was pressing between my legs. Despite the shudder of my body and the racing beat of my heart, I managed to respond, "That's not how talking works."

His chest vibrated with a deep growl, dark laughter filtering past his lips. Hot breath slid down my neck to brush my shoulder when he answered, "Then don't talk and I'll fuck you instead."

Before I could utter a word in protest, his left hand moved to cover my mouth, while his right slid between our bodies to unbutton my pants. He'd managed to unfasten them, shove them to my knees and thrust a finger inside me before I could take my next breath.

Apparently, learning the cues of when a woman was interested in sex would have to happen on another day. At that point, there was no stopping him. Remembering the last time we'd been together, I also knew there was no possibility of this being soft and sweet. And as if spurred on by that thought, Maurice pulled away just enough to flip me so that my stomach was on the couch, lifting my hips so that I was on my knees, my legs still trapped by the pants bunched around them and my face pressed against the cushions when he planted a hand on my upper back to keep me from moving away.

I knew better than to fight, but I couldn't help the squeal when he leaned over to bite down on my ass. More deep laughter as the sound of a zipper opening was a distinct note on the silence of the room.

The bite brought a memory to mind, but it was gone again as his cock thrust in my body, my mouth opening on a sensual moan the instant his width filled me. One of these days I was going to convince him to fuck me sweetly, but for now, I would submit to his whim and enjoy the ride.

As his hips thrust and he pushed himself deeper, his hands crept up the front of my shirt to push my bra up my breasts so that he could grip them possessively. Much taller than me he was able to bend over me, to press his mouth to my ear. His voice was a rough whisper when he said, "I think it's funny that you were already wet. You didn't actually want to talk, did you?"

I couldn't find the strength to answer him, I was too busy trying not to explode from the rush of pleasure he was forcing through my body. Maurice may have not been skilled in regular communication, but the man had a gold medal in the area of sensual torture.

With every powerful thrust of his hips, his breath pulsed against my neck, and as my muscles tightened to grip him and pull his cock deeper, the sounds coming from his mouth became feral. He wasn't simply fucking me, he was claiming me as his.

It was slightly embarrassing how quickly he made me come. And as soon as my body tightened with my release, Maurice thrust harder to find his own. It wasn't long until our bodies were coming down from the moment, his erection still inside me as it softened.

I closed my eyes and listened to his rhythmic breathing, thinking that when I brought him dinner, I'd show him what it meant to be sweet.

CHAPTER THIRTY-ONE

After leaving Maurice at his desk and refraining from sneaking behind him to see what he did on the computer all day, I took a shower in my room and left the hotel to walk the streets of the city and think about everything that had occurred over the past few days.

Remembering the email I'd sent to my sister, I stopped in at the Internet cafe, paid the clerk for a half hour and pulled up my messages to see she'd answered me almost immediately. If I hadn't been in such a bad mood when I sent the email, and if I hadn't shut down the computer almost as soon as hitting send, I would have heard the tell tale ping of her response.

Opening the email, I laughed to see the first several lines written in all caps. Leave it to Meadow to find a way to yell at me from across an ocean.

"FINALLY! I WAS ABOUT TO HIRE AN INVESTIGATOR TO FIND OUT IF YOU ARE DEAD!!"

Reading through the long winded message, I discovered that Meadow was doing well in school even though she was only taking two classes at a time. Between the two of us, I'd been the more academically gifted, but not exactly the smartest when it came to common sense.

Apparently, Meadow was working towards a journalism degree but hadn't yet made it past the basic courses. Luckily, she'd managed to find a program that taught in both English and German, since she was as frustrated with the language barrier over there as I was with two particular men at the hotel.

According to her, mom was doing well in her new marriage and the man she'd married was halfway decent, but had no sense of humor to speak of. It was a far cry to who our father had been, but dad had been one in a million.

Hitting reply, I sent Meadow a response promising her I'd stay in touch on a more frequent basis. My hands must have hovered over the keys as I made my decision whether I'd be staying at Wishing Well or not. If it had been about Vincent alone, I would have begged my sister to buy me the next plane ticket to Germany, but I had Maurice to consider.

I couldn't leave him to waste away beneath the abuse of his older brother. Not after the moment we shared today while eating lunch. Not after I'd seen for a few minutes at least that he had the potential to lead a normal life.

So instead of begging to be rescued, I told my sister how happy I was in my new job and that I'd write to her again in a week.

The day moved quickly after that, the sun setting on the horizon as I let myself into the garden of the hotel through the back employee gate. Seeing that it was six, I made my way to the kitchen to fetch Maurice's dinner. Except when I arrived, I had two trays given to me on a metal courier cart and I glanced up at the kitchen manager in confusion. He glared back, too busy to politely explain.

"Vincent said two meals should be ready." Having barked out the simple sentence, he stormed off to reprimand one of the cooks who was prepping food behind the line.

It didn't take long for me to reach Maurice's basement suite, or for me to find him in the same room as usual. "Dinnertime," I announced.

The typical tapping of his fingers over a keyboard stopped immediately, his eyes flicking up, a forced smile stretching his lips. I had to bite the inside of my cheek to keep from laughing at the odd expression. Pushing the cart to the table, I asked, "Were you the one who ordered two meals?"

Nodding his head once, he answered, "I didn't want you to be hungry."

Praising him, I said, "That was very considerate of you, Maurice. Thank you."

He responded in such a way that the words sounded foreign on his tongue. "You're welcome."

"Would you like to eat now?" I asked.

Cutting his head sharply to the left, he kept his eyes pinned on me. "Not yet."

"Okay," I said, dragging the word out, "what would you like to do instead?"

Already knowing the answer to my question, I waited for him to tell me he wanted to fuck. Except, he didn't...

"Would you like to take a tour of my home?"

If I hadn't been holding on to the handle of the push cart, I would have fallen over. "Um, sure," I answered meekly, surprise weakening my voice.

Maurice must have noticed the odd reaction because his nostrils flared with anger, his shoulders hunching together as his eyes flicked to the computer screen. "Forget it," he barked.

Shit...

"I'm sorry for looking like I didn't want to walk around, it's just that you surprised me with the suggestion."

Shrugging a broad shoulder as if to dismiss what I said, anger rolled behind his startling green eyes. I refused to give up. "What made you think to give me a tour?"

His jaw ticked, uncertainty a shadow beneath his eyes. "The internet," he practically whispered. "I looked it up and it said that friends show friends around their house."

My heart shattered into a million fucking pieces. He was actually researching how to be normal. Gathering myself back together, I focused on a word that he'd said as I approached him. He refused to look up at me, but I stood next to him regardless. With a soft voice, I asked, "Am I your friend, Maurice?"

His gaze darted up to my face and back to his screen, pink darkening his cheeks. "Yes."

I couldn't help my smile. "Then give me the tour."

Reluctantly, he stood from his seat and offered me his hand. I took it, squeezing his fingers between mine as he led me from the room. I should have known the tour wouldn't be normal. Waking down the halls, he pushed open every door we passed saying, "Room. Another room. Another room. Bathroom. Another room. Room with weights. Therapy room. Room."

We reached the last door, "Room with bed." He tugged me inside.

I should have known we'd end up here. It occurred to me that Maurice wasn't quite accurate on his definition of 'friend.'

Glancing around the dark room, I could only see by the flickering light of candle sconces on the wall. There

251

wasn't much furniture to be found, just a giant bed positioned in the center of a wall, the mattress covered in black sheets. Unlike the hallway floors of dark marble, his bedroom floor was a thick, dark carpet. No wonder he spent so much time in the yellow room, the rest of this place felt like a large coffin.

Before I could return my attention to him, he was dragging me deeper inside to shove me down on the mattress. He started to crawl over me, but I stopped him by placing my hands on his strong shoulders. Almost immediately, his expression twisted with rejection, but I spoke before he could react. "Can we try a new way of ..."

"Fucking?" he asked.

I took a breath. "Of being together," I corrected him. It was a struggle not to laugh when his head tilted like a confused puppy.

"There's only one way, unless," his hand found my ass, "you want to try my cock in that hole."

Yeah, no. I wasn't ready for that. "Just trust me, okay. I'm your friend, so I'd like to do something different. You'll like it, I promise."

It took him a minute of staring at me to finally nod his head and roll off me. Pushing to my knees, I climbed off the bed, his hand striking out to grab my wrist and stop me from leaving. Turning, I crooked a corner of my mouth. "I'm not going anywhere. I just need to move out of the way so you can sit down."

Cocking one brow, he pushed himself into a seated position on the edge of the bed. Placing my hands on his shoulders - noticing how big he was compared to me - I climbed up to straddle him. His hands immediately moved to cup my ass and I smiled realizing the need to do so was just a natural part of him.

Cupping his cheeks in my hands, I didn't miss the way his brows tugged together. He was completely still, a snake ready to strike, a man afraid of what the small woman in his lap would do to him.

"I want to go slow this time."

Maurice shook his head, his fingers gripping me tighter.

"Please?"

Another shake of his head.

Lowering my voice, I pressed my forehead to his. He winced, jerking his head away before I could ask, "Have you ever gone slow before?"

Frustration was a tick in his jaw. "No."

Remaining patient, I asked, "Have you ever let a woman fuck you before?"

"No."

"Would you like to try it with me?"

Uncertainty was obvious in his voice. "Okay."

Realizing he didn't like his face touched, I assumed kissing him was out of the question. *Baby steps*, I told myself as I gently pushed on his shoulders to make him lie back. "Can I take off your shirt?"

Several seconds passed, but he nodded his head. My fingertips dragged from his shoulders down to his waist, ripples of hard muscle like deep ridges as I touched his stomach.

Good God, what kind of body does this man have hidden beneath his shirt?

I lost my ability to breath when I lifted the hem, tugging it off him as he moved his arms and showed me. But as my stomach twisted in knots to see an almost perfect physique, anger clouded my eyes to

253

notice the maze of scars that were small white lines across his torso. Knowing better than to focus on those scars or ask questions, I lifted my eyes to his face. "You're a work of art, Maurice. I've never seen someone so beautiful."

Heat blazed behind his eyes, a primal edge to his gaze that made the butterflies in my stomach beat their wings harder. Without unlocking our gaze, I unbuttoned his jeans and freed his erection from his pants. My fingers wrapped the girth, a growl emanating from his chest, letting me know his patience to let me take the lead was running out.

Leaning down, I placed a kiss in the center of his chest and released his cock to unbutton my own pants. Moving so that I could drag them off my legs and kick them from my feet, I stood on the floor at the edge of the bed, and stripped off my shirt. There was no doubt on my mind this man was hungry, not with the way he stared at my breasts.

Slowly, I climbed back on top of him, my body ready, my breath held as I straddled his lap, positioned him so that he could sink inside my body, and lowered myself down. His hands immediately went to my waist, his lips parting as I began to move over him.

Dragging his hands up my body, he palmed my breasts, taking possession of them as he watched me move. I was driving myself to a climax when his patience finally snapped. But instead of shoving me over so that he could climb on top, he simply grabbed my hips, his grip firm, as he set a faster pace.

I came apart almost instantly, my palms on his shoulders, my head falling back as I let him use my body to find his own release, and when his hips bucked up, his cock sinking deeper inside me, I closed my eyes and realized that I was becoming addicted to the savage beast of man who had trusted me enough to call me his friend.

CHAPTER THIRTY-TWO

After the time we spent in Maurice's 'room with a bed', as he called it, we made it back to the 'sunshine room', as I called it, and ate dinner. Not much conversation was had, but I hadn't expected it, at least until I asked about the reason for one yellow room in his basement.

My curiosity won me an angled brow, a moment of silence as he carefully placed his fork on his plate, pulled the cloth napkin from his lap and placed it on the table. A million thoughts rushed behind his downcast eyes, lines of sorrow written across his face.

His voice had little strength when he asked, "What has Vincent told you?" His eyes lifted to mine. "About me? About life before he brought me here?"

Not a damn thing... I thought, bitterly. Well, that wasn't entirely true, he'd admitted Maurice had some issues, and that they'd lived in Paris before coming to the States.

"Not much. He said you lived in Paris before coming here. That you had a place in Paris and a farm outside the city with a well much like the one in the garden."

Nodding, Maurice admitted, "I don't remember that much about Paris. Or the farm. I was younger than Vincent when Maman died. But I do remember a room like this one. It was her favorite place. I could be calm for her in that room."

My heart fractured again. And while trying to swallow past the knot of emotion his words conjured, I realized something about Maurice: it wasn't that he couldn't talk - his vocabulary and tone were normal in that moment - it was something else that made communication difficult for him. Maybe because we were 'friends', the words were coming easier to him.

"I'm sorry about your mom. My dad died a little over two years ago."

Nodding, he refused to look at me. "I didn't like my Papa. He was-"

His teeth clenched together so hard I could hear them scrape. Shaking it off, he said, "You should go," his voice was tightly controlled.

A live wire, frayed at the end, Maurice struggled against some emotional turmoil, his energy - his pain - bleeding across the table. I opened my mouth to ask what I could do, I reached across, but pulled my hand back when his expression twisted, when it was all he could do to tell me to get out. Fear took hold of me, concern, and I found myself bolting for the hallway, running past the dancing flames of fire sconces to shove the key into the elevator slot, my fingers tapping the code as glass shattered in the distance and tears rolled down my cheeks.

Not knowing what I'd said or what I'd done, I pressed my back against the elevator wall as the doors slid closed, my body sinking to the ground, my head snapping up with the expectation that Vincent would be waiting when the doors slid open again.

He wasn't. The employee halls were empty. The hotel silent except for the muted echo of conversations floating in from the lobby.

Forcing myself to my feet, I hit the button for the fifth floor and took the elevator up. My feet were practically dragging as I made my way to my room, let myself in and stripped away my clothes in route to the

257

shower. By the time my skin had turned pink beneath the spray of hot water and steam, I glanced at a clock to see that I was expected in Vincent's suite in a half hour.

I didn't bother to dry my hair or care about the clothes I pulled on, and by the time I was knocking on Vincent's door I resembled a drowned rat. His expression said as much when he pulled the door open, his lips slightly parted as if he'd planned to say something but had lost the words as soon as his eyes caught mine.

"That bad?" He finally asked after clearing his throat.

Stepping inside the suite, absolutely *hating* the man walking behind me, I didn't stop until I was at the sidebar trying to remember what Vincent had mixed to make the drinks he always gave me.

I knew why I was here. I knew the demands he'd make of me, and when his hands landed on my shoulders, his fingers gripping down as if to massage the muscles, I flinched beneath his touch. "Not as bad as right now," I answered. Picking up a bottle to read the label, I set it down, jerked away from his hold and turned to face him. "If you're going to make demands of me, you could at least get me drunk."

Arrogance cocked his brow, amusement curling his lips. "You act like you know why I wanted you up here."

One slow blink and then: "What other reason could there be, Vincent? You told me I have no choice in anything. And knowing you, you'll threaten me with kicking me out of the hotel, leaving me penniless and homeless unless you get your way. So, here I am."

"Yes," he responded, his thumb running across his lip in suspicion. "Here you are. Without a word of complaint, in fact. How very unlike you."

I hadn't intended to submit to anything on my way up to Vincent's suite, but now that I was here - now that I had the opportunity - I decided to play my own games. Vincent wanted to force me to submit to his whims. I wanted answers. Perhaps by giving him what he wanted, by pretending that he still had the ability to hurt me, I could discover the information I needed to help Maurice.

"Will you make me a drink, or not?"

His shoulders shook with a bark of laughter. "Are you really that eager?"

I nodded my head. "Eager to get this over with."

Leaning down, Vincent held his mouth a teasing inch from my ear. "Then why the need for the drink?" Pausing, his breath was a beat trailing down my neck. "Take off your shirt, Penelope."

Stepping out from between Vincent and the sidebar, I stripped off the shirt that was damp at the shoulders and down the back from my hair. I hadn't bothered to wear underwear beneath my frumpy clothes, hadn't cared to seduce a man that was only using me for his own amusement.

Vincent's smile was mistrustful, but he edged closer regardless. When he was near enough to reach out and touch me, I took a step back. "I have a question I want to ask."

His eyes drifted from my breasts to my face. "I might have an answer."

"Where did Maurice get all those scars on his chest?"

259

The humor in Vincent's expression was gone, his body becoming still. "He let you see those?"

Confusion addled my thoughts. "Yes. Why?"

A line of concern wrinkled Vincent's brow, his phone ringing from another room at the same time. Turning to glance in the direction of the sound, he asked, "What happened while you were down there tonight?"

Convinced he was going to be angry that I'd had sex with Maurice after his explicit instruction not to, I said nothing as the phone went to voicemail only to immediately ring again. Cursing under his breath, Vincent shot me a look that could kill before marching into the other room to answer. What I heard from the other room trapped my breath in my lungs, worry seizing my heart between its crushing fingers.

"What do you mean he's lost control? Damn it! Have his medication waiting for me by the elevator. I'll be there in a second."

The fall of angry steps preceded his booming question. "What in the hell have you done to my brother this time?"

"I -" My mouth fell open to answer the question, my heart practically beating in my throat. "I don't know. We were eating dinner and talking -"

Grabbing his suit jacket from the back of his sofa, Vincent's gaze snapped to me. "Talking? About what?"

He'd made it halfway to the door before I answered, "About family."

Stopping suddenly, Vincent spun on his heel to look my direction. "I want you to see the consequences of your actions. Put on your damn shirt and follow me."

Grabbing the damp shirt from the floor, I was pulling it over my head as I chased behind him. "That was what I wanted to ask about. The scars, and Maurice's reaction when I mentioned my dad."

Climbing into the elevator, Vincent pressed the button to the lobby. "Your dad? Why would he give a damn about your dad?"

"He didn't," I explained, shoving my arm through a sleeve, "but it made him think of his dad-"

"Fuck," Vincent breathed out, pinching the skin between his eyes in frustration. "Now I know why he's destroying the basement."

The elevator doors opened and John, the hotel manager stood waiting. Handing a small box to Vincent, he stepped away as Vincent stuck a key on the elevator panel and punched in the code for the basement. The doors slid shut as I asked my next question.

"What did he just give you and how do you know Maurice is destroying the basement?"

Vincent cut me a scathing look, pulling a syringe from the box and uncapping it. "John retrieves the dishes from Maurice when I'm unavailable to do so. Apparently he didn't have to go past the elevator doors to hear the sound of objects being broken. And this," Vincent explained, holding up the syringe to check the clear liquid beneath the light of the elevator, "Is what I have to give Maurice when he won't calm down."

The doors slid open again before I could respond, the sound of shattering glass and splintering wood filtering down from the left hall. As we both stalked toward it, Vincent kept his voice low. "He already tore apart that room once today. I doubt there's much left for him to destroy."

Turning, I froze in the doorway while Vincent charged forward, tears bursting from my eyes to see Maurice so out of control. His mouth was opened wide on a frustrated scream, his eyes vacant, his fists beating holes into the walls. This wasn't the man - the friend - I'd known earlier. This wasn't the man who'd shown me that, despite his aggression, he could be gentle.

So lost in his anger that he didn't notice us come in, Maurice struck out with his arm when Vincent stuck the needle in his neck and pressed the plunger. Vincent was able to move in time to avoid being hit, and within seconds Maurice was off balance, his body stumbling back as Vincent caught him and directed him onto the cushion of the couch. Although his eyes didn't close and he wasn't sleeping, Maurice didn't actually see me when his head lulled in my direction.

Standing over his brother, Vincent released a heavy sigh, actual pain clearly evident in his expression. I was caught off guard to see it.

Still crying, I didn't move until Vincent walked past me and grabbed my arm to pull me down the hall. Stopping when we'd reached the entryway in front of the elevator, he said, "Never, and I fucking mean NEVER, bring up our father around him again."

Puzzle pieces began clicking together in my head, the truth of Maurice's life becoming clearer. "Is your dad responsible for those scars on his chest?"

Vincent's expression shadowed. "Some of them, yes. Some of them are from Maurice himself. He wasn't the easiest child to deal with and our father believed too much that harsh discipline was the answer to keeping Maurice under control."

True agony was a cold chill across my bones. "Is that why you lock him down here?"

With an agonized grin, Vincent answered, "At first I'd believed Maurice was trapped, but lately I've learned that he's had the ability to leave the basement the entire time we've been here. It's not just me that keeps him apart from the world. I believe Maurice traps himself-"

"Because he believes he's bad," I finished for him.

"That's probably exactly right. And most likely the result of my father's words and my continued handling of him."

Regret and guilt flooded his eyes before he turned to push the elevator button. "We should go."

Shifting my weight from one foot to the other, I wrapped my arms around my abdomen. "We can't just leave him like that. What will happen when the drugs wear off?"

"He'll wake up and go to bed."

"I'll stay with him," I offered. "Maybe clean up the room as much as possible and then help him when he comes around."

Vincent looked at me like I was an idiot, but there was something else behind those green eyes of his, something that pleased him. "Suit yourself," he answered, allowing the doors to close and leaving me to stay in the basement with Maurice.

CHAPTER THIRTY-THREE

While Maurice was lying on the couch, not quite sleeping and not quite awake, I spent the next few hours doing my best to clean up the mess he'd made of the room. After finding trash bags, a dustpan and broom in the small kitchen down the hall, I swept up the shattered glass, the blisters of wood and the plaster that had been pummeled into a fine dust over the carpet. Setting the bags near the entryway of the elevator, I returned to the yellow room that now resembled what was left of a hollowed out bomb shelter.

Maurice blinked his eyes every so often, his gaze tracking me in moments where he found some sense of lucidity, and while he continued to lay there from the effects of the drugs, I found a first aid kit in a bathroom and went to work disinfecting and bandaging the cuts and scrapes on his hands.

After finishing, I set the first aid kit aside, sat on the floor next the couch and lay my head on his chest, the motion from his deep, rhythmic breathing reminding me that, even as the world felt like it was closing in, his quiet strength was there.

The silence was too much after a while, so I got up to retrieve a book from his shelf. Not recognizing the title, I sat back down and started reading to him, intentionally keeping my voice soft. The story wasn't all that great, a tragedy I assumed by the somber tone, but I kept reading regardless, not stopping until I felt his arm move and his hand cup the back of my head. Closing the book, I glanced up to see him looking at me, a sleepy haze over his green eyes, surprise written into the line of his brow.

"Hi," I whispered, forcing a smile on my face even when I felt like crying.

"Hello," he answered, his voice gritty and slow.

Not knowing what to say, and not wanting to bring up what he'd done before Vincent knocked him out, I simply stared at him, waiting to see how he would react to my presence. Weaving his fingers through my hair, he watched my face for a while.

"Why are you here?" he asked, confusion mixing with shame.

"I thought I'd help you get to bed when you're finally strong enough to walk to your room."

I don't want you to be alone, I didn't say. *I don't want you to be sad, or angry, or afraid.*

Brows pulling together, he asked again, "Why?"

Shrugging a shoulder, I answered, "That's what friends do."

Nodding his head, he pulled his hand from my hair and struggling to push himself up. There wasn't much I could do to help, Maurice must have been two hundred pounds of pure muscle. But eventually he'd righted himself into a seated position, his wild, dark hair falling down over his face giving him a boyish charm I'd never seen before.

I thought he'd ask me to leave again before heading to bed, but instead he took my hand, his fingers exploring mine. "Will you stay with me?"

"Is it safe?"

His eyes met mine. "I won't hurt you...and I'd like to know if you can chase away the nightmares."

Nodding my head, fighting not to let more tears fall, I accepted his offer. "Okay, Maurice, lead the way."

His fingers squeezed mine, his body unbalanced as he pushed to his feet. For a moment, I worried he'd fall over and take me with him. But somehow we managed to make it out into the hall, and although his shoulder dragged the wall to keep him upright, we made it to his room.

The bed creaked when he crashed down on it. I thought he'd fall asleep with his clothes and shoes on, but he righted himself, pushing up to sit on the edge of the bed, his movements clumsy as he attempted to untie his boots. Moving out from the shadows, I lowered myself to my knees in front of him to untie the laces when he couldn't. Above me, Maurice silently watched, his fingers running through my hair.

After tugging the boots off - and almost toppling over from the effort - I pushed to my feet and said, now the pants and the shirt. He lifted his arms just barely, the bulge of his biceps defined beneath the short sleeves of his black shirt.

Stripping the shirt off him, I reached for the button of the pants. His hand grabbed mine, drawing my eyes to his in question.

"Please don't tell me you're suddenly feeling shy."

Shaking his head, the motion more uncoordinated than fluid, he attempted to smile suggestively. I rolled my eyes. "You can't possibly think you have the strength for sex. Let's sleep tonight, Maurice. Together."

Uncertainty filtered through his gaze, but he relented, allowing me to strip off his pants and toss them aside. They hadn't fully hit the floor by the time he was tugging at my clothes. Raising my arms, I let him strip the shirt from my body, and I balanced myself with my hands on his shoulders as he tugged my pants down my legs.

By the time we were cuddled up next to each other, our bodies tucked beneath blankets and our heads resting on pillows, he'd closed his eyes and fallen asleep.

Brushing the hair from his face, I stared at him for a while, finally doing what he wouldn't allow me to do when he was awake. Pressing my lips to his, I lingered there for a moment, wishing he knew how I cared about him.

Someone had to love this gentle beast of a man. Someone had to see the light that could exist at the end of his dark tunnel and then take him by the hand to show him.

. . .

Weeks passed, each day bringing more of Maurice's playful side out for me to see. Sure, there were still the fits of anger, the days when he worried I'd reject him and run away. There were days that lifted my spirits high just so they could shatter. But there were other days that started out in Maurice's arms and built into the most amazing of crescendos.

In those weeks I spent luring the truth of Maurice's spirit out from beneath the shadow that held him, I noticed that Vincent had backed off from his games. And after Maurice started showing actual improvement, Vincent not only complimented what I was doing, he set out to help me along.

During the day, I'd spend most of my time in Maurice's basement, either sitting quietly by as he typed on his computer or talking to his counselors to learn what I could do to help crack his shell, and of course, my body was always left sore from the countless hours we'd spent exploring each other's bodies to find some form of Heaven within his constant Hell.

Not once had he allowed me to kiss him, and on rare occasion would he let me touch his face. I still didn't understand why he demanded that one barrier, but I knew not to push him by asking too many questions.

Most nights, Vincent would accompany us up to the garden, staying back as Maurice and I wandered the paths. And although he was always close enough to help should Maurice lose control, Vincent was also elated that Maurice never did. It was a turning point in the life of his brother, and for the role I'd played, Vincent rewarded me by becoming a more tolerable human.

That wasn't to say that Vincent didn't still make his sordid comments and rude jokes when Maurice wasn't in the vicinity to hear, but he didn't make demands of me that I'd find inappropriate, he didn't threaten me with homelessness for not playing his games.

I could breathe easier in those weeks, and in the emails I was still sending to my sister, I was finally honest when telling her how happy I'd been. I felt bad that the emails were becoming less frequent and for longer time periods between each one, but Maurice was taking up so much of my time.

On a bright afternoon with the sun beaming down in waves of delicious warmth, I was taking a walk through the garden wondering if the day would come where Maurice could be walking beside me. I didn't think he'd overreact too much to see guests pass by, didn't think he'd panic to be out among society when the dark veil of night wasn't there to keep him hidden. But each time I brought the subject up to Vincent, he was always quick to shut me down.

So, while standing by the well and peering down at the glimmer of coins beneath the surface of the water, I considered how I would convince Vincent to let Maurice out just once. As was always the way with my sadist for a boss, just thinking about him was like whispering his name, calling him to wherever I was standing.

"Tu faites un vœu, et espérons que cela devienne réalité."

Recognizing the deep voice at my ear, I ignored the heat of Vincent's chest against my back. "How many times do I have to tell you that I don't speak French?"

Masculine laughter was a deep note vibrating against my body. "I just said that I'd like to pick you up, dunk your head in the well, and laugh while you struggle to breathe."

Finally turning, I glared at him until he took a step back, his green eyes glittering in the sunlight. Cocking a brow, I asked, "Is that really what you said?"

His smirk curled. "Your name is Penny, is it not? Or at least that's the ridiculous name you like to be called. What I said was only fitting."

Shaking my head, I vacillated between slapping him and laughing. Vincent Mercier deserved a hard smack, but I was in too good of a mood to get violent.

Levity lost, he confessed, "I've been thinking about what you said. And while I'm not yet comfortable

269

bringing Maurice out into the garden during the busiest part of the day, perhaps baby steps can be taken."

"Really?" My heart damn near burst from my chest. "What kind of steps?"

Vincent cocked his head, his eyes darting to an attractive couple that passed by arm in arm. After greeting them with a wave, his eyes returned to mine. "We can try bringing him out around sunset for the first time. There will be a few stragglers out wandering, but most will be inside. We'll see how he reacts."

My cheeks hurt from the stretch of my smile. "Thank you, Vincent."

"You're welcome," he answered, turning to stroll off. But before he was more than a few feet away, he glanced back at me. "I just want you to know that if anything should go wrong, your ass will be on the line for it. Literally."

Giving him the finger, I smiled sweetly, watching him stroll off with his shoulders shaking with laughter.

It didn't matter if Vincent had threatened me directly, not when I realized that, for once, Maurice would witness a sunset.

CHAPTER THIRTY-FOUR

Faiville Prison, 4:53 p.m.

Stretching her neck to ease the muscles, Meadow released a heavy breath, relaxing back in her chair as Vincent digested the portion of the story she told. Studying his face, she wondered about the shadows beneath his eyes, the exhaustion of a man who, until then, had been content to appear unaffected. Not wanting to give him the time to recover - to pull his professional mask back in place - she asked a simple question.

"I've thought about that part of the story quite often. Penny was so happy to learn Maurice would be able to see a sunset, that in the progress he'd made, he would gain new experiences in his life. But as you told me yesterday in our discussions, Maurice had escaped the basement on the night of the masquerade ball. Not just escaped, he'd been around a large group of people without striking out."

Vincent lifted his eyes to give her his attention. The green was flat, the normal smile that curled his lips absent.

"Why could he handle the ball and not a walk through the garden among other people? What was the difference?"

It wasn't until Meadow remembered this particular part of the story that she'd connected the two events, but now that she knew Maurice had been out on his own previously, she couldn't help her curiosity.

Rolling his shoulders, the weight of Maurice's problems were heavy on Vincent's chest. "I often wondered that myself. It was the reason I was so shocked to find him in the hallway the night of the ball. I guess I'd never considered his escape because I knew, for as careful I was to keep Maurice separate from society, he'd internalized my fear and deemed himself unworthy of human interaction. It wasn't that he wanted to strike out at people, it was simply that he couldn't handle the attention or the perceived rejection. Perhaps the mask at the ball made it easier for him to be in a crowd. Nobody could reject him if they didn't know who he was."

Not wanting to see any light within the septic soul of the man across the table, Meadow couldn't help her belief that, despite Vincent's games, despite the mistakes he'd made, there was a spark of compassion inside him. It was that spark that made it impossible for her to celebrate his death like others would do in two days.

However, she also couldn't allowed the weakness he showed when it came to his brother to distract her from the answers she'd come to this interview to ask. One, he still hadn't answered, one she needed to know so that she could soothe her battered heart.

"Who killed Penny?" she asked, her voice calm, her demeanor practiced.

Nostrils flaring with a deep inhaled breath, Vincent's head tipped back, his eyes closing, "If you read the police reports you'll see that I did. Her and several other people. The police did an excellent job of investigating the garden around Wishing Well, the cadaver dogs digging up the past."

Meadow slammed her hand on the surface of the table, "Damn it, Vincent! That's not an answer."

The door popped open to Meadow's left, a guard stepping through to announce, "Day's over. You'll need to end the interview for today and start again tomorrow."

She could see the slow smile stretch across Vincent's face. "For fucking once in the time I've been here, I'm actually happy to see a guard." His head lowered again, his eyes opening as he threaded his fingers together over the table. "I'll see you tomorrow, Meadow. I suggest you use what time you have tonight to focus your thoughts and determine what questions *must* be asked. We only have a few hours remaining before they stick a needle in my vein, and whatever answers you later remember you needed will be forever buried with me in my grave."

Glaring at the pompous expression on his face, she stood from her seat a bit too forcefully before turning to stop the tape and retrieve her recorder. She didn't bother glancing back as she allowed the guard to lead her from the room.

. . .

Spending the night reviewing the tapes, pushing off sleep even when it clutched its greedy fingers over her tired bones, begging her eyes to close her just once, Meadow regretted the loss of the effect she'd hoped Penny's true feelings for Maurice would have had on Vincent. She'd wanted the words to sting, the realization that his games weren't as perfect as he'd believed following him into death. But as usual, Vincent had been one step ahead.

However, there was still one secret he hadn't discovered, a hidden tidbit she intended to use to crush him into dust.

Not all of his victims had been as easy to manipulate as he'd believed. At least one puppet had escaped their strings.

Giving in to the need for sleep, Meadow was flustered to wake with only an hour to get ready and begin the last day of the interview. Not taking the usual care with her appearance as she had before, she quickly grabbed a new set of tapes, her recorder and darted out. Having made the drive faster than what would be considered safe or legal, she was practically running as she approached the gates of Faiville Prison. The same guard from the previous two mornings stood waiting.

"Damn, looks like I just lost fifty bucks. I bet the guys you wouldn't show today."

Ignoring his jab, she tucked her recorder beneath her arm. "I'm only a few minutes late."

Leaning inside the small booth, he tapped in the code on the electronic panel before pulling the heavy key from his belt. "Doesn't matter, you'll have to wait for a few minutes anyway. Mercier's finishing up with another visitor."

Fury arced through her. "What do you mean another visitor? This interview was supposed to be exclusive."

The guard shrugged and opened the gate, the hiss a sharp noise against the tension in the air. "Man's dying tomorrow. His attorney is in there with him squaring up his final wishes." Eyeing her as she passed him, he laughed. "No offense, but it looks like you didn't get much sleep last night. You're not as put together as usual."

Biting the inside of her cheek, she kept from snapping at him again. Smiling sweetly instead, she asked, "How would you sleep after hearing the sordid details of the life of a man who killed four people?"

He rubbed at the back of his neck. "I hate to say it, Ms. Graham, but it wouldn't bother me much. I've worked on death row for thirteen years. I've heard stories that would make your skin crawl. Once these assholes are about to walk the final line, they just love to brag."

Her shoulders sagged, and realizing she was taking out her anxiety on a man who didn't deserve it, she forced herself to relax. "How much longer will his attorney be here?"

They'd reached the interior waiting room by the time he answered. "There's no telling. Usually it's a matter of deciding what will be done with the body following death, but in Mercier's case, I assume there's more to deal with, considering he's rich and all. Just take a seat on the bench and they'll walk you back once he's done."

Dropping her weight onto the uncomfortable bench, Meadow ground her teeth. She had only a few hours left to discover how Penny died, to determine whether it was actually Vincent that killed her sister. Memories raced back, sharp and jagged, the truth of the tragedy unfolding in her mind's eye. She knew more than she was letting on, felt guilt for her role in it, wanted to stab a knife so deep in Vincent's heart that the secret she revealed would be the last thought across his mind as he took his last breath.

And she wanted to cry.

While Vincent worked out the terms of his death and estate with some high-power attorney, Meadow fought tears of rage, of sorrow, of frustration. She had nothing left after this interview. Her sister was gone, her mother was gone, and except for the journalism career she didn't love, she was without direction in her new life.

The tears fell despite her hatred of them. For her sister. For Maurice. For all the people who were caught in the web that Vincent had so expertly weaved.

A noise drew her attention to the gate, a man being allowed through in his slate grey suit, his pressed white shirt and red tie. A file folder was held loosely in his hand, plain durable paper in brown. Approaching her, he dared to meet her eyes with his own, the blue like a clear lake beneath the salt and pepper color of his hair.

Extending a hand, he introduced himself, not that Meadow hadn't already deduced who he was. "You must be Meadow Graham. I'm Stephen Chase, Mr. Mercier's attorney. It is Meadow, correct?"

Nodding, Meadow didn't miss the odd expression on his face. "Of course. Are you finished with Vincent? I need to start the interview if I hope to finish today."

Behind the attorney, two guards waited patiently by the gate, their eyes darting about as if they weren't listening. Meadow knew they were.

"Yes, that's one of the reasons I wanted to stop and talk to you before leaving."

"Is he cancelling the interview? I have one day left!"

"No," he answered, shifting the folder in his grip. "But Mr. Mercier explained to me that there are items at the Wishing Well he'd had stored that he would like given to you."

"What kind of items?"

"Odds and ends. I believe some of the items were from Penelope's room. I'm not sure what exactly. He explained there's a list at the hotel. I'm hoping you'll agree to meet me at the Wishing Well tomorrow morning following Mr. Mercier's execution."

Although the last place Meadow wanted to go was the Wishing Well, she couldn't find it within herself to decline the invitation. Seeing the hotel, walking the halls would be the same as confronting a ghost, the same as confronting a nightmare she feared she could never escape. Perhaps looking the monster in the eye would be the only way to dispel it.

"Fine. I'll meet you there once the execution is over."

Standing from her seat, she gathered her recorder and blank tapes, a hand landing gently on her shoulder. Turning, she backed out of reach of Mr. Chase.

"There is one other matter we need to discuss."

Staring at him, she waited for whatever bomb he would drop. The expression on his face was too apologetic for good news.

Taking a breath, he explained, "Although Mr. Mercier has agreed to conclude the interview with you today, he wishes to do so without the use of recording devices-"

"What?" Her voice echoed, the one question repeating through the halls. The volume of it had attracted the attention of the two waiting guards and they no longer kept up the appearance of not paying attention.

"What do you mean he won't let me record this last part? I have no other way to take notes. I'm not allowed to take so much as a pen inside that room. Am I supposed to write stuff down with a fucking crayon?"

Anger was a pulse beneath her skin. How dare he? How fucking dare Vincent do this to her? He knew she needed these tapes, knew she was approaching the portion of his confession that mattered the most. All the rest of it was a method for him to brag, but this part - THIS admission - was what she needed to finally move on from the heartbreak of what her life had become.

The attorney didn't react to her anger, his expression blank, his posture firm. "I apologize, Ms. Graham, but those are his wishes. He's under no order compelling him to discuss this matter with you. He's doing so voluntarily, but he no longer wants your recorder in the room. I can take it off your hands if you like, and return it when we see each other tomorrow. I assume the tapes you've brought with you are blank, and you won't have to worry about losing the work you've already accomplished by entrusting the recorder with me."

"That son of a bitch," she cursed beneath her breath. But time was running out, the clock ticking forward, stealing the precious minutes she had to pick Vincent's brain, to extract the truth she needed.

"Fine," she said, handing over the recorder and tapes. "But this doesn't mean what he tells me is private. I still have an article to write."

The attorney nodded. "I understand. You'll just have to do so from memory rather than having his words documented on tape."

Without a recording, Meadow wouldn't be able to prove that what she wrote was fact, she wouldn't be able to verify Vincent's words if someone were to question their accuracy. And perhaps that's exactly what Vincent wanted.

Maybe it was a good thing they wouldn't allow her to enter the room with a pen. She wasn't sure she could resist jumping across the table and stabbing him in the eye.

"Thank you, Ms. Graham. I'll see you at the hotel tomorrow."

The attorney sauntered off in one direction while Meadow walked in the other, the guards shaking their heads as she approached. One followed her toward interview room three, his voice low when he commented, "Mercier really is a bastard, isn't he? Asshole's dying tomorrow but still feels the need to screw with people."

Meadow didn't bother to respond, her focus on one man alone, a man who sat grinning on his side of the table as the guard let her into the room. Ignoring the quiet click of the door closing, Meadow took her seat, her arms crossing over her chest in defiance of Vincent's amusement.

"That's a really pretty smile you have for a dead man."

Laughter burst from his lips, actual joy beaming behind his glittering green eyes. "Ah, Meadow. Don't be mad," he finally said once he had calmed enough to speak. "There are reasons for everything I do. You'll learn that eventually."

When she didn't answer, he asked, "Have you decided what questions you'd like to ask today? Seeing as I'm dead tomorrow, I certainly hope you've determined which ones are the most important."

Unclenching her teeth, she glared across the table at him. "I think you already know what my first

279

question will be. I asked it twice yesterday, both times wherein you refused to answer."

Shaking his head, he grinned. "You'll have to excuse me for my forgetfulness. With death on the horizon, I can't seem to think of much else. Please remind me, what is it you would like to know?"

Her fingers curled into her palms, her nails cutting crescent shaped gouges into her skin. "Did you kill Penny? Or was it Maurice?"

Sighing, Vincent relaxed back into his seat, his eyes locking to hers. "I find it funny that you keep asking a question to which you already know the answer. Or, at least you *think* you know."

He was silent for a moment, his gaze distant, as if he'd returned to the years his memories took him. With a voice far more somber than anything she'd heard in the past few days, he said, "When I was a child, I used to adore the hours I spent with Maman reading fairytales-"

"Oh, cut the shit," Meadow burst out. "I don't have time for your musings about pretty stories."

"I think you do, Meadow. At least if you truly want to know this last part. But, I'm actually glad you interrupted me, I was skipping ahead. Tell me, what details do you know about the day your sister died?"

"Are you asking me that so you can formulate a better lie?"

He grinned. "No. In this, I will be honest. I just find it funny that you seem to think it wasn't me who killed your sister. Now, how would you know that? It's not like Penny could record the events of her own death in the diary I sent you. So why do you think the details are any different than what the police know?"

Vincent was edging too close to the secret Meadow had kept close to her chest, the only weapon she had left to use against him. "The police report claimed that two people died that night, that it was due to a lover's spat the deaths occurred. You didn't love Penny, not according to the diary-"

"The *diary*," he repeated, soft laughter shaking his shoulders. "Right. Obviously that's the only way you could possibly know this."

"Two people died," she argued, "one quite viciously from what I recall reading. But viciousness isn't your style, Vincent. You are far more controlled than to lose yourself to that type of violence. And if what the reports say is true, than it wouldn't have been you to kill both Penny and your friend, Barron. However, a man who was jealous, a man such as Maurice, would be able to tear another man apart so cruelly. He had no control over his instincts."

Breathing deeply, Vincent held the air in his lungs for a few seconds before exhaling. "Yes," he agreed, "Maurice was quite capable of that."

"So," Meadow continued, "I believe Maurice killed her because he thought she was with another man. He killed her because she was the only woman he loved, she was his damn obsession, and he mistook seeing her with someone else and slaughtered not just her, but the other man. Perhaps that is why he was so devastated that he took his own life."

A flicker of remorse flashed across his expression, there and then gone, human and then cold, unfeeling monster. "Back to what I was saying," he finally replied, his smile stretching again. "The reason I always loved fairytales was because of their perfect timing, despite how unrealistic that timing might be. And this story *is* a fairytale, I hope you know that."

Rolling her eyes, Meadow knew shoving Vincent along would only make him dig his heels deeper in refusal to budge. Lounging back in her seat, she glared at him, waiting for whatever point it was that he wanted to make.

"Except, in fairytales, the perfect timing has more to do with the prince sweeping in to save the fair maiden, his actions allowing just enough time for the reader to think she'll perish, but then there he is on his white horse, slaying the villain. And as you know the prince and the maiden kiss, their bodies disappearing as they ride off into the sunset. The perfect timing of fairy tales are intricately tied to the happy ending. However, in this particular fable - although there is a prince, there is a maiden, there is a villain, there is a kiss, and there is a sunset - the perfect timing is tied to its tragedy."

A shiver coursed down her spine, pain and sorrow shredding her heart, images flashing through her thoughts. "Just tell me what happened, Vincent. I've lost enough time due to your meeting with your attorney. I don't have much more to go before you die."

Weaving his fingers together over the surface of the table, Vincent leaned forward to close some of the distance between them. "And so it happened, on a night that should have been pure joy for the prince and his maiden, the villain swept in to steal that happiness for himself, if only to exact revenge..."

CHAPTER THIRTY-FIVE

Vincent

"I mean it, Maurice, stop trying to shove food in my mouth in front of Vincent. Your jerk of a brother will get ideas and pretend to try it himself while actually just stabbing me with a fork!"

Penelope's laughter was an infectious joy lighting the face of my brother, my eyes locked on his expression with utter disbelief. In a matter of weeks, Penelope had been able to accomplish what everybody else had not: She'd shown a man who was trapped by his own emotional turmoil how to come out from beneath the weight of it and learn how to live again. The counselors, the doctors, not even my mother, had been able to accomplish that. And for what Penelope had done, I would forever be in her debt.

Not that I would admit that debt. Not to her, at least. Lord knows she would wait for the most inopportune moment to demand her pound of flesh. Although Maurice loved her more than he could even love himself, I still saw her for the rebellious, Dirty Girl I'd discovered on the streets. But that didn't mean I could ignore the gratitude I had for her ability to return a member of my family to me.

Lips pulled into a smile, Maurice shoved the fork at her once again, the food spilling over to dribble down her chin. "I'll kill him if he stabs you. He knows that." Turning to flash me a fake snarl, Maurice asked, "Right, Vincent?"

"*C'est vrai, mon frère.*"

It was in moments like this, I wondered if I was dreaming. This change in him wasn't possible.

Two weeks had passed since I'd agreed to taking Maurice out into the garden at sunset, fourteen days wherein Penelope hunted me down demanding that I make good on my promise. I'll admit nervousness had kept me from finally relenting, and for those two weeks, I found excuses for why it couldn't happen that night. However, I'd run out of excuses, and tonight, while the sun was still partially in the sky and was busy lowering itself over the horizon to become a web of brilliant, beaming color, Penelope and I would walk Maurice out while there were still people lingering around the gardens to see how he reacted to the attention.

In truth, my brother was a good-looking man, not quite as tall as me, but broader, his physique better defined. His hair was just as dark and wild, curled at the ends where it dusted his shoulders. And his eyes, like mine, were the color of emeralds that could lure a saintly woman into the bowels of Hell. He would attract attention whether he liked it or not, but hopefully with Penelope at his side, he could ignore the idle glances and the curious stares.

Penelope took the bite he was offering, her lips sliding slowly along the tines of the fork as he pulled it away, their focus locked on each other. To see him so happy, to feel his contentment from across the room, I had a moment of jealousy for my brother. In all my years, in the freedom I'd had to explore the world, never had I looked at a woman like that.

But, that's fine. I would still fuck them, and that would just have to be good enough for me.

"Well," I said, clearing my throat, "I should probably get going before you two strip down and start mating with each other right in front of me. By the looks you're throwing across the table, I just envisioned a reverse cowgirl occurring on top of your lunch."

Penelope turned her head and glared. "Not funny, Vincent."

Maurice grinned. I was giving him ideas apparently.

Laughing as I left, I returned to my office with a skip to my step. Life had just become less irritating at the Wishing Well, a bit of light added to the secret hidden in the basement. I'd been at my desk for a few hours when a familiar face walked through the door.

"Hello, Vincent. Long time no see. Has your newest toy been keeping you busy and out of touch?"

Glancing up from my computer, I watched Barron stroll in to take a seat. As usual, his blond hair was perfectly styled, his suit impeccable, his eyes focused on me with the arrogance only a man like him could have. As rich as me, as powerful in this city, he walked as if he owned everything within sight, and had he not been currently in my hotel, that would have been true. Barron was a entrepreneur with his name on most of the nightclubs, restaurants and bars around town.

"Barron, it has been quite a while. I'm sorry I couldn't meet you for lunch the last several times you asked. I've had my hands full with the hotel and my brother."

Taking a seat in one of the leather chairs facing my desk, he unbuttoned his suit jacket and relaxed. "How is the monster these days?"

Feathers ruffled by the comment, I couldn't blame him for his use of the term. Three months ago, I'd used the description myself to describe Maurice.

"He's improving, actually. In fact," I glanced at the clock on my computer to see I was supposed to meet Maurice and Penelope in the basement in forty-five minutes, "I'm going to have to keep this visit short. I'm taking Maurice for an activity in a little while. How have you been?"

"Better than you. While you're busy babysitting a grown child, I've been having the time of my life. Making money. Fucking women. Attending party after party with grownups. And everybody has been asking about you, wondering where you've been."

Clicking to exit my email program, I relaxed back in my seat and lifted my feet to rest them on the surface of my desk. "I wouldn't call it babysitting, and I'm glad people have missed me, even if I can't say the same about them."

"Has one particular woman been keeping you busy?"

Brows pulling together, his statement confused me until the past came back to me and the reason for his presence clicked in place. "You're here because of the bet."

Inclining his head, he grinned. "Today is the last day of the three month time period. I've come to see how well you've trained her. I look forward to my taste. Especially after the bruise she left on my cheek the first time we met."

Damn. Losing the profits from the hotel for a full year would sting, but it wouldn't bankrupt me. And being a man of my word, there was no way I was getting out from the wager I'd made. "Looks like I owe you a ton of money, Barron. I didn't complete the bet."

A curious expression flickered across his face. "Are you telling me that a homeless teenager bested Vincent Mercier at his own game?" Shaking his head in disbelief, he laughed. "You're losing your touch. I would have had that girl eating from my hand after not giving her a choice."

My fingers drummed on my desk. "It's not that she bested me, it's just that her usefulness ended up being in a different place in my life. It seems Maurice fell in love with her."

His eyes widened. "Tell me you're fucking kidding? You're giving up millions so that your pest of a brother can be in love? What the hell is going on with you, Vincent? That bitch deserved to get put in her place."

Pausing, he stared at me, thoughts racing in his head. "Unless tossing her to Maurice was your way of training her? Being used by that psycho son of a bitch can't be too enjoyable."

My anger crested as my patience wore thin. It was one thing to disparage Maurice once, but to continue doing it was beyond what I considered tolerable. "Be careful, Barron. You're beginning to anger me. Regardless of his issues, he is still my brother."

"Maybe I'm angry, Vincent. You dragged me into this and even accepted that little bitch struck me. But I allowed it with the understanding I would get to strike her back. You can't possibly be telling me that I have to simply settle for her disrespect. If I'd known you'd backpedal, I would have done something about it a few weeks ago when I saw her."

My eyebrow cocked. "A few weeks ago? Were you at the hotel and didn't tell me?"

Stretching his legs out in front of his body, he tapped a finger against his knee. "No. I went to the cafe to grab some coffee and walked in as she was walking out. When I touched her, she threatened to rake her fingernails down my face. I left it alone, but only because I thought I'd have the opportunity to show her what happens when a girl like her says something so nasty to a man like me."

Seeing the anger in his expression, I had no doubt that Barron was looking forward to teaching Penelope a lesson. Thankfully, she was under lock and key at the moment, down in the basement where Barron couldn't reach her. I would be sure to warn her of his intent, be sure to tell her to keep an eye out for him on the streets.

"Isn't the money you'll receive for winning the bet enough to more than make up for any insult? We're talking millions, Barron."

"I already have millions," he reminded me. "But what I don't have is tolerance for petty little bitches who think they can treat me as if they're somehow better."

Worry crept down my spine at the menace in his voice. "Penelope is off limits to you, Barron. She's a woman who's dragging Maurice out of his shell and also my employee. You'll be smart to leave her alone."

"Is that a threat?"

"It's a pointed request from a friend and business acquaintance to leave this one alone. Penelope may have started as a game, but in the effect she has on my brother, she has become a very important person in my life. And as such, she has my protection. It was a slap,

Barron. That's all. I'm sure a man of your stature can look past it."

He barked out a laugh. "So, you've gone soft? I should have known." Rising from his seat, he straightened the creases from his pants and rebuttoned his jacket. "I'll expect the money I've made off this hotel on the first day of every month."

Nodding my head, I stood and extended my hand to shake his. "And you will receive it. I'm a man of my word."

Flicking a disgusted glance at my hand, he stormed off, closing my office door behind him with considerable force. I dropped my weight into my seat and went about finishing up a few issues that needed my attention before shutting down for the night and heading to the basement. Sunset was in twenty minutes and I didn't want to be late. This was as important to me as it was to Penelope.

Reaching the basement, I heard the standard tapping coming from the left. Assuming Maurice was busying himself with what he was learning about managing aspects of the hotel, I strolled down the hall expecting to find Penelope on the couch curled up with a book. Although I couldn't mention Barron in front of Maurice, I had every intention of warning her when I next saw her alone. Unfortunately, when I entered the room, only Maurice was inside.

Concern was an icy finger scratching at my heart. "Where's Penelope?"

Maurice's eyes never left the screen of his computer. "She left a few hours after lunch to go up to her room and take a shower."

My brow arched. "Why doesn't she just shower down here?"

His eyes sparkled. "Because she never gets clean. I won't let her."

Shaking my head, I said, "Well, I'll just go upstairs and bring her down. Sunset will be happening soon."

I'd barely turned to leave before he answered, "She had to run errands before coming back. If she's not down here on time, she'll meet us by the employee door leading to the garden."

By now, my pulse was absolutely jagged. "Then we should go."

Perhaps it was a note in my tone that caused his eyes to dart up. "Sunset isn't for another ten minutes." Maurice's shoulders went rigid, worry creasing his brow.

Purposely attempting to hide my own feelings, I smiled. "We wouldn't want to keep her waiting. You know how Penelope can be."

The expression on his face was love-struck. "Wonderful?"

"Let's go, Maurice. This will be your first sunset in a long time. I wouldn't want you to miss it."

Watching him rise from his seat, I had to stop myself from rushing him along. My spine was prickling with anxiety, my thoughts racing to the conversation I'd just had with Barron. Telling myself there was no way his path could have crossed with Penelope's, I walked with Maurice down the hall, taking a deep breath as I punched in the code that would take us to the lobby.

CHAPTER THIRTY-SIX

The first indication that something was wrong was Penelope's absence by the employee door leading into the garden. She had been so excited for this step in Maurice's life, so adamant that I let it occur. She was his champion after falling for a man that was learning to love himself as much as he loved her. For Penelope not to be at the door with a selfless smile to give to him, together with her hand for him to hold, was the first warning I needed to turn around and take him back to the basement.

I wish I could say it was just me that tensed to see the hallway empty of her presence, but Maurice grew concerned as well, his eyes searching the distance looking for her. "Maybe she's outside," he posited, "I may have misheard her. I do that all the time."

It was a momentary relief to think the two had simply miscommunicated, and I walked beside my brother through the door. The garden, like the hall, was silent, even as guests strolled by, their hands or arms locked together while they enjoyed the peaceful serenity of the garden I'd commissioned to remind me of home.

I should have turned around. I should have forced him back inside. But doing so would have only set him off. Now that Maurice was outside the confines of the basement beneath the hotel, there would be no stuffing him back in that cage until he had Penelope beside him.

"Maybe," I said, "she's just late. Anything could have held her up. We'll continue walking until we find her."

Nodding his head, Maurice tucked his hands inside his pockets, his shoulders folding in on themselves as self-conscious thoughts attacked his mind. Already he was assuming that Penelope had forgotten about him, that she was rejecting him by not being in the place where she'd promised to meet him.

If she was running late, I would be sure to tear her a new asshole when I had a moment to speak with her alone. This was a big step for Maurice, an important step, and she should have known better than to fuck it up. And even while my anger caused my teeth to clench together, there was still the concern that Penelope would have been on time if something hadn't stopped her.

To say I wanted to run the perimeter of the garden to find her and drag her to us was an understatement, but with Maurice at my side, I had no choice. I had to walk calmly. Running would only cause him to panic. It would cause him to lash out.

"The well," he finally breathed out. "I bet she's there. She always talks about how much she loves it."

"Does she?" I asked, making idle conversation, my eyes scanning every nook and cranny, seeking her out. "Why does she love it so much?"

"Because that's where she met me."

My mind returned to that night, to the fear I'd seen on Penelope's face when I told her to be careful around Maurice. If only I'd known she'd be the catalyst for his change, I would have shoved her at him, chained her to his waist. As it was, Maurice had been the first to pursue her, the only one to love her, but Penelope wasn't aware of that yet.

We were nearing the well when a distant sound drew both our attention, and before I could react by

292

holding Maurice back, he'd taken off at a dead run. It was nothing more but a startled cry, it could have been anybody, really. But Maurice had Penelope's voice dedicated to memory, the pitch of her tone a siren's song that called to him. I was sure he heard her voice in his sleep, was sure he could sniff her out like a dog does a rabbit when on the hunt.

The next scream that cut through the silence of a day turning to night was far more compelling, far more distressed than was normal for a woman playing around. I couldn't run fast enough to keep up with him, couldn't yell loud enough to make him stop.

All hell broke loose when Maurice crashed through a grouping of distant bushes to find Penelope limp on the ground, her attacker standing above her with rage darkening his face. I only caught a glimpse of the gouges across Barron's face before Maurice was on top of him, only caught a peek of the blood that wept from the wounds. If only Maurice had been more in control, those wounds would have been our salvation.

But as it happened, as the fury overtook my brother and he lost the ability to understand reason, Barron was on the ground screaming as Maurice became more dangerous than a wild animal, beating on and breaking every bone in Barron's face. At the time the fighting began, this portion of the garden was empty, but as any loud noise will do, as any terrible fight will cause to happen, the battle between the two men drew attention. As guests ran over to see what the noise was about, I was attempting to jump in and drag Maurice off the man he was beating to a bloody pulp.

The crimson stain was everywhere. On the ground, on the bushes, on my clothes, on Penelope where she lay much too still to be alive and breathing.

Barron managed to break free of Maurice for an instant, long enough to run in the direction of Penelope's body, to fall on top of her, to sink down as Maurice tackled him again. In the fight between the two men, Penelope's body was also being crushed. There was nothing I could do to stop it. My clothes were ripped like theirs, my body, face and hair covered in the blood of Barron and Maurice both. All three of us had wounds consistent with a battle.

The fight was far too brutal, the ripping of skin, the crunching of bones, the viciousness of a man gone mad, creating a scene that caused the guests to scream as they witnessed it, for them to grab their phones and call the police.

Bones protruded from Barron's body, his face unrecognizable as human, and when Maurice made sure that Barron was no longer breathing, he flung me off his back and crawled to Penelope.

As far as the guests had witnessed, the gathering of people who would attest to the facts of what had occurred, my brother and I had killed a man as well as the woman who was with him. They didn't know what caused the fight to occur, they hadn't heard the muted cry of a woman fighting off her attacker. They didn't know that Barron had caused her death with a blow to her face, or by breaking her neck. In truth, and when all the examiners and doctors had their chance to detail the injuries of her body, they wouldn't be able to opine which one had been the blow that killed her.

The sun was setting over the garden, the distant horizon lighting up like a painting over the endless sky, and in the distance, sirens were tearing through the warm spring evening, blue lights swirling within the reds and golds, pinks and violets of a sun sinking beneath the horizon.

On my knees, I watched as Maurice lifted Penelope's limp body from the ground, a roar escaping his chest and mouth as he cradled her to his chest, his lips pressing to hers with a gentleness that brought tears to my eyes. Pulling away, he roared again, the sound that of a man who'd just lost everything. I'd never heard such deep sorrow and pain, and in my entire life, I never wanted to hear it again.

Behind me, the drum of running feet approached, the hurried voices of guests explaining what they'd seen, and in a panic to protect my brother from what I knew was coming, I rushed toward him to make it appear as if I'd been the aggressor. The police had me by the arms, their grip crushing as they dragged me away from a broken man clutching his broken doll, tears streaming from his eyes.

Before they could approach him, I screamed the only words I could think to say. "It was me! Okay? That son of a bitch thought he could fuck her behind my back! My brother tried to stop me, but I wouldn't let him!"

Yes, I'd flipped the roles we'd played, but with the injuries, the blood, the carnage that covered us both, it could have been either of us that had been the one to kill.

How stupid had I been to scream the first words that came into my head when it would have been easier to use logic and explain calmly what had happened? To lay blame at Barron's feet? To go against everything the guests were claiming they'd seen so that I could protect us both from being arrested?

However, instinct isn't always stupid.

As it turned out, it was my immediate confession that had been the only thing protecting my brother from being taken into custody, from being tossed to the ground where he would have fought to the death to get back to Penelope.

Perhaps that's why emotion had clouded my better judgment in that instant: I knew Maurice would have been killed by not listening to a single instruction the police gave him.

I could only be thankful that my hotel manager had come running as soon as he heard the report there was a fight in the garden, that he'd been smart enough to bring the drugs that would neutralize Maurice and keeping him from fighting the police who wanted to take Penelope's body from his arms.

While being handcuffed, I watched Maurice's body crash to the ground, watched John explain something to the officers that kept them from hurting my brother.

Figuring it all could be explained once I knew Maurice was safe, once I had a moment to calm down and come to my senses in the police station, once I had time to speak with my attorney, I let the officers lead me away and place me in their waiting car.

And while waiting for the officer to round the car, climb in and drive away, I heard the slap of the employee gate closing, and turned to see a dark haired woman running away.

. . .

"What do you mean one of us is taking the fall for this? It was Barron who killed Penelope. I only attacked him because he went after my brother next."

"That's not what seven guests had to say. I'm not privy to their exact statements, but from what I'm gathering on what little the police have told me, the guests are pinning the deaths of both the man and the woman on you or your brother." Stephen Chase, the man who had been my attorney for longer than I could remember relaxed back in his seat, obviously uncomfortable with the plastic chairs in the holding room of the local police station.

According to him, I would be staying overnight to attend my arraignment in the morning.

"What are my chances of getting out on bail tomorrow?" I asked, hating the jumpsuit they'd given me to wear after taking my clothes as evidence.

"Slim, considering the brutality of the crime. That man was ripped apart, Vincent. The woman's body crushed in parts. What the hell happened?"

"I already told you-"

"You told me you killed a man for attacking a woman in your garden, but for fuck's sake! The scene was a blood bath!" His palm slapped the table in frustration before he reached up to run it through his hair. After releasing a heavy breath, he leveled his stare on me and lowered his voice. "I know you couldn't have done that. You're not a fucking maniac. Your brother, however-"

"Had nothing to do with it," I insisted. There was no way I would let them drag Maurice into this. If my brother were found to have committed murder, he would end up in a state psychiatric facility. I refused to let that happen to him. "Speaking of which, did you get in touch with John? How is my brother doing?"

"You're worried about your brother? Are you kidding me right now?"

297

I simply stared at him.

"Your manager said they got him to the basement. Whatever the hell that means"

When relief withered my shoulders, he ground his teeth. "You kill me, you know that? This is serious, Vincent. They have cadaver dogs out there looking for the *pieces* of that man who was killed."

That information did not bode well. Scrubbing my palm down my face, I asked, "Just out of curiosity, how deep down can those dogs smell?"

His eyes rounded. "I'm not sure. Why?"

Shaking my head, I answered, "No reason." Except for maybe the two other bodies I'd disposed of when accidents happened.

Fucking Hell, this was bad. "So, what now? We go through the arraignment? The judge sets my bail? What happens then?"

Cursing under his breath, Stephen clicked his pen, the noise an outward symptom of his disbelief and anger. "Then we allow the police to conclude their investigation and decide on charges. As your attorney, I'm highly recommending you come clean about who actually ripped apart that man and killed the woman."

"Penelope, I said, genuine sorrow coating my voice. "Her name was Penelope Graham."

"I don't give a fuck what her name was. All I know is that if you don't come clean, she'll be the woman you get the death penalty for."

CHAPTER THIRTY-SEVEN

Faiville Prison; 12:01 pm

Meadow was in tears as the guard led her from the interview room for shift change, her jaw practically dragging the table after listening to Vincent's reiteration of events. She didn't have a single second to ask him more about it before the door popped open and she was informed she'd need to leave for a half hour.

In truth, and for the first time since she'd started that interview with Vincent, she appreciated the interruption. Meadow felt broken, crushed, suffering the same injuries her sister had suffered as a fight broke out around her.

After being led to the waiting area where she took a seat on the benches that were as uncomfortable - as inhospitable - as all the feelings inside her, she wished she'd brought the police reports and autopsy reports with her, if only to confirm what she thought she knew.

Barron had suffered such brutal injuries that the medical examiner could only guess which one had been the trauma that killed him. As if a pack of animals had taken hold, his body was torn apart, was shredded by the rage of a man who, until now, Meadow believed had been jealous. She'd guessed, she'd KNOWN, Vincent couldn't have been the one to do it, leaving only Maurice to have lost control.

But in all the days she'd spent studying those reports, in all the years she'd thought back to what she'd read, she'd never considered the possibility that the rage of the man who killed Barron had been in protection of her sister from the man who'd intended her harm.

How stupid had she been?

As for her sister's body, the injuries were also inconclusive. Bones broken, skull crushed in, skin ripped and torn. There were several guesses as to what had been the fatal blow. Meadow assumed the injuries had been intentional, not that they'd occurred as one man attempted to protect her body from another man who could have cared less.

In the end, she was right, Vincent hadn't been the aggressor - he hadn't been the villain in this tragic fairytale ending. And he hadn't been wrong to say that it was the *too perfect* timing that had made it possible for the story to end this way. As if fate herself had danced the streets of the city, the sway of her hips causing soft winds to blow and push all the characters into place.

Too perfect, that bitch we call fate and her timing.

But even in that, Vincent didn't know all of it. He didn't understand *just how* perfect the timing had been. Only Meadow knew, and it was her turn to tell him. It had been her one card - the ace that would send him to death screaming.

Not anymore. Now it was just a pathetically sad fact that if she hadn't been so angry and afraid, she could have prevented tragedy and senseless death.

"Are you ready to go back? Or did you need another few minutes?"

Swiping at the tears that dotted her cheeks, Meadow glanced up at the grim faced guard by the gate. Standing on the other side, he peered out at her from between the heavy bars, his hands wrapped around one on each side of his body. Her expression must have set off warning signals in his head. "Did he say something to you in there that made you so upset? You don't have to finish this, you know? You can walk away and let that bastard die all by himself."

His words made her cry harder. For all of his games, for the tangled webs he'd spun and the joy he took in trapping his prey, Vincent Mercier didn't deserve to die at all.

It had all been about his brother. About Maurice. The deaths, the accidents, the cages and chains: it had all occurred because one man hadn't known how to help another. But not because he hadn't tried.

People would celebrate Vincent's death tomorrow.

Meadow wouldn't be one of them.

Slapping away the last tear, Meadow answered, "I'm ready," while hating the crack in her voice. Standing from the bench seat she would never warm again, she took measured steps toward the imposing gate, winced at the sound of the pneumatic hiss and stepped through to finish an interview she wished had been conducted years before.

Before...

She would have done anything in her power to save him.

Led inside interview room three, she didn't lift her head, didn't dare meet Vincent's eyes until she'd steeled her spine and was ready. What she found when she finally glanced across the table broke her even more. For the first time since they'd started this dance, Vincent looked at her with pity behind his emerald green eyes.

"I'm sorry," he said, his voice a soft whisper.

"For what?"

Vincent was too still in his seat, too remorseful and calm. For some strange reason she suddenly missed the arrogance, the humor, the razor-edged wit of the man now looking at her with keen understanding in his expression. "You just heard the details of your sister's death. That can't be easy for anyone."

If only he knew...

Wrapping her arms around her abdomen, she attempted to hold herself together. And with minimal strength in her voice, she said, "You weren't the villain in this story. I mean...you were...but at the same time, you were not."

A quick shake of his head, just one soft movement. "No, not in that part, at least. In others?" He shrugged. "Perhaps I was."

A journalist shouldn't lose herself this way, not a real one, not the type that is tough as nails, that could set herself aside from the story and look at it from an objective place.

She couldn't. She'd lost the ability to fight.

"How," she asked, her throat clogged by emotion, her lungs struggling to take a steady breath. "How did Barron end up in the garden with my sister?"

Seconds passed in silence, Vincent studying her, dissecting her, before breathing out and admitting, "That, I don't know. From what my attorney told me, the police reviewed the security tapes from the hotel. They saw your sister arrive, they saw Barron come and go, but how those two ended up together is a mystery I fear we'll never solve. It's the *timing* I mentioned."

I glanced up at him to see him flare his fingers in resignation. "How did the woodcutter show up just in time to save Little Red from the wolf? How do the

302

princes of every fairytale appear at exactly the moment they're needed? I used to think those stories were comical for the way everything just neatly fell in place. I used to think they were so opposite to reality. But after this story, after countless other tragedies where people were simply in the wrong place at precisely the wrong time, I don't laugh at fairytales anymore. Even life has its neat and tidy endings that we have no choice but to accept."

Another short period of time where the only sound in the room was the gentle hum of the air conditioning. Meadow was lost for that moment, at least until Vincent rattled his chains.

"But that's not all there is to know about this particular ending, is there?"

Lifting her eyes, she found him leaning toward her, closing the distance she so desperately needed.

Meadow needed space from the tragedy, the shattered lives, the secrets and the pain.

Oh, God, the pain...

"I don't know what you mean," she answered weakly, her own lies crushing her beneath their pathetic weight.

"Don't lie," he answered softly, "not now, not after we've reached the end."

Tension traced across her bones. *He can't know. There's no possible way.*

Reaching as far as the shackles would allow him, Vincent could only touch the tip of his finger to her chin. She wanted to straighten her posture, to stop curling her body over the edge of the table just so she could move out of reach. But, yet, that small bit of contact comforted her more than she wanted to admit.

"How could you let Maurice die?" she asked, pure agony coating her words.

"I didn't mean to. I did everything I could to help him. He's why I walk voluntarily to my death. But that's not what we need to discuss at the moment, is it? We have time for that after locking in the final piece of this tragic puzzle."

Meadow lifted her eyes, the truth of her secret written clearly across her face.

"Barron finding your sister, the choice of which night Maurice and I would go to the garden, those weren't the only factors with perfect timing, were they? There was one more factor that added to this fairytale ending, and I think it's only fair you tell me."

Her eyes locked to his, gold-flecked brown meeting the emerald green as all veils and pretenses were torn aside, the secrets finally being revealed.

Vincent blinked, his dark lashes a fan across his skin for only a moment before the green pinned her again.

"How is it your sister was at the hotel that night? And why did you choose to run after witnessing what happened, *Penelope*?"

Heart seizing, she clenched her eyes shut, opening them again to see him staring at her with knowledge written into the color.

"You know?" she asked, her mind drowning in disbelief.

Vincent simply nodded his head. "I've known since the moment you first entered this room to start the interview. I've known the entire time."

CHAPTER THIRTY-EIGHT

Penny

Vincent left the room with his shoulders shaking. Lately it seemed he no longer got his enjoyment by torturing me with games, but rather by torturing me with making suggestions Maurice would take to heart. Five seconds ago and we'd merely been eating lunch, even if messily so due to Maurice's fun in force feeding me. But now, the beautiful man with glimmering green eyes was staring at me like I'd become the meal he would eat, the food on the table no longer holding his interest.

"What's a reverse cowgirl?" he asked, his head tilting slightly to the side.

My face fell into my palms. Mumbling against my hands, I answered, "It's nothing. Just forget Vincent ever said anything."

Deep laughter floated across the table, his hand reaching out to tug mine from my face. "It doesn't sound like nothing."

Shaking my head in disbelief, I laughed along with him. "I'll teach you what it is after our walk in the garden tonight. Deal?"

Cocking a brow, he smirked. "Deal. But what can you teach me now?"

When he looked at me like that, I wanted nothing more than to grab his face between my hands and kiss him until we were both breathless. But for as long as we'd been 'friends', he still hadn't allowed me that one bit of intimacy. Sex, Maurice could handle. In fact, it was a demand he made several times a day. But kissing, he wasn't there yet. I didn't know if it was a trust thing and I'd asked Vincent if he understood why Maurice had that issue. Even Vincent didn't know. The only guess he could make was that the last person Maurice had willingly let kiss him had been their mother.

And then a few months later, she'd died.

So, perhaps it was fear - a fear I was determined to show him was misplaced. Vincent had given me some ridiculous speech about how a kiss gives life or brings death, whatever the hell that meant, but I refused to let Maurice continue walling himself off from any of the best experiences in life.

So, at night while he was sleeping, I would kiss him all over his face. And one day, I would do it when his eyes were open, when he was looking at me like I was his world, when I'd finally reached a point with him that he could trust I would never leave his side.

"I can teach you patience," I answered, grinning like an idiot to see the content expression of his ridiculously beautiful face. It wasn't fair how handsome both Maurice and Vincent were, and perhaps Maurice's issues, those problems that kept him apart, had been a favor to the women of the world. Dealing with one was enough to suck you into a vortex of sensual confusion and leave you with the inability to breathe, but if these two had ever gone out on the town together, I knew there would have been a slew of broken hearts left in their wake.

"Patience? Why?"

"Because I need to get a shower and I have errands I need to run today," I explained, my sister on my mind.

It had been a few weeks since I last sent an email and after stopping by the Internet cafe to answer whatever messages Meadow had sent me, I had every intention of stopping by a store to purchase a phone with the earnings from my last paycheck. No longer concerned that Vincent would boot me onto the streets, I wanted to make my life more convenient. Why I hadn't bought one weeks ago was beyond my understanding, but perhaps my own fear of what could happen with Vincent's mercurial moods had made me a bit too leery of draining her savings.

His moods didn't matter anymore. Nothing would strip me away from Maurice.

Concern edged his eyes. "Will you be back in time for the walk?"

Smiling to comfort him, I wanted to reach out to wipe the worried lines from his face, but knowing he would only pull away, I curled my fingers into my palms. "I wouldn't miss it for anything. Not one damn thing. Okay? And if I don't make it down the basement in time, I'll wait for you by the employee door leading outside."

Maurice nodded his head before settling back into his seat. "Okay."

And if I wanted to keep that promise, I would have to get going. Already, the day was getting late. Standing from my seat, I pressed two fingers to my lips and blew him a kiss. "I'll be back, Maurice, and then we'll find out what I can teach you later."

He nodded his head and it killed my not to be able to hug him, to hold him in a way he still wouldn't

307

allow. Maurice's idea of physical affection often led to rough sex, and there was no time for that, not if I wanted to send the email to my sister, buy a phone and make it back in time.

Not only that, but I needed to shower. Doing so in the basement only led to Maurice climbing in to dirty my body after I got it clean.

"I'll see you when I get back," I called out, leaving the yellow room to race down the hall to the elevator. After going to my room on the fifth floor, showering and getting dressed, I left the hotel via the back employee gate of the garden.

It didn't take long for me to reach the Internet cafe, and by now the clerk recognized me well enough to call out my name as I entered. "Penny! How are you today?"

"Good," I answered, tossing enough money to buy myself a half hour.

Shaking his head, he opened the cash register and handed me a receipt with the login code. "Why haven't you bought a phone yet? Coming here all the time has to be a pain in the ass."

"I'm buying one after leaving here today."

The cashier grinned. "Well, in that case, I'll miss you. Desk three is open."

"Thanks!"

Within seconds, I was at desk three, logging into my email provider to find dozens of emails spanning the past few weeks, each subject line becoming more panicked and urgent. When I reached the email with the subject line, **MOM IS DEAD!!**, my heart was a drumbeat in my throat and I clicked to open it.

Tears burst from my eyes, my hand flying to my mouth as if that would stop the loud sobs from escaping my lips. I could barely read the words through my tears that wouldn't stop streaming, could hardly understand what Meadow's email was saying.

Apparently, she'd been sending me emails for over a week to let me know my mom and her new husband were in a car accident, that neither of them had survived. When I didn't answer, she'd lost her patience and had written me this email with the horrible subject line, hoping it would catch my attention.

Meadow was an intelligent girl. She had a good head on her shoulders. She knew where to find me. Why hadn't she called the hotel to let me know the news? Perhaps, her shock, her pain, her agony from losing mom had made it impossible for her to think logically. Telling myself I would ask her that question when I had a chance, I scrolled through the next several emails with the details of the funeral she was planning. Refusing to have it without me there, she made plans to come to the city to find me, and her last email, dated that morning, told me she'd arrived into town safe and sound.

She was staying with her best friend, Gia, at her house in our old neighborhood. Glancing at the clock on the computer screen, I calculated driving distances and determined I could make it there to see her and get back to the hotel on time.

Panic and grief have a way of scrambling the mental wires, logic becoming absent as emotion takes control. I should have gone back to the hotel and called Gia. Meadow should have called the hotel to get in touch with me. When you take all the 'should haves' and wrap them up in a neat little package, you see just how ridiculous the mistakes had been. But who has time for that when their heart is tearing in two? My sister needed me just as desperately as I needed her.

Racing from the cafe, I flagged down a cab, and after jumping in the back without concern for cost, I rattled off Gia's address.

The cabby turned to me, his brows pulled tightly together. "That's a forty-five minute drive. Do you know how much that will cost?"

"I don't care," I practically yelled, tears still streaming, "just get me there now!"

After looking at me like I was insane, he shrugged a shoulder and took off down the road. The drive felt like it took days instead of less than an hour.

Gia's house was exactly as I remembered it, a single story ranch style with blue shutters and a red door. The yard her mother had always meticulously maintained was in full bloom now that we were in the middle of spring, and from what I could see the white picket fence had just received a fresh coat of paint. I tossed some cash to the driver when he told me the ridiculous fee, but before climbing out and letting him drive away, a moment of logic took over.

"Can you wait for me to come back out? I'll need a ride back to the city."

Shaking his head in disbelief, he pulled out his phone and started scrolling through. "Whatever you want. The fare's the same whether the car is moving or not."

"Thanks," I said, my voice distracted as I ran down the small sidewalk leading to Gia's door. Ringing the bell, I tapped my foot anxiously waiting for someone to answer. Gia finally pulled it open, confusion wrinkling her brow. "Meadow? You could have just walked inside."

"No. I'm Penelope."

"Holy shit!" she said, laughing, "It's still impossible to tell you two apart. But what are you doing here? Meadow went into the city to look for you. She said you've been out of touch the past few weeks."

"Damn it!" Tears burst from my eyes. I was not in the mood for this. "I got her emails and came here looking for her. I didn't even know she was coming into town."

Cocking a hip, Gia leaned a shoulder against the door. "Neither did I until yesterday. She called me in a panic as she was boarding the plane. All she brought with her was a small carry on, which -"

Glancing over her shoulder, she said, "Damn, she must have rushed out the door when she left a little bit ago. She forgot her stuff. Are you heading back to the city?"

Her gaze flicked past my shoulder to see the waiting cab. "Looks like it. Why don't you take her bag with you? I have a feeling once you two find each other, she won't want to come all the way back here."

"Yeah, okay. I really need to get back."

Not only to find Meadow, but to be at the hotel in time for sunset. Maurice would have a panic attack if I wasn't there. There was no telling what he would think happened to me.

Handing me the cross body bag, which was no bigger than a purse, she touched my shoulder as I turned to leave. "Hey, Penelope. I'm really sorry to hear about your mom. Meadow was inconsolable. I've never seen her so flustered and out of it. She's really taking it hard."

Nodding because I didn't know what to say, I walked off, but turned again before reaching the cab.

311

"Gia, if Meadow left her stuff here, how did she get to the city? She wouldn't have been able to pay for a cab."

"My mom said she'd drop her off since she was heading over there for some business meeting. She probably hasn't even noticed she left it here. It's like I said, she's really messed up right now."

"Thanks." She was still waving goodbye as I climbed into the cab.

"Back to where I picked you up?" The driver asked.

"Yes. And hurry."

I should have remembered to plan for traffic when deciding whether I could make it to Gia's and back to the city on time. I should have remembered that at five in the afternoon, the streets leading between the city and suburbs became a practical parking lot. Here I was again listing out the 'should haves', the mistakes that made a night like this possible.

By the time we were able to get remotely close to the Wishing Well, the sun was already settling over the horizon, my hands clenched painfully over the strap of Meadow's bag. Unable to endure sitting in the back of a cab doing nothing, I snapped, more worried about Maurice than anything else. Although I knew Meadow was in a state of mourning, even though Gia had mentioned that Meadow hadn't been herself, I knew she couldn't be so bad that she wouldn't simply wait at the hotel for me to return. If she went there, the people at the front desk would have contacted Vincent -

Crap, I thought. He didn't know I have an identical twin. I'd mentioned my family to him, but never that Meadow was my twin.

I didn't want to think what Vincent would say or do after sauntering into the lobby to discover Meadow standing there. I could only hope he controlled himself enough not to say or do anything to freak her out, that he showed her to my room so she could wait there, or perhaps to a table in the dining room.

Why the fuck didn't I have a phone? It would have prevented all of this.

I couldn't sit in the cab any longer. Running the rest of the way was faster at that point.

"How much for me to get out here?" I asked, urgency edging my voice.

Sirens cut through the night air, so ear-splitting in their volume that the driver couldn't speak loud enough to be heard over them. Blue lights flashed as police cars fought to race past us, the traffic eventually moving enough so that they could squeeze by. As the sound eased with their distance, the driver finally told me the amount. Wincing at the cost, I tossed him the cash and let myself out of the car.

Still several blocks away, I saw the lights of emergency vehicles battling against the brilliant colors of the setting sun, and after turning several corners, I heard the distant screams, the murmurs, the shouting police, a heart-shattering roar of pure pain rising above it all. I couldn't catch my breath, couldn't gather my thoughts, couldn't do anything but keep running toward the hotel. And as I approached it, I knew something terrible had occurred.

What I didn't I know was that my entire life had just fallen apart. Not until I unlocked the employee gate into the garden. Not until I stood off to the side, a large flowering bush hiding me from easy sight as I witnessed the scene that was playing out before me.

Logic was lost to me, agony sliding in to take its place in my thoughts. And my heart didn't just splinter, it buckled and stopped. Hand flying to my mouth to prevent the scream that never came, I first saw Vincent being handcuffed and led away, his clothes bloody, injuries dotting his body and face.

Beyond him, beyond the man who had taken me from the streets and somehow given my life new meaning, I saw my sister's body being pulled from Maurice's arms. John had just enough time to inject Maurice with the medicine Vincent had used on him before, and as Maurice's body crashed down, as Meadow lay lifeless over a bed of grass, blood and gore, as the guests kept insisting to the police that Maurice and Vincent had killed her, I no longer had the ability to think rationally.

So instead of running up to the scene to discover what happened, instead of taking just one fucking second to gather myself together and *think*, I *reacted* to my fear and instinct by leaving through the back gate. Glancing at the police car where they'd taken Vincent, I turned and I ran.

CHAPTER THIRTY-NINE

Faiville Prison, 2:07 pm

Silence.

Pure, aggravating, hypnotizing, agonizing, penetrating silence.

Vincent and Penelope both were caught in its thrall. Neither moving, neither blinking, both barely breathing as they absorbed the facts of a story that had destroyed so many lives. And hanging over the horror of the events like a lingering shroud that still hadn't been swept aside to reveal the last bit of tragedy to be found, was the ticking clock counting down the hours to when the last act of injustice would occur.

Vincent was being put to death at six o'clock the following morning, and there wasn't a damn thing either of them could do to stop it.

One would think the man with death hanging over him would be more lost than the woman who could walk away, but in testament to his fortitude, to his acceptance of fate, Vincent was the first to break the enduring silence when he closed his eyes, opened them and spoke.

"You took over your sister's identity. At first I told myself I was crazy for even thinking it, but for a year now, I've wondered. I offered you the interview just so I could confirm one way or the other."

Penelope's tear-dappled gaze met his.

"How? Why?" he asked, confusion drawing lines across his forehead.

For those questions, she had a simple answer. "Fear." Shaking her head at her own stupidity, thinking of all the mistakes, the 'should haves', she swiped the back of her hand across her face to chase away the tears that slid slowly down her cheeks.

"After running off, I didn't know what to do. The last thing I wanted was to return to the hotel, and having nowhere else to go, I checked into a cheap motel on the outskirts of the city. What happened...it was all over the local news that night, so I sat glued to a television in my room with horrible reception and tried to see through what was being reported. I wanted the truth, but I was in too poor a state of mind to process any of it. I made irrational and horrible decisions in the weeks that followed."

"We both did," Vincent offered, his words intended to comfort when they only drove the weight of the tragedy deeper.

"We both did," she agreed, her voice lacking conviction and strength. Sad laughter escaped her lips. "Perhaps it was your mistake that caused mine. I'll blame this on you if you'll let me."

Shackles scraping across the table, Vincent reached for her. For the first time, Penelope reached back. Their fingers threaded together as he said, "You have my permission to blame me for whatever you want. But at least explain what blame I'm taking."

Remembering back, Penelope breathed deeply, the pain, the fear, the confusion and hatred she'd felt coming back in crashing waves. "The news that night was nothing more than speculation. They interviewed a few of the guests who witnessed it and could only guess as to what caused the fight. The only thing the guests thought they knew for sure was that both you and Maurice had been the aggressors. It wasn't until your arraignment that I started putting the pieces together. They televised it, you know?"

Nodding his head, he admitted, "I knew they would. Apparently the brutality of Barron's death made for excellent television. People are such vultures."

Enjoying the warmth of his hand, comforted by the contact, Penelope admitted, "When you claimed at the arraignment that you had lost control out of jealousy - that it was a crime of passion, or whatever - I knew better. You had no reason to be jealous. Maurice, on the other hand, he had reason. They hadn't released the victim's names as they were waiting to contact next of kin, and although I knew one had been Meadow, I wasn't sure about the other. By the time they finally named the victims as Penelope Graham and Barron Billings, I'd already made my decision as to what I would do."

"And why did you make that choice? Didn't you question why Meadow was with Barron? Didn't you want to talk to me, at least, knowing I hadn't been the one to cause that fight?"

It's insane what emotions will do to a person. For some, they're able to think rationally. They're able to calm down and decide on a course of action that helps improve a situation instead of making it worse. But Penelope, at that time, wasn't able to make sense of anything. All she knew was that her entire family was gone, she only had a thousand dollars to her name, and she was once again unemployed and homeless. If only she would have stopped to think about another way to handle it.

"I was angry and scared. Heartbroken. I know they released you on bail, but the last thing I wanted to do

317

was return to the hotel. It scared me to think that Maurice had killed both Barron and Meadow. He could have killed me. As for why my sister was with Barron..."

Penelope shrugged, releasing a breath before saying, "The guy was a jerk. I knew that much about him, but I didn't consider him to be dangerous. I'd seen him in public since that incident in your office and he didn't attack me. He let me go and he wasn't violent. It didn't occur to me that he'd tried to hurt Meadow. I thought maybe he was just harassing her like he did me. I thought that Maurice had seen them together and flipped out, and that you took the blame to protect him. I was right on that last part. You always protected him, even if keeping him in the basement was wrong."

Nodding, Vincent squeezed her hand. "It was wrong. What my father did was wrong. What I did following my father's death even more so. I had one group of physicians and counselors telling me there was no hope for Maurice, and another set that told me he could live a normal life if he would just comply with a medication schedule and therapy, but I was too frightened for him. And that fear, that lack of trust rubbed off on him until not even he could believe in himself. Perhaps, if I'd made different decisions, Maurice could have lived a different life. I know for a fact it was my actions that kept him from becoming what he should have been. It was my fault he hadn't reached his true potential."

Tears streamed down Penelope's face. "He was only trying to protect me, and now he's dead and you're being put to death because of it."

Without responding to what she'd said, Vincent asked, "How did you become Meadow?"

"After the arraignment, after the belief was in my head that Maurice had killed Meadow and Barron out of jealousy, I bought a plane ticket and flew to Germany using her identification. I had her bag, and since we were identical, nobody questioned it. As far as the world knew, Penelope Graham had died that night, not Meadow. And since I had nothing - no family, no job, no money, no home - I took over what she had. I continued the education program she was in. I handled my mother's estate and took the house and the bank accounts. I became someone else and forgot all about the mistakes I'd made as Penelope. I started over as my sister since she'd never had the same problems as me. And here I am. A journalist with a life in another country."

He let the statement linger before asking, "But are you happy?"

"No," she confessed, the one word a weight being stripped from her shoulders. Every day she tried to convince herself that it wasn't true, that she had found happiness in a life she never wanted. But despite the lies she attempted to tell herself, Penelope knew she was miserable. "Being a journalist was Meadow's dream, not mine. I absolutely hate it. Looking at the constant evils of the world is awful. And as for a personal life?" She laughed. "I haven't been with another man since Maurice."

Surprise drew Vincent's brows together. "No one else? In the seven years since that night?"

"I loved him," she said, sorrow coating every syllable. "Despite his problems, despite what he'd done, I loved him. I still do, and to find out he died alone, that he-"

319

Unable to finish the thought, she choked back a sob.

Releasing her hand, Vincent leaned back in his seat. "I'm sorry. For everything. For what you've lost."

Slapping away tears, she laughed pathetically. "This is a really shitty fairy tale."

Grinning, Vincent answered, "Most of the true ones are. It wasn't until people sought a better ending and changed them that they had the characters riding off into the sunset to live happily ever after. Most fables and fairy tales were cautionary stories when first told. It makes this particular one fitting, don't you think?"

"At least I get to walk away from all of this. You're the one losing your life." Panic tore through her, sorrow chasing its wake. "Why don't you tell the truth now that Maurice is gone? Why don't you attempt to save your own life? You shouldn't have to die for what happened."

His smile was full of melancholy and regret. "You're upset *for* me instead of *at* me." A statement more than a question, Vincent appeared amused by Penelope's reaction. "I never thought I'd see the day."

"I don't want you to die."

His green eyes softened. "*Ma chérie, sois forte. Aie un peu de courage.*"

"I'm not strong, Vincent, and my courage is all tapped out," she answered.

His laughter drew her gaze across the table. "So you have learned French? It's about time. Your refusal always drove Maurice and I crazy."

Weakly, she smiled. "And I learned German. It wasn't easy." Growing quiet, she asked, "Will you not try to save yourself?"

Vincent shook his head. "I'm afraid it's too late for that. I took the blame for those deaths in an attempt to save my brother, and I do not regret going to my death. If he had been blamed, his final years would have been more tortured than mine. They would have put him in a state psychiatric institution instead of a regular prison. I didn't want that for him. And, in truth, those lives were lost because of me. Maurice's life was held back because of me. He spent far too many years in that cage. I may not have killed those people myself, not your sister, not Barron, not Émilie or the other woman that was found, but I was the indirect cause. Dying tomorrow is fitting for the mistakes I made, and for the crimes I committed. I'll take my punishment without remorse for what is done to me."

Penelope knew their time was quickly running out, that she would be asked to leave the prison so that they could begin the preparations for Vincent's execution. She needed to focus on what was important, on the last questions she needed answered before it was too late.

"I would like to know one thing." Sniffling, Penelope relaxed into her seat, her tear-swollen eyes lifting to meet Vincent's stare. "Why did you give me to Maurice in the end? Especially after the sexual relationship we'd shared? Did I mean so little to you that you could just toss me off to him without being hurt by it? Was I just another one of your women?"

Sympathy was obvious in his expression, that and the open intimacy of a man who truly cared for a woman. "I guess there's one more mystery we haven't yet solved, one secret I never mentioned." His lips curled at the corners. "I never slept with you, Penelope. Not once. All those nights in my room had been my brother."

"What?" Her eyes widened, disbelief a shadow over her thoughts. "I don't understand."

"Are you angry?" he asked, genuine curiosity a note on his fluid voice.

"No," she answered. "I think I should be, but in a way, it only makes me more sad to know I'd been his all along."

Inclining his head in agreement, Vincent explained, "From the night he stole you from the masquerade ball, I knew you were special to him. You were the first woman he felt compelled to chase after. That night was the first that he'd stepped out of his self-imposed prison. And I couldn't take that from him. But," he paused, the hint of a grin on his lips, "knowing how he was and knowing how rebellious you could be, I couldn't just slap the two of you together without both of you learning how to behave. You needed to learn submission to a man such as him, and Maurice needed to learn how to control his urges. I didn't want either of you to walk away injured, physically or emotionally. Once I felt you were both ready to know each other, I sent you down to the basement that day."

Cocking a brow, Penelope mentioned, "Yet you let me go down on you in your office?"

Vincent's laughter boomed through the small room, true joy in the sound and in the expression on his face. "I am but a man, Penelope. Sometimes these things cannot be helped."

She would have laughed herself if the door hadn't opened, if the guard hadn't stepped through to lead her away. Vincent darted a glance in his direction and sighed. "It seems it's time for this interview to end. Thank you for agreeing to come talk to me."

Hating the tears that poured from her eyes, Penelope could barely speak around the lump clogging her throat. "And thank you for being honest."

With the guard standing and listening, she couldn't say everything else she wanted. Like how she would miss him. Like how she didn't hate him. Like how she would mourn him when he was no longer in the world.

By the look on his face, he knew what she was thinking without her having to speak a word. "Will I see you tomorrow?"

She nodded. "Yes. I'll be there to walk with you into whatever comes next."

"Thank you," he answered as she stood to leave.

And with one last glance over her shoulder, Penelope saw Vincent watching her leave, his shoulders rolled back, his face masculine and refined, his arrogance still obvious in the green of his eyes. Both he and Maurice both had been far too beautiful to be real.

"Goodbye, Vincent," she called out.

"Goodbye, Meadow," he answered.

Led through the gates, Penelope was escorted out of Faiville Prison, and she would return for the last time the following morning to watch Vincent Mercier die.

CHAPTER FORTY

Penny

The sun hadn't so much as crested the horizon when I sat on my small hotel balcony the next morning, my eyes practically swollen shut by the tears that wouldn't stop falling, my heart barely beating as my mind begged this day to never begin. If it were possible to stop time, I would have done so, remaining in permanent stasis, giving up the next rising sun, the next hour, the next second just to keep Vincent Mercier from never being executed.

Already the city was applauding his death, the media setting up their camps outside Faiville Prison, the reporters keeping in touch by delivering brief live broadcasts detailing the anxious energy of the people camped outside the prison's gates.

And the reporters who wouldn't be telling their tales live from on scene were busy behind their desks reminding their viewers why Vincent Mercier was being killed.

Four lives lost: Barron Billings, Émilie Lapierre, Penelope Graham and another woman it had taken them months and dental records to identify. Her name was Candace Ray, an exotic dancer who had given a show at the Wishing Well on the night of their annual ball, and who had disappeared four days later never to be heard from again. At least until the cadaver dogs had sniffed out her bones. Her initial disappearance had never been connected to Wishing Well since she'd given two other performances since that night, but the media had speculated that Vincent had invited her back, had slept with her and killed her before burying her in the garden.

Her parents would be in attendance for the execution, happy for the justice their daughter would receive. It was too bad they didn't know that justice had already been given on the night Maurice Mercier had taken his life. Barron's parents would be there as well, with absolutely no idea that their precious son was a fucking rapist.

I didn't believe Maurice killed Candace on purpose, and I was sure her death occurred during one of his fits, but Vincent had taken the blame for that death onto himself in order to protect his younger brother, had claimed in court that he'd enjoyed taking her life.

Anything to distract the police, the lawyers, the judges or jury from looking in Maurice's direction. Vincent made himself a monster in their eyes so that they had no reason to suspect another man.

I wanted to slap him for his stupidity, and kiss him at the same time for the selflessness of what he'd done. When I first met that man, he was all about himself. People were nothing but pawns to be played. Nothing mattered except that which benefited him. The world revolved around Vincent Mercier and every other person's value was worthless unless they had something they could contribute to him.

I had been a game when he pulled me from the streets, a means to earn some easy money and keep himself entertained. I was only supposed to be a trophy he could set on his shelf and allow to collect dust until some other person came along to dust it off.

But Vincent, despite his selfish ways, had a weakness in his brother, Maurice. It was the only reason Vincent would deign to give up the world he believed he owned, to give up the life he'd built on the backs of every person he'd used to achieve his ridiculously lavish dreams.

As usual, however, Vincent was right in what he said. If Maurice had been dragged into the fray, if the police had suspected his part, they would have locked him away in a state psychiatric facility with all the other criminally insane. His last years would have been horrendous. He would have suffered those years even more bitterly than he suffered his basement prison beneath the lobby of Wishing Well.

Vincent seemed convinced that the bulk of Maurice's problems had been the fault of his family and him. And I didn't doubt that Vincent would walk into that execution room this morning believing he was dying not just because he'd attempted to save Maurice from being blamed, but also believing he deserved to die because he felt guilty for having screwed up his brother's life by never believing Maurice could have been more than he was.

The first belief was an act of pure love for his brother. The second, well, that was simply a man atoning for his sins. He was sentencing himself to death for not knowing the best thing to do for Maurice, even if he'd spent his life trying to do what was right.

The thought broke my heart, splintering it into a million pieces and scattering the shards.

Regardless of how I felt, I would be there until the bitter end, just to ensure that Vincent didn't die alone.

The first mist of fire on the horizon had me standing from my seat to walk inside and get dressed. Only two hours remained of Vincent Mercier's life.

Despite knowing that it didn't matter how I looked for this event, I still took the time to select nice clothes - a white flowing top with a navy blue skirt - to stuff my feet in heels and twist my hair up into a professional knot. I took the time to hide my swollen, red eyes beneath a generous amount of concealer, and took the time to apply mascara and lip gloss to finish the look.

To everybody in attendance, I would look like the unaffected journalist, there to record the facts and nothing more. But to Vincent and me, I would be the Dirty Girl from the streets whose heart was breaking.

The drive to the prison didn't take long, the morning so young that traffic hadn't yet accumulated on the streets. Approaching the gates leading to the parking area, however, was a different story altogether. The addition of rides, game booths and food vendors would have been a nice touch to make it look more like the carnival it was.

News vans filled the parking area, their floodlights glaring, their antennas scratching the sky as the reporters, cameramen, sound engineers and other technical crew littered the grounds around them.

I guessed it wasn't too often that the world got to witness a millionaire being put to death. Driving past the chaos, I realized quickly how much I hated those people, the *vultures* as Vincent had so accurately described them.

After flashing my credentials to one of the prison guards, I was directed to park in a smaller lot reserved for the people who were being allowed inside. A line had formed outside the door, two grieving parents holding each other as they waited, several high power reporters watching them from feet away wondering if they should allow them privacy or approach. In the

327

end, I knew those assholes wouldn't be able to help themselves to the feast of heartache and pain the parents would give.

Not me. I was there for one purpose alone, even if it wasn't the purpose I'd intended before starting the interview. Originally I'd wanted to stare Vincent in the face as the puppet who'd broken free of her strings, but now I would watch as they stuck the needle in his veins and let him know there was at least one person who would grieve.

As I approached the line, I was reminded of one other role I'd originally intended to play: that of the grieving twin sister.

It wasn't that I wasn't grieving for the loss of Meadow, it was simply that I didn't blame Vincent for it. The only person I blamed for that was Barron. So when his parents glanced up at me, and when the reporters came rushing forward, I simply glared in their direction, even if they didn't deserve my anger.

"Ms. Graham!" the reporters shouted, "How does it feel to know that your sister's murderer is being put to death today? Are you looking forward to the execution? Is it true Vincent Mercier spent the past three days giving you an exclusive interview?"

Fucking vultures...

Pasting on a professional smile, I answered, "If you don't mind, I'd like to keep to myself at the moment, as I'm sure you all can understand. Perhaps after the execution, I'll be better able to answer your questions."

They backed away, but only after one of the guards came over to direct me to where the other family members were standing. We would be afforded a front row seat, as if that would make up for the losses we'd suffered.

After a few minutes, we were allowed inside, and after passing through two large, heavy gates and two sets of doors, we entered a room with three rows of folding seats facing a large glass window with the partition pulled closed. Lucky me, I was given the seat that was front row center, stuffed between two sets of parents who would be cheering the executioner on.

Already, their whispers were making me bite the inside of my cheek to keep from telling them how wrong they were about Vincent. Was he a jackass? Yes. Did he deserve this? No. Not at all.

I guessed some would argue that he buried the bodies of both Candace and Émilie. He stole from them a proper burial. And with Candace, at least, his actions had left them to suffer not knowing what happened to their daughter. But, even in that, he was protecting Maurice. He made stupid decisions, but he hadn't been a heartless monster.

Barron's parents could just fuck off for all I thought about their son, and keeping myself from turning to them and admitting the truth as to what he had done was extremely difficult. Not that anybody would believe me if I came out with the truth. There was no evidence to prove Vincent's claims of what occurred that night to set off Maurice's fury.

The partition opened revealing a sterile room with a medical bench, a machine with several dials and tubes, and three plain white walls with a steel door set into one of them. I closed my eyes, tried to hide from what was happening, attempted to breathe when I knew who would soon walk through that door.

Fuck, I wasn't sure I could watch it. Not without screaming, not without banging on the glass and telling them to stop. Vincent hadn't been walked inside the room and I was already crying.

A hand patted my back. "I know it's hard, honey. But it will be over soon."

I opened my eyes to see Candace's elderly mother attempting to comfort me. Slapping away a tear, I forced as much of a smile as I could and redirected my eyes to the window.

The steel door opened, all six foot five inches of Vincent's muscular frame being led through, his hands locked behind his back, his shoulders pulled wide and his hair a dark, wavy mess dusting his white prison jumpsuit ... his green eyes locking on me where I sat.

A sob shuddered through me, so violent it shook the legs of my chair. Candace's mother took my hand in hers, patting the top like a mother would to comfort an upset child. She meant well, so I didn't snatch my hand away. I pretended it was my mom or sister sitting next to me and comforting me to watch this event.

Led by two officers to stand in front of the glass window, Vincent was positioned in the center, an intercom turning on with some quiet static. When the warden at the back of the room starting speaking it was a jolt of harsh noise against the silence of where we were seated.

"Vincent Mercier, you have been sentenced to death for the murders of four people. Having been found guilty by a jury of your peers, your punishment for those crimes will be carried out today. Prior to the execution, are there any last words you would like to say?"

My eyes locked to his, and it felt like I was the only person in the room. The usual glitter was in the green of his gaze, the humor, the arrogance, the laughter I

330

remember seeing in him when we'd both shared in the joy of seeing Maurice improve. Despite knowing he would take his last breath, he didn't beg or cry, didn't lose any part of who he'd always been. Vincent stood tall, and he stood proud.

Still watching only me, Vincent opened his mouth to say, "*Tu faites un vœu, et espérons que cela devienne réalité.*"

It was exactly what he'd said to me at the well in the garden on the day he told me we would take Maurice out to see a sunset. Back then, I'd had no clue what it meant, but I knew now.

You make a wish, and hope it comes true...

My tears wouldn't stop falling, my entire world crumbling down on top of me as they led him away from the window, laid him down on the bench and hooked him to the drip line.

He didn't fight. He simply closed his eyes.

And at 6:27 a.m., on a chilly Thursday morning, Vincent Mercier was officially declared dead.

I felt like I'd died beside him.

CHAPTER FORTY-ONE

It was nine in the morning before I was in my car again, emotionally stable enough to leave the parking lot and make the hour and a half drive to the hotel where all of this had started. Just like I felt seven years ago after my sister was killed, I had no desire to walk into the Wishing Well, to see the opulent interiors, to meet the eyes of the employees or Vincent's attorney. But he had my recorder, and I couldn't contain my curiosity as to what items Vincent had set aside in the belief that I'd want them.

I couldn't turn on the radio without having to listen to all the news reports concerning Vincent's death, so I listened to the smooth white noise of the tires rolling over the asphalt. My thoughts were in the past, my mind conjuring images of happier times, and my quiet meditation didn't end until the noises of the city drew my attention. I turned off the freeway exit to drive down the main boulevard. Finding parking at a public lot a few blocks from the hotel, I walked slowly to approach the six story structure that stood tall in the bright sunlight. It was just as I remembered it, surrounded by a beautiful stone wall that held all the secrets of the garden behind it.

Entering beneath the large wrought-iron courtyard gate with purple and pink wisteria that hung down in a breathtaking display, I strolled up the cobblestone walkway to the front doors, smiling at the doorman as he opened them for me. My heels clicked across the gold scarred marble floors, the white shined to a brilliant polish. Above my head, the crystal chandeliers cast their light is a prism of color and at the large front desk that stood to my left, three impeccably dressed employees waited to welcome me to this heavenly place.

Only it wasn't heaven to me, it was a ghost of a memory, a nightmare I had to face if I ever hoped to breath easy again. Thankfully, I didn't recognize any of the clerks who stood waiting.

"Bonjour! Welcome to the Wishing Well. Are you checking in?"

"Um, no," I answered, attempting to smile politely at the pretty brunette clerk. "I'm actually here to see Stephen Chase. He was the attorney for-"

"I know Mr. Chase," she answered, interrupting me before I could mention Vincent's name. "He's in a meeting with the hotel manager, but if you'll have a seat on one of the sofas in the waiting area, I'll let him know you're here. May I tell him your name?"

"Meadow Graham."

Her eyes widened just barely before she gained control of her expression. "Of course, Ms. Graham. I'm sure it will only be a short wait."

She wasn't wrong. Within ten minutes of my having taken a seat on a large, white sofa that had elegant curves and carved wood detailing, Stephen Chase, with his salt and pepper hair, and his power suit glory, came strolling out to the waiting area with a manila envelope in hand.

"Ms. Graham. How nice to see you again."

Sad laughter tumbled from my lips as I stood to shake his hand. "I can't believe you'd actually say that to me considering the horrible circumstances. I noticed your absence today at the -"

"Why don't we go out into the garden to discuss this?" he suggested, interrupting me just as the desk clerk had. After glancing over his shoulder to ensure no guests had overheard us, he motioned for me to walk ahead of him. "It's just outside these doors. The gardens are stunning actually. I'm sure you'll enjoy them."

Apparently, he'd neglected to remember the gardens are where my sister had died. I would have to ask him at some point if he would like some salt with his shoe.

Walking became more difficult with every step we took toward the gardens, not only because of the images flashing through my thoughts of what I'd seen the night my sister died, but also because I could hear Vincent's laughter, his accented voice that was always teasing or mocking me. Regardless of what happened that morning, Vincent was still very much alive inside this building, his memory engrained in the walls, his vision still standing in elegant wonder as his body turned cold.

And more painful than that was what lay beneath my feet, in a basement where the man I would always love had taken his life when he believed that everyone who'd ever cared for him was gone.

I was struggling for breath by the time we made it outside, gulping down the fresh air as fast as I could drag it into my lungs. My distress was not lost on the grim faced attorney who followed behind me.

Lowering his voice to a gentle whisper, he said, "I'm sorry for what you've gone through today, Ms. Graham. I'm sure it wasn't easy." He placed his hand on my back as if to escort me, but I pulled away from the contact.

I didn't want to be touched or comforted. I wanted to feel this pain for what it was if only to purge it from my body. "It is what it is," I answered. "And I'm here to retrieve my recorder from you as well as whatever items Vincent had set aside for me."

"Ah, yes. Of course." Handing me the manila envelope, he explained, "Mr. Mercier asked me to give this to you. I'll ask that you take it somewhere away from the guests' view. We're attempting to keep mention of Mr. Mercier's name to a minimum, and you're rather recognizable this morning due to pictures of your sister being shown on the news. While you look at that, I'll go back and speak with the hotel manager to determine where the other items can be located. I'll return momentarily to take you to them."

Nodding absently, I stared at my name written in masculine script across the envelope. Not my name, really. My sister's. Mr. Chase walked off and I continued along the cobblestone path until arriving at a familiar place. The wishing well in the center of the garden looked exactly as I remembered it.

"If you could wish for anything in the world, Penelope, what would you wish for?"

Memories assaulted me. Of Vincent. Of Maurice. It took everything I had not to buckle where I stood. Finally moving to sit on one of the iron benches, I tore open the envelope to pull out a single sheet of paper.

Penelope,

If you're reading this, then I must be dead. Okay, so it's an awful way to start a letter, but my gifts in life had never been in writing. My point in the sentence is that I know this letter wouldn't have been given to you unless my execution had taken place and you'd gone to Wishing Well as I hoped you would.

I also hope you don't expect some long-winded apology or some other similar nonsense. Whatever I had to say to you I'm positive was said in our interview. But knowing myself, and knowing my refusal to give any person leverage over me while I'm still alive and breathing, I know there was one thing I wouldn't have brought myself to tell you.

I want to thank you, Penelope, for everything you were to Maurice and me. Despite the less than honorable reasons for pulling you from that alleyway the night I met you, and despite your atrocious manners and rebellious behavior, you turned out to be a blessing I never saw coming.

As you well know, both Maurice's and my lives had been mired in many tragedies. We'd both suffered the grief of his issues, the loneliness not only affected him, but me as well. I may have had wealth, women and businesses to keep me company, but I was never truly happy until you came along. I've spent many years trying to figure out what it is you did for the two of us, and then one night while I remembered an afternoon spent in the yellow room that I'd watched my brother smile as I teased you, it hit me.

You gave us both back the sense of family. And while you became the light that shone in Maurice's dark prison, you also became a sister figure to me. For all the money, for the lavish lifestyle I led, for all the comforts I had at my fingertips in life, you were more valuable than any of it. Those afternoons spent with you and my brother are what I take with me to my grave. I can promise you that while I waited on the gurney for the drugs to steal my breath, it was that yellow room I imagined last, it was your face looking at me with annoyed exasperation and Maurice's beaming smile as he watched us talk back and forth.

He always had faith in you. He knew from the first second he saw you that night by the well, that you belonged to him, and he belonged to you.

I owe you everything for the role you played in our lives.

If this was our fairy tale, Penelope, than you were the hero that rode in on the white horse to rescue Maurice and I both. But even more than that, you were the beauty that soothed the violence of the beast, you were the sunrise and sunset in both of our lives.

I want you to continue being the hero, in every choice you make and in everything that you do. I truly believe you were put on the Earth to make it a better place, and I believe that whatever man ends up with you will be the luckiest man because of it.

Continue soothing the beast, Penelope. Even when he roars. Especially when he roars. And even when he tells you to play the maiden so he can be the hero, you continue simply being you.

My heart belongs with you, in this life and in whatever comes next.

I am forever in your debt,

Vincent Mercier

P.S. You must forgive me, Penelope. I am just a man...and a liar.

More tears. How my body was still able to produce them was a mystery to me. How I hadn't gone blind from their heat was a mystery as well. I could drown in them, I thought, could fill the wishing well to the rim, until it, too, cried as those tears leaked over to slide down the stone and nourish the ground beneath it.

337

Even now, it felt like I could barely hold my head above water.

The stain of my tears dabbled the note I held, the ink running along the edges where the tears had bled the words Vincent left for me knowing he would be gone. And in a bright spot where even the sunlight felt cold, I swiped them away wondering what I would do with my life now.

Being Meadow had been a disguise to hide from my past, but after learning the intricate details, after facing what had been done, I no longer felt the need to hide, no longer wanted to assume the life of my sister who was long gone.

My job didn't make me happy. The country where I lived wasn't my home. The name by which every person knew me was a lie I could no longer choke down.

I was as lost today as I had been the day Vincent found me in an alley beneath the freezing rain. Except he wasn't here anymore. There was nobody who could pull me from the streets and lead me to my new home.

"Are you okay?" a deep voice asked

Wiping away another tear, I shook myself from the spectacle I was making, opening my mouth to answer, "Yes, I'm -"

My neck wrenched from how fast my head shot up in recognition of the familiar voice, my eyes locking to a memory, to a man that couldn't be flesh and blood.

"You're -" my voice failed, the word cracked through as it crumbled apart. Swallowing to shove my heart back down to my chest from where it had lodged in my throat, I said, "You're supposed to be dead."

Arrogance was the arch of a single brow over his green eyes, the sunlight capturing the color and turning it into a glimmering, rare jewel.

"So are you," he answered, his hands tucked in the pockets of his slacks, his suit jacket perfectly tailored to the breadth of his broad shoulders. With his dark hair a disheveled, wavy mess, his strong cheekbones cutting lines beneath those mesmerizing green eyes, and his mouth set in a cruel, yet compelling hint of amusement, he could have been Vincent on the night we met - a man of wealth, of power, of secrets and sound mind.

This wasn't the Maurice I remembered from the basement where we'd spent so many hours. This was a man I didn't recognize, except for how closely he resembled his older brother.

"How?" The single word slipped out from between my lips on a rush of exhaled breath. Before I understood I was moving, I'd stood from the bench and crossed the distance to approach him. Maurice didn't move away or give ground, but he didn't step toward me or give any indication that he was as surprised by my presence as I was by his.

"I now own the Wishing Well," he explained, his voice absent of familiarity, of happiness to see me, of the love we once had shared. Also absent was the self-doubt, the self-loathing, the confusion and sorrow that had always been present seven years ago when I'd known him. "I've managed it for the past several years under a corporate name."

"You-"

Fuck...how was this even possible?

Beyond the shock of seeing him standing here, beyond the shock of understanding what Vincent meant in the letter by calling himself a liar, beyond the

339

shock of standing in a garden I'd swore to never see again, was the shock of seeing Maurice staring down at me with confidence in the set of his shoulders, arrogance in the glimmer of his eyes, anger in the thin line of his lips as if daring me to admit that what I'd done to him was wrong.

I'd blamed him for my sister's death. I'd walked away and stayed hidden. I'd deserted him while still loving him for all these years.

And in that time, he'd become another person.

It made sense, finally, in how Vincent could have known *for a fact* that keeping Maurice away from the world had hindered his brother's true potential. Vincent must have seen the changes in Maurice, must have known his brother had grown into a man as beautiful and strong as the one standing before me now.

So, instead of hiding behind false pretenses, instead of lying or exhibiting a strength I didn't have, I abandoned the fake persona I'd kept for seven years and morphed back into the girl I'd been when I called myself Penny.

"I've missed you," I confessed, exposing my heart, my soul, my weaknesses and injuries for him to do with as he pleased.

A bark of laughter shook his shoulders. "You lied to me. You ran from me. You never came back. And now you tell me you missed me?"

"How long have you known?"

"Two years," he admitted, the shadow of anger rolling behind his eyes. "It wasn't Vincent that figured it out. He only invited you to the interview because I asked him to. We didn't know you had an identical twin, and even when we discovered it, we didn't think it was your sister that died that night. But then you started your journalism career and I scoured the photos of you, watched the broadcasts, saw the subtle signs of who you were. Even twins don't share all the same expressions, the same tells and body language. You might have been able to fool the rest of the world, but you couldn't fool me. And I hated you for it."

"I'm sorry," I whispered.

His lips crooked in challenge, his brow arching again. It was such a Vincent-esque expression that it should have been foreign on the face of Maurice. Pure masculine mischief was written into the glimmer of his eyes. "Make it up to me."

"How?"

His lips crooked higher, his eyes darting suggestively toward the small, hidden alcove that was down the path from the well. Following his gaze, I shook my head in disbelief before returning my attention to the man who was now staring at me like I was his next conquest.

"You can't be serious. Here? Now? Like this?"

He shrugged a disinterested shoulder. "Or not. Goodbye, Penelope."

I watched helplessly as he turned to walk off, his stride powerful and assured. Panic tore at my heart with clawed fingers. "Wait!" I called out. Maurice turned to glance at me from over his shoulder.

Son of a bitch...He was just like his brother now.

"Fine," I relented, trying to ignore how my heart swelled in my chest, how heat bloomed between my thighs.

Carnal satisfaction curled his lips. Following slowly behind me, Maurice stood at the opening to the alcove while I backed up against the stone wall. We were hidden from view by the flowering bushes, shielded from the bright sunlight by the tree branch that stretched lazily above our heads.

"Turn around," he demanded, his voice a deep vibration against my senses.

Our eyes locked, and I would have accused him of challenging me to do something he had no intention to do if not for the dark heat behind his gaze. On shaky legs, I did as I was told, turning slowly to splay my palms against the wall and leave myself defenseless to whatever he desired.

He was on me before I could take another breath, his chest a wall of heat against my back, his hips so tight against my ass that there was no mistaken how serious he was about taking what had always been his.

Seven years later and I still belonged to him alone.

I trembled when the tip of his nose trailed the line of my neck, his nostrils flaring as he breathed in my scent.

There he is...the Maurice I remember.

His teeth locked on the lobe of my ear, one hand moving up to cover my mouth and mute my cry of surprise. And with the other hand, he fisted my skirt, lifting it to give him access to everything he wanted.

It was so easy to submit to him...so natural. The years, the pain, the lies and the tears had done nothing to dampen the love I had for him.

But, he did nothing, simply laughed and moved away.

Spinning, I narrowed my eyes on him, the first touch of anger edging my thoughts. "Where are you going?"

Sliding his hands in his pockets, he twisted around just enough to look at me. "Back to work. Where do you think? I'm a busy man now."

Pulling my clothes into place, my forehead wrinkled with confusion. "But, you didn't-"

"You didn't deserve it," he interrupted, amusement curling his lips. "But if you think that would fix everything, you have a lot to learn."

"I thought you wanted me back? I thought-"

"You can come back. You're always welcome here. But that doesn't mean you won't have to work to regain what we once had."

"You can't be serious, Maurice? How can I come back here? I have no home, no job. My entire life is in Germany."

I was beginning to hate the way he so easily shrugged his shoulder as if to dismiss what I had to say. "There's a room available on the fifth floor, and we have a position open in housekeeping, if I'm not mistaken. You're welcome to both."

My jaw fell open as he turned to walk away again, his stride satisfied and in no hurry as he wound his way up the path. My eyes flared open with anger, my teeth set in frustration with this impossible man. Chasing after him on shaky legs, I called out, "You can't be serious! Are you seriously offering me a job in housekeeping? After everything that's happened?"

I was going to kill him. For real this time. So that he was actually dead. It was like Maurice had taken over Vincent's persona to become the most aggravating man in the world.

Stopping in place, he spun slowly to face me, a wicked grin tilting the corners of his lips.

"If I'm not mistaken, even in some fairy tales, the princess started out as the maid. It's your choice, Penelope. I've made my offer."

And after flashing me another knowing grin, he turned to walk away, his shoulders shaking with silent laughter.

Oh, yeah. He was going to be a dead man when I was done with him.

But what could I do? I had to say yes. At the end of our fairy tale, the beast had become the prince, and I was the beauty chasing after him.

Knowing what my decision would be, knowing that I would return to Wishing Well to be with the man I'd never stopped wanting, I followed behind him wanting to slam my fist into the back of his pretty head.

But I did so with the hope that our stories would finally become what they should have been all along, knowing that we both would live happily ever ...

...Oh, who am I kidding?...

We would drive each other crazy, every day and every hour, for the rest of our fairy tale lives.

THE END

If you are interested in reading additional books by Lily White or would like to know when new books are being released, Lily White can be found on:
Facebook and
Twitter

Join the Mailing List!!!

If you are interested in receiving email updates regarding additional books by Lily White or would like to know when new books are announced or being released, join the mailing list via this link.

http://eepurl.com/Onoeb

Join the Facebook Fan Group!!!

If you are interested in receiving exclusive previews for upcoming novels, or to participate in giveaways, join the fan group for Lily White Books.

FAN GROUP LINK